'This is a very individual piece of work, with a satisfying plot involving Syrian refugees, snobbish dons and nimble interaction between the ill-assorted protagonists. There is real craftsmanship at work here' *Financial Times*

'Ryan Wilkins is about as far removed from George Smiley as a protagonist can be, he may in time become as memorable. He's an extraordinary creation, and demonstrates that even in the most suspenseful thrillers, character is king' *Spectator*

SIMON MASON has pursued parallel careers as a publisher and an author, whose YA crime novels *Running Girl*, *Kid Got Shot* and *Hey, Sherlock!* feature the sixteen-year-old slacker genius Garvie Smith. A former managing director of David Fickling Books, where he worked with many wonderful writers, including Philip Pullman, he has also taught at Oxford Brookes University and is currently a Royal Literary Fund Fellow at Exeter College, Oxford.

His novels have been shortlisted for a number of awards, including the Branford Boase Prize for Best First Children's Novel, the *Guardian* Children's Fiction Prize, the Costa Prize for Best Children's Book, and have won the Betty Trask for Best First Novel and the Crimefest Prize for Best YA Crime Novel.

A KILLING
IN NOVEMBER

Simon Mason

riverrun

First published in Great Britain in 2022
This paperback edition published in 2022 by

riverrun

An imprint of

Quercus Editions Limited
Carmelite House
50 Victoria Embankment
London EC4Y 0DZ

An Hachette UK company

A CIP catalogue record for this book is available
from the British Library

Paperback ISBN 978 1 52941 570 4
EBOOK ISBN 978 1 52941 568 1

10 9 8 7 6 5 4 3 2 1

Typeset by CC Book Production

Printed and bound in Great Britain by Clays Ltd, Elcograf S.p.A.

Papers used by riverrun are from well-managed forests and other responsible sources.

For Eluned

ONE

Everyone said the security at Barnabas was a joke.

Folded gracefully into an irregular space at the back of the High, Barnabas Hall is one of the prettiest Oxford colleges. It possesses many features of outstanding charm: the sixteenth-century buildings in Old Court, for example, their low slate roofs blown by age into gentle waves, their brick facades a shade of rust; or the chapel with its late-medieval stained glass and Elizabethan brass lectern in the shape of a swan. But the exquisite wrought-iron gate at the end of Butter Passage doesn't close properly, and the Victorian 'castle' gate in Logic Lane, with its unpredictable locking mechanism, can usually be opened with a brisk shove. The main gateway itself, elaborately decorated with scenes of Christ in the wilderness, is manned by a slow-moving elderly porter almost as picturesque as his lodge.

It seems the undisturbed dream of an otherworldly mind. But this is deceptive. Like all Oxbridge colleges, it is a high-value business, linked to corporations and governments round the world, a hub in a global network of high-speed information, its professors and scholars selling their specialised expertise to a hundred different enterprises. Which is why, on a damp evening in the middle of November, with cold drizzle coming down and jelly-like water hanging on the college's carved stone lintels and sills, the Provost of Barnabas was in the Burton Suite making conversation with his distinguished guest, Sheikh al-Medina.

The Burton dining room is one of the glories of Barnabas. Situated at the top of staircase IV in the north wing of Old Court, it appears at first sight to be carved from a single piece of timber, blackened and hardened by age. The plaster ceiling is intricately mazed with Dutch strapwork and supported by warped beams of oak; the fantastically historical floorboards creak if you so much as breathe on them; and around the walls the painted faces of the college's founding fathers – pale, stern men in Tudor bonnets – float against the lacquered darkness of the panelling, sober businessmen all.

It was these paintings, or the figures in them, that the Provost was attempting to make interesting to the Sheikh.

'Cropwell,' he said, peering. 'Bishop of Winchester to Henry VI. He was the king who went mad, as I mentioned before. His is a curious case.'

The Sheikh said nothing.

The Provost was a short man, his ponderous bald head speckled with age spots, his voice smooth but nervous. Formidably well educated, a geographer by training, he was lacking in common sense and not averse to using outright aggression to conceal the fact. His short-fingered hands made heavy shapes while he talked. The Sheikh was large and stooped, with a fleshy nose, hooded eyes, and a habit of disconcerting stillness. He was the Emir of the least well known of the seven United Arab Emirates, a multi-billionaire, of course, and for three years the Provost had been trying to induce him to fund the university's new Institute for Peace Studies. He did not yet know if he was likely to succeed. The Sheikh was enigmatic. Also, controversial; persistent rumours linked him to human-rights abuses in his own country and acts of atrocity in others. In the university, there had been fierce opposition to his patronage.

It was half past seven. The Provost was anxious. Conversation with al-Medina so far had been stilted. Earlier in the day, there had been a tour of the grounds, a viewing of the college's collection of Islamic art and a recital of English fantasias, played in the chapel by the organ scholar. But the Sheikh had appeared unmoved. He had been the victim of a recent assassination attempt in Istanbul, and when he spoke it was usually to ask some question about security arrangements; he had noticed, for instance, the rudimentary nature of the college's CCTV. For his part, the Provost, a man with little interest in such matters, suspected that his reassurances had not been wholly effective. As he talked now about the sour-faced Bishop of Winchester, he was uneasily aware of the Sheikh's bodyguard, a handsome man with anxious eyes, pacing up and down at the top of the staircase outside.

Making the slightest of gestures with a hand half-hidden beneath his white robe, al-Medina excused himself from the Provost's historical lecture and went to confer again with his bodyguard; and the Provost took the opportunity to make a phone call.

*

In the lodge adjoining the main gate, the porter, Leonard Gamp, was sitting with a mug of tea, looking at the roadworks outside the entrance, which had temporarily closed Merton Street. Leonard was seventy-four, a cockney veteran of the Royal Gibraltar Constabulary and the British Metropolitan Police force. He had the impeccable footwear and scrupulous hair of a man of strictly traditional views. His respect for the institution of the university, which he had served now for nearly twenty years, was boundless. When the lodge phone rang, he answered it in his usual suave 'lodge' voice: 'Barnabas Hall, porter's lodge. May I be of assistance?'

The Provost's voice said impatiently, 'Leonard, have you seen Dr Goodman this evening?'

'Can't say I have, sir.'

'Do you know if he's in college? I've been trying his rooms.'

'He was certainly in earlier this afternoon; he came across to check his pigeonhole. I haven't seen him go out. Would you like me to run across and see?'

'That would be kind. I can't go myself; I'm in Burton, with our guest.'

'Of course.'

'He might still be in the collections room. You could try there, as well.'

'Yes, sir.'

'Another thing, Leonard. We're waiting for our drinks from the buttery, but something seems to have gone wrong. We were expecting them at least half an hour ago. And they're not answering my calls.'

'Shall I go and enquire, sir?'

'Yes, please. A sherry and some sparkling water – the Blenheim, preferably. And, Leonard, do try to instil in them a little urgency. They know how important our guest is.'

'I'll go right away, sir.'

That buttery, Leonard thought to himself as he hung up, doesn't know its arse from its elbow. There's the Provost with Sheikh Camel-bollocks, and they've forgotten all about him. He put a cardboard *Back Soon* notice in the window, went out through the empty porch into the wet gleaming darkness of New Court and hurried stiffly in the direction of the buttery.

At that moment, carrying a tray containing a schooner of sherry and a bottle of Blenheim sparkling water, Ameena Najib from the buttery was lost in one of the labyrinthine corridors between the medieval Stable Yard block and the new Fitzgerald Conference Suite. She had been employed by the college for only five weeks, the first beneficiary of the college's Syrian refugee programme, and everything was still unfamiliar to her. England itself was unfamiliar, and in many ways unsatisfactory. In Syria, she had been a law graduate; here, she was a kitchen porter, someone who could be given any menial task, to clean the ovens or take out the rubbish. This evening, for example, like a common household help, she had to collect a bag of clothing for charity from the porch of the Provost's lodge.

Tonight was going to be different, though.

She had a narrow face and judgemental eyes. Her dark brown hair was hidden under a close-fitting hijab, navy blue, to match the college kitchen jacket, which she wore over her jeans and T-shirt. Glancing from left to right, she went rapidly along the corridor with her tray. She did not need reminding how important the guest was. The defiler Emir Sheikh Fahim bin Sultan al-Medina was well known to her, though she had never imagined that one day their paths would cross. It was not a coincidence, however. God was the dispenser of all opportunities. Also, she had received a message from a compatriot who monitored al-Medina's movements from a safe place in the city of Dubai.

First, she had to navigate her way out of the conference suite. The college's only brand-new building, a tasteful addition by a distinguished French-Moroccan architect, it still smelled of carpenter's oil and overheated glass. Few of the rooms had yet been fitted with notices of their functions. Looking for the passage which connected the new suite with Old Court, she went quickly down the corridor, past blank doors, to another corridor, where she found yet more blank doors, and went past them to a final blank door, on its own, at the end. For a moment, she listened at it, then reached for her keys, before realising she no longer had them with her. She tried the door anyway – and it opened.

She saw at once that she had made a mistake. It was not the connecting corridor she was looking for, not a corridor at all, but a room lined with glass cabinets containing archaeological objects and hung with paintings and tapestries. Crouching on the floor in the middle of the room, a man wearing large round glasses was busy with a packing crate. Vaguely, she recognised him as a 'don' – a tutor. Phone squeezed between shoulder and chin, he was telling someone not to worry. He smiled at her, and the smile was so unexpected and cold, so full of difficulty and, above all, so English, that, without saying anything, she

6

nervously backed out of the room and hurried away down the corridor. It was quarter to eight and she was later than ever.

In the Burton Suite, the Provost and al-Medina resumed their one-sided conversation. Mentally cursing the buttery for taking so long with the drinks, the Provost tried to think of a way to turn the conversation from the Burton portraits back to the more promising subject of Arabic art. He knew little about it, but the college's collection of Islamic pieces, the bequest of an alumnus who had been a director of the Iraq Petroleum Company in the 1930s, was impressive, and he had been prompt to show it off to al-Medina. He had also taken the trouble to mug up on the history of one of the illuminations, from a late-medieval Persian album in the collection, depicting a sultry young lady reclining after a bath, a reproduction of which hung in the Provost's own study. But he was unsure how to raise so sensual a subject with the Sheikh, whose religious views he could not determine.

He ventured a smile, which seemed to be absorbed without trace in al-Medina's answering expression of utter impassivity.

Before the Provost could speak, al-Medina received a call. Withdrawing his phone from his robes, he looked at the Provost in his usual heavy-lidded way, without speaking.

'Please,' the Provost said, 'take it, by all means.' Gesturing, he added, 'If you'd like some privacy, perhaps you'd be comfortable in the other room.'

Without reply, the Sheikh went into the small office next door, closing the door behind him, cutting himself off from both the Provost and his own bodyguard.

★

7

By this time, Ameena Najib had made her way into New Court. She stopped and looked round. Through the misty darkness, the chapel appeared in front of her, an enormous stone snail patterned with faintly luminous plum-coloured windows. It would be empty, she knew; its purpose was decorative. To her right was Cranmer Library, throwing lozenges of fuzzy-edged light across the darkened quadrangle lawn. She was in the wrong place. Turning sharply, almost spilling her drinks, she reversed through the cloisters, went round into Old Court and saw, at last, the north wing ahead of her.

By force of will, she focused her thoughts on the Emir Sheikh waiting for his refreshment. As she went, she pictured him in her mind, a heavy, sleepy-looking man, famous in her country for biding his time, for awaiting the right moment. And for other things. She imagined his face photographed against a background of smashed grey buildings and the smoking rubble of Kafr Jamal, which she had once called her home. No such photographs existed: the Sheikh was famously elusive.

But God had found him out.

In the mild, damp darkness of an English town, she felt suddenly at one with her lost family, and with those still living, somehow, among the ruins of their homes. She was weak, but luckily not alone. She saw the Sheikh as God saw him, with implacable judgement. She saw him as her sister Anushka might have seen him, if only she had lived. Under her breath, she began to recite.

Allāhu akbar, God is the greatest. *Ana la 'kafr Jamal'*, I can't forget Kafr Jamal.

It was nearly eight o'clock. But now she was ready.

*

8

Standing alone and irritable between the dinner table and the portrait of Bishop Cropwell, the Provost called the buttery again. No response. He called Dr Goodman, the college curator, and this time the man answered.

'Where the hell have you been?' the Provost hissed. 'I thought you were joining us.'

Goodman said, 'No. I've been busy. The tour of the collection this afternoon has created a lot of extra work. I shall be there for the dinner, if I can finish up here in time.' His tone was openly hostile.

'You better be,' the Provost said rudely. 'And, this time,' he added, 'I expect you not to mention the bloody Koran. If you think . . .' he began angrily – but Dr Goodman had rung off, and the Provost sat there, staring furiously at the phone. The Farquar Koran was part of the college collection, one of Barnabas's most valuable antiquities, but the Saudis wanted it back, and Goodman, the college's only Arabist, was sympathetic to their cause. The Provost was anxious to avoid it being mentioned again at dinner. His temper, never good, was aroused.

Glancing at the shut door of the office where the Sheikh was talking on the phone, he checked his watch and, to pass the time, went over to the dining table and began to check the glassware and silver cutlery, brought out specially for the occasion. The plan was to impress his benefactor with the sort of relaxed, intimate, intellectually high-powered gathering for which Oxford was famous, a final act of persuasion in the effort to secure the Sheikh's commitment to the new institute. But he could not stop fretting. In particular, he wished that his guest would stop complaining about security. It spoke of a negative attitude.

The bodyguard had inspected the Burton rooms for nearly an hour before allowing his employer to enter, and had visited the kitchens to question the staff and examine the food. Several times the Provost had been on the point of telling the man that he ought to realise he was now in a country with the rule of law.

He was released from these troublesome thoughts by the much-delayed arrival of the drinks.

The young woman came in carrying a tray.

'Thank God!' the Provost exclaimed, and did not notice her frown. 'Has there been a problem?'

Ignoring him, the girl said, with a heavy accent, 'There is man outside, question me.' She was flushed, her chest heaving as if she'd been running. An attractive girl, the Provost thought, noticing her figure. She did not look at him as he eyed her, but glanced around the room, as if searching for something, continuing to mutter to herself under her breath, rhythmic syllables he did not catch.

The bodyguard appeared in the doorway behind her, and the Provost, exasperated, ignored him, ushering the girl inside. 'Don't worry about that,' he said to her, curtly. 'The amontillado for me, thank you. And the sparkling water . . .' He gestured towards the other room. 'Our guest is on a call. Take it in and leave it on the table. Please don't disturb him.' He waved her through.

Ameena Najib took a breath, went quietly into the antechamber and closed the door softly behind her.

The defiler was sitting in a swivel chair, facing away from her, talking on his phone in Arabic, oblivious to her presence only a few feet from him. His shoulders were visible to her, and the top of his head vulnerable under his white keffiyeh. She took a cautious step towards him. Then, hearing the sounds of her own language, she hesitated; an expression came over her face, a listening trance.

Suddenly, as if he had felt her presence, the Sheikh stopped talking and spun round in his chair towards her, and they faced each other in silence.

The thought came to him at once: At last, they have found me.

The girl was nothing – merely an instrument, a face without a meaning.

He was tired suddenly. Exhausted.

The girl said nothing, nor needed to. Eyes fixed on his, she seemed to be willing him to read her mind and hear the words she spoke there. He could imagine them.

Last wahida, I am not alone. *Tdhakkar annak batmut.* Remember you will die. And other slogans, other taunts.

He watched her intently, immobilised by fear, but intensely curious to see what she would do. She would have instructions from her associates. What was concealed under that uniform? Still she did nothing. What was her role?

For a long, agonising moment, neither of them did anything.

Then her eyes suddenly widened, she sucked in her breath, and, as if dismissing him forever from this world, she turned abruptly and went quickly out of the room.

The Provost did not at first notice the Sheikh's agitation as he emerged, immediately after the girl, from the study. He beamed

11

as he raised his glass of amontillado. 'Better late than never,' he said. 'Cheers.'

'Who is that girl?' the Sheikh asked.

The Provost looked at him curiously. 'From the kitchen? She's new to the college. Aneesha, I think. Or Anika, perhaps.'

The Sheikh clapped his hands and his bodyguard came rapidly across the room.

What was his interest in the girl? the Provost wondered as he sipped his sherry, watching them talk. Al-Medina had unexpectedly cast off his sleepiness; he spoke now to his man in abrupt bursts of Arabic, as if seized by some excitement. The Provost knew nothing about al-Medina's private life, but allowed himself to imagine that the Sheikh had many wives. He had once been told intimate details about Arab princes' sexual arrangements by a salacious diplomat, whom he had not discouraged.

Al-Medina ended his speech on a note of command and the bodyguard ran out of the room and quickly down the stairs.

The Provost was puzzled. 'She's a refugee,' he ventured, 'from Syria. We have an aid programme, just up and running. She's only been with us since noughth week,' he added. 'I think she's finding it hard.'

The Sheikh did not respond.

'Noughth week,' the Provost said helpfully, 'is the week immediately prior to the beginning of term. Michaelmas term, I mean,' he went on, after a moment, 'which always begins on the Sunday after the Feast of St Michael and All Angels.'

His explanation made no impression. He frowned. Perhaps the difficulty lay in some aspect of al-Medina's foreignness. He tried to remember the arcane differences between Shia and Sunni Muslims, about which he was vague.

The Sheikh turned and glared at him. 'How did she come to be here?'

The Provost was taken aback by the ferocity of his tone. He said, 'I don't remember off the top of my head. Doubtless her journey was very difficult.'

'Who are her associates?'

What was he to do with such a wild question? 'I think her experiences have made it hard for her to make friends easily,' he said.

He was beginning to feel browbeaten. He noticed how pale al-Medina was, how intent his manner. Now, the Sheikh rephrased his question: 'Are there others of her kind here?'

Belatedly, the Provost understood. The man was frightened of the girl, he thought she was plotting something against him. What paranoia! He said, with dignity, 'She's been thoroughly vetted, of course. Thoroughly.'

But the Sheikh ignored this. He said in a low voice, 'Who did you tell of my visit? Who?'

Feeling, now, the subject of an unfair accusation, the Provost said, 'No one at all. Beyond those who needed to know,' he added.

The Sheikh's only response was to prolong his stare. With a nausea-like feeling of fear, it struck the Provost that the Sheikh was about to walk out – taking with him upwards of thirty-five million pounds of funding. Indeed, as the Provost stood there helplessly, al-Medina made an impatient gesture of dismissal – but, at that moment, to the Provost's relief, the other members

13

of the dinner party arrived up the stairs, led by his wife, and he immediately began introductions, talking rapidly. His wife, who had suffered a stroke three years earlier, limped forward with a strained expression, accosting the Sheikh with a smile her husband recognised as forced and engaging him brightly in conversation. The guests were followed by a waitress with two bottles of Mumm and a little silver platter of hors d'oeuvres. The bell of Barnabas struck half past eight and al-Medina was engulfed by his hosts, preventing his departure.

Outside, Ameena Najib watched the bodyguard approach, head swivelling, walking quickly in the direction of the kitchen. Half-crouching on the gravel strip that ran around the Great Hall, she pressed herself against its wall as he drew level with her, slowing down, peering into the shadow. He came nearer, and nearer still, and stopped. His eyes met hers, a brief moment of recognition passed between them, then he turned away and walked briskly on. She lifted her face to the mild, damp sky, feeling herself tremble. Tested, she had come through. The first part of her task was over. Taking out her phone, she hurriedly composed a text.

Hadha huwa. It is him. *Ihna jahizeen.* We are ready.

But, before she could send it, she heard her name called from nearby – 'Ameena! What you doing in there?' – and she turned in alarm, caught with the phone in her hand, text unsent.

In the Burton Suite, the champagne was being poured. Besides the Provost and his wife, there were four other guests to entertain the Sheikh. Humourless Dr Goodman, the necessary Arabist. The Dean of the college, whose silvery, smooth looks were familiar

14

from his many television appearances. A zoologist called Arabella Parker, dressed in a bright flowing kaftan. And a junior visiting fellow from the States, called Kent Dodge, an art historian from Harvard, who had once spent a semester at the University of Abu Dhabi and had already been useful during the tour of the college collection, earlier in the day. All of them noticed how uneasy the Sheikh was, but none was able to rouse him from his introversion, which persisted through the preprandial drinks. Disengaged, he refused all conversational gambits from his lively, intelligent hosts – questions concerning the Middle East, witty chit-chat about orientalism and the discontents of globalism. When his bodyguard returned, he engaged in a long, agitated conversation with him, ignoring everyone else. It was a relief when the meal was served and they were able to take their places round the table.

Hoping, now, for a fresh start, the Provost stood, with an anxious smile on his flushed face, to propose a toast of fellowship between Barnabas and the house of al-Medina, and to the continuation of their joint efforts to promote peace in all parts of the world. But the polite echoes of his colleagues and their light applause could not divert attention from the unresponsive expression of the Sheikh, who remained impassive and immobile, and there was a hint of panic in the Provost's voice as he sat down and immediately began to repeat to his guest all he had learned about the picture of the reclining girl from the Persian album in the college collection.

Stepping out of the shadows, Ameena stood in front of Jason Birch, the college handyman, who nodded at her. He was a thickset young man, with big hands, gingery stubble and a default expression of glazed friendliness. He took an interest in foreign girls and Ameena had caught his eye. She made him nervous, but he remained hopeful. He hadn't expected her to be working so late.

'Won't get no signal in that hidey-hole,' he said, grinning. His accent was broad rural Oxfordshire, all lazy vowels and muddy consonants.

She said nothing.

'Just saw you,' he said awkwardly. 'That's all. Need a hand with anything?'

She shook her head. 'I must go.'

'You alright? You look a bit, what's the word?'

'I have been lost.'

He ignored her curtness. 'Easy done, place like this. Where was you trying to get to?'

'Burton Room.'

'Ah. I bet you was in the north side. Next to the chapel. All them little old corridors.'

'No,' she said impatiently. 'Conference building.'

'Even worse, then. All them little new corridors. Sure you're okay? People treating you alright?'

He could tell this was a conversation she did not want to have, but he believed in his good-natured appeal, and in fact he was rewarded, because, as if she suddenly felt a need to express pent-up feelings, she began to speak quickly: 'No,' she said. 'People do not treat me.' Gesturing, she told him about the Provost, the way he spoke to her, the way he *looked* at her.

Jason, pleased to be confided in, made exaggerated dis-

16

approving expressions with his rubbery face. 'No surprise there. He's got a reputation, he has. All touchy-feely.'

And there was a man in the room of treasures who frightened her just with his smile. She made a gesture with her hands to indicate glasses.

'Collections room? That's Goodman, that is. He's a weirdo. To be honest, this place is full of them. Now you're here, you got to be careful how you go.'

To his surprise, her eyes filled with tears, and he took a protective step towards her. 'What is it?'

She went on, emotion fracturing her voice. 'In Burton Room . . .'

Jason's mouth fell open a little as he leaned forward, agog. 'In Burton Room, what?'

'The Sheikh Emir,' she whispered. '*The defiler.*'

She was pale with fury or fear, Jason wasn't sure which. The word 'defiler' made him feel suddenly out of his depth.

'That man,' she said, musing to herself. 'What was he talking about on the telephone? What was he *doing*?' Raising her voice, she said loudly, 'He is a defiler of the Holy Book.' She glared at Jason.

'Oh, right,' he said, after a moment. He peered at Ameena nervously. 'You don't have to worry about him,' he said at last. 'He's just a bloke, same as everyone. Don't matter how many wives he's got,' he added, without meaning to. He made a sympathetic clucking noise and blew out his cheeks, rummaging in his mind for something else to say. 'Tell you what, though,' he said at last. 'I been thinking. Security in this place is something shocking. Anyone can just waltz right in. What if something happens? You know, to old Emir.'

She looked at him sharply. 'Why do you say this?'

'No reason. Just that I—'

'I have no time to talk with you,' she said. 'What do you do here?'

'Nothing. I was just—'

'I have things to do. You have made me late.'

He watched her sadly as she hurried across New Court, then turned and went the other way. He did not see her pass through the archway into the Fellows' Garden, nor stop in the shadow of the library, carefully looking around her, to finally sent her text.

There, she sighed with relief. The garden ahead of her was hidden in darkness, the path around it dim in the lamplit mist, but, for a moment, she thought she saw someone in a kitchen uniform disappearing round the far side, towards the Provost's lodge. She frowned. The only other member of the kitchen staff on duty, apart from the chef, was Ashley Turner, and she would be busy in the Burton Room. It puzzled her. Heart thumping, she set off in the same direction.

Meanwhile, in the Burton Suite, the dinner was a disaster. The Provost's attempt to coax the Sheikh into a distracting conversation about the picture of the reclining girl in the Persian album ended in personal humiliation when his wife jovially corrected him on a basic point of detail, which he was afraid to dispute. Conversation slackened, died and was replaced by the scraping noise of the silverware on fine china. The foie gras came and went, then the lobster ravioli – but, before the Herdwick lamb with vegetables 'navarin' could be served, the Sheikh suddenly announced his decision to leave.

It was only nine forty-five. There was general embarrassment.

Helped to his feet by his bodyguard, he stood, heavy but still pristine, and for a moment he dispassionately examined the other guests, who had all fallen silent. He inclined his head, briefly lifted his arms, and, in English, wished them goodnight.

From across the table, the Provost's wife said, 'Must you go? Such a shame.' Her partial paralysis gave her face a sour expression, but her tone was sincere and encouraging.

The Sheikh ignored her. He conferred with his bodyguard. His departure was premature; arrangements would have to be brought forward.

The bodyguard approached the Provost. The Emir's car would arrive in twenty minutes' time. How near to the college entrance could it park? Merton Street was closed because of the roadworks.

The Provost was in no mood to be helpful. He sensed that the three years he had spent soliciting the Sheikh's money had been a waste of time. He could hardly bring himself to look at the man.

'Get your driver to park on the High. You can walk up Logic Lane to meet him.'

The bodyguard asked if the lighting was good in the lane.

'Not particularly.'

The bodyguard asked for a better option.

The Provost struggled to suppress his exasperation. 'Use the gate on the other side of the Fellows' Garden, then. It lets you out virtually on the High. I'll give you the exit code. It's a bit rickety, but you just have to give it a push. You can manage that, I suppose.'

The bodyguard conferred with al-Medina, who grudgingly

19

accepted this new arrangement. He still appeared uneasy, however. Ignoring the Provost and making an ambiguous gesture with his hands, he retreated with his man into the antechamber to wait for the arrival of the car.

Not knowing quite what to do, the other guests continued to sit, talking in low voices, the Provost standing apart, silently contemplating the ruin of his plans.

After a moment, he went over to his wife.

'I can't stand this,' he said to her in a low voice. 'I'm going out for a minute.' Before she could remonstrate, he left the room and went down the stairs.

He felt a familiar urgent craving.

Outside, the rain had worsened. He hurried through clinging drizzle along the side of the north wing and ducked under an archway into Benet's Yard. Here, in the wall of an outhouse, next to Butter Passage, was a recess hidden by shadows. He stood in its shelter and, with trembling fingers – strictly against college regulations and, worse, against his wife's express wishes – lit up a Parliament Light, desperately needed.

On the opposite side of Old Court, in other shadows, Ameena Najib had been waiting all this time in the damp chill. She could not stop shaking, though more from a violence of emotion than the damp. Her feelings would not be still. At last, she saw movement at the bottom of the far staircase, across the oval lawn, and, without hesitating, sent another, final text.

Han al-waqt. It is time.

It was done. Her part was finally over. It had been a far more difficult night than she had expected, but she had come through.

With great force of will, she turned her mind away from individual sufferings and fixed it on important things: death and judgement, heaven and hell. She had asked God for justice, and He would not fail her. She was free to go. Arranging her face in an attitude of calm, keeping a wary eye out, she left her hiding place at last.

In his damp alcove, the Provost sucked in smoke and held it deep inside his lungs until the longed-for moment of stillness came over him. Then again. And then again.

Finally, he began to relax.

Several minutes passed. He stood there, drained, staring blankly at the darkened yard in front of him, letting his thoughts drift. He remembered moments from the long, difficult day, irritating gestures the Sheikh had made, the disdain in his face while the Provost attempted to make conversation with him about the picture from the Persian album; above all, he remembered the constant carping about the supposed lack of security in college.

Quietly smoking, the Provost let the image of the girl in the Persian picture come into his mind. As always, it comforted him. He had often gazed at it as he worked at his desk, admiring the woman's careless beauty. Nestled inside a concertina of golden rectangles, she lay half-sleeping, her hips draped with a blue cloth decorated with golden ducks, white breasts pendant, one ear exposed in a cascade of thick dark hair. It was an erotic image over which he liked to superimpose the faces of various junior research fellows. He sighed through his nose, gazing unfocused into the drizzly darkness of Butter Passage, out of which four figures wearing black balaclavas and ski masks quietly appeared

21

from the direction of the badly fitting wrought-iron gate, jogged past without seeing him, and disappeared in single file, through the archway, towards Old Court.

For several moments, the glassy-eyed Provost did not register what he had just seen; he smoked on, dreaming. Then, with a sudden belch, he spat out his cigarette. Four masked men, heading towards Burton!

In a sudden flux of terror, he stood rigid, thinking helplessly of the Sheikh's persistent questions about security. Then, with a jolt, he lurched out of the recess, turned sloppily on the wet gravel and began to run after them.

Meanwhile, in the Burton dining room, conversation was continuing as before – awkwardly. The Provost's wife, talking to Kent Dodge about his experiences in Abu Dhabi, had adopted an inappropriately teasing tone; the young man was easily embarrassed. He never knew which part of her face to look at – her eyes, which had an unnatural fixed shape, or her lopsided mouth. The Dean and the zoologist were arguing in a low, elegant murmur about some imminent elections to the senior common room. Dr Goodman sat apart in bitter silence; his tenure at the college was coming to an end and the Provost had made it clear to him that he would not be missed. He watched the others.

They were all taken by surprise by the sound of footsteps coming rapidly up the stairs. Several people, it seemed, accelerating with intent. Kent Dodge instinctively shrank back, and the Provost's wife, alarmed, got to her feet as her husband appeared in the doorway, staggering and purple-faced, looking wildly round the room, making inarticulate noises.

'What on earth?' his wife said.

Flapping angrily at her to be quiet, he pointed at the ante-chamber. Gasping, he made a long, disjointed noise, which they eventually interpreted as 'Is he safe?'

His wife frowned. 'The Emir? He left a few minutes ago.'

'But . . .'

'His car arrived early. I gave him the code to the gate. I thought that was alright. My only worry was that the Fellows' Garden is so dark they might lose their way. But perhaps they'll run into someone to assist them.'

For a second, the Provost just stared at her. Then, wrenching himself around with another cry of pain, he staggered back down the stairs, leaving them looking after him with astonishment.

The Fellows' Garden lies north-east of New Court. One side is flanked by the chapel, another by an end of the library, a third by a tall municipal building facing the High. The fourth side is bounded by the low rubble wall that runs along Logic Lane as far as 'castle' gate and the neoclassical Provost's lodge. A gravel path leads round the garden in that direction.

Along this path, al-Medina and his bodyguard cautiously proceeded. Once they had left New Court, it was unexpectedly dark. There were no more than two or three antique lamp posts along the way, shimmering dimly. It was a clouded night. Mist and drizzle further obscured things. Ahead of them, they could see nothing much beyond the wavering inky outlines of bushes and trees in the small park-like garden.

They walked close together, in silence, listening. Occasionally, the bodyguard put his hand on the Sheikh's arm to bring him to a halt, before making an all-clear signal and going on again in the same wary way.

Since his encounter with the girl from the kitchen, al-Medina had grown increasingly perturbed. His mood of fatalism had passed; now, he wanted to survive whatever threat faced him. His irritation with the basic failures of security in the English college had grown into a fearful anger.

Near the final bend, his bodyguard stopped him again. He had heard something pattering in the garden. For several minutes, they stood there in the damp darkness, peering across iron railings at a small copse of ornamental trees, black and dripping in the gloom. Then, cautiously, they went on again.

At last, as they rounded the bend, the lodge and gate came into view. At the same moment, the last lamp post ahead of them flickered and went out, casting the path into near-total darkness.

They stood there in confusion.

Al-Medina spoke in an undertone: 'What is happening now?'

The bodyguard took a moment to reply. 'Only an electrical fault. Nothing works in England.'

'This place,' al-Medina said contemptuously. 'No one loves us here. Let us go on.'

For a moment, neither of them moved. Darkness surrounded them, very thick. But, slowly, through the mist, they discerned gleams of light from the windows of the Provost's lodge, ahead, where the gate was. They began to walk towards it. For twenty yards or more, there was no sound except the crunch and scrape of their feet on the gravel path and al-Medina's heavy breathing. And then, hideously, the quiet was broken by sudden violent cries and the sound of running feet.

'Quickly, now!' al-Medina cried, and they lurched forward together.

The Provost was aghast to see them running away from him. Still crying out ragged noises of warning, unintelligible as the howls of animals, he staggered faster down the path behind them, waving his arms.

But he was too late.

As he watched, four masked men leaped out of the undergrowth in front of al-Medina and blocked his path.

'No!' the Provost cried, one last despairing shout.

Confusion ensued. The bodyguard leaped forward, yelling, to shield al-Medina, who went down like an elephant on his knees, and everything blurred and whirled in the darkness, shadows leaping in a long and ragged moment of panic, until finally the scene came clear – and, to his horror, the Provost saw the four figures bending over, mooning at the Sheikh, their pale arses gleaming in the faint light from the windows of the lodge.

When his wife finally caught up with him, she found him speechless, sitting on the ground against the garden railings, and assumed he had suffered some sort of fit.

She arrived with Kent Dodge, whom she had persuaded to help carry certain items of silverware and porcelain which needed returning to the lodge. They fussed intently around the fallen Provost, until he waved them away and got to his feet.

'What happened?' his wife asked. 'Did you fall? Are you ill?'

He looked at her with fury. 'Fucking students,' he said in a choking voice.

His wife drew him away from Kent, who hung back, embarrassed.

'What on earth are you talking about?'

Tight-lipped, he explained. 'It's not funny,' he added.

'I'm sorry. Was he very put out?'

'Put out?' He rolled his eyes. 'It wouldn't surprise me if he had us all killed. Or our hands chopped off. That's what they do, over there, to people who violate their sense of honour.' Turning petulantly, he tottered towards the lodge. 'At the very least,' he added bitterly, 'he's sure to pull out of the institute.'

'Really?'

He turned and glared at her. 'You didn't help.'

'What do you mean?'

'At dinner. Contradicting me about that picture.'

She knew better than to reply. Turning, she went with some effort up the stone steps to the portico of the lodge and the outer door to their rooms, blushing Kent Dodge following self-consciously with an armful of silverware.

'It's over now,' his wife said, over her shoulder, to her husband. 'You can relax.'

He muttered to himself.

'Relax,' she said. 'He's gone. Safe. Nothing can happen to him now.' She tried the door; shook it. 'That's odd.'

'What is?'

'The porch door's locked.'

'What's odd about it?'

'You always leave it open.'

He glared at her again. 'In point of fact, I generally lock it.'

'So, you locked it this evening?'

'I must have done, mustn't I?'

Again, she bit her lip. Sighing, she unlocked the door with her own key and they went into the porch, pausing there together while she unlocked the inner door, and finally into the house. Kent carried the silverware, as directed, into the dining room. The Provost slumped against the dresser in the lobby.

'I'm not happy with the state you're in,' she said to him. 'Think of your heart. You need your medication.'

'I'm alright.'

But his tone was conciliatory. It was, in fact, a huge relief to be in the familiar surroundings of his home. The furniture was his, the decor – a comforting scheme of classic wallpapers and pale carpets – the paintings along the wall.

'Come on. The tablets are in your study.'

He nodded feebly. Everything had been too much. He gave in to his wife's ministrations and allowed himself to be supported down the hallway.

His study was a square room, elegantly decorated. There were long drapes of grey chenille at either side of the French windows, a mahogany desk and leather chair. Along the walls, papered in pale cream, were several pictures, including, to one side of the desk, a framed print of the reclining girl from the Persian album, the source of their disagreement at dinner. But neither the Provost nor his wife looked at the picture.

They looked at the floor.

On the pale grey carpet lay a young woman in T-shirt and jeans. Her T-shirt had ridden up, exposing her midriff. One of her shoes had come off and lay apart on the carpet. Sprawled on her back, head twisted sideways, she glared at the wall, her face bloated and discoloured in the puddle of her dark brown hair, her mouth stretched wide, as if forced open by her protruding, swollen tongue.

It was obvious that she was dead.

Kent Dodge came up behind them to say goodnight, and his mouth fell open too.

The Provost's wife looked at her husband. Controlling her tone, she said at last, 'Well, I see I was right about the picture. But I agree with you. Once this gets out, you can kiss goodbye to the Arab's money.'

From behind them, there was a sliding noise and a crash. Young Kent Dodge had fainted away.

TWO

Four hours later, five miles away, in an untidy room in a nondescript brick house in Bayworth, a mobile phone began to ring. It lit up in the darkness where it twitched on the floorboards, bumping to the beat of the 'Bad and Boujee' ringtone, and an arm stretched out from a mattress and groped around. At last, the ringtone stopped. Eyes closed, a thin-faced youth with shiny traces of scar tissue down his left cheek slowly brought the phone to the side of his head and breathed into it for a moment before he spoke.

'What?'

A voice told him that something had gone wrong.

'What's gone wrong?'

The voice said that a new job had come up.

'What job?'

The voice explained.

'What, now?'

The voice gave him perfunctory details and rang off.

The youth sat up, head bowed, and groaned. He rubbed his

itchy scar with the ball of his thumb. Holding his phone close to his face, squinting, he read the time.

'You're shitting me,' he said out loud.

He dialled a different number, eyes closed again until it was answered.

'Yeah,' he said, yawning. 'Listen. I got to come round. Yeah, now. Yeah, I know it's the middle of the night.'

Hauling himself off the mattress, he stood for a moment, awkward and angular, in his Carling Black Label T-shirt, scratching his groin, looking out of the uncurtained window at the Oxfordshire farmland rising beyond the road to the crest of the hill, where corrugated cattle sheds stood silhouetted against the agricultural night. Everything was silent and still.

There was a washbasin in the corner of the room, and he went over and rinsed his face and gargled, pressing his hair down flat with his wet hands and wiping them dry on his T-shirt. It was cold in the room and he shivered as he began to put on his clothes. A jumper over his T-shirt, a pair of trackies, his Nike trainers. His Loop jacket.

Yawning again, he went over to a chest of drawers and took out a gun, a Glock 26, black and plastic-looking, small and light enough to fit in his jacket pocket. Then he went quietly out, along the landing to another room.

This room was different. There was chunky colourful furniture and a freshly painted frieze of teddy bears round the edge of the yellow walls. In a small bed, covered with a duvet patterned with red tractors against a green background, a blond-haired boy of about two lay sleeping, and the youth reached down and lifted him out.

'Wake up,' he whispered. 'Wake up.'

The boy made a mewling noise and pushed his face against the youth's arm.

'Oi, Ry. You got to wake up. Daddy's taking you to Auntie Jade's. Come on, now, there's a good boy.'

But the boy wouldn't wake up. He was boneless with sleep. It took nearly quarter of an hour for the youth to patiently insert him into his coat, shoes, hat and gloves, and it had gone three thirty before, at last, he carried the sleeping child downstairs and out to the Peugeot 306, parked on a patch of waste ground in front of the house.

The noise of the engine seemed enormous as he drove up the dark, silent lane to Foxcombe Road and turned right, past the mansions of the nouveau riche, towards town. Northward, across the dim undulations of fields, the city below came into view, tiny under the cloud-filled sky, a nest of dim, speckled lights. The engine banged as he accelerated along the empty road.

'Hear that?' the youth said conversationally to the sleeping child next to him. 'This car's a piece of shit, mate.'

He checked his phone: three messages already.

He accelerated down Hinksey Hill to the roundabout, over the ring road to the turn-off and past Hinksey Point trailer park, comatose in its circle of garbage. He went clanking up the long straight ribbon of Kennington Road, humped every hundred yards with speed bumps to deter the joy riders, and came at last to Kenville Road, a short side street of untidy semis.

His sister was waiting in the kitchen in a short, towelling

31

dressing gown, a petite young woman with the same overlarge nose as the youth, her blond hair scraped back over her scalp.

'Not even four,' she said bitterly.

He said nothing.

'You never said nothing before about four o' bloody clock in the bloody morning,' she said.

She put her arms out to take the boy and the youth handed him over.

'You get the call, don't you?' he said. 'That's how it works. They call, you go. You don't get to chat about it.'

'What is it?'

'You know I can't say.'

She looked disgusted. 'Don't fuck it up, then. Like last time.'

He shrugged. He stooped, kissed the back of his son's bonneted head and walked away towards the door.

His sister said, 'When you picking him up, then?'

'Not late.'

'Not later than five. I got work.'

'Alright.'

'After you get back, you've got to go and see Mam.'

'Yeah, yeah. Tomorrow.'

'Today. You promised. He's been at her again.'

Muttering, he turned and went out into the quiet street.

She shouted after him, 'Don't fuck up, knobhead!'

He lifted a lazy finger backwards as he went. In the car, he took the Glock out of the glove compartment and put it in his trackie pocket. It felt awkward and he took it out and put it in the waistband instead. It still felt awkward. He put it in his jacket pocket, where it hung loosely against his thigh.

'Fuck it,' he said quietly. He put it back in the glove compartment.

He put the car in gear and set off, engine banging, back down the Kennington Road.

In the porter's lodge of Barnabas Hall, Leonard Gamp limped up and down with a mug of tea, reviewing the situation. Although he had been on full alert for over five hours, he wasn't tired. On the contrary, he felt something of the old pep and certainty that had sustained him in his younger days during emergencies in Gibraltar town and Tottenham.

He had received the Provost's call at half past ten. His first task had been to assist the Provost and his wife, and, more particularly, the young American, who was in a state of shock and needed some minor medical attention (small gash to the forehead). Americans, in his opinion, tended to lack gumption. To his disappointment, Leonard had not been invited into the room where the body was, but the Provost had taken him into his confidence with a full description. He had even asked Leonard's advice, though he had not listened for an answer. The man was, naturally, distracted. Twice, strangely, he had addressed Leonard as 'security'. Leonard had been struck by his appearance, his eyes enormous and wandering, his voice hoarse. In the end, the Provost's wife had put her husband in a chair with a glass of brandy and sent Leonard back to the porter's lodge to make the all-important first call to the authorities. After that, Leonard had been constantly busy, first with the night-duty officers who arrived to secure the crime scene, then, for an hour or so, with the forensics team, all the while continuing to provide updates for the Provost and his wife, who had vacated their lodge and were now in the Provost's new office in Old Court, awaiting the arrival of the investigating detective, who was unaccountably late.

Sipping his tea as he walked, Leonard told himself that it made no material difference that he had not actually seen the body. He had gathered from the Provost's detailed, if sometimes incoherent, comments that the young woman had been garrotted and trussed, and had something terrible wedged into her mouth. Perhaps, he mused, it had been some sort of sexual game. He had heard of such things. Fruit, he thought, was often involved – though, why, he could not guess. He fingered his jaw nervously as he thought about it, and winced. It would come down hard on the Provost, he knew that. In his own study! There were rumours about the Provost's marital relations. And, now Leonard thought of it, there had been something hard – betrayed, almost – in the way the Provost's wife had avoided looking at her husband as they stood together in the study, communicating the awful news to him. If the Provost had seemed shrunken and confused, she had been fiercely herself.

These thoughts invigorated him. Sipping his tea, he felt calm and alert. Then, he glanced over towards the porch, and frowned. What now?

He stumped over and rapped smartly on the window. 'Oi!' he called. 'Oi, you!'

A youth was standing there. He seemed to have come in to shelter from the rain. He was skinny and white, sloppily dressed in the manner of the idle poor, in white Adidas trackies, a garish jacket and unlaced Nike trainers. His fairish hair was plastered against his forehead. His nose and chin seemed too big for his

34

thin face. There was something on his cheek – Leonard thought it was tears, until he realised it was a scar of some sort. Brazen as you like, he stood there sipping from a can of energy drink and fiddling with his phone.

Leonard slid open the window. 'College is closed,' he said loudly. 'It's the middle of the night,' he added.

The youth ignored him.

Leonard felt a surge of masterful anger. 'Nothing to say, eh?'

The youth took another drink. Glanced across, looked down again.

'Not surprised,' Leonard went on. 'I know your sort. I dealt with your sort at Broadwater Farm in eighty-five. Don't matter. I'm seventy-four,' he added. 'I'm going to call 999.'

The youth spoke: '101. Non-emergency.'

Leonard hesitated.

'841148, if you want to report antisocial,' the youth added.

Confused, Leonard Gamp said, with dignity, 'I've no doubt you're known at both of those numbers, but I'll call who I want. And that's the police.'

He hesitated, however, as the youth pushed himself off the wall and sauntered towards him, scratching himself, pushing his hand around in his baggy tracksuit pocket. For a sickening moment, Leonard thought he was going to expose himself. But instead he took out some sort of passport and held it up in an oddly familiar manner.

'Already here, mate.'

Leonard's face lurched at the sight of the well-known badge.

The ID read: *Ryan Wilkins, detective inspector, Thames Valley CID.*

35

The youth wiped his nose with a finger, while Leonard stared at him in horror.

'Get your head on, Gramps,' Ryan said. 'There's been a murder. Thought you'd be expecting me.'

Leonard found his voice at last – his formal one, slightly shaky: 'The Provost and his wife are waiting in his office.'

'Crime scene first. You should know that.'

'What do you mean?'

'Broadwater Farm, you said. With the Met, were you?'

Leonard swallowed. 'Fifteen years.'

'Get in gear, then.'

'They've been waiting hours already.'

'Going to be waiting longer, then, aren't they?'

Leonard clenched his jaw. 'Very well. I'll escort you to the lodge.'

'Can't you just point me in the right direction? What's the matter? Think I'm going to nick something on the way?'

Leonard breathed. He said slowly, as if with difficulty, 'Most people find the layout of the college complicated.'

'Well, lucky for you, I'm a fucking homing pigeon.'

The world suddenly seemed a far more unsatisfactory place to Leonard Gamp. This sort of thing would not happen in the Royal Gibraltar, nor, indeed, at the Met. Limping badly, he emerged from the lodge and reluctantly began to give Detective Inspector Wilkins directions.

THREE

At six o'clock, the sun had still not come up in Oxford. The small damp city slept on under drizzling darkness. In the heavy gloom of Christ Church Meadow, beyond St Aldates Police Station, ghost trees stood half-submerged in pools of mist.

Out of this darkness a woman appeared, moving steadily at pace along the river towpath, next to the black flow of water. She ran across the footbridge behind the Salters building, up the path out of the shadows to the Abingdon Road, then turned towards town, passing under the milky blooms of obscure light hanging from the street lamps over Folly Bridge, as far as the police station, where she came to rest.

She was a slightly built woman of fifty-six, with a wiry frame and a small, neat head of close-cropped black hair. Damp, now, from the mist, in running tights and jacket, she appeared sleek and grizzled. She had a silent, efficient way of holding her body, a habit developed gradually out of private discipline, partly to combat the sciatica in her hip, partly to cope with the pressures of her job. Her mood was sometimes bitter, her fitness regime more important than ever in controlling it. But, today, she had different preoccupations.

After a moment, she went inside.

'Morning, ma'am,' the officer on duty said.

'Morning, Janine.' She made a point of knowing the names of all her staff. 'What's the news from the Leys?'

'Been quiet since about four.'

'How many arrests, in the end?'

'Seventeen.'

'Damage?'

'Three cars in Merlin Road burned out. Shop windows smashed along Blackbird Leys Road.'

'Are we in touch with the family of the boy?'

'Yes, ma'am.'

'I want to go out to see them as soon as possible. Is the body at the JR?'

'Yes, ma'am.'

'I want complete privacy. No leaks.'

'Understood, ma'am.'

Blackbird Leys was a tight community – also, by various metrics, one of the most deprived urban areas in the country. One of the poorest, side-by-side with one of the richest. Feelings would be running very high.

The Super looked at Janine. 'Thank you,' she said, smiling slightly. 'It's going to be a long day. But we'll get through it.'

She went through security, past Operations and Admin and up the stairs, heading for the showers next to the senior-management suite above.

She didn't get there. In the corridor, she encountered one of her inspectors.

'Ray!' she said, in surprise.

'Super?'

Raymond Wilkins was one of the force's high flyers, of a new generation of young black detectives coming through. Thirty years old, Oxford educated (PPE, Balliol, 2006), thoughtful and articulate, he had risen rapidly, via the fast-track graduate programme in criminal investigation, to his current position of detective inspector. He was strikingly good-looking, with a steady, attentive way of looking at women that made them overly conscious of his shapely mouth, his shining skin, his intelligent dark eyes. He was suave dresser too, this morning wearing a grey blazer with a pink box-check pattern, over a sky-blue gingham shirt and navy khaki trousers. His chic glasses gave him a thoughtful air. He had been with Thames Valley three years already and had formed a close working relationship with the Superintendent. She liked him. She had been a detective herself, and chief detective inspector too, before going back into uniform, and she thought of all the detectives as hers.

'I'm surprised you're back so soon.'

He paused. 'What?'

'From Barnabas.'

He looked blank.

'You got the call last night, right?'

'What call?'

There was a moment when they just looked at each other; then they went into her office, and she went straight to her desk phone and dialled.

'What have we heard this morning from Barnabas? . . . When was that? . . . Who?' As she listened, she glanced over at Ray, who was watching her closely. 'No,' she said into the phone. 'He's with me here, now; he doesn't know anything about it.' She listened only a few seconds before interrupting. 'Doesn't matter. Get me the night dispatch team.' A moment later, she spoke again. 'Who put the call out about Barnabas last night? I need to know who it went to. Call me. Yes, straight away.'

Replacing the receiver, she looked steadily at Ray. 'There was a body found in the college last night. A girl. In the Provost's lodge.'

Ray raised his eyebrows.

'In his private study, actually. I know. Today of all days. Goes without saying, it needs careful handling. I asked for you to be called.'

'I didn't get a call. What happened?'

'I don't know yet.'

'But someone got the call?'

'Yes, someone did. Someone's there now.'

'Who?'

She hesitated. 'I don't know yet,' she said again. 'They thought it was you. Something's gone wrong.'

She was conscious of sitting there, still sweating, in her running kit, but she forced her mind away from that. 'I don't have time for this,' she said quietly. The phone rang and she answered and listened for a moment. 'How long for? . . . Alright, what then? . . . How did that happen? Christ almighty. Doesn't matter. Get him on the phone. Yes, now!'

After she replaced the receiver, she didn't speak for a while.

Ray said nothing either. Finally, she said, 'We've got a new detective joining today.'

'I heard.'

'His name's also Wilkins.' She paused. 'Ryan.' She looked at him. 'Another R. Wilkins.'

After a moment, Ray said, 'You're kidding me.'

'It seems he got the call by mistake. First there was a delay – nearly four hours; the night team got distracted by the Leys incidents. Then your numbers got mixed up in dispatch records.'

'Embarrassing.'

She winced. 'Worse than embarrassing, actually.'

He raised his eyebrows, but she said no more. Her phone rang again and she answered it. 'Have you got him for me?' she said. 'What do you mean? Why would he do that? . . . Yes, keep trying,' she said. 'Yes, immediately.'

'What's wrong now?' Ray asked softly. He waited patiently, but the Super only shook her head.

'I'll call if I need you,' she said.

Outside her office, Ray stood a moment, thoughtfully. Then he went down the stairs. Though it was still early, he could feel the tension in the building, in the sudden bursts of footsteps, the doors shutting tight on clipped conversations. The disturbances in Blackbird Leys were only going to get worse when news spread that, in the early hours of the morning, a local boy had been knocked down and killed by a police car. He went down to the floor below and along the corridor, until he came to COMINT – Communications Intelligence.

Nadim worked an early shift; she was already at her desk,

hitting the keyboard. She was the keenest and also the best of the IT specialists on the force.

'Hey, Ray.'

He nodded. 'Do me a favour?'

Without moving her head, she glanced sideways at him. She liked Ray. All the staff liked Ray, especially the women. 'Maybe. Not got much time. Fallout from the Leys.'

'What's happened now?'

'Three officers suspended. She's about to brief the media. Going to announce an independent inquiry. Local feeling's running very high. It's a war zone, basically.' She looked at him again. 'So, what favour?'

'Ryan Wilkins, the detective inspector joining us today. What do you know about him?'

'Only what's in the classified file. Which you don't have access to.' She typed on impassively, eyes fixed on her screen.

'Come on, Nadim,' Ray said, after a moment. 'It's not a big deal.' He hesitated. 'Is it?'

She pursed her lips.

'You know how it works here,' he persisted. 'Everyone's going to know inside a week, anyway.'

'I don't know much. The file's redacted, obviously.'

'Just tell me what you do know.'

'He's coming to us from Wiltshire division.'

'Okay.'

'Under a cloud.'

'What cloud?'

She hesitated before she spoke: 'Gross misconduct.'

Ray shook his head. 'Can't be right. He would've been dismissed, not transferred.'

'Mitigated on appeal.'

'What happened?'

'He lost it with someone down there.'

'Verbal?'

'Physical.'

'Bad?'

'The guy went to A & E.'

Ray thought about that. 'What guy?' he said.

'That's the thing.'

'What do you mean?'

'Wasn't just some guy off the street. Not a suspect or contact. Or a passer-by.'

'Who was it, then?'

'The Bishop of Salisbury.'

Silence.

'You're winding me up,' Ray said, at last.

She shrugged. 'Everyone'll be talking about it within a week – you said so yourself.'

Ray stood there, mystified. 'What, he doesn't like bishops?'

'File says he has, quote, "problems with privileged elites", unquote. Must be good, though,' she added. 'Came top of his year in the fast track.'

'Obviously the treatment of bishops wasn't part of the course. Why're we getting him?'

'He grew up here.'

'Where?'

She hesitated. 'Hinksey Point trailer park.'

'*Trailer park?*' He made a helpless face, then turned to go.

'Ray?'

'What?'

'You know the Super. She'll look after him, bring him in slowly, keep him away from sensitive cases to begin with.'

Ray made no reply. He was imagining Ryan Wilkins of Hinksey Point trailer park with the famously pompous Provost of Barnabas Hall. He went, without speaking, from the room. It was half past six in the morning, still raining.

FOUR

At seven o'clock, Ryan was just leaving the crime scene, where he had spent the previous few hours with the forensics team, and was on his way to see the Provost and his wife. Picking his teeth, flicking through a copy of the college magazine, which he had found in the Provost's lodge, he ambled down the stone steps, round the Fellows' Garden and under the archway into New Court. Still reading, he went past the chapel, round the cloisters, through to Old Court and cut across the lawn towards staircase XII and the Provost's office. He didn't miss a turn. His sense of direction was uncanny. A gift, unasked for, like the scar on his face or his son.

Before he went up the stairs, he took a moment to have a smoke and glance around. An oval of shaven grass, with a sundial in the middle. Wavy low roofs, orangey brick facades. One wall of crisp stone and glass, only recently completed – some of the windowpanes still had the manufacturer's labels on them. Lots of small new rooms. A labyrinth of staircases and corridors. He could imagine it.

He had always noticed things. They stuck to his eyes. Sometimes, things he didn't want to see. Police training had taught him not to look away – an ambiguous skill. Luckily, he'd always known how to forget, how to lose himself – in the sight of his son sleeping under his tractor-print duvet, or at a club, dissolving into the moving crowd, lost in the raking lights, the thumping music.

He took a last drag and dropped the butt next to a sign saying *No Smoking*. His phone rang again, but he didn't recognise the number and didn't want the distraction. He had a new job, a new boss. Get in quickly, stir things up, that was his style. He climbed the old stairs to the second floor and went, without knocking, into an old-fashioned study, expensively decorated in cream and pale green, with a dove-grey carpet, elegant desk and a vase of dried flowers in an empty ornate fireplace. Framed photographs of college events and sporting teams, captioned with fancy calligraphy, covered the walls.

The Provost was a dumpy guy with a wobbly head. Despite the fact that the old porter must have told him all about Ryan, the man stared at him in surprised silence, as if he'd never seen someone wearing trackies or a baseball cap before. Ryan rummaged around in his trackie pocket, flashed his badge. The Provost didn't react; he was still reacting to Ryan's appearance in the room. Ryan put his hands back in his pockets, looking round sceptically.

Without getting up from behind his desk, the Provost said slowly, in a rising crescendo, 'Assuming that you are, in fact, Detective Inspector Wilkins of the Thames Valley CID, we have been waiting here to speak to you for eight and a half hours. Could you explain why?' His voice trembled slightly as he spoke.

'Yeah,' Ryan said. 'I could.'

He glanced round at the Provost's wife, who gazed back at him coolly from an easy chair in the corner. She had something wrong with her face: it was handsome and twisted. Her mouth was half-dead, but her eyes were alert. Ryan immediately liked her.

'Who's the girl?' he asked her.

She composed herself before she spoke. Perhaps it was a habit she had, perhaps something to do with her stroke. 'I don't know.' There was irritation in her eyes, though not for him. She did not look at her husband.

'What about you?' Ryan asked the Provost.

'The girl? We'd never met her, we don't know anything about her, she's a total stranger. And, before you ask, no, we don't know how her body came to be in our house. It's an outrage. And, now,' he said, 'are you going to answer my question?'

Ryan ignored him. 'So, you'd never seen her before?'

The Provost made a show of controlling his exasperation. 'As I just said,' he said, at last.

'Why's she in your study, then?'

'I have no idea. *As I just said.*'

A glance passed between him and his wife, a tiny involuntary flicker. Most people would have missed it. Not Ryan.

He said to the Provost's wife, 'Who found her?'

The Provost spoke first: 'We both found her.'

'Who's "we"?'

'Who do you think? My wife and I.'

His wife said, 'There was another person with us too – a young art historian. Kent Dodge.'

47

'He won't be of much use,' the Provost said. 'He passed out. He's from America,' he added.

'What time?'

'Quarter past ten, last night,' the Provost said.

'Nearly half past,' his wife said.

Ryan nodded at her. 'And where were you earlier, between eight thirty and nine thirty?'

The Provost said, 'That's your estimated time of death, is it?'

Ryan said nothing. He listened while the Provost explained about the reception drinks and dinner, about al-Medina and his bodyguard and their departure. He mentioned in passing the issue of the Koran, the disagreement about the picture. His account was pedantic, shapeless, like a lopsided story; nothing in it connected to the body in his study. Occasionally, he lost the thread of what he was saying, and Ryan prompted him, and he repeated himself angrily. His attitude to Ryan was resentful and contemptuous.

Ryan kept calm. He made no notes. He listened, looking round the elegant room.

'Anything odd?' he asked, at last. 'Apart from finding a dead stranger on the floor of your study, which we'll assume for the minute is odd. Anything else out of the ordinary when you got back, after your dinner?'

'No.'

'The front door was locked,' his wife said, after a moment.

The Provost breathed heavily as he turned to her. 'That's because, as I told you, I locked it when we went out.'

He looked at Ryan, who said, 'You sure?'

'Of course I'm sure.'

48

Ryan nodded, thought for a moment. 'What painting were you arguing about?'

The Provost was taken aback. 'Does it matter?'

'Pretend, for a second, I'm someone who knows what a painting is.'

'It's not a painting, in fact. It's an illuminated page from a Persian album. Sixteenth century. It's in our college collection.'

Ryan waited.

The Provost went on, 'It shows a young woman reclining after bathing. Is that enough detail for you? You can look it up online, in our catalogue. The Gunter Matthias bequest. I have a reproduction of it hanging in my study,' he added, 'though I wouldn't expect you to have noticed it.'

Ryan didn't hesitate. 'Between the windows on the south wall? Gold and blue. White skin, black hair, duck pattern on a towel.'

The Provost shrugged.

'Small, really small. Like, about this big.'

The Provost looked at him scornfully. 'Its size is immaterial. The feeling in it accounts for its interest.'

After a moment, Ryan nodded. 'And who was right?'

'What do you mean?'

'You were arguing about it. Some "point of detail", you said. Who was right?'

The Provost was silent. His wife said, 'I was.'

Ryan turned to her. 'So, now we've established who's good with detail, I can ask you: did he lock the door?'

If she was flustered, she didn't show it. She said carefully, out of the side of her mouth, 'Perhaps. But I was surprised. Usually he leaves it unlocked.'

The Provost became agitated. 'I lock the door,' he said. 'It's my habit to lock the door; the idea that I always leave the door—'

'Calm the fuck down, alright?' Ryan said. 'It's not about the door. It's about the key.'

Momentarily speechless, the Provost looked blank.

'You still got your key, right?'

He didn't deny it.

'So obviously someone else had a key. They locked the door behind them when they left. What we're doing now, right, is sorting out how come they could have got hold of it.'

The Provost made a dismissive noise and Ryan got angry.

'Tell you what I think. I think that, if you can't be arsed to lock your own front door, and you're the head or whatever you call it of this place, security here's probably a bit crap all round. Probably the sort of place where, I don't know, keys get hung up in great big labelled bunches on wooden pegs in some open-access office, waiting for someone to come and borrow them.'

The Provost gritted his teeth. 'The bursary is manned at all times,' he said. 'All the keys have to be signed out.'

'Yeah, yeah, in a great big . . . What do you call it?'

The Provost looked at him, puzzled.

'Come on,' Ryan said. 'Book. Great big book, with handwriting. What's the posh word?'

'Ledger?'

'Yeah, ledger. Think I'll stroll over to this bursar place and have a squint at the ledger. Don't go away. I'll be back.'

'Is that it?' the Provost asked, incredulously. 'Is that what we waited eight and a half hours for?'

'No. You waited to tell me what you know, which you haven't done yet. So, I'll give you a little rest, so you can think about what you've missed out.'

'Are you implying that I'm a suspect?'

'You were busy sipping champagne at the time of death, weren't you? What you are is a material witness, and what I want to know from you is who's the girl and what's she doing in your study?'

'I've told you already, I don't know!'

Ryan merely moved towards the door.

'Before you go,' the Provost said, 'I want to impress on you the need for total discretion. For reasons which I don't need to explain here, this is an extraordinarily sensitive matter. Confidentiality is absolutely vital. You understand? I shall be phoning Superintendent Waddington now, to emphasise this. She's a personal friend. I hope I make myself clear.'

He was looking belligerently at Ryan. He was still a dumpy guy with a wobbly head, but he had the tone of voice to make you think he was President of Neverland.

Ryan said, 'Hasn't sunk in yet, has it? There's a dead girl in your private study, right? Someone put their hands round her throat and squeezed and squeezed until she was actually dead. Right?' He paused. 'The feeling in it accounts for the interest, I think you'll find,' he said.

The Provost's wife made a noise, immediately smothered.

Ryan pointed at him. 'And there'll be plenty of interest. I'd expect headlines, if I were you.'

The Provost's face shook. 'Would you indeed?'

'Yeah. Buckle up.'

51

The Provost was on his feet as Ryan left. 'Buckle up?' he shouted. '*Buckle up?*'

But Ryan had gone. He sauntered down the old worn stairs, checking his phone as he went. Three missed calls. Fuck it. He had a job to do.

FIVE

In her office, in the St Aldates Station, Detective Superintendent Waddington – still unshowered, still dressed in her running kit – spoke clearly into her phone. 'I don't understand,' she said. She listened. 'What do you mean he's blocking your calls? Are you sure you have the right number? You know what, forget it.'

She hung up, and dialled again.

'Ray? I need you.'

A minute later, he knocked and entered.

'He's not answering his phone,' she said. 'This is absurd. As if I haven't got enough to do today, without babysitting a new detective. I want you to go up to Barnabas now and find him. What can he be doing? Whatever it is, stop him and bring him back here.'

Ray nodded, stepping back out of her office. On his way to the sally port, he stopped again in COMINT.

'The other Wilkins. I need a picture.'

Nadim said, 'There's one about to go up on the website.'

'Show me.'

He looked at the face on screen.

'What's he done to his face?'

'Scar tissue. Childhood injury, apparently.'

Ray sighed. 'How old is he?'

'Twenty-seven.'

'Really? He looks about fifteen.'

'Why do you need his picture?'

'He's gone rogue at Barnabas. His first morning! I'm going to fetch him.'

'Good luck.'

'I don't need luck. What I could do with is support from the youth offending team.'

It was a five-minute walk from the St Aldates Station to Barnabas Hall, but Ray took his car, and left it, blue lights blinking, on the cobbles outside the college gate, behind the forensics wagon at the edge of the cordon. In the cordon, he noticed, was a beaten-up Peugeot 306, now clamped.

The arthritic old porter's attitude was strained and wary. Yes, a detective inspector had arrived earlier.

'Young fellow,' he said cautiously, watching Ray's face. 'Dressed like . . . I made him show me the badge,' he said, as if expecting to be asked why he had let him in.

'Where is he?'

'He went over, first, to the Provost's lodge. Made his own way. Wouldn't let me take him there.'

'Where's the lodge?'

'He's not there now. I got a call from my colleague to say he was going into the Provost's new office in Old Court.' The porter consulted his watch. 'That's only a quarter of an hour ago, so he'll still be there.'

'How do I get there?'

'I can take you.'

'Just point me. I'll find my way.'

Sighing, Leonard led him to the edge of the quad and began to give directions.

SIX

Emerging from staircase XII into Old Court, Ryan stood on the flagstones a moment, thinking about the dead girl. No ID as yet. Unidentified dead female. He remembered the rigid sprawl of her body on the pretty grey carpet of the Provost's study, the angry look towards the wall, her bloated, frozen fury. Alive, she must have been beautiful. Her body had that magazine perfection, solid and taut. Incredible skin. Tight midriff exposed under the forensics photographer's lights. Great breasts. Long toned thighs. And she'd known how beautiful she was: her hair was chic, her make-up immaculate, fingernails precisely glossed.

But then there was her expression, that fat, protruding tongue, those bulging black eyes. Police pathologists advised you not to read meaning into the expressions of dead people. They're not expressions at all, just brute, fanciful shapes made by violence. But Ryan couldn't help thinking how angry she looked. Angry, and something else. Outraged.

He was outraged himself, though he was careful not to show it.

Just thinking about her now, he could feel pity start to flood him. He took another drag on his cigarette to calm himself. He never allowed his sympathies for victims to show. That wasn't something they'd taught him at the police academy; it was something he'd already learned. He came from a world where sympathy was the wrong look altogether. Anger was better, rage at the thought that someone had choked her life out, made her ugly, dropped her on the carpet like trash and walked away. But – and he knew this, as well – his anger was a risky thing, it carried him away, got him into trouble. Insolence was best. People understood insolence in someone like him; everything fell into place if he was rude to them.

He ground out his butt and looked about him. After a moment, he hitched up his trackies and ambled through an archway into a small garden laid out in a corner between the walls of the chapel and the New Court halls.

On the other side of the garden was a young woman and an East Asian girl carrying a schoolgirl satchel. The girl was complaining about an unannounced closure to the library the evening before. They talked together briefly before the girl went off, holding her bag against her chest.

The woman turned and saw Ryan.

'Thought uni students didn't do any work,' he said.

'They work very hard, here. Though Kim's exceptional. Always in the library. Up early, stays late.'

Her voice was brisk and polite. She had long blonde hair, very fine and straight, and a pretty, narrow face, with the big fawn eyes and cute nose of a certain class of Englishwoman, bringing to mind Barbour jackets and well-behaved horses. At a guess, she was in her late twenties. Her grey skirt and jacket were formal, her shoes chic: slimline clothes and a sexy, weasel-slim body.

'You're up early too,' Ryan said. 'Preparing for classes?'

'No. I'm not a don,' the woman said. She looked at him with curiosity. 'Do you think I look like one?'

'Don't know what a don is, to be honest.'

'A don's a tutor. From the Spanish. *Don*, meaning gentleman.'

'So, they look a bit Spanish?'

She smiled. She said, in a low, mock-serious voice, 'Some of them even *are* Spanish. Full Spaniards.'

'I can tell you got them sussed. Anyway, you're not a don, you're not a student, so I'm guessing you're on the business side of things here.'

'Maybe I am.' She looked at him coyly.

'Organised type. Good discipline and that.'

'And how do you know?'

'Up early, like I say. Got to have spent a bit of time making yourself look so good. Or is it all natural?'

She made a face of comic disapproval. 'A lot of time, actually. But, unless you know university life, you won't be able to guess what I actually do.'

'Oh, I know what you do. I've just been arsing around.'

'What, then?'

'You're the Bursar.'

She was so surprised, she stopped looking mischievous. 'How do you know that?'

'Just got that look. Sort of bursarish.'

'Really?' She looked disconcerted.

'Nah. Just clowning. Saw your picture in the college mag.

58

Jumped out at me. But it's lucky I've run into you, right, 'cause I wanted to ask you something. About a key. Or, maybe, bunch of keys.'

She stared at him. An expression he'd seen before: part frown, part incredulity. 'Are you . . . a policeman?'

He did the flashing-badge thing. 'There you go. Sorted. We're both good at working stuff out. Anyway, about these keys.'

'Yes, you're quite right. There's a bunch missing. I was just going to the lodge to report it.'

'Check the ledger?'

'Yes. Not signed for. Just gone.'

'Right.' He sighed. 'And who has access to the bursary?'

She coloured.

'Yeah, thought so. The world.'

'Well,' she said, 'we generally manage to keep an eye on things. But . . .'

He sighed, scratched, looked at her. 'Happened before?' he asked, at last. 'Keys gone missing, turned up later sort of thing?'

'Yes, actually. Last week. Ameena Najib. She's new. Kitchen staff. She forgot to sign them out.'

'Change the locks and that?'

'No need. I had a feeling she might have been the culprit. I had a quiet word with her and, in fact, we found them almost immediately, in her locker.'

'Ameena . . .'

'Najib. She's had a very difficult time recently, a lot of stress. I think she's having trouble settling in. She seems to mislay a lot of things. Anyway, in the end, no one needed to know about the keys.'

He drifted off again, rubbing his cheek with a finger, while she looked at him with undisguised curiosity. She was almost smiling.

'What else was on the bunch?' he said, at last.

'Which other keys? Key for the lodge, for the chapel, the library, the collections room. Oh, and the bursary.'

He nodded and turned.

'Is it true?' she asked.

'What?'

'What Leonard's saying. About . . . a dead woman.'

He nodded again. 'She's dead alright. You can tell.'

'In the Provost's lodge?'

'No need to be so delicate. I bet Gramps couldn't wait to tell you everything. In the Provost's study.'

She nodded. 'And . . .'

'And what?'

'And . . . something in her mouth?'

Ryan scratched his head, frowned. 'Yeah. Her tongue. Partly in her mouth, partly out of it, if you want to know.'

'Nothing else?'

'What *has* Gramps been imagining?'

'Fruit of some sort, I think. He didn't specify.' She looked apologetic.

There was a short silence.

'What's your view of the Provost?' Ryan asked, suddenly.

Taken aback, she hesitated, slowly colouring again.

He prompted her. 'Dumpy guy. Wobbly head. You'd recognise him.'

She scowled. 'I know who he is. Why do you ask? Surely he's not a suspect.'

There was a moment of strained silence, which Ryan was careful not to break. Looking at her all the time, he nodded thoughtfully and turned to go.

'I'm careful not to find myself alone with him,' she said suddenly. Her face was very red.

Ryan raised his eyebrows. 'One of those, eh?'

'Nothing vicious. But his hands have a habit of putting in an appearance without introducing themselves.'

He nodded.

'Not to be repeated,' she said.

'Fair enough.'

'Am I free to go, now?'

'Oh, no.' He gave her a sudden smile. 'I'll be wanting to see you again.'

'More questions?'

'Don't worry, I'll think of something.'

'Where are you going, now?'

'Just going to have a wander, to be honest. See the sights, you know. Back to the Fellows' Garden, maybe. Looks like a pretty spot. Not often someone like me gets into a place like this. By the way, what *is* a fellows' garden?'

'Fellows are members of the college.'

'Spaniards?'

'Some of them. The Fellows' Garden is a garden especially for them. Fellows only.'

'Sounds like a dirty mag.' He turned to go.

'By the way,' she said, 'I'm not sure the security here's absolutely as bad as you think. It's not high-tech, not even low-tech, but there's a sort of unofficial surveillance going on all the time.

61

People-watching. In a place like this, you get to know very quickly the sort of person who belongs and who doesn't.'

'Like me.'

'I don't just mean an individual. I mean a type.'

'Yeah. Like me.'

She didn't lower her eyes. 'Alright, yes, like you. Anyone here can tell straight away you don't fit in. I mention it just because, well, if there was someone here from outside, last night, even someone doing their best to fit in, there's a chance someone noticed. Even if they weren't conscious of it at the time. They might remember.'

He nodded. 'Alright. Good shout. See you later, then.'

He went up the steps and sauntered into the chapel porch, and she turned the other way and went through the archway to Old Court and round the curving path towards staircase XII.

At the bottom of the stairs, she passed a young black guy coming out. Good-looking – remarkably so – but distracted. He was dressed in a fancy grey blazer with a pink box-check pattern, and he went at speed towards the main gate, looking about him. She put him down as a visiting academic, late for an early-morning appointment, and continued up the stairs to see the Provost.

SEVEN

It was another hour before Ray caught up with Ryan, nine o'clock before Ryan finally made it into the Superintendent's office. He stood in front of her desk, blinking, while she looked at him.

She had showered and changed, and sat there immaculately dressed in her uniform. Her mood, however, was still in disarray.

'All go, then, eh?' Ryan said, to break the hostile silence. 'Non-stop, or what? Things kicking off in the Leys.' His voice was nervous, hopeful. He wiped his nose with a finger. 'Didn't expect Thames Valley to be such a madhouse. Three o'clock start, first day.' He grinned uncertainly. 'Not complaining. Said to my sister—'

'Shut up.'

He stood there, rubbing the palm of his hand over his cheek.

'Why did you block our calls?'

'Didn't know they was from here, to be fair.'

'Why didn't you know?'

'Well. First day and that. Just—'

'It's taken us over two hours to pull you out of there. I don't know how long it will take to undo the damage you've managed to do.'

He frowned.

'I've had two telephone calls already this morning. The first from Sir James.'

'Who's he?'

'He's the Provost of Barnabas, the man you tormented this morning. I know Sir James socially. He sounded as if he was about to have a breakdown. He feels demeaned, insulted, abused, ignored.'

'Don't remember abusing him. Told him to calm the fuck down, I think, but—'

'The second call was from a national media outlet.'

'Don't know anything about that. Nothing at all. I did warn him, though. And I was tempted, I got to be honest.'

'Tempted? You're not aware that unauthorised contact with the media is a misdemeanour in the police code of conduct?'

'Yeah, course. Everyone does it, though.'

'No one does it here.'

'I wasn't going to do it. It's just he needed something to think about. Bring him down a bit.'

The Superintendent took a breath. 'What do you know about the Oxford colleges?'

'Well, they're pretty weird—'

'They've educated half of our prime ministers, an extremely high proportion of our politicians, judges, journalists, captains of industry, educationalists, analysts and activists. They are the heart of the establishment. A closed world. A world with its own rules, its own way of doing things. We don't blunder in without taking care. We don't risk offending them, because, for all we know, they're advising the government on law-enforcement policy or police funding, or they have the ear of the producer of the *News at Ten*. We don't tell the Provost of one of the colleges to calm the fuck down. Do you understand me?' Her face pointed at him, wren-like and fierce.

'Got it.' He shuffled his feet. 'Only that . . .'

'Only what?'

'He's obviously hiding something.'

The Super looked at him silently for a full thirty seconds. Then she made a call.

'Ray? Can you come up? Yes, now, please.'

She said nothing else. Ryan looked around. You can tell a lot about a person from their office. The Superintendent's was unfussy, bare, tidy. Her uniform correct, her desk empty. Ryan wondered where all her untidiness went. He liked her. Mid-fifties. Small head; dark, close-cropped hair; thin lips. A hint of pain somewhere in the corners of her eyes. At her age, arthritis maybe, or sciatica. A medical condition is a sort of untidiness, perhaps. But she looked neat and efficient and fair.

Ray came in and stood next to Ryan, slightly behind him.

'Ray – you'll be taking over the case at Barnabas, as of now. You know some of the details already. Ryan, you'll brief Ray to make sure he's not missing anything. Understood?'

Ryan shuffled about, head down, hands in trackie pockets. He made preparatory noises.

'Well?' she said.

'It's not right.'

'Pardon?'

'It's my case.'

'You've handled it badly. I'm taking it off you.'

'Not on my first day; it's not right.'

'Before it gets worse. We're not having another Salisbury here.'

Ryan flushed. He looked at Ray. Ray looked at the Superintendent.

Ryan said to Ray, 'Did you go to an Oxford college yourself, then?'

The Superintendent said, angrily, 'The point is he knows how to handle it, and you don't.'

'You've only given me a few hours. Haven't even reported yet. Still picking things up.'

'What have you picked up? ID on the dead girl?'

'Not yet.'

'Where she came from? What she was doing there? Why she was killed?'

'No.'

'Suspects?'

He shook his head.

'Witnesses? What have you got? Nothing.'

Ryan bit his lip.

'That's why it's the right time for Ray to take over. You can tell him what you've picked up so far; it won't take long.'

Ryan turned to Ray. 'Write this down, then: that Provost fella's a bit suspicious.'

Ray said, quietly, 'We can do this downstairs.'

Ryan ignored him. 'And this: bit weird that it all kicks off on a night they've got some old Sheikh over, everyone running round like meth heads. He stormed off early doors, so I hear – what's going on there?' He turned to the Superintendent. 'You say they're all closed up, yeah? I totally get that. But you have a read of their mags, and you look at their collections of foreign stuff, and all the foreign students queuing up for the library, and all these sheikhs giving them millions of sheks, or whatever it is – you can't help thinking they're plugged into the great big international world of money alright. And I don't know who the dead girl is, but frankly she looked a bit foreign to me. Yeah. Shape of the nose, I think.'

This was the moment when a superintendent would usually tell him to tone it down, but she didn't; she just looked at him. He couldn't read her expression.

'Let's go,' Ray said.

But Ryan went on: 'One other thing, right. The key. Obvious the perp don't need it to get in – security's a fucking joke. Why's he need it, then? Locked the door behind him. Why?'

Ray said, promptly, without meaning to, 'Delay the finding of the body.'

'Yeah. But here's a funny thing. Library was locked yesterday evening as well. Meant to be open twenty-four seven. Open again this morning when I went to have a gander. Bit weird. Someone locks themselves in the Provost's Lodge, leaves behind a body. Someone locks themselves in the library, leaves behind . . . this.'

He smacked something down with a crack on the Super's empty desk.

They all looked at it. A little transparent evidence bag, and in it a woman's ring.

The Superintendent said, 'Why isn't this with Forensics?'

'That's what I'm saying. Not had a chance yet.'

67

She looked grim. 'You found it in the library?'

'On a desk. Could be hers, I reckon – the dead woman's. Looks sort of foreign, to me.'

Ray made an exasperated noise.

Ryan said, 'Tests'll show. Could be that, first, she's in the locked library; then, she's in the locked Provost's lodge. What's going on? Interesting, though.' He grinned hopefully.

The Superintendent said, 'Are you saying that Sir James is a suspect?'

He shook his head. 'Not if he was having drinks with the Sheikh. He might know the girl, though. I've got a hunch about it. He definitely knows more than he's saying.'

The Super's phone rang. 'Yes,' she said. She hesitated. 'Alright. Put her through.' She turned away from the two men and faced the near wall while she spoke. 'Penelope . . . Yes. I know you did. I can only repeat what I said to Sir— . . . I see. Yes, he's here.' With an unreadable expression, she handed the phone to Ryan. 'Lady Penelope,' she said. 'The Provost's wife. Wants to speak to you.'

Ryan took the phone, looked at it a moment, held it to his ear. 'Yeah?'

The Provost's wife said, in her slightly blurred voice, 'We feel we got off on the wrong foot when you visited this morning. Shall we make another try?'

'Yeah, alright.'

'There are things, perhaps, we didn't have a chance to discuss, so can I suggest you return at your convenience?'

'Alright. Will do.'

'We'll see you later, then. Goodbye.'

Ryan handed the phone back to the Super. 'She wants me to go back, talk to them again.'

The Superintendent looked at him.

'Think she trusts me,' he said. 'We were starting to have a laugh, me and her.'

The Superintendent's expression hardened.

'Listen,' he said. 'I know I can be a dipstick, right. But I do my best. And I'm good at it, I know I am. I see stuff.'

For a moment, she continued to stare at him in silence. 'Sir James is not a suspect, correct?'

'Yeah.'

'Therefore, you won't be treating him as a suspect.'

'No, course.'

Again, she contemplated him without speaking. Her phone began to ring and she glanced at her watch. 'Alright. Work the case together. The two of you. Starting with Forensics.'

Ryan said, 'I got it covered. Trust me.'

Ray looked grim.

The Super said, exasperated, 'No, I don't trust you. I trust Ray. But you'll work together till I say otherwise. I'll expect an update on my desk every evening. Understood?'

Ryan sighed. He nodded.

Ray made no response at all. He turned and went out of the office, and, after a moment, Ryan followed him.

EIGHT

Thames Valley Police Forensics is housed in a hangar-like building, twenty minutes into the countryside, a smooth silver splinter in the sticky ribbed fields of Oxfordshire.

Ray drove – Ryan's car was still clamped – and Ryan briefed him on the way.

Inside the building, the offices and laboratories were decorated pale grey, all clean surfaces, sharp edges and squeaky floors. Taken through to the autopsy suite and dressed in white CSI suits, they stood on either side of a metal table on which the naked body of the dead woman lay, mottled cream and fish-scale blue, emptied out and zipped up again with stiches.

The Chief Pathologist, also paper-suited, addressed them, her birdlike voice coming through her respirator mask in short crackly bursts. Mainly, she addressed Ray, whom she assumed to be the senior officer. It had taken her a while, in fact, to realise that Ryan wasn't doing work experience.

'Time of death: between 20.30 and 21.30 yesterday evening.'

Ray nodded.

Ryan said, 'Can't narrow it down a bit?'

'Not without running the risk of error. Significant cooling of the body had taken place, but the heating in the room was timed to go off at ten, so it's hard to know the ambient temperature throughout the relevant period. If I had to guess, I'd say the murder took place earlier rather than later. But we can't be sure.'

She went on. 'Manner of death: asphyxiation caused by strangulation. Maximum strength was used; unusually, the windpipe was broken. Round the throat are the imprints of all ten fingers and thumbs. From the grip and slight twist, the perp was almost certainly right-handed,' she said. 'Hands medium-sized, but strong.'

She drew their attention to small nicks across the face, bloodied nose, bruising on the wrists. 'Signs of a struggle. Intense but brief. Frenzied, even.'

'A man?'

'Most likely. I couldn't categorically rule out a woman, but the strength and frankly the violence are more characteristic of a male.'

They all looked in silence at the body, the beautiful pelvis, graceful arms, delicate clavicle, breasts bulging soft-cheese-like over her ribs, the scuffed and swollen face, orderly now, but still faintly angry in expression.

'ID?' the Chief Pathologist asked.

Ray shook his head. 'Not yet.'

They stood in silence again.

Ryan picked nervously at the material of his smock. He jutted his chin towards the woman's chest. 'Impressive. Had some work done, had she?'

There was a pause.

'Breast uplift, yes,' the Chief Pathologist said to Ray. 'Augmentation to her lips too. High-quality work, within the last couple of years, probably.'

'Would've cost her, then.'

Again, the Chief Pathologist looked at Ray when she answered: 'Expensive procedures, yes.' She gestured towards the corpse. 'Signs of high-end beauty treatment in general. Haircut, skin condition, for example.'

Ray said, quietly, 'How old was she?'

'Twenty-eight, twenty-nine.'

'Toxicology?'

'Traces of cocaine.'

'Recent sexual contact?'

'None.'

'Anything else of interest?'

'Ten years ago, she had an abortion.'

There was silence again.

'Foreign, I bet,' Ryan said. 'The nose.' He fidgeted with his smock. 'I hate these things, don't you?'

Ray and the Chief Pathologist ignored him. Ray said to her, 'We'll need a full clean-up of the face.'

'For an information request?'

'Soon as.'

'We'll get on it now.'

He nodded. 'Thanks. Anything else? How about the clothing?'

She ushered them to a screen, where she began to call up images of shoes, socks, underwear, jeans and T-shirt.

'Again, high-end items. Tasteful, you might say. A young

woman who liked to dress well. Details are in the report: likely age, provenance and so on.'

They came to the end of the slide show.

Ray nodded. 'Thanks. Maybe there'll be something there to give us a steer.'

Ryan said, suddenly, 'T-shirt's a bit clean.'

This time, the Chief Pathologist turned to him.

'She got a bloody nose, didn't she?' he said.

'Minor abrasions. Interesting point, though. Some dark fibres were found on the T-shirt. They might just be from another article of clothing worn on top. But just as likely to be from contact with something worn by the perp. At this stage, inconclusive.'

Ryan was fidgeting again with his smock. 'What about the ring?'

The Chief Pathologist said, 'The ring you gave us ten minutes ago? We'll let you know when we've had a chance to analyse it.'

'Fair enough. That it, then?'

She looked at them. 'The room's still being worked on. These are the latest images.'

She showed them pictures on the screen of the Provost's study: the mahogany desk with its lamp overturned; the leather chair on its side; the long drapes of grey chenille at either side of the French windows; the back of the study door, where the Provost's scarlet robes and black velvet cap were hanging; walls blamelessly papered in pale cream; and, from a dozen different angles, the same stretch of dove-grey carpet, where the dead girl lay, twisted and furious, staring at nothing with contempt.

Ryan said, 'Any interesting fingerprints?'

She shook her head. 'The perp wore gloves and cleaned up afterwards.'

'And that's where she was killed, right? She wasn't dumped there after?'

'That's right.'

Ryan drifted off, scratching his cheek. 'Good-looking,' he said, turning to Ray.

Ray said nothing.

'Well built,' Ryan said. 'Especially up top.'

Ray ignored him.

'Dressed nice, too. Knickers and that. So, what's she doing in the groper's den?'

There was a moment's silence, then the Chief Pathologist said, 'I'll leave you to figure that out,' and walked away.

Ryan and Ray gave the body a last look as they went out, and left it lying on its gurney, one more object in the cool, silent room, inanimate except for that persistent expression on its face, furious at being killed, still furious at being talked about.

In the car, Ray said, 'Do you want to tone it down a bit?'

'Don't know what you mean.'

'It's not amusing.'

They drove back to Oxford, passing ploughed fields darkened with drizzle, the sky ahead blotted with low cloud. The car's interior was immaculate, like Ray himself. The music system, tuned to a classical station, played Bach very quietly.

'Why'd you call him a groper?' Ray asked.

'Been told it.'

'Who told you?'

'That good-looking Bursar, Claire. Can't keep his hands to himself, she said. Wouldn't mind letting my hands get to know her, I got to say. But what was the dead girl doing in his study, then? Feels personal. There's a connection, got to be.' He caught Ray's eye. 'Course,' he added, 'he's not a suspect. Still.'

'Let's concentrate, first, on getting an ID for her, shall we?'

Ryan sniffed, wiped his nose with a finger. 'Good-looking rich girl. Foreign. University type, maybe. Lots of them are rich and foreign. Academic, mature student, whatever. There to see the Provost.'

'Sir James has already said he doesn't recognise her.'

'Yeah, well. I'm keeping an open mind about what Sir Grope-a-lot says.' He mused to himself. 'Brutal job. "Frenzied, even." Lot of passion in it, whatever.'

'Evidently.'

'Accounts for the interest, I think you'll find.'

Ray frowned. 'What?'

'Not raped. No sign of theft. Just violent. Going to be hard getting hold of a motive.'

Ray said nothing.

Ryan went on: 'But what was she doing in the library earlier?' He blew out his cheeks. 'Know what? Could be a cock-up. Most things are cock-ups.'

Ray looked at him again, sideways. Nodded. 'There's no point in getting ahead of ourselves. First thing: an ID.'

'Yeah. We need to work on Slippy Bob. His study, after all.'

Ray said, 'Not you. Definitely not. Work with the office. Get a description out for display round the college. You said yourself, it's full of people-watchers. There's a chance someone noticed her.'

'Dunno. Place is full of posh foreigners.'

'Any news from Missing Persons?'

Ryan made no reply.

'You did contact them, right?'

'Do it now, when we get back.'

'What about the university checking their staff records?'

Ryan shuffled about in his seat. 'Oh, yeah, I was going to ask who sorts that kind of thing.'

'Jesus. Listen, I don't know what you were used to before, but here we work the process. Alright?'

'Alright, Mum.'

They drove on in silence. As they crossed the Frilford Road at Marcham, there was a downpour. Players on the golf course, crouching under umbrellas, dissolving like sugar statues in rain-mist. Spray from the articulated lorry in front of them blurring the windscreen.

'Bunch of tossers, anyway,' Ryan said.

'Who now?'

'Academics. Keys on pegs. Bursary manned at all times. All those fucking Spaniards.'

'What the hell are you talking about?'

'He knows more than he's telling. The Provost. His missus, too. I like her, though. Shame about her face. Talking of for-eigners . . .'

'What now?'

'Old Sheikh Money-Nuts. We need to have a chat with him, too.'

Ray looked at him, astonished. 'There's no way you're having a chat with him.'

'Why not?'

'Because the Super'll be anxious to avoid a major diplomatic incident. He's officially a foreign friend of the country.'

'You mean he's rich. If I want to interview the migrants in the kitchen, you're not going to stop me, are you?'

'Jesus Christ! Are you like this all the time? Do something useful and get on to Missing Persons.'

By the time they reached Oxford, Ryan had finished his calls. The rain had eased, but they met heavy traffic caused by roadworks at Osney and crawled up the Botley Road in awkward silence.

A call came though on the car phone, and Ray spoke to the windscreen. 'Hey, babe.'

A woman's voice, soft and educated, floated into the car. 'Hi, sugar. Just wanted to know what time you'll be home.'

'Not sure yet.'

'Having fun today?'

Ray hesitated. 'Every day is a barrel of cherries. I'll call you later.'

'Okay. Love you.'

'Love you, too.'

He glanced at Ryan, who was staring at him.

'My wife.'

'Nice.'

There was a short silence.

Ryan fidgeted. 'Call you Ray, then?' he said at last.

'What?'

'Can't call each other DI Wilkins, can we?'

Ray said, stiffly, 'I prefer Raymond, actually.'

A minute or so passed. Bach gave way, at last, to Prokofiev.

'So, Raymond. You were a student here, yeah?'

'I was, yes.'

'Nice. You know Barnabas of old, then.'

'I was at Balliol. Different college.'

'Oh. Nice, was it?'

'Good for sports.'

'Oh, yeah? Study crown green bowling or something, did you?'

'Politics, Philosophy and Economics. But I got my Blue boxing. Blue,' he said, 'is the top sporting award at the university.'

'Better watch myself, then, eh? Joke. Where d'you grow up?'

'London. Ealing Broadway.'

'Nice. Been there. Leafy and that.'

Ray said, 'What about you?'

'Here.'

'Where?'

'South.'

'Where south?'

Ryan shifted uncomfortably in his seat. 'Here and there. Moved around a bit. My dad was a . . . Don't matter what my dad was.'

There was silence for a moment. Ray pressed on: 'Got friends here still?'

'A few. Course,' he added, after a moment, 'most of them are in prison.'

Ray couldn't help glancing at him.

'That's a *joke*,' Ryan said.

He turned his face away, gazing at the eyesores of Botley Road, thinking about Baz and Mick Dick, both of them at Grendon, a category-B facility out in Bucks. Manslaughter and aggravated burglary, ten and five. Mick Dick had only been twenty-two when he went down. Ryan remembered him from the Leys, a big, lazy lad with a loose grin. Bloodshot eyes in a black face. Good at sports: boxing, football. Even tried out for Wantage Town, one time. He liked Mick, they'd been friendly for a couple of years. Baz was nuts, though. No hope for Baz. He killed his father. Still, some fathers should be killed.

He caught Ray squinting sideways at the tattoo on his wrist, trying to decipher it.

'Checking if I've spelled it right?'

'I can't read what it says.'

'Ryan.'

'Oh.' Ray looked puzzled.

'My son's name.'

Ray couldn't stop his eyes widening. 'You've got a son?'

'Two years, three months. Yeah. Handsome, like me – that's why I give him the same name.'

Finally, Ray laughed.

'Funny, though,' Ryan said. 'Don't have my temper. Quiet little chap. Polite. Don't know where he gets it from.'

'From his mother, perhaps.'

Ryan said nothing, peering out of the window as they drew up outside the gate of Barnabas.

Ray checked his phone. 'Photo's done.'

'Right, then,' Ryan said. 'Let's tackle the Provost. You know he's a dickhead, right?'

Ray left a pause. 'Best if I do it.'

Ryan shook his head. '"Work together" is what she said. My case as much as yours. More.'

'You've messed up; we need to calm things down. I'll talk to him. You talk to Ameena Najib, the girl who served the drinks.'

'Oh, yeah, kitchen staff, just my level. Not fucking happening. I want to see the Provost again. And it was me she invited back, not you.'

'Wait. *Wait!*'

Ryan had already got out of the car. Scratching his groin, he ambled away through the gateway. By the time Ray caught up with him, he was in New Court.

'I'm serious,' Ray said. 'We can't afford to upset him again.'

Ryan grinned. 'Relax. I'm cool. I'm not going to take another pop at him.' He held Ray's gaze for a moment. 'Unless he deserves it, of course,' he added.

Ray caught hold of him.

'Joking, for fuck's sake.'

Ray kept hold of his arm. He put his face close to Ryan's and spoke in a low voice: 'Well, I'm not joking.'

'Oh, yeah? What's this? Queensberry Rules?'

'Listen to me. You kick off, I report it to the Super, she takes you off the case. That's how it happens. It only takes a minute. Got it?'

'Course.' Ryan's eyes were big with innocence. 'Wouldn't want to go toe to toe with you, anyway, big man.'

Ray said, 'He's not a suspect. He was having drinks with other people at the time she was killed.'

'I know that.'

'Not. A. Suspect.' He tapped the side of his head. 'Keep it in your mind. In fact, it'd be good if you were pretty much silent in this one.'

They came apart, backed away from each other. Ray nodded at last, and Ryan grinned, and they continued together round the trim disc of lawn towards staircase XII and the Provost's office, where the Provost and his wife were waiting.

NINE

The Provost's wife poured coffee from a silver pot into china cups. 'Too early for sherry, I think,' she said. 'Though I expect you'd tell me you don't drink while you're on duty. Isn't that the cliché?'

Brief smiles. She gave Ray a steady, appraising look as she handed him his cup. In armchairs too low for comfort, they sat around a coffee table in a corner of the elegant room, overlooked by bookshelves and framed prints of sports teams and college events.

The Provost wore a blue suit and aggressively upbeat tie, though his cheeks were waxy and his eyelids thickened from lack of sleep. He didn't look at Ryan. He sipped coffee and said conversationally to Ray, 'At Balliol, weren't you?'

'Class of 2004.'

'In Beloff's day.'

'He was President, yes.'

'Good man. Met him at Chequers, once or twice.' One of his eyes twitched.

Ray passed on the Superintendent's sympathies. His voice was open and soothing. It was kind of them, he said, to invite them back to ask a few more questions. And he would be frank. The most basic question remained unanswered. They didn't know who the victim was.

'You've had a little more time to reflect, now,' he said. 'Do you have any recollection of seeing her before?'

The Provost gazed back at Ray. 'None whatsoever,' he said.

'She was a complete stranger to you?'

'Absolutely.'

'Lady Penelope?'

'Penelope, please.' Her eyes lingered on Ray appreciatively. 'No, I didn't recognise her at all.'

He said, carefully, 'Can you think of any reason why she should be in your room?'

'I have literally no idea,' the Provost said.

'Is there anyone you can think of, perhaps unknown to you personally, who might have their own reasons for being there?'

'Such as what?'

'Someone determined to see you privately. Someone in the academic community, for instance.'

'No.'

'No one who might be connected in some way with your circle of family or friends?'

'No.'

'No one with – forgive me for saying this – a grievance against you?'

'Absolutely not.'

There was a silence after this.

Ray said, 'Can you remind me, how many people have keys to your lodge?'

'I do. My wife does. And the bursary does. Because I have a study there, the college needs to have access.'

'No one else? Family? Friends?'

'No one.'

There was another, longer, silence.

Ryan lay almost horizontal in his over-soft chair, fidgeting, a surly, almost embarrassing presence, saying nothing, staring idly across everyone at the wall where the photographs hung.

The Provost's wife said, 'This is obviously frustrating for you. For us too, of course. All night we were asking ourselves who she was, what she was doing there, but I'm afraid, as my husband says, we have simply no idea. It's grotesque.'

'An outrage,' the Provost said.

'We understand,' Ray said. 'As you can appreciate, we need to explore all avenues as we try to identify her. We're working with Missing Persons, and with the university and the academic community more widely. With your permission, we'd like to put up pictures of the victim around college, to see if anyone recognises her.'

'Fine,' the Provost said shortly.

Ray nodded. 'Thank you.'

There was a deflating silence. Ray put down his coffee cup.

'See you got a picture missing,' Ryan said suddenly. He nodded at the wall.

They all turned in their chairs to look.

The Provost frowned. 'I wouldn't know. They're not my pictures. I'm only here temporarily while my own office is being refurbished.' He made an expression which might have passed for a smile. 'You seem to have a thing about pictures.'

Ryan was about to reply when Ray hastily spoke across him: 'May I ask a question about your guest of honour, yesterday evening?'

The Provost turned away from Ryan. 'Of course.'

'I understand he left early.'

The Provost began to explain. Unfortunately, the Sheikh had been overcome by anxiety. From the beginning, he'd been nervous. 'And, before dinner,' the Provost said, 'he was unsettled for some reason by the appearance of one of our new members of staff, who brought drinks over from the buttery.'

Ray said, 'Ameena Najib.'

'That's right.'

'What was the problem?'

The Provost's wife intervened smoothly: 'Ameena can be a little unsettling. When I asked her to pick up a bag of things for charity at the end of her shift, she was clearly unhappy and made no attempt to hide it. I expect she was brusque with him. For his part, and I say this in confidence, the Emir was quite unsettle-able. He had issues,' she added, 'about a perceived lack of security in the college.'

Ryan gave a snort. Ray scowled at him.

'Also,' the Provost's wife went on in her composed manner, 'although this isn't at all relevant, there was a . . . minor incident as the Sheikh made his way out of college.' Briefly, she described the mooning.

'Students,' the Provost said, shortly.

There was a brief silence, broken by Ryan muttering something under his breath.

'Didn't catch that,' the Provost said at once, aggressively.

'Your future prime ministers. Hilarious.'

'They weren't from this college, as a matter of fact.'

'How do you know? Shape of their arses?'

The Provost's expression stiffened and bulged; he seemed to be tightening his grip on something held inside his mouth. 'I happened to see them coming into college, down the passage from Butter Lane,' he said.

'From the gate that'll open with a quick kick?'

The Provost glared, nostrils widening.

'And you think it's odd your guest of honour was worried about security?' Ryan added.

There was another silence, in which they could all hear the Provost breathing through his nose.

'Well, thank you, anyway,' Ray said to Lady Penelope. 'As you say, it's not directly relevant.' He glanced furiously in Ryan's direction. 'And I don't think we need to take up any more of your time, just now.'

'Hang on.' Ryan turned his head and raised his eyebrows at Lady Penelope. 'Got the impression, on the blower, you had something new you wanted to tell us. Isn't that what we've been waiting for?'

It wasn't clear from her face whether she smiled or grimaced. 'That's right, in fact. It won't take a moment.' She looked coolly towards her husband. 'James?'

They all looked at the Provost, who cleared his throat and pursed his lips. 'Oh, that. Yes. The reason for us asking you back is . . . I don't see that it alters anything, but we thought we ought to . . .' He cleared his throat again. 'My wife has reminded me that, as it happens, I left our preprandial drinks last night for a brief period, to go and make a phone call.'

'Right,' Ray said. 'What time?'

'Between about half past eight and nine o'clock.'

He suddenly didn't know what to do with his hands. He folded his arms, unfolded them, put his hands in his lap.

Ryan sat forward. 'Having a fucking laugh, aren't you?'

Ray interrupted so fast, his words came out as a yelp. He cleared his throat and began again: 'The thing is, Sir James,' he said, 'as you know, that's in the window of the time of death.'

'That's the reason I'm telling you now,' the Provost said testily.

'Of course. Can you tell us a little more? Where did you make the call from?'

The Provost elaborated. At around eight thirty, just after the arrival of his other guests, he'd left the Burton Suite to make a phone call, in his office, to a firm of lawyers called Kriegstein, in Los Angeles. Kriegstein had been acting for a client interested in co-funding the new Peace Studies Institute. This client, an American, had been waiting for the Sheikh's buy-in, which the Provost had hoped to secure that evening. The original arrangement had been for Kriegstein's client to talk directly to the Sheikh later in the evening and confirm the deal.

'However,' the Provost said, his tone tightening, 'he became unsettled, as my wife has said, and informed me he no longer wished to have the conversation, so I took the opportunity, before the meal was served, to phone ahead and cancel.'

Ray nodded. 'And you made the call on the landline, here?'

'Yes.'

'Did you come straight here from the Burton Suite?'

'Yes. Yes, I did.'

'You weren't, at any point, near your lodge?'

'The lodge is on the other side of New Court, beyond the Fellows' Garden. It could hardly be further away.'

'Did you meet anyone as you came and went?'

'No. There was no one about.'

'And were you alone while making the call?'

'Naturally.'

'And how long did the call last?'

'I got back to Burton just as they began to serve dinner. Nine o'clock. You can check with Ashley, from the buttery. She was on duty.'

There was a silence.

'That's all,' the Provost said. 'It's a small point, but we just felt you should know. For the sake of completeness.'

Before Ray could speak, Ryan said, 'Small point? You just told us you can't prove where you were at the time she was killed.'

The Provost flushed. 'On the contrary, I have told you exactly where I was: here, making a phone call. Do you seriously think I would lie?'

'No idea. Be stupid of you, though, 'cause we can check your phone use.'

'I don't believe you can, legally.'

'We can do it, anyway.'

The Provost mimed tremendous surprise. 'Oh, can you? Well, that's very interesting! Is it official police policy, I wonder?' His head wobbled with indignation.

'Want me to give you a rundown on official policy for dealing with suspects?' Ryan said.

'So, I'm a suspect now?'

'Just made yourself one, pal.'

Ray stood up smartly. 'I think we've taken this as far as we can.' Bending to Ryan, he said in a low, violent voice, 'We're leaving.' He got hold of Ryan by the arm and, without saying anything else, propelled him out of the office, along the hall and down the stairs.

'Alright, alright,' Ryan said as they went.

Ray kept hold of him, even after they reached the bottom of the staircase. He said, in a hoarse voice, 'I honestly can't believe you, goading him like that. What were you going to do next? Nut him?'

'I said alright, alright? He'll be okay.'

'Not a suspect, we said. *Not* a suspect! Jesus *Christ*.'

They glared at each other.

'He'll be on the phone right now to the Super,' Ray said, 'asking if the police are going to break the law by checking his phone use. And, you know what? She's going to take you off the case. And, you know what else? She's going to rip me for not babysitting you properly. Congratulations – you've just wrecked this for both of us. You *idiot!*'

He let go of Ryan with a flick of his fingers, and Ryan rocked loosely back and stood there, nodding and gazing mildly across the quad. He said nothing. He seemed to have zoned out.

Ray shook his head in amazement. 'Well?'

Ryan said, 'Did you notice her?'

'What?'

89

'The way she was looking at him. She knows he's hiding something.'

Ray shook his head in amazement. 'You really are . . .'

Ryan said, 'What's a gaudy?'

Ray looked dumbfounded. '*What?*'

'Something called a gaudy. What is it? I bet you know.'

Ray let out a long groan.

'Come on, could be important.'

Ray controlled himself. 'It's a college event. A dinner, picnic, whatever. Gaudy. From the Latin for *feast*,' he added, without meaning to. 'Why? What's a gaudy got to do with anything?'

'I was looking at the pictures, a row of them, year by year, right? All labelled *Gaudy*. The one from ten years ago's missing. Someone's taken it down since this morning. Why would they do that?'

'I don't know. I've no idea if you're even right about this.'

'Sort of thing I notice. Why would someone take it down? Come on, it's interesting.'

Ray paused. He'd got his breath back, now. Ryan's face was stupidly eager. Despite himself, Ray caught the edge of an idea and unpeeled it. He said, slowly, 'To conceal the identities of the people in it.'

Ryan grinned, nodded. 'Because?'

Ray said, 'Because . . . one of them is the dead girl.'

'See? Told you it was interesting. My guess is, she's got some connection with the college and someone wants to hide it.'

'It's only a supposition.'

'Only a what?'

'A . . . a theory.'

90

'Yeah. So, come on. Let's go back and get at him again.'

Ray caught hold of him. 'Absolutely not. You're not going anywhere near him again. Ever.' His phone rang, and he turned aside to answer it. 'Yes,' he said. There was a long pause. 'Are you sure? When?' There was a further pause. 'Okay. Thanks.' He turned back to Ryan. 'That was Forensics,' he said slowly. 'Two things. The ring was hers.'

'Knew it.'

'But then there's something odd. His robes.'

'What robes?'

'The Provost's academic gown, hanging on the back of his study door. She'd been wearing it. Could have been that evening, could have been earlier – but, at some point, she'd had it on.'

Ryan grinned. 'See? Hiding stuff. He's the dog with the shifty eyes, man. Peter Pervert. Let's get back up there and—'

Ray grabbed him. 'We've got about two hours before we're pulled off this case, and we're going to spend that time proceeding in a *completely normal manner*. Do you understand? *I'll* talk to Sir James, and I'll ask him about it *after* I've apologised on your behalf. You can go and find Ameena Najib.'

'Fucking typical. Kitchen staff.'

'You don't talk to anyone else, you don't go near anyone else. Understood? Or I phone the Super right now, straight away, and suggest she begins disciplinary proceedings. Have you got that?' He was shaking with anger again.

'Alright, alright. Don't chuck your sandwich.'

Ray turned to go.

Ryan called out, 'Don't forget to ask him whose office it was before his.'

Ray said, 'Don't think about what I'm doing. Think about yourself. Keep a lid on it.'

Then he was gone, back up the stairs, and Ryan turned, grinning, and went across the quad, scratching his armpits.

TEN

Barnabas kitchen is located in a large barrel-vaulted room adja-
cent to the hall, a high-tech lab inserted into a medieval basilica,
stainless-steel panels and scrub-down surfaces gleaming under
narrow shafts of churchy light pouring through old arched windows. Next to it, off a stone-flagged corridor, is a low-ceilinged
storeroom smelling tartly of damp, and here, crouched among
bins and cupboards containing minor tools, college handyman
Jason Birch, wearing stained white overalls over an Arsenal shirt,
was whispering into his phone.

'Pick up! Pick up! Come *on*, you fucker. Come *on!*' He
glanced through the doorway into the kitchen, grimacing. His
head hurt after a sleepless night of panic attacks. The inside
of his mouth tasted like pet food. 'Listen,' he hissed, his lips
glued to the plastic, 'you promised it'd be straightforward.
Well, it's fucking not straightforward. It's *all fucked up*. Call
me, soon as. Got it?'

Hearing footsteps on the stone flags of the corridor outside,
he straightened up smartly and put his phone away, arranging

his face into a semblance of affability as a youth wearing Adidas trackies and a baseball cap slouched into the room.

'Come from conference, have you? After the room signs? Hang on – they're in a bag over here; I'll get them for you.'

Fishing in his trackies, the youth flashed his ID and Jason stiffened. A fed!

'Sorry, I thought . . .'

'Ameena what's-her-name,' the fed said. 'She around?'

For a moment, Jason just stared. He licked his lower lip nervously. 'What do you want Ameena for?'

The fed looked at him. 'Thought I might ask her to do me a cheese sandwich.'

Jason's face registered incomprehension, one of his most popular expressions. He felt a sudden, deep unease. 'What?'

'She here?'

'Her day off.'

The fed continued to look at him and Jason shifted about a bit. 'How'd you know that?'

'Well.' Jason thought about his answer for a long time, then gave up. 'She told me.'

'Know her well, do you?'

'A bit.'

'What's she like?'

The fed's face was mesmerisingly intent. Jason was confused by the rapidity of his questions. Trying to slow things down, he thought hard again. 'Yeah,' he said at last. 'She's alright.'

The fed waited.

'People should cut her some slack, is what,' Jason blurted out, without meaning to.

Still the fed waited, watching him carefully, and Jason felt compelled to continue, almost babbling now with nerves.

'All this kitchen stuff, see – she's not used to it. She's a trained lawyer is what she is, back home. And, what with that war over there . . . So what if she's a bit late for work or loses her keys or whatever? Her mind's not on it. Only natural, with what she's been through.' He came suddenly to the end of what he had to say, and stood there, surprised at himself, breathing heavily. He was distracted by the feel of his phone in his pocket and the fear that it might ring at any moment.

'When did you last see her?' the fed asked.

'What do you mean?'

'Did you see her last night?'

Jason could feel himself beginning to sweat. The guy was deliberately trying to trip him up. 'Yeah,' he admitted, at last.

'What time?'

Jason scratched his scalp. 'Eight? I lose track, but I was working late 'cause of that dinner,' he added quickly.

'What was she doing?'

'Nothing. On the phone.'

'On the phone to who?'

'I don't know!' He rubbed his gingery bristles with the palm of his hand, grimacing. 'She was having a hard time, see. I stopped by, had a quick word. You know.'

'Not really.'

'Well, she was upset.'

'About what?'

'I don't know. Working late, serving drinks, picking up bags. People not treating her right.'

'Like who?'

'Like that Emir fella. All his wives, thinks he can do whatever he likes.'

'What did he do?'

'I don't know; she didn't say. Scared her, though. She was proper shook up.' He was panting now, with all the questions. 'He's a defiler,' he added, recklessly.

The fed stared at him. 'Is he?' he said, at last.

'Yeah. Ameena said.'

Jason braced himself for more questions, but the fed nodded, as if to bring the conversation to an end. 'Alright. Interesting. Someone else, now, I need to see in the kitchens: Ashley someone.'

'Ashley Turner, yeah.' Jason took a step forward and pointed through the open doorway. 'Blonde, at the end. Ponytail.'

Ryan nodded again.

Jason said, 'She'll be busy with lunch, though. If you want a sandwich . . .'

But Ryan was on his way through to the kitchen, and Jason slumped against the wall, exhausted.

In the front room of a house, less than a mile away, a man sat on a sofa, listening to Jason's message on speakerphone: 'Pick up! Pick up! Come *on*, you fucker. Come *on!*'

He was a thickset man, with a wide, flattish face and dark hair plastered on his forehead, and he sat, leaning forward, with his hands pressed down on a coffee table. One of his hands was deformed; it lay on the table like an unshelled crab. Outside, a car was turning in the cul-de-sac with a brief panic-roar of slipped gears; he lifted his head, blinked at the net curtains and looked away again.

When the message ended, the room was unbearably quiet. The man got up and went into the kitchen. There were two articles of clothing in the sink and he took out a small can and doused them in cigarette-lighter fluid, then dropped a match on to them, jabbing them with the fingers of his good hand and swearing under his breath as they flared up and slowly shrivelled.

Then he sat on the sofa again with a glass of whisky. Hours passed.

When his phone rang a second time, he grabbed it, but, before he could say anything, a suave, well-educated voice spoke: 'Don't speak. I don't know what you've done or why you've done it, but you're on your own. Do you understand? You don't work for me. You've never worked for me. Don't try to contact me again.'

He stared at the phone for a long time after the speaker had rung off, drinking his whisky. Then he took the SIM card out of the phone, went into the kitchen and stamped on it, putting it into the bin before sitting on the sofa again, breathing in the sickly smell of burning, his mouth bending and tightening and bending, as if some mental struggle were going on inside him.

In the kitchen of Barnabas, at lunchtime, there was a constant muted percussion of metal utensils. Ryan made his way between the great aluminium ranges towards the far end, where Ashley Turner was working. She was a sharp-featured, good-looking twenty-three-year-old, with a bold expression and brisk manner, and she carried on working while Ryan introduced himself.

'Can't stop. Soup's behind.'

'It's alright; we can talk here.'

'Go on, then. Pass me that ladle. What do you want to know?'

He asked what Ameena Najib was like.

'You should ask Jason.'

'Why d'you say that?'

'She's his latest project. Going nowhere, if you ask me. Don't think she likes boys. She's got God. Thing is,' she said, 'she thinks she's too good for this sort of thing.'

Ameena had been housed, temporarily, in a college building, down the Abingdon Road, where Ashley also roomed. Ameena spent a lot of time praying in her room, Ashley said. 'I can hear her, droning on. Must have a lot to say to Him. Guilty secrets, eh?'

She took up a knife and chopped herbs intently, glancing around once or twice, as if to check the readiness of the next object for her attention. They all looked ready. She had that kind of presence.

'Did you know that, a couple of weeks ago, she lost some keys?'

'No, but –' she shrugged – 'gloves, tunics, hairnets – you name it, she's lost it. Told you, her mind's on higher things. Pan, please. No, the other one.'

Ryan turned to the events of the night before.

'Total shambles,' she said as she poured cream. 'Should've heard the Head Chef! Hadn't even had their mains! We had to throw them away. All 'cause the guest of honour gets it into his head someone's trying to kill him. I could tell there was something wrong, soon as I served the foie gras. He had a face on him like a slapped arse.' She paused. 'Funny, you asking about

Ameena, though, 'cause he was the same. "Who's your, what's the word, *associate?* Where does she come from?" And then his bodyguard.'

'What do you mean?'

'Roaming round college, asking people if they'd seen her. Wanted to talk to her, he said. Good-looking fella, I got to say. But useless. I told him to buzz off. She'd've gone home by then, anyway. All in all, I wasn't impressed with last night's VIP. Served him right, what happened after.'

'Yeah, heard about that. Bit of a surprise, in a place like this. Thought they'd have better manners, somehow.'

'Sort of thing they do. Pranks. Drive a sports car into the Great Hall, jack it up on top of the tables – they did that, once. Paint something rude on the roof. You know, in Latin. Yesterday, someone went to the bother of taking all the electric lamps in the chapel, from the choir stalls and the vestry and that, to build a sort of pyramid on the altar. I mean, what's the point? Ladle again. Hello? Ladle!'

He'd gone blank. It was a thing he did. Zoning out. Not thinking, more like the opposite of thinking. He stood there, gazing slack-faced at her, absently fiddling with his tracksuit zip.

'You alright?'

'What? Yeah. Interesting, though, innit?'

'Don't know what's interesting about it, just more work for people like me.'

'Fair enough.' He sniffed and scratched. 'By the way, Provost says he left the others having a drink, about half eight, went to make a phone call, didn't come back till nine.'

'Could be. Half past, his other guests were just arriving, and

I remember him leaving after I started pouring the Mumms for them, and, when I went back with the foie gras, he came in just after me, so, yeah, about nine.'

He nodded.

'That it, then?' she said, glancing across at him.

There was a different sort of expression on his face, as if he'd tightened it a notch. 'What do you think of him?' he asked.

'Who? Sir James?' She smiled, and her mouth was wide and generous. 'He's got a reputation, I know that. With the young academics.'

'Not tried it on with you, then?'

'He knows better than to do that, Ryan.'

She held his gaze and, a second later, he felt himself colour up; it made him feel childish suddenly.

'How d'you know my name? It's not on my ID.'

For the first time, she stopped working and looked at him, slyly, folding her arms. 'What's it like being back, then, Ryan Wilkins? You won't remember me,' she went on. 'That bit younger than you. My older sister was in your year – Michaela. Not that you were there that much, right? But I used to see you sometimes at Point Park. Off your face.'

'Yeah, well.' He dropped his gaze and shuffled from side to side. Looked at his watch. Felt something deep in the nub of his stomach twist itself inside out.

'I know. Times change. You won't be back in the park, will you? Not with you being a police detective now. There's a turn-up. Parents still there?'

He got to his feet. 'Listen, I got to—'

'And how's Shel?'

100

Now, he couldn't take his eyes off her. 'She's . . .' His mouth stayed open, but his voice went out. Something happened in his face, a spasm. Shaking his head, he backed away. A metal bowl fell on to the floor with a crash and he got his balance and went, without looking back, out of the kitchen.

ELEVEN

Several hours later, young Kent Dodge stood in Old Court, gazing round at the sixteenth-century buildings with their rusty brickwork and low-brimmed slate roofs gilded with Oxford damp in the last glimmerings of the afternoon light. Exquisite, tranquil . . . panic inducing.

Man, he thought. I'm a long way from home.

He was a fresh-faced Midwesterner from Johnsburg, Illinois, with a shock of blond hair, conservatively cut, a trim blond beard and naïve blue eyes, enlarged by round plastic-framed glasses. Generally, he was an even-keeled sort of guy. Not today. His night had been troubled by sickness and bad dreams, nauseating flashbacks of a young woman sprawled on the carpet of the Provost's study. Dead and ugly with it. Hopped the twig, as they said in Johnsburg. He fingered the medical plaster on his forehead where he'd gashed it falling against the chest of drawers. He knew he wasn't a strong person, a fact for which he had compensated all his life by being clever, and now, though it was hours later, he still felt trembly, and he sensibly paused for a moment in Old Court, eyes closed, until his feelings of panic had passed and he could continue up staircase XII to the Provost's office.

He realised at once that he was interrupting. Someone was in there already – a young black guy, impeccably dressed in a grey blazer and navy khaki trousers. A visiting fellow, perhaps. Kent noticed, with envy, how neat his head was, how beautiful his features. Then the Provost beckoned him in, and he went across and held out the copy of the article he'd brought: 'Demon Figures in Qajar Tiles in Early Nineteenth-Century Persia'.

'What's this?' the Provost said blankly.

'The article I wrote. You asked yesterday if I had a copy.'

'Did I?' The Provost put it on his desk without looking at it. He made no attempt to introduce Kent to the man, who was scrolling through his texts.

As so often with the Provost, Kent felt a sense of invisibility.

'Well, anyway,' he said, 'I was just dropping it off.'

He was ignored. But, as he turned to go, the other man asked to be directed to the kitchen, and the Provost said, abruptly, 'Kent, here, will walk you over, won't you, Kent?'

Kent hesitated. 'Oh, sure. No problem. I was just going that way.'

He gave the man a sidelong look as they went down the stairs. Tall, very smooth black skin. Well built, athletic. Good-looking – head-turning, in fact. And interested in his appearance – you could tell from his clothes. Kent watched him texting on his phone. He reappraised him. Perhaps not a visiting fellow, after all. One of the city's businessmen whom the Provost liked to cultivate. Kent was good at sizing people up. He began to make conversation – a nervous habit he had.

'To be honest, I still get lost sometimes. I've only been here since the summer. I'm from the States, you probably realised. In the US, we generally stick to the obvious, we don't really do subtle. This place is just nothing but subtle – I mean, including the buildings. I'm like, What? Were they designed by rabbits?'

The man continued, unsmiling, to look at his texts.

'Of course,' Kent went on, 'I like subtle. Goes with the territory, you know. Academics. I've wanted to come here ever since I was in high school, and I was lucky enough to get a Fulbright. Only for a semester, and, frankly, it pays nothing, but still. I'm an art historian, at Harvard,' he said, after a pause. 'Identity and cultural appropriation. Oxford was a little slow getting into my field, but there are some really smart people here now, and it's just been a great chance to, you know, work the libraries and talk to these guys.'

Still the man made no reply.

'And I just love England,' he added.

The man briefly looked him up and down. 'Thomas Pink.'

'The shirt? You got it. English tailors are the best.'

The man said no more, however. They walked in silence round Old Court, through to New Court and along the cloisters, their footsteps echoing in the stone passageway. When the man's phone rang, he spoke into it briefly, some sort of domestic conversation, with a partner, perhaps, soon over.

'Of course,' Kent went on, 'I won't say it hasn't been a culture shock. I mean, gowns and mortar boards, and high table and battels bills, and all that goofy shit. My first dinner here, they offered me snuff. I'm from the Midwest. Freaked me out.

I mean, I went to Dubai once, and that was weird, but nowhere near as weird as this. And, last night . . . Well, I don't know if you heard about last night . . .'

The man had stopped walking and was looking at him.

'I know,' Kent said. 'I'm sorry. I talk too much.'

But the man was looking at the plaster on his forehead. He said, 'Are you Kent Dodge?'

He felt a sudden impulse to deny it, but he said, nervously, 'Yes. Yes, I am. Why?' He put a hand up and adjusted his glasses, a defensive habit he had.

'I was coming to see you later.'

The penny dropped. 'Are you . . . something to do with the investigation?'

A badge came out. 'DI Wilkins. You were with them last night, when they found the body.'

'Well, yes, but I can't tell you much.'

'You fainted.'

'Always had that susceptibility. When I was a child—'

'Had you ever seen the victim, before last night?'

'No, sir.'

'Never seen her round college?'

'No, sir.'

'You don't think she could have been a student, or visiting academic, or someone with some other connection to the university?'

Kent looked at him and blinked. 'You don't know who she is yet?'

The detective didn't respond for a moment. 'You were at the drinks and dinner earlier, too, right?'

105

'That's right.'

'Impressions?'

Kent described the gathering in the Burton Suite, the attempts at conversation with the unforthcoming Emir, his early departure. 'To be honest, the whole thing was just a little embarrassing. I really felt for Sir James. He didn't get much help, either.'

'What do you mean?'

There had been an argument at dinner, he explained. 'Robin Goodman – he's the Arabist, here – he really attacked the college's policy about the copy of the Koran they have in their collection. Do you know about that?'

'No. Is it important?'

'Well, the Saudis want it back. Goodman agrees. It infuriates the Provost. Still, it doesn't take much to . . .'

'What?'

Kent hesitated before he spoke, and lowered his voice: 'He's like this Jekyll-and-Hyde character, the Provost. One minute he's charming, the next he's really quite nasty.'

'How do you mean?'

'I'll give you an example. Because of my stint in the Middle East, and because I speak a little Arabic, when I arrived, they asked me to help out with the college collection, and yesterday afternoon I helped with the tour – and he was just so appreciative. Charming, kind. And then, just a few hours later, I met him as I was arriving for the drinks; he came down the staircase, rushing into the quad, and I guess he didn't see me, but he more or less knocked me over, and he didn't apologise, didn't even stop, just snarled at me and off he went.'

'Didn't recognise you, perhaps.'

'Oh, he knew who I was. He looked right at me.' Kent shrugged. 'He's been under pressure, I know, with the Emir. Funding issues. I guess things weren't working out too well. Still, it shook me up a little, I don't mind saying. The look on his face. Contempt.' After a moment, he smiled. 'Well, the kitchen's just down those steps there. Take care, now.'

The detective ignored him. He said, thoughtfully, 'Where was he going? When he took off.'

'I don't know. Back to his lodge, I assumed.'

Ray looked at him a moment. 'Why did you assume that?'

'Well, that's just the way he was heading.'

'Not to his office?'

'Where we just were? No, no. The other way completely.'

He was going to say more, but the detective thanked him and went briskly down the steps towards the kitchen, and, after a moment, Kent went on towards the hall.

107

TWELVE

Three squad cars had been left in front of the station, blue lights buzzing, agitating the twilight. Reporters were huddled by the entrance with their cameras and booms, their breath steaming about their faces. Occasionally, one of the them caught sight of movement inside the entrance and called out.

Inside, the tension gave everything a speeded-up, over-loud air. Nadim came running down the corridor on her way to an emergency briefing, speaking to them as she passed: 'Man down in the Leys – one of the riot team. Third-degree burns. They don't even know if he'll make it.' Then she was gone.

They ran upstairs to the management suite and along the corridor to the Super's office, going in quietly.

'Don't sit,' she said, after a moment.

Ryan stood up again.

She stared at him, her face tight and pale. 'I don't have time for this. Everything's kicking off, there's an officer in intensive care. In fifteen minutes, I have to call the Home Secretary.' Ryan opened his mouth and she said, 'You don't speak until I ask you to. Understood?' She looked at Ray. 'Sir James called me. Why did this happen?'

'I'm sorry; I stopped it as soon as I could.'

'Not soon enough. He was asking questions about call monitoring.'

Ray nodded.

'He wanted to know why he was being treated like a suspect. I thought I'd been clear about that. He highlighted several points of what he called "striking divergence from the police code of conduct," which, as you may know, the Dean of Barnabas had a hand in drafting.'

Ray grimaced, nodded again.

Ryan opened his mouth again; the Superintendent's gaze swivelled on to him and he closed it.

'You stand still and listen. Do you really need me to say you shouldn't tell the Provost of Barnabas he's, quote, "having a fucking laugh", unquote?'

Ryan looked down.

'Don't look at the floor, look at me. I don't have time to teach you basics. Sir James said Ray had to drag you out of his office before you lost control completely. Stand there till I decide what to do with you.' She glanced at her watch and turned again to Ray. 'Ray, give me a summary. Make it quick.'

Ray began to speak, a little too quickly, tripping over his words. The Provost was not a suspect, he said, but, as it turned out, he had no alibi for the time of death.

Ryan made an eager noise, immediately smothered when the Super looked at him, and Ray went on. There was also the puzzling discovery that the victim had been wearing the Provost's academic robes. And something else, in fact, just mentioned to him by the young American, Kent Dodge. Although Sir James had told them quite categorically that he went from the Burton Suite directly to his office in Old Court, Dodge remembered him going the other way, towards his lodge, where, of course, the murder took place a few minutes later.

Ryan couldn't contain himself any longer, and the Superintendent turned to him furiously.

'What did you say? Did you just say, "*Peter Pervert*"?' She turned again to Ray. 'Well?'

'He doesn't seem to have been as honest as he might.'

'And another thing,' Ryan blurted out, 'everyone you talk to says he's a sex pest.'

The Super ignored him. 'Ray?'

'Haven't heard that myself, but Dodge described him as a Jekyll-and-Hyde character, with an unpredictable temper.'

'A sketch ball, for sure,' Ryan said. 'Gets them in there, dresses them up, has his—'

'Shut up. Ray? We're running out of time.'

'We need to talk to him again.'

'Do it. On your own. And do it properly. Where are you with ID of the victim?'

They were silent.

'You don't know who she is yet?'

They shook their heads.

'Any response to the photo that went up?'

Ray said, 'No one we've talked to noticed any strangers in college last night—'

'Yeah, well,' Ryan interrupted again, 'there were four strangers we actually know about – the guys showing off their arses – not to mention the victim, so I don't reckon we can rely on this unofficial people-watching shit.'

Ray began to speak, but the Super said, 'No, he's right. Who were they, these four?'

'Pranksters,' Ryan said. 'Hilarious stuff. Cars on tables, Latin on roofs. Arses. Future prime ministers, innit?'

The Super ignored him. She said to Ray, 'What about the guest of honour? He's the reason they went in. Is there a connection? Seems far-fetched.'

'He's not a suspect; he was at the drinks and in the dinner the whole time.'

'His bodyguard wasn't,' Ryan said. 'Got to be talked to. Him and the Sheikh.'

Ray turned to him angrily and the Superintendent said, 'No, he's right.'

'I'll go do it, if you like,' Ryan said.

There was a silence as they both looked at him.

'I can get on with anyone, me,' he said hopefully.

The Superintendent said, 'There's zero evidence of that. Ray, you talk to al-Medina. He has a house in Spain, I think, so you've got something in common.' She held them with her eyes while she thought further. 'You don't know who she is, you don't know why she was there. Do you have any idea – any idea at all – why she might have been killed?'

They shook their heads, looked at the floor.

'Christ,' she said. She turned her gaze on Ryan. 'Right, I've decided what to do with you. I should pull you, but I don't have the cover just now. So, from now on, you report to Ray, you

111

don't do anything without Ray's permission. Got it? You stay away from Sir James, you stay away from Sheikh al-Medina. Ray? What does he need to do next?'

'Ameena Najib, in the kitchen, still needs talking to.'

'That's what you do. Understood? And when you've done that, you ask Ray what to do next.'

Ryan shuffled his feet.

'Out.'

He went. Ray stayed behind.

'What is it, Ray? I'm out of time.'

'I think you should know how difficult he is. I've literally never met anyone like him. I even wonder if it's some sort of condition, but—'

'Then you need to deal with it.'

'I've got to be frank. I know we're short, but I think he should be taken off the case altogether.'

'I'll be frank too, Ray. You need to step up. This department is currently under enormous pressure. You need to do what's necessary, not what's most comfortable. This is a new test for you.' She looked at him. 'So far, you're failing it.'

Ray breathed deeply, nodded, a little curtly, and left as the Superintendent reached for her phone.

The office they had to share was a small box, with plain white walls, a single desk and two chairs, lit by the dull glow of panel lights in the low ceiling. On the corridor side was a window striped with the metal slats of a blind; on the other, a map of Oxford, prickly with coloured pins. Stacked against one wall was a bank of filing cabinets; on another was a large evidence board, the 'crazy wall', empty now except for a single photograph stuck crookedly in the centre. It had a utilitarian, unloved feel to it.

Ryan was lying horizontal in one of the chairs, feet on the desk, a careless expression on his narrow face; Ray felt his own face clench. The Super's words were echoing in his mind. For three years at Thames Valley he'd enjoyed her constant approval and encouragement; in each yearly appraisal he'd received official commendation for his professional progress, recognition of his talent, work ethic and judgement. This is who he was, the fast-tracked high-flyer. Until now.

'What's wrong with you?' he said.

Ryan squinted at him. Picked his teeth. 'Don't know what you mean.'

'Is it medical?'

'Don't know what you're talking about.'

'Why you behave like this.'

Ryan shrugged.

Ray looked beyond him, at the crazy wall. 'What's that?' he said.

Ryan swivelled round, looked across and grinned. 'The photo? Ryan Junior. Keeping an eye on us. Sort of a good-luck thing.'

'Take it down.'

Ryan didn't move. His expression shifted just a little, from careless to fuck-you.

Before he realised he was doing it, Ray had moved across the room, yanked it off the board and dropped it on to the desk. He could feel the stress of adrenaline in his muscles. His breathing was shallow. He unclenched his mouth and said, 'You know what? You shouldn't be on this case. You shouldn't even be in

113

the force. But, now you report to me, you'll keep your Tourette's or whatever it is under control. What are you doing?'

Ryan had been checking his phone and now he got to his feet. 'That's it. Car's unclamped. Going home.'

Ray was bewildered. 'It's not even six.'

'Got to pick up Ryan from my sister's.'

'We're busy. Make some other arrangement.'

'Never miss bath and bedtime.'

'What about his mother?'

An ugly change came over Ryan's face. 'What about *your* fucking mother? You know what gets me about people like you? You don't actually give a toss about anyone else. So, do yourself a favour and have a read of the Police Handbook, section on single parents. You can translate it into fucking Latin as you go.'

Ray strode across the office and closed the door, standing with his back against it. He said, 'I can't actually believe this. You're telling *me* how to behave?' He could feel himself breathing. 'What are you doing now?' he said.

Ryan was fiddling with his phone. 'Text from my sister. Third one I've had in the last half hour.' He held up his phone as if to prove it. 'I'm late. She's doing her fucking nut.' He hitched up his trackies and pulled the baseball cap round on his head. 'So, yeah, yeah, whatever, big man.' He jabbed a finger at him. 'Why don't you fucking go back inside your cosy fucking little head and keep telling yourself that you're the greatest, with the greatest wife, and the greatest education, and the greatest fucking house in Spain, and let me get on with my life, 'cause I've got to go and pick up my son before it gets any later. Alright?'

114

Ray lost it. He felt it physically, an instant before it happened, like the thud of a punch before the pain kicks in. He flooded. He could feel himself pantomiming astonishment, gesturing wildly. 'I can't believe you. I cannot believe that you speak to people like this. You . . . you . . .'

Ryan sauntered up close. 'Yeah, go on, say it. Say it!'

Ray panted, struggling to control himself.

'Chav!' Ryan said for him. 'Poor white trash! Trailer-park ratboy. Think I haven't heard it all before, from people just like you?' He stepped a little closer and lowered his voice. 'Tell you what, Raymundo. Think I can't call *you* names? Some pretty fucking obvious ones, eh?'

Ray could see in his eyes what he meant. He felt cold. No one had said anything racist to him for many years. He said, in a low voice, 'Be very careful.'

'University graduates like you don't use these words, do they? Liberals. You think I do it 'cause I'm ignorant, 'cause I'm not politically correct. Don't bother me.'

Ray stood rigid. His voice was an ugly whisper. 'Say it, then.'

'You want to hear it?'

'Say it.'

Ryan's eyes were small and nasty. He said, 'Here it is then, Raymundo. Don't matter about your education, don't matter about your leafy Ealing Broadway and shit, this is what you are and always will be, and you can't do a thing about it. You're just a . . .'

'Say it.'

'Just a . . .'

'Go on!'

Ryan paused for a long beat as they looked into each other's eyes. '*Snob*,' he said.

Ray's eyes bulged as Ryan laughed. He opened the door and went out into the corridor, calling back, 'Don't work too late. See you tomorrow!'

THIRTEEN

It was late when Ray left the office. He was tired, but no less unsettled. Putting on the consoling prelude of Bach's first Cello Suite, he drove slowly home. The great blue clock face of Worcester College showed eight o'clock as he turned on to Beaumont Street and drove by the familiar floodlit monuments of old Oxford, the fluted columns of the Ashmolean, the intricate spire of the Martyrs' Memorial, the crenellated walls of St John's College, all immaculately preserved and soothingly antique, as cream-coloured and waxy-looking as old candles. He drove up the wide leafy avenue of St Giles, past the frumpy Victorian villas on the Banbury Road, the trendy cafes and bars of Summertown, and finally into Grove Street, a narrow road of box-like terrace houses, small but expensive, embellished with knock-throughs, observatories, loft conversions and bespoke garden offices, where he pulled up, turned off the engine and realised that he'd heard nothing at all of Bach's consolations.

He walked from the car, let himself in and said loudly, 'You would not believe the day I've had.'

*

He sat with his wife in their knock-through, eating gnocchi. Diane was a petite woman, with the clear, arched eyebrows of a child, the delicate figure of a ballerina and loose, messy hair. Like Ray, whom she had met at Balliol, she was a middle-class Londoner with Nigerian ancestors.

Ray had changed into his old Stüssy T-shirt and brushed-cotton lounge pants; finally, he began to relax. For a while, they talked about the riots in Blackbird Leys, which Diane had seen reported on national news. The shocking death of a boy knocked down by a squad car in the early hours had been followed by street protests through the night, with extensive damage to property; the protests continued into the morning and had escalated sharply in the last few hours, with a petrol-bomb ambush by masked men on uniformed officers, one of whom had been hospitalised with life-threatening burns. In many of the news reports, Detective Superintendent Waddington had appeared, answering questions, expressing regret for the death of the child and appealing for calm. However, the suspension of three of her officers and immediate confirmation of an independent inquiry had done nothing to pacify the Leys, parts of which were now effective no-go areas for the police.

Talk turned, at last, to the new guy.

'So, what's he like?' Diane said.

Ray put down his cutlery, briefly rested his head in his hands, and let out a sigh he'd been holding in for the last three hours.

'That bad?'

'Obstructive. Obnoxious. Rude. Sexist. Misogynist. Hyper. Out of control. Totally – ideally – incorrect. Think England flag, big dog on a chain, mouthing off about immigrants.

And unstable. I'm thinking Tourette's, ADHD maybe. He's twenty-seven, looks fifteen, acts like he's seven. He grew up on a trailer park – Hinksey Point. I don't even know where that is. He's come to us because he was up on a gross-misconduct charge in Wiltshire, where – get this – he nutted the Bishop of Salisbury.'

'Wow. What's he doing in the police?'

'Maybe it's his way of staying out of prison – where most of his friends are. He can't possibly last. I'd give him a couple of weeks.'

'No point in asking if you're getting on.'

'You can ask.'

'Are you getting on?'

'At six o'clock, in the office, I thought we were actually, physically, going to have a fight. I think we would've done, if he hadn't gone home early to pick up his son.'

'He has a son?'

He caught the change in her tone of voice and looked at her warily. 'Lord knows what he's like as a father. He doesn't know how to behave himself.'

'How old?'

'Two, I think. Three. Guess what his name is. Ryan. Ryan, son of Ryan.'

'Does his mother work? Why didn't she pick him up?'

'Not around. Don't know the story. But gone. In prison, for all I know – or rehab, perhaps. He's touchy about it, very touchy. Who knows what sort of mother she would've been, anyway.'

He held out the wine bottle and hesitated as she put her hand over her glass.

They exchanged a look, and his eyes widened.

'Oh God,' he said. 'Babe, I forgot! I'm so sorry. Was it today?'

Her small face tightened; his heart threw a turn to see it.

'Doesn't matter,' she said.

'It was today, wasn't it? What happened?'

She made a tiny distressed gesture and shook her head.

He got up and went round the table and held her in his arms. 'Babe, I'm sorry. I'm so, so sorry.'

'It's okay,' she said, as she burst into tears.

He held her as she shook, comforting her, asking questions. What did the consultant say? Why didn't the implant work? What was the problem with the embryo?

'You're sorry. *I'm* sorry,' she said. 'It's just, every time it happens, I can't help thinking it's never going to work.'

He held her hard. 'Listen to me, babe. We're not giving up. We're going to make it work. You and me, that's what we do.'

She smiled, nodded, wiped her eyes, whispered, 'I keep thinking of Zack.'

'Don't think of Zack.'

'I won't,' she said, thinking of him.

Ray thought of him too – their two-month-old son, who hadn't woken up one morning, three years earlier. 'Cot death' isn't a term used any more by doctors, 'sudden infant death syndrome' is the preferred description, but it was the cot they both thought of, its shallow oval dish of white cotton sheet, its slender wooden railings, the hand-painted stars and clouds of the musical mobile dancing to a pavane above Zack's tiny face, curled up like a new leaf, as he slept on and on.

120

Diane wiped her eyes with the sleeve of her cardigan. 'Well,' she said, 'I guess I can have that glass of wine, anyway.'

And he poured the Pinot Grigio and sat down again.

Five miles away, in an unlit, silent house in Bayworth, a small child slept, breathing softly under a duvet printed with pictures of tractors, while his father stood in the next room, with head-phones on, rave music from the nineties pounding in his head like factory noise as he gazed through the uncurtained window at the darkened field opposite. Grinning.

He was remembering picking up his son from his sister's, earlier that evening. The way the small boy came stumping fast across the room to greet him, blond hair loose, cheeks pink, his tiny hands scrabbling softly at his father's face, talking immediately, with complete seriousness: 'Daddy, today I saw a tunnel. Daddy, how much poo have you got in the world? As much as to fill the bathroom? As much as to fill England?' All the time, picking gently in amazement at his father's ears, as if he'd only just discovered them, still talking.

Ryan's sister had not been so cheerful. She'd hustled him into the kitchen.

'Listen, knobhead, get your act together. I should have been at the Co-op an hour ago.'

'Alright, alright, don't lose your blob. It was just 'cause it was my first day.'

'Don't tell me you fucked up like last time.'

'Just this guy I'm working with.'

'What guy?'

'This guy. Don't matter. He's alright. A bit up himself.'

'Yeah, well, don't even start about the day I've had.' He didn't, but she went on, anyway. 'Mylee's mucking about on Darren's old computer, right, and you'll never guess what pops up. Porn. I'm not even kidding.'

Ryan's mind was on his son. 'Oh, yeah?' he said absently. 'Any good?'

'Any good? I'm talking about porn, Ryan. Nurses wanking off doctors, and air hostesses giving guys in first class blow jobs. Do you think it matters if it's any good? Do you think it's the sort of stuff a three-year-old girl should see? Would you be happy if Ryan saw it? Would you?'

'Alright, alright, point made.'

He moved towards the door, but his sister wanted to talk about their parents again.

'Did you go and see her, like I said?'

'You know I didn't. I haven't had time.'

'I told you this morning, you got to go and see her. He's been at her again. I know he has. She won't say anything on the phone, but I can feel it.'

He looked doubtful. 'I don't know. Better call social services.'

'You know we can't do that. They'll get the police involved; chances are they'll be evicted. You know what happened last time. You got to go round yourself, have a look at her.'

He didn't want to listen. 'Yeah, okay, I'll do it tomorrow.'

'You said that yesterday.'

'Tomorrow. Promise, alright? Scout's fucking honour.'

Now, he stood at the window, nodding his head, letting the music fill him up, grinning again. Thinking again about Ry.

122

They had a routine at bedtime. A bottle of warm milk and a chat, then a bedtime story. Lying on their backs, side by side on the child's little bed.

'Daddy?'

'Yeah?'

'Haylee's mummy's hair is yellow.'

'Okay.'

'What colour hair does my mummy have, Daddy?'

'Sort of brown, I think.'

'She's beautiful, isn't she, my mummy?'

'Oh, yeah. Like I told you. Hair like . . . yeah, brown. Anyway, what sort of day did you have?'

And he lay there, listening to everything that had happened, a whole world of conversations recalled word for word.

'What day did you have, Daddy?'

'Bit shit, if I'm honest with you, but thanks for asking.'

'Auntie Jade says you shouldn't say "shit".'

'Fair enough. What about a story?'

'Have we finished our conversation?'

'I think so.'

'What *is* a conversation?'

'Tell you what, let's have the story.'

'Alright, Daddy. You win.'

He lay on his back with the open book held above his face, and Ryan Junior lay on his back next to him, pointing his bottle at the ceiling, sucking, and he began to read.

'Once upon a time, there was a mouse and a mole, and they were the best of friends . . .'

Ryan Junior always fell asleep before the story ended, and

sometimes Ryan carried on reading out loud to himself, just to make it last longer.

But, now, he stood alone in front of the window in the darkness, listening to music on his headphones in the silent house. In his mind, he went back over the day, remembering the people, conversations, the gestures and expressions: the Provost, his plump mouth pursed as his watery eyes shifted sideways towards his wife; his wife's measured calm, so like supressed anger; Claire, the Bursar, her blonde hair, so fine, so straight, swishing in a single wave against the curve of her neck; Leonard Gamp, mouth clamped on the remains of his dignity, like an old dog with a stick. Ray, Raymond, another posh boy come from the world of money and manners. And the good-looking dead girl, glaring at them all, like, What the fuck are you looking at? What the fuck are you going to do about it? Her tongue dark and thick as steak, her face blue and yellow, all her sex appeal gone ugly.

Just a dead girl. She didn't even have an identity. He felt again his helpless pity, the sudden prickle of tears behind his eyes. But he caught it and stopped it, turned it to anger and felt his rage begin to spread inside him like a physical pain. Someone had killed her and walked away because they could. And, before he could stop it, a memory came to him from childhood: his father's big hand around his throat, lifting him off the ground, the electrifying jolt of panic as his air was cut off, the rasp of his eyes being squeezed out of their sockets. Briefly, he heard Ashley Turner's voice in his head again – 'How's Shel?' – and, as quick as he could, he pushed it all away, as far as possible, away from himself, away from Ryan Junior sleeping next door, into the darkness of the fields outside.

He breathed.

He had a problem with anger, he knew it; he hadn't needed the report of the police review team in Salisbury to tell him. The red mist came down. Like a noise hitting a nerve – the singing of a kettle, the screaming of a child – an acceleration of rage in him as physical as muscle and blood.

He emptied his mind and gave himself up to the music. Music helped. He felt the beat in his body. Slowly, he began to move. He moved his feet, rolled his shoulders; he moved his arms, lifted them into the air; he went from side to side, faster and faster. He threw a shape or two and bobbed up again and kept moving. He drifted down tunnels of noise into the centre of himself, where he could think.

He thought of three doors. Lodge. Chapel. Library. Doors that hid secrets.

What secrets?

She knew. The ugly beautiful girl with the look of fury on her dead face. If he was right, she'd been in each of them.

But why? What had she been doing?

The music pulsed through him as he threw shapes in the silent house at midnight, dancing down its tunnels towards the answers to his questions.

And, back in the city, in her room in a college house on the Abingdon Road, Ameena Najib sat cross-legged on her bed, leaning over her laptop, trawling through images of war-damaged Kafr Jamal on a website routinely monitored by antiterrorism government agencies. Grey slumped buildings, nibbled at the edges like papier mâché left out in the rain; grey

125

debris in drifts; everything the colour of dust, as if not only life but also colour had been lost. A world of dead grey. As she scrolled, she talked rapidly into her phone in Arabic. 'We have to meet, to talk. When it is safe. *Faealt ma kan adl.* I did what was right.' Despite the softness of her voice, her tone was defiant. '*Allah, taealaa, yudammar 'aedayah.* Allah, may he be exalted, destroys his enemies. Even as they turn their hands to new sins.' Though she was alone, she lowered her voice. '*Fasid.* Yes, a defiler . . . No,' she added, still whispering, 'I was not seen.'

Briefly, she remembered Jason Birch, but dismissed the thought.

'Sometimes,' she said fiercely, 'I think God wishes us to take retribution for ourselves . . . *Why?*' Her voice was contemptuous. 'Because here we have no justice.'

Putting down her phone, she continued to scroll through the images on her laptop. Mangled cars, incinerated school buses crash-landed on a moonscape of dust. People used to live there. Now, it was empty like the moon. A dead place, a place of the dead.

And then, without warning, before she could prevent it, flashes of the other thing came into her mind: the journey that had brought her away from the bombs. She saw again the grey metal box they lived in all those months; smelled the diesel, garbage, excrement; saw Anushka's yellow face, her eyes staring up at her, startled as a rabbit's eyes, as she pulled the froth out of her mouth; heard again the footsteps of the men coming at night, as they always came, with their boots and swinging buckles and trousers round their ankles.

In the next room, the ignorant girl Ashley Turner snored, and Ameena forced her mind on to higher things, the mourning of the lost and the reparations of the guilty, and carried on scrolling as she began at last to weep.

FOURTEEN

The next morning was dull and slick with damp, and Leonard Gamp shivered in his porter's lodge as he sat at the window, surreptitiously watching the chav talk to the Bursar at the south-western corner of New Court. He could see him making gestures and the Bursar laughing, and he felt, as he'd felt before, the wrongness of the man being a detective; it was an affront, really, to veterans like himself, not to mention a blunder – like putting a criminal into uniform, or – worse – a leftie.

He hastily shut down this thinking (he had a superstitious belief in the porousness of minds) and prepared an irreproachable but stony face as Ryan came up to the lodge window and gave it a rap.

'Ameena Najib. Off sick today. Got an address for me?'

Making no reply, but going to a filing cabinet at the back of his room and retrieving an index card, Leonard sat with his back to Ryan and began to copy out the Abingdon Road address.

There was another rap on the window. 'Can't you just tell me?'

After handing over the slip of paper with Ameena's address,

Leonard waited until Ryan had ambled off as far as the gateway, then rapped on the window in his turn and was childishly pleased to see him stop and trudge back.

'Yeah?'

Leonard held up the envelope which had been left in the lodge overnight.

'What? For me?'

'For your superior officer,' Leonard said with satisfaction as he passed it over, a plain A4 Manila envelope addressed *FAO: senior investigating detective*, and, as if dismissing Ryan from his thoughts as well as his sight, he immediately bent his head to his desk.

Ryan ripped open the envelope. Inside was a single sheet of paper with two words printed on it in fading ink: *Chiara Belotti*.

Ray was sitting in his car on the drive outside al-Medina's Buckinghamshire home when he got the call. His conversation with the Sheikh had been interrupted by a visitor from the UAE and he was waiting to resume it.

'Wilkins.'

'Yeah, Wilkins here too. Listen, I got something. Anonymous note.'

Ray listened.

'Could be the dead girl,' Ryan said. 'I had a feeling she was foreign. My bet's she's some sort of junior academic – sort of type he goes for.'

'Why hasn't she shown up in Missing Persons?'

'Dunno. 'Cause she was on holiday, 'cause she was on sick leave, 'cause of something else – you know what it's like. Never neat, is it? Thing is, this note, I reckon someone in college knows who she is. Someone's had their eye on Sir Grope-a-lot. What's he been up to in that nice little study of his?'

He began to go on, and Ray cut him off.

'Work with Nadim in COMINT,' he said. 'Don't jump to conclusions. And I don't want you talking to anyone else in college. Above all, you don't go anywhere near Sir James. Understood? Under any circumstances. We're clear on that, right?'

'Alright, Mum.'

'What about Ameena Najib?'

'On my way, now. She's off sick. Malingering, whatever. I'll pick up her file from Nadim and go down the house. What about you? How you doing with old Money-Nuts?'

'Listen,' Ray said, 'do you want to dial down the silly names?'

'Not really. Reminds me what they're all about.'

Sighing, Ray told him that he was waiting to finish his conversation with the Sheikh. 'All he wants to talk about, though, is Ameena. He's convinced she's a member of a Shia terrorist organisation; he's given me the names of three or four different groups to investigate. The prank that night wasn't just a humiliation, he says, it was a warning, and she was the identifier, the person who goes ahead to confirm his identity and monitor his movements. He thinks they're coming to get him. Next time, assassination.'

'Yeah? What do you reckon?'

'A little bit of paranoia, perhaps. But maybe she was involved in the prank.'

'He sent his bodyguard after her, did you know that? Ashley said.'

130

'Yes, the Sheikh told me.'

'Have you talked to the bodyguard?'

'He's not here. I got the impression, in fact, that he's not in the Sheikh's favour, at the moment.'

'Interesting. Ashley said he was useless, anyway. I'll see what I can get out of Ameena Najib, give her a bit of a shake.'

There was a pause. Ray said, 'What do you know about the Syrian civil war?'

A sigh. 'What's this, now? School test?'

'Al-Medina's rumoured to be implicated in some of the sectarian violence there. He's Sunni. Ameena Najib's Shia. It's in her file.'

'Been doing your research like a good boy.'

'Do you know the difference between the two?'

'You know I don't.'

'My point. When you talk to Ameena, don't shoot your mouth off, don't give her a "bit of a shake", because there are things you don't know, things that other people take very, very seriously. It's counterproductive to cause unnecessary offence. Enough,' he said, as Ryan began to speak. 'Work with Nadim to get some light on this Chiara Belotti. And *nothing else* without my say-so.'

He got out of his car and stood there in his flecked slim-fit wool blazer and navy twill trousers, feeling the damp breeze on his face, looking across parkland, calming himself. Ryan was a disturbance, an unexpected splash in the water, spray in the face, ripples setting everything rocking. He thought of Diane's pillow, damp this morning when he made the bed. He heard in his head the new tone of disappointment in the Super's voice. Breathing evenly, he scanned the tranquil arrangement of grass slopes and copses of trees, grown together by design. Gradually, he began to simplify things in his mind. His first requirement was self-control. Ryan would explode all on his own; Ray just had to make sure he wasn't caught in the blast. His second requirement, no less urgent, was tangible results. He was spending too long babysitting Ryan. He needed ideas of his own.

He began to feel better. He was famous for his discipline, after all. It only required a little more focus on the facts. He unbuttoned his blazer and relaxed at last into a new sort of alertness, reviewing the features of the case, stress-testing possible connections between the kitchen girl and the Sheikh, between the dead girl and the Provost of an Oxford college, standing there patiently by the car, gazing over the English parkland of the Sheikh's estate.

Hurrying round Old Court, zipping up a kitbag as he went, Jason Birch had just reached the entrance when he saw the odd-looking fed he'd talked to yesterday come into college through the gate, and he veered sideways, behind one of the portico's columns, just in time. Peering round the edge of the stone, he saw the fed put something back inside an envelope and bang on the window of the porter's lodge, and Leonard Gamp slide back the pane warily.

He heard the fed say, 'Provost around?'

'Until this afternoon.'

'What then?'

'He's flying to Oslo, I believe, to attend a conference.'

'What time?'

'A car is coming for him at two o'clock.'

As Jason watched, the fed said no more, but turned and drifted away, back out of the gate. Jason waited a minute, then hurried out too. Gamp, who had stayed at the open window as if guarding against further intrusions, called out to him as he went by, but he didn't stop. The coast was clear and he lugged his bag down Merton Street as fast as he could go.

Luckily for Jason, Ryan had gone the other way, through Oriel Square to the High, his Peugeot 306 banging.

'Piece of junk,' Ryan muttered.

As he drove, he googled 'Chiara Belotti' on his phone, but got nothing more interesting than the Twitter and Instagram accounts of pouting Italian teenagers, and he soon gave up, focusing instead on driving down St Aldates, towards the station.

There was a camp of journos round the entrance, television vans double-parked in Floyds Row. A little earlier, a statement had been released by a group calling themselves Defenders of the Leys, saying that any police found in the area would be 'dealt with as we have been dealt with', and the whole of the Greater Leys was now under lockdown, with road blocks and security crews in place. The Super had spent the morning negotiating with a residents' association for access to a venue for a public meeting. In the meantime, a general instruction had been issued prohibiting any officers from entering the area in groups of fewer than six, and only then with specific approval from the Superintendent and equipped with the appropriate resources.

Ryan got into the sally port and found his way through the confusion to Nadim Khan in COMINT. It was the first time they'd met, but she looked up from her desk and smiled at him.

'Hello, Ryan.'

'Quick work. Got me sussed. You should be in the police.'

'Your photo's just gone up on the portal.'

'Oh, yeah? What do I look like?' She turned her screen towards him and he stooped to look at it. 'Makes my nose look a bit big.'

'Nose is fine.'

'You think? You're not just trying to make me feel good?'

'It's the ears that are the problem, Ryan.'

'What's wrong with my ears?'

'They're crooked.'

He instinctively put his hands up. 'I never knew that. No one ever told me that before.'

'You need to get yourself some better friends.'

'Or some better ears.'

Nadim said, 'You've come for the file on Ameena Najib. Here it is.'

He sat on the corner of her desk, flicking through it. 'Hang on – what's this? She's on a watch list. Contact with groups, here, I can't even say the names of.'

'Kata'ib Hezbollah and Asa'ib Ahl al-Haq.'

'Yeah –' squinting at the report – 'that looks right.'

'Shia militia.'

He nodded, read on. 'Came out of Syria two years ago. Long journey – six months, or something. Turkey, Greece, Serbia – all over.' He paused, flicking back and forward. 'Don't understand this. Says here, she reached the UK over a year ago, but didn't apply for asylum till six months back. So, what's she's been doing?'

'You can ask her.'

'I will do.' He slid off her desk. 'Before I go, though, got something for you.' He gave her the note with *Chiara Belotti* on it and began to explain. 'Ray, Ray Wilkins – he's the guy I'm—'

'I know who Ray is, Ryan; he's a good friend of mine.'

'Fair enough.'

When he finished explaining, she said she'd get on it, and he nodded.

'Junior academic, something like that, I bet.'

'Got it. I'll give you a call when I've got something.'

'Cheers.'

'In the meantime,' she said, looking at him, 'take good care of Ray. He's one of the best.'

He said nothing to that, but went back out into the corridor and made for the sally port.

FIFTEEN

The college house was a tall Victorian building on the busy Abingdon Road, just over Folly Bridge. Pincushions of moss on the cracked window sills, brickwork grimy as a butcher's apron. Its entrance was round the side, on Western Road, through a small yard smelling of garbage, and in this yard Ryan stood for a moment, thinking, as he gazed up at the stretch of brickwork, windows and jumbled pipes above him.

The colleges owned property all over the city: new-build conference centres and institutes, old buildings converted cheaply into rooms for staff or visiting academics. Perhaps Chiara Belotti had come from overseas on some sort of fellowship, perhaps she'd been staying in a house like this, somewhere along the Abingdon Road, or in the mews and cobbled streets around Barnabas.

The door opened and two young men came out. They stopped when they saw him and they all stared at each other. They looked Middle Eastern, tall and stocky, wearing black leather jackets and bandanas. Both of them bigger than Ryan. One of them had a lazy eye; he said something sideways, in what sounded like Arabic, and the other grunted, neither of them taking their eyes off Ryan.

He fished out his badge and waved it laconically at them. 'Been visiting?'

They didn't even hesitate, but pushed past him as if he were a child and then they were gone; he heard them talking to each other in the street as they walked away.

He pressed the door buzzer, muttering to himself. Interesting, though, he thought.

Wearing a pale blue hijab and black knee-length blouse over grey jeans, Ameena Najib sat on an armchair with a sagging seat in the communal living room, her hands between her knees, looking at him coldly as he described the two men he'd met outside.

'Friends of yours?'

There was the littlest, tiniest hesitation. 'No. I have seen no one.'

'I thought maybe they're jihadi boys, friends of yours from those groups you hang out with. Assa . . . Assa Al . . . Hang on.' He opened the folder. 'Asa'ib Ahl al-Haq. Or –' he hesitated – 'or that other one.'

'No.'

'And they're not the guys who showed off their arses to the Sheikh, couple of nights ago?'

'I do not know what you are talking about.'

'Did something to upset him, though, didn't you? Give him the willies, I heard. Even sent his bodyguard after you.'

137

She looked at him without interest. Her nose was sharp and curved, her eyes glowed black. Her hair, just visible below the rim of her headscarf, was black too, almost blue-black, the same colour as the dead girl's. There was bitterness in her downturned mouth. Her voice was harsh, her manner indifferent. But he noticed her hands trembling in her lap. A little thing, but his soft eyes caught it. She said, with some bitterness, 'I am kitchen porter. I served him drink, that is all. Allah will judge him,' she added, 'not me.'

Ryan handed her a photograph. 'Know her?'

Ameena dropped the picture on to the coffee table. 'No. Is this the person who died?'

Ryan made no reply. Her indifference was perfect, as if practised.

Glancing at her watch, she said, 'I have no time to talk this morning; my work begins soon.'

'Thought you'd called in sick.'

'I am late today because I look for my uniform. It is missing.'

'You lose things easy, is what I hear.'

'Someone has taken it. You English like to play games. Take things from my locker, put things in my locker. It is very funny.' She looked at him with the same lack of interest, blank eyes under heavy eyelids.

'Lose any keys, the other night?'

'No.'

'You had to get into the Provost's lodge, pick up some clothes.'

'I did not need keys. She told me, the door is open.'

'And was it open?'

'Yes, of course.'

138

'And you took the bag?'

'Yes.'

'What time?'

She thought a moment, hesitated. 'A little past eight o'clock,' she said at last. 'My shift had ended. You may ask Jason Birch; he was there when I went.'

'Hear anything at the lodge? See anything unusual?'

'No.'

'Lock the door after you?'

'How? I had no keys. I do not know,' she said, 'why you talk to me of keys.'

'Have you ever lost any keys in college?'

She hesitated again. Straightened her back. 'Yes,' she said. 'Once before, it happened. But I found them, very soon. You may ask the Bursar; she was with me.' She glanced at the photograph lying on the table. 'May Allah punish those who did this. But I do not know her, I cannot help you. Now, I must go.'

They looked at each other for a moment. He was about to look away when her eyes flicked sideways.

'There's a gap in your file,' he said, still watching her. 'Ten months, between getting here and applying for asylum. It don't say here what you was doing.'

She said nothing.

'Just wondering,' he said. He glanced to the side and saw what she had looked at: her laptop, lying on a sofa.

Still, she was silent.

'You know what? I get the impression you don't like us very much.'

'English people?' She shrugged. 'All different: some are slow,

139

some stupid, others not so. I do not think they know enough about the world.'

'And you do? That why you're angry?'

She said nothing. But her eyes never left his.

He pushed harder. 'Scared, too. I can see it.'

'I am not scared.'

'Not what Jason Birch told me, yesterday. Scared at something the Sheikh said.'

Now he'd touched a nerve. She got to her feet. 'Jason Birch! You think this Jason Birch knows anything? Anything at all? No. Now I am going.'

'I haven't finished my questions.'

'Then come to me again when you bring my lawyer. Yes,' she said, 'I know the rights I have. I am trained in law. You have not finished your questions? I have finished my answers.'

She stared at him impassively with the clear intention of saying nothing else and, before he could speak, a text came through and he glanced at his phone. It was from Nadim. It said, *Found something. Get here quick.*

'Yeah, well,' he said, also getting up. 'I'll be seeing you again.'

Her silence made it clear that she judged it an irrelevance.

He got to COMINT just as Nadim was leaving. She'd been pulled into the Superintendent's meeting in Blackbird Leys and, even as she spoke, she was gathering her stuff together.

'Can't stop, Ryan – sorry. The good news or the bad news?'

'I'm a good news sort of person.'

'I got an interesting hit for Chiara Belotti.'

His face lit up. 'Oh, yeah?'

'Visiting junior research fellow at Barnabas Hall, three years ago. Physical geography. Any good?'

'Fucking bingo! I fucking well knew it. Fits the bill perfect. Nice work.' He hesitated. 'What's the bad news?'

'She doesn't exist any more.'

'Well, we know that. She's dead.'

'I mean no record. Nothing. No address, no next of kin, no bank account, no tax ID, no vehicle registration. No online presence of any kind for the last three years. Disappeared. Gone.'

Ryan thought about that.

Nadim said, 'So, anyway—'

A shout came from along the corridor and she grabbed her bag and stood up. 'Got to go. Sorry.'

'No, wait. What else?'

She hesitated. Another shout came, more urgently.

'Okay, very quickly. Three years ago, her national insurance number was transferred to someone else.'

He frowned. 'Which means . . . she changed her name?'

'Can't be sure till we square it with the deed-poll records; there's a process attached to that which I haven't got time for now.'

A third call came, more loudly still.

She ran for the door. 'Wait till I get confirmation. I'll let you know.'

'What was the new name?' he called.

'Chloe Belton,' she called back. 'But don't do anything till I get the process done.' Then she was gone.

Ryan sat on her desk and immediately googled 'Chloe Belton'. Almost at once, he got a hit: lecturer in language geography at the University of Edinburgh – a new post, beginning in January. Her biography lacked a photograph, but *Research Fellow at Oxford University* was included in the list of her previous roles.

'Fucking bingo,' he said again, softly, and dialled the number.

'School of Geosciences,' answered the polite Scots voice of a young woman.

'Yeah. Chloe Belton – she there?'

'Dr Belton hasn't taken up her post yet. Can I help you?'

'What's she look like?'

'Excuse me?'

'There isn't a photo of her on your website. Can you describe her to me?'

There was silence at the other end. Ryan said, 'Oh, yeah, I forgot. It's the police, here. DI Wilkins. I need to know what she looks like.'

'Well, I don't know. I haven't met her yet.' There was a pause. 'She was due to come in for induction a couple of days ago, actually, but she didn't turn up and we haven't been able to contact her. Is there some kind of problem?'

'Anyone there who has met her?'

'Just our head of department.'

'That'll do.'

'She's not here, right now.'

'Fuck. Scuse me. Well, get her to call me, soon as, alright? It's urgent.' He gave his number and rang off, then continued to sit on Nadim's desk, picking his teeth. After a while, he went up to Senior Management, where he was told that the Super had already left for her meeting, so he ambled back down into his own office and sat on the desk there, staring at the empty crazy wall.

A few minutes passed, and then he called Ray.

'Hey, Raymundo, not still at the Arabian Nights, are you?'

'I'm in Buckinghamshire, if that's what you mean.'

'Better get back here pronto, or the whole thing's going to be sewn up. I'm on fire, mate.'

He heard Ray sigh. 'What have you done?'

'Lead on the dead girl is panning out nicely. Academic, just as I thought.' He explained. 'Didn't show up for work a couple of days ago, hasn't been seen since. And she was just his type: young, female, junior research whatsit. Even studied the same subject. Definite fish-bait.'

There was a pause. 'Nadim gave you this information?'

'Yeah.'

'All confirmed?'

'Yeah, course.'

'Okay. What about Ameena Najib?'

'Yeah, interesting. She's a bit shonky, too. Wouldn't surprise me if she had something to do with the mooning. There were a couple of guys visiting her this morning. Could've been them. She hates old Money-Nuts. And she's angry. Maybe even angry enough to get involved in something, you know, a little bit jihadi. But she says she went over to the lodge at eight, so that's too early to put her in the frame for the murder. Jason give me the same time. She grabbed the bags, closed the door behind her, left it unlocked. Half an hour, maybe more, before the time of death. And there's nothing we know of to link her to the dead girl.'

'Alright. Listen, I've got to go now.'

'One thing, though.'

'What?'

'Got to be quick if we're going to get anything out of the shonky bastard at Barnabas. He's about to fly off somewhere.'

'For Christ's sake, enough with the name-calling! Just sit tight till I get back, alright?'

'Tell you what'd be stupid: letting him go.'

'On no account go anywhere near him. In fact, don't do anything without calling me first.'

Ryan sat a moment longer, looking at his phone. Sighing, he got to his feet and ambled up and down the office. He took out his photo of Ryan Junior and pinned it on the crazy wall, took it down again and ambled about a bit more. He looked at his watch.

'Fuck it,' he said at last, and went out of the office at speed.

SIXTEEN

The morning drizzle had dried up and the sun had come out. The poky windows of Barnabas shone like a nest of blades under the low winter sun. Bells struck one thirty as Ryan walked past the porter's lodge into New Court, thinking about Chiara Belotti. Why had she changed her name three years ago, just after her employment at Barnabas? Why then had she returned to the college just now? Why had she been wearing the Provost's robes?

He thought about Ameena Najib telling him he didn't know enough about the world. He gave a snort; he'd learned more about how the world works by growing up at Hinksey Point than he could have done in a lifetime's travelling.

Students were coming out of the dining hall in small groups, dispersing around the quad. At the far side, the Provost came briefly into view and disappeared again into the cloisters. I'm coming for you, Slippy Bob, Ryan thought. If not now, later. You're going to tell me what you know. I don't care about your wobbly head, your high-up friends. Ryan went under the archway and past the garden, along the chapel walls to where the bursary was situated in a small, blond row of converted cottages.

'Hello. Knock knock. Anyone home?'

Claire stepped out of her office and smiled at him. 'Come to interrogate me? I have an alibi. I was having a drink with a friend in town.'

'Oh, yeah? Boyfriend?'

'Is that relevant?'

'Depends what we're talking about. Tell you what's relevant to the enquiry, though: Ameena's boyfriend.'

Claire peered at him quizzically. 'I wouldn't have thought Ameena had a boyfriend.'

'Jason Birch.'

She laughed. 'It's true, I saw him talking to her the other day, but I really don't think he's her type.' She watched him as he chewed his thumbnail. 'Any other questions?'

'Yeah. What's the difference between Shia and Sunni?'

She laughed again, in surprise. Hesitated when she saw he was serious. 'Disagreements about theology, I think,' she said.

'Oh, great, thanks, yeah, that's a big help.'

'If you want more detail, you could talk to Dr Goodman; he's an Arabist. It's his last day soon, though, so you'd better catch him quick.'

Ryan did not cease to bite his nail and she watched him, smiling.

'Anything else? Any other world religion you need to know about?'

He said, 'Anyone changed their printer ink today?'

She stopped smiling. 'How did you know that?'

'Don't know. I'm so fucking ignorant, must have been a lucky guess.'

She coloured. 'One of the PAs in Fitzgerald collected a new cartridge just now.'

'Office printer?'

'Yes.'

'What office?'

'Top floor of the conference suite: humanities, HR and collections.'

'Sweet.' He hitched up his trackies.

'Helpful to the enquiry?'

'You're a model citizen. Can't ask for more. 'Cept for you need to brush up on your theology.' He was going to say something else, but his phone rang. An Edinburgh number. He walked away, back round the garden towards New Court, talking as he went.

'Yeah?'

'Is that DI Wilkins?' A lady's voice, well spoken, with a faint Scots accent. 'I was asked to call you.'

'From Edinburgh Uni? Geosciences?'

'That's right.'

'Listen. I got to be a bit tactful, here. Following information received, we're concerned about the whereabouts of a member of your department: Chloe Belton.'

There was a pause. 'May I ask why?'

'There's no good way to say this, sorry.' He cleared his throat. 'We think she might be a murder victim.'

There was another, longer pause. 'I doubt that.'

'Why?'

'Because she's not dead.'

Ryan frowned. 'How do you know?'

'Because I am Chloe Belton.'

Ryan came to a stop under the walls of the chapel. 'Oh.'

'You sound disappointed.'

'It's not that. It's just . . .' He re-evaluated the situation. 'Can I ask you something else, then? It's going to sound a bit odd.' Taking her hesitation for assent, he said, 'Were you Chiara Belotti?' And he stood, gazing unfocused at the chapel wall, listening to the silence at the other end of the line. 'Hello? Hello?'

When she spoke again, her voice was hoarse and anxious. 'Why do you ask me that?'

Ryan winced as he explained.

There was a longer pause before she spoke. 'You thought the dead woman was me? Why?'

Ryan said, 'Don't know yet, to be honest. What I think is, it'll come a bit clearer if you tell me something about what happened to you when you were at Barnabas, three years ago.'

He could hear her breathing and, when she spoke again, her voice was no more than a whisper. 'It's so difficult, talking about it.'

'Understood. Take it as slow as you like.'

'I've been in therapy.'

He could hear her breathing, as if gathering herself for a plunge. He waited.

Finally, she took a breath and spoke: 'I don't know if you've met the Provost of Barnabas . . .'

The bells sounded the quarter hour as he went at speed across New Court, towards the Fellows' Garden, yelling into his phone, looking at his watch.

'Ray! Ray, mate! Pick up, for fuck's sake.' He got on to the path and increased his pace, yelling again at voicemail: 'Listen, some new shit's come in. Yeah, about the Finger-Dipper. Game-changer, mate. We've got to talk to him before he goes off. Absolutely can't wait. Sorry.'

He rounded the corner of the garden railings and jogged towards the Provost's lodge, dialling another number.

'Come on, come on, come on,' he muttered. Then the Super's voicemail kicked in and he groaned.

For a moment, he stood indecisively at the bottom of the stone steps leading to the porch door, frowning and chewing his bottom lip. He picked anxiously at the scar tissue on his cheek, holding his breath, then breathed out suddenly.

'Ah, fuck it,' he said, and ran up the steps.

SEVENTEEN

The Provost closed his laptop and stood up as his wife came into the lounge, a lavender and cream room of comfortable armchairs, coffee tables and knick-knacks on mantelpieces, a period piece for television.

'Leonard phoned,' she said. 'The car's here.'

He made no reply, but walked across the room to where his bags were waiting.

'Have you got your medication?'

'I'm not likely to have forgotten it.'

She watched him as he put on his overcoat. He looked jaundiced – he always did, when stressed. His face was sallow, hands greyish, and he grunted to himself as he fumbled his arms into the sleeves of his coat. But, when she went over to him, he turned away petulantly, pursing his lips.

'Just trying to help.'

'I'm getting used to doing without.'

'What do you mean?'

He told her about Ray's visit the previous afternoon, the

further questions about the picture allegedly missing from his office wall, the scepticism with which his answers were received. 'He called later with still more questions.''

'What questions?'

'Nitpicking.' She waited and he glanced over and went on bitterly, 'That interfering little American told him that, when I left the drinks before dinner, I'd been heading back here, not to my office.' She looked at him for an answer but he went on, 'He's a strange little man, that Kent Dodge. One of the new wave. I read his paper on Islamic tiles and it made no sense to me whatsoever.'

She waited longer. 'And did you?'

'Did I what?'

'Come back here?'

'For heaven's sake! I told you what happened. I've told everyone.' He stood with his overcoat rumpled up his back, his cheeks quivering, glaring at her. He dropped his eyes at last. 'Look, I needed a breather, I'd had al-Medina to cosset all day and I was bloody well tired. Before I went to the office to make my call to Kriegstein, I took five minutes to relax, over by the chapel.'

His wife regarded him through half-closed eyes. 'What does that mean, "to relax"?'

For a moment, he was defiantly silent, then he made a sudden dithering gesture with his hands. 'I had a cigarette, alright?'

She made the face that he feared so much. Good job he hadn't mentioned the other cigarette he'd had later, after al-Medina had left. Or, indeed, the many other cigarettes he usually squeezed into his days.

151

'Just the one. It was absolutely necessary.' Before she could say anything else, he went on, 'And it's all the fault of that American, stirring things up with the detective. The black one, not the poor-white-trash one. At least he has some basic manners. I hear from Claire, by the way, that Dodge has run up an enormous battels bill. I've asked her to demand immediate payment in full.' As his wife turned away without speaking, he said, angrily, 'I meant what I said about getting used to not having help. No one believes me. Not even you.'

'Nonsense.'

'This is all about trust, you know.'

She made a sceptical noise.

'You're the one who made it an issue,' he said. 'I made a promise to you and I've kept it. Now,' he said, '*you* have to keep *yours*.'

Before she could reply, there was a banging outside and they looked at each other.

'What on earth?'

His eyes widened as he heard the front door crash open and footsteps in the hall. 'Good God, what . . .'

He was hovering over his suitcases in a badly buttoned overcoat, like a fugitive panicking at a railway station, when Ryan went into the room. His wife, more poised, raised an eyebrow, and Ryan nodded at her, glancing round. He said to the Provost, 'We need to talk.'

'Too late, I'm afraid.'

'It's important. New stuff's come up.'

The Provost indicated his cases. 'I'm just leaving. A car is waiting to take me to the airport.'

Ryan considered him, his bulldoggish face, his brisk scorn, and reminded himself that this was a man who had the ear of the Superintendent – a fact he began to forget straight away. What he saw in front of him was someone who did not believe he had to tell the truth.

'Don't worry about that,' he said.

The Provost let out a dismissive snort.

'I give Gramps a bell to tell it to go away again.'

'*You did what?*'

'Helping the police with their enquiries, I said.'

The Provost opened his mouth.

'Chiara Belotti,' Ryan said. 'Ring a bell?'

The Provost closed it again.

'Yeah. Thought it might.' Ryan went further into the room, hands in trackie pockets, as far as a floral-patterned armchair and footstool. 'Do you want to sit down?'

The Provost cast a glance at his wife.

'James,' she said quietly.

His face stiffened as he turned to Ryan. 'I remember Chiara, of course. But I assure you she has nothing to do with any of this. And I deeply – deeply – suspect your motives for bringing her into it.'

'We can talk about motives in a minute. Sure you don't want to sit down?'

No one made a move.

Ryan went on: 'Thing is, I was just talking to Ms Belotti. She's not called that any more, by the way. Changed her name.'

The Provost's face became congested. It made his eyes more prominent. 'You come in here,' he began in a blustering voice, 'you just barge in here, like some—'

153

'Had a breakdown,' Ryan said. ''Cause of what happened here, she told me. Result of being subjected to, quote, "unwanted advances of a sexual nature", unquote.' He turned to the Provost's wife, who was looking at her husband. 'Sorry you got to hear this.'

'I know about Chiara already,' she murmured.

The Provost was breathing heavily. 'She also knows,' he said, glaring, 'that you are grossly misrepresenting what was nothing more than a brief flirtation and a totally private affair, about which you have no right—'

'In the bedroom, a few times.'

The Provost looked around wildly, as if for escape.

'In the library,' Ryan went on. 'Once, in the chapel, she told me.'

'I didn't know *that*,' the Provost's wife said.

'Mainly in your study, though,' Ryan said. 'Which is interesting.'

The Provost flushed, a rapid mottling. 'I've had enough of this. Who do you think you are?' He made his mouth narrow and began to talk in a rapid, compressed manner. 'My relationship with Chiara was a . . . nothing but a . . . and if you think—'

'Told her you could help with her career, didn't you? Sort of a way of telling her she might *not* get on, if she didn't play along.'

Fumbling his phone out of a trouser pocket, the Provost adopted a different tone: a sneering bray. 'Well, this has been an eye-opener. I shall have one or two things to say to my colleagues on the Civic Responsibility Select Committee about the professionalism of the Thames Valley police force. And, in the meantime, we'll see what thoughts Superintendent Waddington

154

has about the sort of policeman who slouches into a private residence without permission, looking like the local juvenile drug-dealer, and begins to browbeat an innocent witness in front of his wife.'

Ryan did his best not to get riled. But he wasn't very good at it. Echoes of other conversations across the years came back to him: *Let's see what the headmaster thinks about it, shall we? Let's get the warden down. Let's ask your father in . . .* He recognised the tone of voice too, the modulated scorn, expansive yelping. It goaded him.

As casually as he could, he said, 'Did you know she had a boyfriend?'

The Provost struggled clumsily to unlock his phone, and bit his lip.

'No? Didn't know he had issues, then,' Ryan went on. 'Anger management. What's known as a bit mental.'

Muttering to himself, the Provost pushed buttons wildly.

Ryan said, 'Kicked her head in when he found out what she'd been doing for you. Month in the Trauma Centre. Can't see out of one eye no more. Funny thing is, she still thinks she was partly to blame.'

There was a rawness in his voice now – he could hear it himself. He saw not just a dead girl in the study, but a whole string of girls, helplessly giving in to the guy at the desk with his flies undone.

With a glance at his wife, the Provost abandoned his phone and his aloof manner. 'Listen to me, you . . . you . . .' His head wobbled, his mouth was wet. His whole face said, *How dare you?* 'You're not going to hold me responsible for another man's—'

155

'James!' his wife murmured.

He turned on her, almost panting. 'I won't have it! I knew nothing about this so-called boyfriend. Nothing in that regrettable little episode is in any way relevant to the discovery of a dead stranger in my study. *Has everyone forgotten what this is actually about?*' He turned to Ryan. 'Is it some sort of vendetta? Is that it?'

Ryan said, 'If she was a stranger, why'd she get dressed up in your robes, then?'

The Provost stared at him wildly. 'In my robes? Are you a fantasist? Is there nothing between your ears?'

'Like dressing them up, did you?'

The Provost lost it. Ryan saw it happen in his eyes – they went horse-like suddenly.

'You ignorant piece of . . . *lowlife!*'

That was it. Ryan lost it now, too. He'd tried. He couldn't help himself any more. He said, 'Get them in your study and dress them up, did you? Make them do a little dance? Maybe that's the only way you can get it up. What happened this time? Went a bit too far?'

The Provost scoffed. 'You know something about going too far, don't you? In Salisbury. Oh, yes, I've been informed of the gross-misconduct charges you faced. You won't get off this time, I promise you that. This,' he said pompously, 'is an outrage!'

'*Outrage?*' Ryan took a step towards him. 'Tell you what's an outrage – dogging your junior staff in your study, you sordid little fuckrat.'

Astonishment made the Provost more shapeless than ever inside his badly fitting coat. He stood aghast, face the colour of raw liver, quivering. Even the skin of his eyes seemed to quiver. He began to shout incoherently, and that was the moment Ray ran in.

Ray looked in horror from one to the other, and the whole lower part of his face seemed to come loose.

'Oh, hello,' Ryan said. 'Glad you showed up. Thought I was going to have to beat the truth out of Peter Pervert, here, on my own.'

'Peter Pervert?' the Provost spluttered. 'Peter *Pervert?*'

Ray, not knowing what to do, found himself making gestures like a traffic officer – huge, sudden hand signs – and, surprised, Ryan and the Provost broke apart, panting.

In the momentary silence, the Provost's wife stepped forward. 'If I may,' she said calmly, addressing Ryan. 'I feel sure that, on this last point, you're mistaken about my husband. He may be vain and arrogant, and, yes, he may have made unwanted advances to many women, nearly always those whose careers were in his hands, but – and I can absolutely promise you this – he doesn't dress them up in his robes and strangle them in some sort of pornographic fantasy.'

The Provost turned. 'Vain?' he said to her, indignantly. 'Arrogant?'

He would have gone on, but Ryan interrupted him. 'Wait,' he said to the Provost's wife. 'Say that again.'

All the anger had gone out of him and she frowned at him, puzzled. 'I said, he may have made unwanted—'

He clicked his fingers impatiently. 'Not that bit. The other bit.'

'Pornographic fantasies?'

Inappropriately, Ryan did his drifting-off thing. It was as if the

157

enormous shouting match had never occurred. He was suddenly remote, disconnected. He couldn't even see the others any more. He went zombie-like into a zone of numbing quietness, like almost-fainting, where everything was gone except a few images, swimming dreamlike out of the rubbish of days, and they were: a pyramid of lamps piled up on a chapel altar; an exceptionally good-looking dead woman; three closed doors concealing secrets; the sharp voice of his sister, talking about doctors and nurses ...

He sighed a long sigh, gazing unfocused at nothing.

'Ryan? *Ryan?*'

He came out of it and went over to the sofa, where the Provost's laptop lay. 'What's your password?'

Bewildered, the Provost just stared at him. His wife said, 'Maladroit. All lower case.' She spelled it. 'A private joke,' she murmured.

Ray began to speak and Ryan shushed him.

The Provost found his voice at last: 'What the hell do you think you're doing?'

'Googling porn on your laptop.'

The Provost turned to Ray. 'Has he gone mad?'

Ryan finished his search, lay back on the sofa and rolled his eyes. 'Bingo!' He laughed out loud. 'Took thirty seconds.' He turned the laptop round to face them, and they all peered forward. On the screen was a photograph of the murder victim – not dead, but very much alive – lying on the Provost's desk, naked except for the long black academic robes, and pleasuring herself with a fluorescent pink sex toy of bizarre shape.

No one said anything.

Ryan slowly clicked through the gallery. Same naked girl straddling a pile of books in the Barnabas library; teasingly resting her breasts on an antique globe; spreadeagled and dumbfounded against a bookcase. Same naked girl bending over the altar in the Barnabas chapel, pious and filthy.

'That's a cheeky one.' Ryan squinted. 'There's more, if you want to browse. Shoots at other places, too. See? Different models.' There was a whole archive of photographs, with various tags: *Reading Room of the British Museum*; *St Paul's Cathedral*; *HQ MI5*; *Buckingham Palace*. And *Barnabas Hall, Oxford*.

'She was in your study for a photo shoot. And in the chapel, and in the library. It's like a feature: porn star in places you wouldn't expect to find a porn star. Funny. I kinda like it. What do you think?'

The Provost was pale and bewildered. There was a tremor in one of his hands. He seemed to be on the verge of tears. But he gathered himself. 'This girl –' he pointed tremulously at the screen – 'has nothing to do with me.' His eyes wandered accusingly to Ryan.

'As it turns out,' Ryan said. 'And lucky for you I've proved it, and saved you from speculation in the national press about your so-called regrettable but brief flirtations. Unless, of course,' he added, 'they're your sex toys she's playing with. 'Cause that would interest the press.'

The Provost glanced at his wife and looked away, lip trembling, and Ryan started to laugh.

EIGHTEEN

He'd stopped laughing by the time they got to the Superintendent's office. The usual post-meltdown process had taken place and the memory of what he'd done was lodged uncomfortably in the front of his mind.

The office seemed bare and functional after the Provost's lavish lounge. He was reminded again of other rooms where he had waited for punishment: headmasters' offices, social services interview pods, police cells. Or in the trailer, waiting for his father to come back from the house where he went to get his brew. A familiar nausea churned in his stomach.

He began to whistle. That was familiar too, the off-key note of defiance.

Ray said, 'Word of advice.'

'What?'

'Think about apologising.'

He bridled. 'Got results, didn't I? We know who she is, now.'

'We don't. We just know what she did.'

'It's a start. Anyway, I was just doing my job.'

'Is that what you told the Bishop of Salisbury?'

That brought back the other memory, of listening to the Super in Wiltshire read out the conclusions of his disciplinary procedure. He remembered the tone of disgust as the man read certain phrases: *Disgrace to the service*; *Unprecedented and unjustified behaviour*; *Intention to cause actual bodily harm*.

He found himself sneering at the floor.

Ray was speaking again. 'What did you actually *do* to the Bishop, by the way?' he asked.

Before Ryan could reply, there were light footsteps in the corridor and the door opened.

'I've been pulled out of an important meeting in the Leys for this,' the Super said. 'Incident at Barnabas, I was told. Involving one of my inspectors.' She looked at Ray. 'Start explaining.'

Ray said, 'I picked up DI Wilkins's message on my way back from al-Medina's. He sounded emotional, so I went straight to Barnabas, where I found him in the Provost's lodge, having an altercation with Sir James. Obviously, my main concern was to defuse the situation.' His eyes flicked at Ryan. 'Some sort of normality was restored.'

The Superintendent continued to look at him after he stopped speaking.

He added, delicately, 'There were things said that I'm sure will be regretted.'

The Super made a noise of exasperation and turned to Ryan, who was shuffling from foot to foot like a little boy.

'Shortly after you left the college,' she said, 'Sir James collapsed and was taken to hospital for a check-up.'

He did his best to put on a sympathetic face. It only made him look devious.

She said, 'You were told repeatedly not to go near him without approval from either Ray or myself. What happened?'

'Tried to get hold of you. Both of you. Thing is, I'd got this new stuff, it was urgent, but I was really running out of time – he was about to leave the country, see, and . . .' He trailed away.

'And when you went ahead and confronted him on your own,' the Super said, 'you broke just about every guideline in the police-conduct handbook. So, I'll ask you again. *What happened?*'

This was the moment – there was one in every conversation of this sort – when you hit out or backed down. He took a breath. 'Alright. Got to hold my hands up. I did lose it a bit.'

'A bit!'

'So did he, though,' he added. 'Though it was regrettable, like Ray says. But it's funny, isn't it? Sometimes, in all the yelling, something gets said that moves you on a bit. That's what led to us ID'ing the girl.'

The Super looked across at Ray and back to Ryan. 'You've got an ID?'

'Pretty much,' Ryan said.

She frowned. 'Explain.'

He began. 'You know what they say: it's all about location.'

'What?'

'I mean, that's what I'd been thinking about. The places she went into. Felt like the college tourist highlights – lodge, chapel, library. Why them? Why did she lock the door behind her each time?'

'Wait. We know she was in the lodge and the library. How do we know she was in the chapel?'

Ray was looking at him.

Ryan said, ''Cause of the lamps.'

'Lamps?'

'Ashley told me someone had piled up the lamps in the chapel, on the altar. She thought it was just another student prank. Didn't sound right to me.' He paused. 'Not enough wit, somehow, for your future prime ministers. But someone might do it to throw a bit more light on the steps in front of the altar. Like a photographer. Then there was the ring.'

'In the library?'

'Yeah. She's wearing it in some of the library photos, but not in any of the chapel or the lodge ones. So she must have been in the library first, where she took it off and left it behind, then in the chapel, then the lodge. It was the robes,' he said, 'that made me think of dressing up. And the fancy knickers and high-end haircare, not to mention the, what'd you call it, enhancement, that made me think of modelling. And porn was on my mind 'cause of my sister.'

'Your sister?'

'Found porn on her computer. Nurses tossing off doctors, air hostesses giving—'

'I know what porn is.'

'Right. So, anyway, when things got a bit verbal and his missus says something about pornographic fantasies, it sort of brought things together in my mind.'

There was a pause, after he said this, in which he tried to be hopeful.

'It's not actually an ID.'

'No. But nearly. It's definitely better than before. 'Cause, before, we knew fuck all, didn't we, Ray?'

Ray looked uncomfortable about being brought into the conversation. Ignoring Ryan, he said, 'We've moved on. With the information we've got now, I think we'll get to an ID fairly quickly.'

The Super turned to Ryan. 'And Sir James?'

Ryan shuffled uncomfortably.

'We're assuming no connection between him and the victim, correct?'

Ryan reluctantly nodded.

'And, as I understand it, Ray, someone at college has come forward to say they saw him smoking by the chapel at the time he told us. Eight forty-five.'

'Yes.'

'And his phone records show he made a half-hour call from his study immediately after that.'

'That's right.'

'So, he's not a suspect, it turns out. No reason for him ever to have been treated as a suspect. Of course, if it comes to that, there's no reason for any suspect to be treated as you treated him. It's no wonder he feels victimised.'

Ryan said, 'Alright, alright, I get it, it's true.' He faced the Super. 'He made me lose my blob.'

The Super said nothing. Ray cleared his throat.

Ryan said, 'But the way he was speaking to me like I was trash, calling me lowlife and stuff, and all the time he's been forcing his junior staff to do stuff for him in his study. Jerk him off, I mean,' he added helpfully. 'Chiara Belotti was in hospital for a month, in therapy for three years. I mean, fuck. Who's the victim, here? Who's the perp? Anyway, I'm sorry,' he said. 'It just made me mad.'

The Super's gaze hardened further. The silence went on and on.

'Will Ms Belotti be pressing charges?' she said at last.

'Doubt it. Think she wants to put it all behind her.'

The Super made a note. 'I'll talk to her, then. We have a responsibility to victims of historic crimes.' She looked up at Ryan. 'And a duty to bring their perpetrators to justice. Now,' she said, 'where are we with the investigation? Ray?'

'It's opened things up. We've got two people, now, we don't know anything about.'

'Go on.'

'The model – and her photographer. *Two* strangers getting into college, going into the library, moving on to the chapel, moving on to the lodge. It all took time; they covered a lot of ground. So why did no one notice them?'

Suddenly they were talking detail.

The Super said, 'It's a college, people are coming and going all the time. And it was dinner hour; guests were arriving, leaving, milling round.'

'No, Ray's right,' Ryan said. 'It's odd. The photographer must have had some kit with him. Something made them blend in.'

Ray said, 'And how did they get into Barnabas in the first place?'

'Security's poor,' the Super said. 'They just walked in.'

'And knew where everything was? Including the bursary?'

165

'Why would they need to know about the bursary?'

'For the keys,' Ryan said.

Ray said, 'Someone helped them out.'

Ryan nodded. 'That's it. Inside job. Some squirrel lets them in, gives them the keys, tells them the layout. I got ideas about that, too.' He risked a grin. 'Hey, we're cooking with gas now, in't we?'

The smile died on his lips while the Super continued to look at him. There was a long and awkward pause. 'Follow it up,' she said at last. 'Where's Nadim got to with the website?'

'Registered in the Caymans,' Ray said. 'She's tracing the owner now.'

'I'll talk to him, if you like,' Ryan said. 'I could pop over.'

The Super ignored him. She said to Ray, 'Ask Nadim to set up a call for me. Obviously we need IDs for the girl and the photographer, soon as.'

'Got it.'

She held them, for a moment, with a level gaze.

'Ray, you need to talk to the press. Do it tonight. Tell them we're making *some* progress, but make it brief. No details on the victim till we know her name, okay? That's it.'

She looked at Ryan. 'You – you stay behind.'

Ray went out alone and shut the door behind him. Caught in her gaze, Ryan shifted his weight from foot to foot, looking round the room. After a long moment's silence, he knew what was coming.

'Pressing charges, is he?'

'No. But he immediately submitted an official complaint.'

'Just his style.'

166

'Copies have gone to three ministers, one of whom is the Home Secretary. I expect to be informed in the next day or two that a misconduct investigation is being initiated.'

He sneered at the floor, suddenly upset. A childish feeling, as if he were ten years old again, standing in the headmaster's office or in the social worker's office. He'd always been the same, indifferent when he could be, shocked when it finally went against him. 'Surprised he's not copied in the Bishop,' he said bitterly. 'Maybe they didn't go to the same school.'

She looked at him without expression.

'Still, least he's not pressing charges,' he said, after a while. That too was familiar – the defiance, the jauntiness, the make-believe. But his attempt to look on the bright side did not survive her continuing silence.

'Am I suspended?'

'Not till I tell you.'

'How long will it take?'

'I don't get to decide that.'

'It's not like in Wiltshire, then?'

'It'll be handled out of Canary Wharf. Sir James complained directly to the IOPC. No doubt he knows someone there. Thames Valley involvement will be restricted to witness statements. Your job,' she said, 'is to focus on the murder investigation until I say otherwise. You're extremely lucky I haven't suspended you.' Her eyes didn't leave his, her expression didn't change.

He began to shuffle from side to side again.

'You can go now,' she said, at last. 'Ray will be waiting.'

He stayed where he was, shuffling.

'What is it?'

167

'You'll give a statement, then? In the disciplinary.'

'Yes, I will.'

There was a longer pause.

'Put my case, then. If you want to.'

She said nothing and her eyes gave nothing away. After a moment, she opened a folder on her desk and, as if he were no longer there, bent to her work, and he turned and went out of her office.

In their office, Ray unbuttoned his jacket and sat brooding. He recalled his wasted day at al-Medina's Buckinghamshire estate, sitting in the great hall, intimidated by its two-storey baroque marble fireplace, snubbed by the pale-faced ladies looking down their noses at him from portraits hanging on the coral-pink papered walls, only, in the end, to have his time wasted by the Sheikh. His questions about the murder had been met with shrugs. His patience and tact had got him nowhere. In the meantime, Ryan had behaved like a delinquent and got away with it – he'd even got results.

Ray looked at him now, pinning pictures on the crazy wall, whistling to himself. He was childlike in his moods. When he'd first come back into the office after his private talk with the Super, he'd paced about, face twitching, as if blinking back tears. Once or twice, he'd let out a scoffing laugh, sneering at Ray. Now, within minutes, he was behaving as if nothing had happened.

Ryan looked back over his shoulder. 'Always something to cheer us up, eh? Look at her in this one. And get a load of this. Makes sense, now we know she was in porn – that work she'd

168

had done. Should've guessed, maybe, but I don't do porn that much. You?'

'What? No. Of course not.'

Standing back, Ryan gave the pictures an appraising look. 'Wouldn't mind seeing that Bursar with some of this kit on,' he said.

Unsmiling, Ray bent to his work again, and Ryan detached himself from the wall and stood there, watching him.

'What *is* a bursar, by the way? Come on, Ray! Raymond, don't sulk. We're on it now, we've even got a suspect come into the frame, right? The photographer, like you said. And, look, if anyone's going to get mashed for what happened, it'll be me, and I've been getting mashed all my life, so you needn't worry.'

Ray didn't look up. 'I don't care enough about you to worry.'

Ryan forced a smile. 'Fair enough.' He ambled over to the door. 'I'll give your best wishes to Ryan Junior. He likes the sound of you, did I say? I told him you were a bit of a mole.'

'What?'

'And I'm a bit of a mouse.'

'I've no idea what you're talking about.'

'Book we're reading: *Mouse and Mole*. Mole's a bit up himself, to be honest.' Ray muttered under his breath, and Ryan added, 'But he's alright, really.' He hesitated. 'You got kids? Never asked.'

Ray kept his head bent to his work. 'No kids.'

'Yeah, they can be a pain. Not Ryan – he's a gent. I'm off, then.'

Ray ignored him.

'By the way,' Ryan said, by the door, 'I'm pretty sure who the inside help was. Tell you now, if you like.'

Now Ray looked up.

'Jason Birch.'

'Why do you think that?'

'Got a vibe.'

Ray snorted.

'Here's the thing: he knew about Ameena mislaying her keys, when no one had been told. Also,' Ryan said, 'he's a fucking Arsenal fan. Bound to be dodgy.'

After he'd gone, Ray sat for a while, grim-faced, doing nothing. Then he called his wife and told her he'd be late. He finished working on his press presentation and went over to look at the photographs on the crazy wall. A woman working in the porn industry. He tried to imagine it. It wouldn't be all play-acting. A photo shoot in an Oxford college had a semi-glamorous feel, with comic undertones, but what else did her job require? Live work? Pole-dancing in bars? Prostitution, turning tricks, visits to out-of-the-way sailors' hostels? Who were the people in her life? Photographers, pimps, enforcers – men with no plan and little control.

He thought about these things and, after a while, called Leonard Gamp at Barnabas and asked for the Bursar's home number.

After the news shout, he went over to COMINT, where Nadim was also working late. It was seven o'clock.

She said, 'What's the matter?'

'How do you know something's the matter?'

'You've got that look – sort of humpy round the eyes.'

He instinctively put his fingers up and touched his temples.

'How were the press?' she asked.

'Overeager. Lots of questions about the Provost's private life, one of them about sex toys. God knows how they got hold of that. And it's hard to claim progress when you still don't know who the victim is.'

'Still, it was a win. Moved things on. That's what people are saying.'

Ray grunted.

Nadim studied him for a moment. 'A win's a win, Ray; doesn't matter who gets it.'

Ray nodded, unsmiling. 'You met him this morning, didn't you? What did you think?'

She thought about it with her head on one side. 'Childish. Funny. Inarticulate. Sharp. A nightmare to work with, I bet.' She paused. 'I liked him.'

He nodded minimally and gave another grunt. 'How are you doing with the owner of the website?'

'Michael Seagrave's his name. Calls himself an "entertainments entrepreneur". Well connected. High-profile political donor.'

'English?'

'Domiciled in Monaco. Super's got a call with him tomorrow morning.'

It occurred to him that the Superintendent didn't trust him to make the call himself, and his jealous thoughts began to drift again, back to Ryan.

Nadim was asking him if he was going home. 'It's late. Your lovely wife will be waiting for you.'

He nodded. 'Just going. Can you pull an address for me, first? Jason Birch – handyman at Barnabas.'

'What's Jason done?'

'Don't know yet. He was around that night and we think – that genius Ryan thinks – he knew more about a set of college keys than he should've done. According to Jason, he was working late, but I just talked to the Bursar and she says he wasn't signed up for those hours. A bit of a Jack the Lad, she said. Up for a laugh. Not the brightest. Gets into scrapes.'

Nadim bent to her computer. 'Field Avenue,' she said, after a moment. 'Blackbird Leys.'

He nodded blandly and took the printed slip. 'Thanks.'

'Right in the middle of the war zone,' she added.

He nodded again and moved off, and she said, 'Ray? You need clearance to go in. Minimum six officers.'

'Yeah, yeah, I know.'

'Ray!' She looked at him suspiciously. 'Field Avenue's where our man got burned.'

He looked at her. 'Come on, Nadim. You don't need to tell me. I always work to the rule book, you know that.'

He went, and she sat looking after him, frowning.

Back in his office, he called his wife again and told her not to wait up.

NINETEEN

When Ryan got to his sister's that evening, he found her waiting outside with Ryan Junior already in his coat.

'I don't even want you in the house, if you haven't been to see her.'

He winced. 'Fuck's sake, Jade – you know I haven't had time.'

'What do I have to do, Ryan? Do I have to do everything myself?'

'I'll go now,' he said.

'You only say that 'cause you know you can't. I've got to get to work, and you're not taking Ryan there.'

'I'll call her, then.' Kneeling down, grinning, he held out his arms to his son, who said, solemnly, 'You shouldn't say "fuck", Daddy.'

'Yeah, fair enough. But, here, look what I got you.' He dangled the bag.

'Gummy bears!'

His sister said, 'More sweets? That's thoughtful. Why don't you just brush his teeth with sugar?'

'Can't do anything right, can I?'

'Call her tonight,' his sister said, as she went inside the house and slammed the door.

Just dialling the number, he began to sweat. He felt the fear burning his stomach – a feeling as disgustingly intimate as the smell of his own shit.

In the bath, Ryan Junior played happily with a purple grinning shark, whispering to himself, and Ryan watched him as he sat on the toilet, the phone clamped to the side of his head, his mouth clamped shut until the call was answered and there was a sort of swaying silence at the other end.

'I want to talk to her,' he said. 'Not you. Put her on,' he added loudly.

There was a dead sound, like the phone being dropped, then nothing for two or three minutes, then the scrunched noise of someone picking it up.

'Listen,' Ryan said. 'We know something's going on.' There was breathing at the other end, faint and intermittent. 'Has he been at you again?' A stupid question: he knew she would never answer with him there. 'We know he has,' he said.

His mother said nothing.

'Come on. What's been going on?'

No answer.

'Useless, this is,' Ryan said. 'I'm going to come round.'

She made a noise, small and distressed; it made him suddenly, shockingly angry.

'Yeah, well, I am, and I'm going to fucking sort him out, you

174

can fucking well tell him.' He had to pause for breath, he was panting so hard. 'No,' he said, when he could. 'No, don't say that – don't say anything. If he asks, tell him I was calling to ask when your birthday is. Alright? We're not putting up with it, though – you got that? We're not . . .'

When he realised she'd hung up, he sat in silence on the toilet seat, his mouth half-open.

Ryan zoomed the shark in and out of the bath water, whispering. Even his whispers sounded polite.

'Daddy?' he said quietly, after a while.

Ryan looked at him and made a hideous attempt to smile. 'Yeah?'

'You shouldn't say "fucking".'

He sighed. 'You're right.'

'Or . . .'

'Or what?'

'Or "fucking *well*".'

'Yeah, okay. I won't say that one either.'

'Daddy?'

'What?'

'Is it hard being a daddy?'

Something inflated balloon-like in his chest and he leaned forward on the toilet seat and grinned. 'Being *your* daddy? Nah, no way. Easy-peasy, mate.'

His son grinned all the way up his fat cheeks. 'Is it really?'

'Yeah. Straight up. Piece of piss.'

Ryan Junior adopted a solemn expression. 'Daddy, you shouldn't—'

'Yeah, yeah, alright. Point taken. Won't say that either. Come on, let's get you out of the bath.'

His son stood on the bath mat, wriggling slightly, shark in mouth, staring at the ceiling as his father rubbed him dry.

'Daddy?'

'Yeah?'

'Mummy's hair was brown, wasn't it, Daddy?'

'Yeah. Sort of brown. Brownish.'

'And she was beautiful, wasn't she, Daddy?'

'Most beautiful thing I ever saw, mate. 'Cept for you, course.'

The boy studied his father's nose intently, pressing the end of it with his finger.

'When she went, why did she go?'

Ryan paused. A muscle jumped in his cheek. 'We talked about this before, didn't we, Ry?'

'She wasn't a happy bunny.'

'That's it. Well remembered.'

'But she loved me very much.'

'Oh, yeah. Big time.'

There was a longer pause. 'Is she happy now, Daddy?'

Crouching on the bathroom floor, towel in hand, Ryan closed his eyes briefly, and felt his son's pudgy hands on his eyelids, and he took hold of him and squeezed him inside the towel until he started to giggle in short gasping breaths.

'Thing about you, you little pudge bucket, is you like conversations too much.'

'But what *is* a conversation?' his son cried out, laughing.

'Don't think I'm ever going to tell you; I'd never get you to shut up. Quick, now, into your sleepsuit, and if you're good we'll

176

have the story about the mouse and the mole. That mole's a bit up himself, isn't he?'

Ryan Junior began to chant: 'I like mole! I like mole!'

Now, at midnight, Ryan stood at the darkened window with his headphones on. The events of the day came back to him in feelings, as they always did; he was washed to and fro like seaweed in the tide by his emotions, his joy at the sound of his son's piping voice, his misery talking to his mother, his helpless rage in the Provost's lodge. He winced at some of the memories. His temper again. He couldn't seem to get it under control. After Wiltshire, he'd even been put on an anger-management course. He made yet another resolution to control it.

And now, as usual, he was weakened, needy; he had his phone out, scrolling through images, at the mercy of other emotions. Picture after picture of a thin, laughing woman with savagely cropped brown hair and shadows in her face. Gone ugly, but still precious. Her hair, her eyes, her rasping laughter – all still beautiful, all of it accusing him still.

Closing his eyes at last, he tossed the phone on to the mattress on the floor; he let the pounding music flood him, lift him clear and take him away.

TWENTY

Fifty miles away, in a windowless office of a club called Wire, its walls covered in framed photographs of forgotten movie stars, three men talked together in a mixture of Arabic and English. Two of them wore black leather jackets and bandanas, and they stood in the centre of the room, looking sullen, while the man sitting at the desk smoked and studied the photograph in front of him.

The photograph showed a thin white youth in trackies. The angle of the picture made his nose look big.

The man prodded it with a disdainful forefinger, moving it from side to side on the polished surface of the desk. He was a handsome man, with a wide, hard jaw furred with bristles, and stiff-gelled hair rising brush-like from his smooth forehead, and he wore a navy-blue suit over a brightly clean white T-shirt. In the lobe of his right ear was a discreet gold stud. Stubbing out his cigarette in a round glass ashtray, he spoke in a quiet voice.

'This man. *Hu alshurta?*' He is police?

'*Heh*, Hassan.' Yes, Hassan.

Hassan frowned. 'He doesn't look like police. *Laqad rik?*' He saw you there?

'*Heh.*'

'*Fi almakan aldhy taeish fih?*' At the place where she lives?

'*Heh.*' Quieter, this time.

'*Hu alshurta,*' he repeated, as if thoughtfully. 'He is police. And he saw you there. At the place where she lives.'

The one with the lazy eye began to speak urgently, moving his hands, as if running out of time, and Hassan nodded, smiling without humour, and took hold of the heavy glass ashtray and flung it suddenly upwards into his face.

For a moment, there was only the dull clonk of the ashtray thumping across the floor, then the man straightened up and stood there, the mark already livid along his cheek and one nostril rimmed with blood. ''*Ana asif*, Hassan,' he said. I am sorry, Hassan. And he stood, breathing hard.

Hassan waited a long time before he spoke again. He said, 'This is not good. This is very bad. *Iidha ja' hdha alrayyal hun.* First her, now him. Do what you need to do. But, if this man comes here . . . *Baqtalik.* I kill you myself.'

He looked towards the door without moving his head, and the two men went backwards and left the room.

TWENTY-ONE

As he drove over the ring road, Ray put on the satnav; he didn't know Blackbird Leys too well. He followed the wide main road as far as the junction of Sandy Lane, where a patrol car and wagon sat on the grass verge, blue lights stirring the darkness, and went past them without even turning his head, driving on towards the two central tower blocks that came into view, black and still against the churning grey sky. Outside the Blackbird pub, a group of men standing on the concrete fore-court watched him as he went by. On the central reservation, more men had gathered round the burnt-out shell of a car, and they too watched as he turned into Cuddesdon Way. He had a glimpse of the parade of shops with their boarded-up windows and charred metal grilles, then he was driving down Blackbird Leys Road towards the second tower. Here, there was no one in the streets and no other cars, and he turned into Pegasus Road, peering from side to side.

As he went, his phone rang, and after a moment he answered it.

'Hey, babe.'

'Hey. Just wanted to know what time you'll be finishing.'

'Had to go out.'

'Anything exciting?'

'Just routine. It'll only take a minute.'

'Your partner with you?'

'He's sitting this one out.'

'Don't be too late.'

'I'll call you when I'm on my way.'

'Okay.'

'Love you.'

'Love you, too.'

Field Avenue lay in the shadow of the leisure centre. The street lamps had been smashed, the road was dark; he had an impression of pebble-dash houses behind low brick walls, maisonettes hung with satellite dishes and washing, garage doors in a row, wheelie bins, wire fences. Vans and pickups sat on bald verges. Sixties development: all good intentions and cheap materials. At last, he slowed and stopped at the end of a row of two-storey maisonette flats, turning off the engine.

There was a hush. Everything was very still. In the distance, sirens set up a frail wail, which the breeze blew away at once.

He buttoned his jacket and walked from the car across cracked concrete, looking about him. His rap on the front door was loud and harsh, and he rapped again, as if in defiance of the quietness, and stood back to look up and down the unlit house front. The radio in his car crackled in a robotic burst; across the road, someone briefly parted the curtains to look out. Turning away, he went calmly through a wooden door at the side of the building, down a narrow passage, broken glass crunching underfoot, to another door, and banged on that, with the same result.

He was still at the back door when he heard the car coming, a sudden noise in the stillness, a long squeal of cornering rubber and engine roar. Briefly, he thought of the person in the house opposite who had heard his police radio, but, by the time he'd got back down the passage, the car was approaching at speed and he had time only to wonder how many men were in it and calculate the odds of four or five against one before it screeched to a halt in front of him.

He stepped forward on to the concrete, where he would have more room to move.

Ryan got out of the car.

After a moment's reflection, it seemed worse than any other outcome.

'What the hell are you doing here?' Ray said.

Ryan ambled across the concrete towards him. 'This where he lives?'

'Yes, this is where he lives. I want to know what you're doing here.'

'Giving you a hand. Is he out?'

'How did you know where I was?'

'Got a text from Nadim. Worried you were going to do something stupid. "UnRay-like" is what she actually said. So I dropped Ryan off with my sister and come over.' He looked up at the block of maisonettes. 'Yeah, thought he'd've fucked off by now. Have you had a look round the back?'

'Yes, I've had a look round the back! I'm doing fine on my own, thanks.'

'Not got your minimum five officers with you, I see. But you're in luck.'

'What do you mean?'

'Not going to dob you in – this time.'

Ray took a step towards him. 'Look, I didn't ask for your help. I don't need your help.'

'Know your way around the Leys, do you? It's a fucking war zone, mate.'

'I did actually read the notices, you know.'

'No, it's always a war zone. Yeah, used to come here a bit when I was a kid. Fucking psychos. That bobblehead, the other day? They weren't fucking around, you know. They were trying to kill him. So, what's round the back?'

'I don't need your help.'

'You will if it kicks off.'

Ray snorted. 'What are you going to do, call them names?'

'I'm stronger than I look, mate,' Ryan said. He went past Ray, through the wooden door. 'He's not very tidy, is he?' he said as he stepped on the broken glass. 'Or just doesn't want visitors.'

'Frightened of someone.'

'Yeah, could be. Interesting.'

They stood together at the back door, banging on it.

'He told you he was working late that night?' Ray said.

'Yeah. Why?'

'He wasn't. I talked to the Bursar.'

'That's interesting too.'

They stood there, looking up at the darkened house.

Ray said, 'I talked to Leonard.'

'Who's Leonard?'

183

'Night porter at Barnabas.'

'Oh, yeah. Gramps.'

'He told me Jason left work this morning and didn't come back.'

Ryan considered this. 'He's got himself into trouble, Jason, and now he's pissed off before the shit hits the fan. There's nothing for us here. Better get a shout going.'

Ray said, 'I'd worked that out before you came along, you know.'

'Fair enough. Don't matter who takes credit.'

'Not my point.'

'Call it in yourself, don't bother me.'

'That's not my point either.'

They walked back down the passage, still bickering, and when they got to the front they found two more cars pulled up across the road and eight men in balaclavas waiting for them with a selection of low-grade weapons: pool cues, chair legs, chains. Three of them had taken off their belts and held them, dangling.

A little jolt of adrenaline passed between them.

After a moment, Ray stepped in front of Ryan and held up his badge.

'Wait a minute, Ray,' Ryan said.

Ray ignored him. He said to the men, 'You'd better be very sure of what you're doing. Get this wrong, you're going down for the rest of your lives.'

The men said nothing, did not look at each other, closed in a pace or two. Ray took off his glasses and put them neatly in the inside pocket of his blazer, took off his blazer and handed it to Ryan.

'Don't think they know Queensberry Rules, mate.'

Ray began to roll up his shirt sleeves. It was a Thomas Pink shirt, white with a faint mauve stripe.

'Wait,' Ryan said to Ray, 'you don't know these fuckers.'

'I'm guessing none of them's the Bishop of Salisbury,' Ray said over his shoulder. 'So I'm not expecting you to be any help.'

'Don't be like that. We can get to the car, call it in.'

'You're forgetting we shouldn't be here.'

Ryan hesitated. 'Oh, yeah, that's a point.'

Ray took another step forward, put up his guard and said to the men, 'You really want to do this?'

Two of them went for him. One had a pool cue, one a chain. Stepping sideways on his toes, Ray cuffed the chain guy off balance and punched through him. The pool cue slapped wildly across his head, but he drove forward hard, jabbing the guy in the face, who reeled backwards, and they all broke and retreated, panting. Ray was bleeding from the ear.

'Ray, mate,' Ryan said.

'Just getting started,' Ray said through gritted teeth. 'Isn't that right?' he called to the men.

One of them stepped to the front – a tall, wide man in a motor-cycle jacket. He said, through the mouth-hole in his balaclava, 'You made a big mistake. After what you done, you don't come here. We look after our own.'

From behind Ray, Ryan called out, 'We're trying to solve a murder, you fucking moron.'

The guy turned his balaclava'd head towards him. 'No one's going to miss you, you trailer-park runt.'

Ryan rolled his eyes. 'Oh, nice. Very pleasant.'

'Or you, choc ice,' the man said to Ray.

Ray opened his mouth, but before he could speak Ryan barged past him and went forward. '*What you say?*' he said to the man. 'What did you just call him? Choc ice? *Choc ice?*' He didn't stop walking, but went on towards the man, who began to laugh. He was twice as wide and a foot and a half taller than Ryan, and Ryan marched all the way up to him, and, pivoting suddenly from the hip like a circus gymnast, flung his right leg into the air and kicked him in the side of the head.

The man went down and lay still on the road.

Ignoring him, Ryan carried on shouting at the others. 'What you looking at, you racist scumbags? Get back in your fucking ripped-off motors and do one, and take Earl with you and hope he fucking well lives and he's not drooling or pissing his nappy for the rest of his miserable fucking brain-dead life, and if I have to come back here, I'm going to come round yours, Darren, and yours, Wesley, and yours, Slick, you fucking perv, and sort you out, and sort out your little brothers and your mothers and your fucking pets, you scumbag racist cunts. Now, piss off.'

At some point early on in this speech, everyone had realised he had his Glock out, waving it round in an unstable way, and they stood there, motionless, in shock, until he finished, and when he turned to walk back to Ray, they said nothing, but went quietly to pick up the unconscious man and carry him to a car.

Ray was staring at Ryan.

'I know, I know,' Ryan said. 'Don't look at me like that. Almost lost it, didn't I? What they called you, though, that was well out of order. And that Earl's been brain-dead all his life, so no harm done.' He limped a step and rubbed his groin, wincing.

'Think I might have twanged something, though. Regional youth kick-boxing champion five years in a row when I was a kid, look at me now. Drink and drugs take their toll, eh?' He grinned. 'Joke, for fuck's sake. Anyway, I know these tosspots, even with their balaclavas on. Bunch of fucking amateurs.'

There was a silence in which the men drove off.

'Well?' he said.

Ray, still bewildered, said, 'The gun? Did you sign it out?'

'Come on, will you? It's not like I had time to do any paperwork, is it?'

'It *is* a police gun, right?'

'Look, I just happened to have it on me. To be honest, it's a fucking pain to carry round – I lost the holster somewhere.'

'Christ almighty,' Ray said.

'Oh, there's always something, isn't there?' Ryan said. 'Some nitpicking little thing. Look, I won't dob you in for coming out here on your own, you don't dob me in for having a gun. Alright?'

Before Ray could say anything, his phone rang. He looked at it for a moment before answering. 'Babe,' he said at last. 'Yes, yes, I'm coming now. No, no problem. Just routine stuff. Okay? I'm on my way. Love you, too.'

Scowling at each other, they made their way to their cars.

'Get that APW out,' Ryan called.

'Don't tell me what to do,' Ray called back. 'And, by the way, next time I give you my blazer, don't just drop it on the ground. It's a Tommy Hilfiger!'

They slammed their car doors and drove off in different directions.

TWENTY-TWO

At six o'clock in the morning, Jason Birch was apprehended letting himself back into his flat; he'd left his bank card behind. He was escorted to St Aldates Police Station and alerts were sent out to DIs Wilkins and Wilkins.

LOCATION: C3, smallest and dimmest of the windowless St Aldates interview rooms, where the overhead light illuminates no more than a functional office table, empty except for a recording device, and three stackable conference chairs, two on one side of the table, one on the other.

INTERVIEWERS: DI Wilkins (Raymond), in black jeans, matching sweatshirt and blazer, and DI Wilkins (Ryan), wearing Adidas trackies, Loop jacket and baseball cap.

INTERVIEWEE: Jason Michael Birch, wearing sweatpants and puffa jacket – recently slept in and slightly soiled.

WILKINS (RAYMOND): Police interview of Jason Birch, in C3. Present: Detective Inspector Ryan Wilkins and Detective

188

Inspector Raymond Wilkins. Time: seven twenty-five in the morning. Jason – so, you just took off. Why's that?

BIRCH: Yeah. It's like this. My mother's been ill. I mean, she got ill. And I got a call to go and see her.

WILKINS (RAYMOND): So, why didn't you go?

BIRCH: Yeah. Thing is, I forgot my bank card, right, and—

WILKINS (RAYMOND): So, why didn't you go straight back to your flat? Why did you spend the night in . . . where was it? Littlemore Community Centre car park.

BIRCH: Yeah. Well. I've been a bit . . .

WILKINS (RYAN): Fuck this. Listen, Jason, just start with the keys. No, wait. Start with the contact. What happened? All your idea, was it?

BIRCH: No!

WILKINS (RYAN): Give him a call, did you?

BIRCH: No! I didn't know him from Adam.

WILKINS (RYAN): Thing is, if that's right, Jason, you might just slip this one, but if it was you pulling the strings, basically you're fucked, know what I mean? Do you know what they do to Arsenal fans inside?

BIRCH: I never even see him before, I swear.

WILKINS (RYAN): Don't know if I can believe you, Jason. Ray. Raymond. What do you think?

WILKINS (RAYMOND): Jason, it's okay, you don't need to be alarmed by my colleague. He's just impatient. We want to help you, Jason. But you need to tell us exactly what happened. Everything. Do you understand?

BIRCH: Okay, okay, alright. It was like this. I was in the Lamb and Flag and he got chatting. Said he was a photographer.

Bought a round. After a bit, he said what sort of pictures he took. Well, it was funny. Told me about this special feature, how he'd taken pictures in Buckingham Palace and stuff. Then he said he really wanted to do an Oxford college – library, chapel and that – but he couldn't think of a way in, didn't have any contacts. And I said, 'Well, you'll never guess what?' Thinking about it afterwards, though . . .

WILKINS (RYAN): Yeah?

BIRCH: I wondered if maybe he'd already found out who I was.

WILKINS (RYAN): No shit, Sherlock. What next? You offered to get him in?

BIRCH: He said there was money in it, cash. And I didn't think there was any harm in it – I mean, it's just a bit of fun, right? Just let them in, he said, lend them the keys, give them a bit of detail about the layout, that's it, all done.

WILKINS (RAYMOND): How did you get hold of the keys?

BIRCH: Got lucky, to be honest. My thought was, I'd borrow them from the bursary, so, about four o'clock, I'm hanging around waiting for a good moment, and Ameena comes out and we get talking. She's had a rough time, Ameena; I like to have a word with her. Comforts her, you know, to have someone here she can . . . Anyway, when she went off, she just left the keys lying there. She loses things easy. So I never even had to go into the bursary, after all.

WILKINS (RAYMOND): What next?

BIRCH: I let them in at seven, at the Stable Yard door.

190

WILKINS (RYAN): The girl was with him?

BIRCH: Yeah. Didn't say anything to her. Don't know anything about her, nothing. I never even—

WILKINS (RAYMOND): Just the two of them?

BIRCH: Yeah.

WILKINS (RAYMOND): Stable Yard door's on Merton Street, right?

BIRCH: That's it. Tradesman's entrance. Passage goes down past the kitchen stores and kitchen, out into New Court, by the hall there. They were going to wait a bit in the stores till the coast was clear, then just go for it. I legged it straight off, though.

WILKINS (RAYMOND): And the keys? What was the plan?

BIRCH: They'd leave them back in the stores, they said. Eight o'clock, at the latest. I was waiting and waiting, and the keys didn't show up, and I was getting more and more worried. I went walkabout. That's when I ran into Ameena again. I didn't know what to do. About nine, I went home, but I thought to myself, Summat's gone wrong, here. I never dreamed what, though, till I heard, next morning.

WILKINS (RAY): So, you were in college till nine?

BIRCH: Yeah. You know, just hanging about, really.

WILKINS (RAY): Anyone corroborate that?

BIRCH: I saw Ashley once or twice. She told me to get lost. Thing is—

WILKINS (RYAN): These stores, Jason.

BIRCH: Yeah?

WILKINS (RYAN): Kitchen uniforms kept there?

BIRCH: Most kitchen things. Smocks, gloves, hats – they all

191

have to wear them, now. Equipment, utensils, fuel, all sorts of—

WILKINS (RYAN): Fucking bingo! That's why they didn't stand out. Uniforms, Ray! They put on kitchen uniforms. Ameena's was missing the next day. Ten to one, those fibres on her T-shirt match.

WILKINS (RAYMOND): The photographer, Jason. Did he give you his contacts?

BIRCH: Yeah, he did. So, after I knew something had really happened, something bad, I give him a call. No answer. And later the number stopped working altogether.

WILKINS (RYAN): Big surprise.

WILKINS (RAYMOND): So, who was he?

BIRCH: I dunno. He never give me a name. I been thinking, since. He never said who he was or who he worked for, or anything like that.

WILKINS (RYAN): We'll need a description. What did he look like?

BIRCH: He looked a bit . . . what's the word? Not fat, but he looked fat. You know.

WILKINS (RYAN): Great – thanks, Jason. Listen, try hard not to be stupid.

BIRCH: Wide is what I'm saying, sort of wide.

WILKINS (RAYMOND): Did he say anything to the model? Call her by her name, for instance?

BIRCH: Don't think so. No.

WILKINS (RAYMOND): What about her? Did she say anything?

BIRCH: Nothing. Didn't really get a good look at her, neither.

She just come in after him, when I opened the door. He was acting a bit . . . I don't know. I did think to myself it was funny, because, before, in the Lamb and Flag, he was friendly, like I say, but that night, when I let them in, he was different – sort of, I don't know what . . . tense.

WILKINS (RYAN): Well, course he was; he was breaking and entering and taking dirty pictures in the Provost's study.

BIRCH: Not that sort of tense. Tense with her. Like maybe they'd had an argument about something, him and her. He'd got a face on. Like I say, he was sort of wide. Big arms he had, big chest. Not exactly fat, but—

WILKINS (RYAN): Fuck me, Jason, save it for your psychiatrist.

WILKINS (RAYMOND): Interview terminated, seven fifty-nine.

Jason lifted his head, calf-like, and looked at them bleakly. 'How much trouble am I in?' he said.

Ryan rolled his eyes.

'Am I going to lose my job?'

'Lose your job? Fucking hell, Jason, just pray you're not going down. Not being funny, but you never heard of aiding and abetting? Did you come forward to identify the dead woman when her picture went up? Did you call this photographer guy on the quiet instead? If they handed down sentences for stupidity, you'd be getting five to ten, no time off for good behaviour. Know what I mean?'

Head in hands, Jason began to weep, making the inappropriate noises of a man in the desperate throes of passion, and they left him there.

Outside the interview room, they hesitated, wary of each other.

'Went well,' Ryan said. 'Do you think it went well?'

'No.'

'Neither do I. When are we going to get something decent to work with?' He puffed out his cheeks, wiped his nose with a finger. 'Well. What next?'

'We need to get a kitchen uniform to Forensics, see if they can get a match for the fibres on her T-shirt.'

'I'll give Claire a call. Been meaning to do that, anyway. What about you?'

'Don't worry about me. I've got stuff to do.'

Ryan watched him go, striding across the open-plan, blazer swishing from side to side, then stuck his hands in his trackie pockets and sauntered off the other way.

TWENTY-THREE

Half a mile away, a man stood at an open bedroom window above a cul-de-sac, looking out at rooftops – the cramped roofs of neighbouring houses, the shallow roofs of the big brick boxes of the business park beyond – and the cold, empty sky.

He had a wide face and an unpleasant expression. He took out a disposable phone and clumsily dialled a number.

'Where are you?' he said. He had a thick, unemotional voice; his words fell out in lumps.

'But you're not me,' he said, after a while. Then, 'Not yet, but they will . . . I can't wait, that's why.'

He listened, staring at the empty sky.

'Not where I'm going, they won't.'

He listened again.

'I got out of Fallujah, didn't I?' he said. 'You just get here with the stuff.'

The sky was completely flat, a pale, even emptiness. He watched it carefully.

'Stop talking,' he said, 'and get here. The tattoo place. Yes, they know.'

A speck appeared in a corner of the sky and he fixed his eyes on it.

'You can talk to Carl. He knows I'm good for it.'

The speck began to slowly draw a careful line across the sky and he watched it move.

'Nothing too old. Not a Colt . . . Yes, the tattoo place, I just said. Carl knows . . . No, I can't fucking wait. Any second now, they're going to know my name. A second after that, they'll be here. Enough. I need it by five, no later. Five o'clock – got that?'

After he hung up, he carried on watching the line being drawn across the sky – so slowly, so carefully, so agonisingly, it was like he was sticking pins under his fingernails.

TWENTY-FOUR

Ray had never been to the IOPC before. He emerged from the car park at Canary Wharf, nestled among the snug, vast buildings of money and power, and walked across Cabot Square towards 10 South Colonnade, its smooth masonry snout like the hull of an ocean liner beached up out of the river beyond. It was a dark, slick November morning in the city, overcast, as if dawn had malfunctioned, fairy lights brittle white in the shadow-hung ornamental trees, the fountain making a steady fuss. The square was quiet, groups of people standing without interest by the rim of pattering water, and he went past them, round the large bronze statue of a thick-hipped woman with a floorboard-nail head, into the building. He sat briefly in the lobby, attracting frequent looks from the three female receptionists, and, ten minutes later, he was taken up to a room on the thirteenth floor, where investigator Alec Todd, senior solicitor Meg Ayers and director of people Tisi Phou were waiting for him.

He took off his Brooks Brothers single-breasted trench coat, unbuttoned his blazer and settled himself in the chair.

Ms Ayers thanked him for coming and reminded him of the seriousness of the allegations. 'What we want from you is detail. We appreciate,' she said, 'that, in this case, it might take a while.' No one smiled.

She began by asking him how long he'd worked with Ryan, and about the formal nature of their partnership and how they managed day-to-day operations between them, and about the briefings and instructions received from Detective Superintendent Waddington. Then she handed over to Todd.

'Tell us about your two joint interviews with Sir James and Lady Penelope.'

Ray described them. He kept his tone neutral, focusing on verifiable facts.

'Can you remember the exact words used by DI Wilkins, in the first interview, when Sir James informed him that he had not been present at the preprandial drinks the previous evening?'

Ray cleared his throat. 'Something like, "You're having a laugh, aren't you?"'

'"Having a *fucking* laugh," wasn't it?'

Ray paused a moment. 'Yes, I think so,' he said at last.

'Thank you. And did he call Sir James, quote, "stupid", unquote?'

'He implied it. "It would be stupid of you," or something.'

'And did he, in the second interview, refer to Sir James as, quote, "a sordid little fuckrat", unquote.'

Ray closed his eyes briefly. 'I believe so. I came into the room just afterwards.'

'And as, quote, "Peter Pervert", unquote?'

'Yes, he said that.'

'And would you agree that, in those two interviews, DI Wilkins displayed a remarkable degree of verbal aggression towards Sir James?'

'Yes.'

'Thank you. Can we now turn to the interview with Jason Birch? After that, we'll be asking you to provide details of your own conversations with DI Wilkins.'

Another hour passed before Todd was satisfied. By way of conclusion, he allowed himself a moment's reflection on the extraordinary lack of oversight and management by Ryan's senior officer, which had allowed such flagrant breaches of conduct to occur. A little jolt of indignation went through Ray. Then Tisi Phou took over. She wanted to know about Ray's personal view of DI Wilkins.

'I'd prefer to confine myself to the facts.'

'I'm sure you would. We require a little more gumption.'

'He's difficult,' Ray said.

'Can you elaborate?'

'He has anger-management issues. His upbringing, as I understand it—'

'No need to reference his upbringing, at this point. He has difficulty controlling himself?'

Ray began a number of different answers in his head. 'Yes, I think so,' he said, at last.

'Verbally?'

'Yes.'

'Physically?'

Ray remembered the man, Earl, lying in the road. 'In certain situations.'

'Such as in his final meeting with Sir James?'

He said, 'To be candid, yes, I was concerned that he might have been about to lose control.'

Todd said, 'Of course, it's your responsibility as his senior officer to prevent that.'

'We're not always together.'

'You were together in the Provost's lodge, were you not?'

'For some of the time.'

Todd and Phou consulted, and Ms Phou made a note.

Reminding Ray of the new police guidelines on discrimination and their new diversity agenda, Ms Phou wanted to know what Ray thought about Ryan's attitude towards racial minorities, women and the upper middle classes. What did he think of derogatory comments made, in Ray's hearing, to the Chief Pathologist, Sir James and Lady Penelope, Detective Superintendent Waddington, the staff of Barnabas Hall and to Ray himself?

Quote, 'Money-Nuts', unquote.

He couldn't defend it.

Quote, 'Fucking jihadis', unquote. Quote, 'Fucking immigrants', unquote.

'I note for the record that these aren't his private thoughts, these are his spoken comments, voiced ignorantly or intentionally to give offence. Many made while you stood by.'

Ray said, irritably, 'I didn't stand by. When he made them, I reprimanded him. I don't have special powers to prevent him saying them in the first place.'

'Your reprimands should have deterred him from repeating them. But, for some reason, they didn't.'

Ray breathed heavily. 'Because he is what he is. I can't change him.'

'And what sort of person is he, DI Wilkins? Is he racist?'

Ray frowned.

'I repeat: is he racist?'

'No, actually.'

'Xenophobic?'

'Yes.'

'Sexist?'

'Look, you've got records of what he's said. Yes, he's xeno-phobic; yes, he's sexist. He's bad mannered. He's a chav. He's got a chip on his shoulder; the people he hates the most are rich, privileged people. He's casually abusive, he can't bite his tongue. His behaviour's totally inappropriate. Maybe he's got some medical condition, I don't know. But don't make out I've failed to control him. The truth is, he can't control himself.'

'So, in your opinion, he's out of control?'

'I've just said so.'

'He's not fit to be a police officer, in fact?'

For a moment, Ray made no reply.

'You can't have it both ways, DI Wilkins,' Tisi Phou said. 'Either he's in control and you should have—'

'No, he's not fit to be a police officer.'

There was a pause in which he regretted what he'd said.

'Thank you,' Ms Phou said. 'No further questions.'

He sat for a moment, hearing himself breathe in the silence, then he got up, pushed his chair away and left without looking at them.

TWENTY-FIVE

'Thomas Dubin,' Nadim said. 'That's his name.' She stood with Ray and Ryan in the Superintendent's office, presenting the results of her research. 'Forty years old. Born Walthamstow, trained at the London College of Communication. Went to Iraq at the time of the invasion in 2003; was in Fallujah when the killings happened. Mental-health breakdown shortly afterwards. No photojournalism after that. For a while, some paparazzi stuff for the tabloids. Now, it's just porn.'

They peered at the picture of Dubin on the screen. Jason had been spot on: a wide man, with a wide face. Black hair plastered across his forehead, Hitler-wise. Pasty skin. Shadows and creases under dead-fish eyes. Lipless mouth curled downwards.

The Superintendent said, 'Two cautions after complaints of harassment from young women working in the sex trade. Thank you, Nadim.'

Nadim left the office.

Ryan said, 'How was Mr Adult Entertainment? The guy in Monaco.'

'Mr Seagrave has a personal mission to restore the integrity of the glamour industry. He told me so himself. He's passionate about ethical business. And, as an old boy of Christ Church College, he was keen to be as helpful as possible. He gave me Dubin's name at once – and stressed that Dubin was not on the payroll, had never been on the payroll, and that he, personally, had never even met the man. I suspect, in fact, he called him immediately, as soon as news broke, to cut his ties. Perhaps Nadim can trace that, later.'

'And the girl?'

She looked at Ryan. 'She was in her late twenties, we think. So, just to be clear, Ryan, not a *girl*.'

He felt the force of her stare. 'Yeah, alright.'

'No,' she went on, 'he doesn't know who she is.'

'Really?'

She briefly outlined the logistics of Michael Seagrave's ethical business. The photographers, all employed on a freelance basis, submitted their pictures for approval and, once approval was given, were responsible for uploading their pictures to the site themselves, remotely. Minimal contact. Good for business. But no contact *at all*, under any circumstances, with the models. The photographers acted as their agents; they paid them out of their own fees. Even better for business.

'So, no,' the Super said, 'Seagrave doesn't know who the young woman is, and I believe him. He had his staff run records which show she hasn't worked for them before. The models in the other features on his site are all different. He wonders, again helpfully, if she's new to the industry. I wonder that, too. Nadim has been running face-recognition software all morning; nothing's come up.'

Ryan made disgruntled noises.

'What is it?'

'Just, this posh-boy porn-meister in Monaco's a bit hard to take.'

'Is it his pornography that bothers you, Ryan, or the fact he went to Oxford? In fact, he's been helpful. Though, yes, it's true, he's a bit hard to take, and that's why I took care to pass various details on to HMRC to support their ongoing inquiry into irregularities in his taxation history. But, so far as our investigation goes, I don't think he's going to be more helpful to us than he has been already.' She turned to Ray. 'What next?'

'Does Nadim have the photographer's address?'

'She does.'

'Then that's where we go.'

She nodded, paused a moment. 'By the way, there was an incident last night in the Leys. A man living there was left unconscious outside the hospital. The man is well known to us – he was a member of the Defenders of the Leys group. But we don't know why he's there. He hasn't regained consciousness yet.'

She examined their faces.

'We're picking up comments on social media about rogue policemen in the area,' she said. 'Do either of you know anything about it?'

They each put on the same half-puzzled, half-disengaged expression and shook their heads.

TWENTY-SIX

Ray drove to London for the second time that day. A firearms unit was waiting for them at the photographer's address. They went out of Oxford through tattered fringes of mist and climbed the Chilterns into cold winter sunlight, speeding on past High Wycombe towards Uxbridge and the grey edge of the city, sprawling in the distance like a blanket left out in the rain. Ryan crouched in his seat with his knees hugged to his chest, almost foetal, making Ray nervous.

'What the hell are you doing?' he said, at last.

'Got something to tell you. A heads-up.'

'What?'

'There's a misconduct thing against me. At the IOPC.'

Ray didn't reply.

'Not going to let it bother me. Like I say, I'm always getting mashed.'

Ray drove on.

'It's just, I thought this was working out alright. You and me.'

Ray swallowed a noise.

'Anyway, you'll probably get called to give a statement. That's the way they do it.'

A muscle twitched in Ray's cheek.

'So, you'll get a chance to tell them what you think of me.'

Ray spoke at last: 'I know how it works.'

'Yeah. Well, that's it, really. Know what?'

'What?'

'Not going to let it bother me.'

'Good.'

They drove on. Ryan straightened his legs, took out his phone and began to fiddle with it, humming to himself.

Ray glanced over and frowned. 'What are you doing now?'

Ryan grinned. 'Wait for this. Wait.'

He held the phone in front of his face and a voice came from it, piping and serious: 'Daddy?'

'Yeah?'

'You've got a funny nose.'

'Must be the phone. What my ears look like?'

Ray said, sideways, 'Listen, not being funny, but we're at work. There'll be an update from the FT coming.'

The piping voice came through again. 'Daddy?'

'Yeah?'

'Rhinocer-horses are very big, aren't they, Daddy?'

Ryan began to laugh. 'Rhinocer-horses!' he said to Ray. 'Did you hear that? Kid's a fucking genius.'

Ray said, 'Can you stop it?'

'Daddy! You shouldn't say—'

'Yeah, alright, good point. What you been doing with Auntie Jade, then?'

Ray said, 'Are you listening to me? Not now; we're working.'

Ryan pointed the phone at him. 'Hey, Ry, look! This is Daddy's partner. He's called Ray. Come on, Ray, say hello to Ryan.'

Ray glared at the road ahead.

'Daddy? He's *not* a mole, Daddy.'

'You might be right about that. Maybe he's a Rhinocer-horse. He's pretty big. Check out that jacket. What's that, then, Ray? Is it a Tommy Hilfugger? Know what, Ryan? I thought he was a bit up himself, at first. He is, a bit. *Joking*. He's alright, really. Come on, Ray. Say hello.'

Ray muttered, 'Hello.'

'Are you Daddy's friend?'

Ray forced a wary smile. 'Yes, I am,' he said, after a long pause. 'But your Daddy and I have to go now, because we—'

A new voice came on the phone suddenly: 'Listen to me, knobhead!'

The car swerved slightly as Ray turned, startled, towards the phone, where a young woman's pixilated face swam in and out of focus.

'Ryan!' her voice said. 'You listening? I don't want no more of your excuses. Are you going to do it? Are you?'

Ryan held the phone close to his face and spoke quietly: 'Yes, I'm going to do it,' he said. 'Yes. I told you. Enough, now. I can't talk; I'm at work. You can't just call me like this.'

'When you going to do it?'

'Tonight. I'll do it tonight, alright?'

'That's what you said before.'

'Jade, listen, I'm at work.'

'I don't care where you are. Do you want her to end up in the hospital again? Do you?'

'I'll go round tonight,' he whispered. 'I'll do it, I promise. Tonight.'

The last thing Ray heard was the voice on the phone shouting, 'Knobhead!' Then there was silence in the car.

'Sister,' Ryan said, after a moment. 'Looks after Ryan. She can get a bit . . .'

Ray said nothing. He asked no questions. He gave a Ryan a look and Ryan turned away without saying anything.

At Northolt, they hit traffic, and Ray pulled off the M40 and went south through the suburbs.

Ryan asked Ray about Jason. 'You think he's in the frame?'

'Not really. I talked to Ashley. Like he said, she saw him hanging round, looking nervous. I don't think he's the type.'

'You mean he's too stupid. Stupid people commit crimes too, you know.'

'I didn't say stupid.'

Before they could bicker further, a call came into the car phone from a London jeweller Ray had consulted earlier about the dead woman's ring. Apparently, it was a distinctive piece in a modern style, made in the eighties or nineties, almost certainly in France.

'How distinctive?' Ray asked. 'Can it be traced?'

'I can circulate details to the right sort of dealers in Paris and Lyon.'

'Please. Let us know as soon as you hear.'

Ryan grinned. 'Nice,' he said. 'Thought that ring'd be useful. And I keep saying she was foreign.'

'She could have bought it on holiday. Or on a shoot. Or been given it by someone French.'

'Just got a feeling.'

'Really? Shape of the nose?'

'Bit French-looking all round, I think.'

They drove on for a while.

'Have you ever been to France?' Ray said.

'No need. Fucking thousands of them over here.'

They went down Ruislip Road, past parks and playing fields, into wide, leafy avenues of stuccoed villas and art-deco apartment blocks, and finally into streets of Victorian terraces, sycamores overhanging the roads, plump hedges snug behind wrought-iron railings, high-end cars showcased on patterned brick driveways. The pavements were empty except for a few schoolchildren in uniform and nannies with pushchairs.

'So, this is where you grew up,' Ryan said. 'Ealing Broadway.'

'Near here, yes.'

'Nice. Nanny take you to school?'

'You know what, Ryan?'

'What, Raymond?'

'Fuck off.'

Ryan began to laugh, and after a moment Ray shook his head and smiled.

He looked at his watch. 'ETA in five,' he said.

Ryan radioed the firearms team, and then they were there.

They left the car in Jubilee Lane, a narrow street of brick walls and parked BMWs and Mini Coopers, and walked with the FT leader to the corner of Haven Road. The photographer's house

209

was fifty yards away, a terraced cottage in biscuit-coloured brick, small and smart behind a tiny square of neat front garden.

'Must pay alright,' Ryan said, 'all that porn. Anyone home?'

The FT leader said, 'We don't think so, sir.'

'Makes no difference,' Ray said. 'Usual procedure. Ready?'

'Yes, sir.'

His phone rang and he hesitated.

Ryan said, grinning, 'Fuck's sake, Ray, tell her not now, we're working.'

Ray turned away in irritation and whispered into the phone, 'Babe, I'll call you back.' He gave the FT leader the nod and they watched his team move in.

In silence, a dozen men in matt black boiler suits and helmets, their faces hidden by black masks, with chunky guns hoisted forward, crouch-jogged along the street towards the house, taking up momentary positions in postures of textbook vigilance, peeling away again, taking up new positions – by variation on their knees or flattened against a wall – the whole thing as choreographed as a movement of *Swan Lake*, until they came to rest in different poses around the tiny front garden, waiting motionless, as if for applause. Still silent, two of them flanked the door, while a third waited for the radio crackle of instruction; then he beat down the smart red front door with an equally smart handheld battering ram, and they all burst into the house, shouting, to be met by another team entering through the back door, and, mingling together, they spread quickly through the rooms.

'Know what you should do?' Ryan said to Ray, conversationally. 'You should keep your phone switched off, so we don't get interrupted.'

Ray scowled. They walked together to the house.

In it, there was absolutely nothing of interest, least of all Thomas Dubin, and within an hour they'd left the Forensics team to their work and gone back outside.

Neighbours loitered in the street, quietly watching, pretending not to. Beyond the barricade tapes at each end of the road, cars had drawn up, and people stood there watching, too; some of them held up press passes, in vain. As Ryan lounged, smoking, in the street, Dubin's next-door neighbour came into his garden. He was a white-haired man dressed English-style in over-bright mustard-coloured corduroys and hairy jacket, and Ryan got to his feet and ambled over to him.

'Wake you up, did they? All the crashing and shouting and that.'

The man looked at him coldly. 'The police are just doing their job.'

Ryan tried again. 'Yeah, course. Know him well, do you, this Dubin guy?'

The man said, 'I'm going to save any information I have for the police, thank you.'

Ryan was in the middle of rummaging in his trackie pocket for his badge when Ray came past him and shook hands with the old man. 'Morning,' he said. 'DI Wilkins. Sorry we had to disturb you today. I know what a peaceful spot this is; I grew up here, just round the corner. Corton Road.'

'Really?' the man said. 'Nice road. One of my bridge partners lives there.'

Ray smiled, nodded. 'May I ask you a few questions?'

211

'Of course,' the man said, with a glance at Ryan. 'Shall we go inside, so we can be private?'

Ryan watched them go. Squatted in the road. Lit up.

As he smoked, he thought about the dead woman. It made him angry she didn't even have a name yet. Despite what he'd said to the Super, they knew nothing about her except that she'd done a porn shoot – perhaps just the one. Odd to be making a start in that line of business at her age. Odd . . . and interesting. He wondered how much money had been in it for her, how badly she'd needed it and why. He imagined her that evening, walking with Dubin across New Court towards the library, wearing a kitchen jacket and perhaps one of those funny hygiene caps; keyed up with a little cocaine buzz, nervous with the risk of it; one eye on Dubin, her money man, keeping tabs on his foul mood; thinking about ordinary things like her make-up, her hair, her underwear; trying to remember where to go after the library, in and out, nice and quick; then back in her jeans and T-shirt, cash in hand, and at last the walk to the station, shaking free of it all, catch a train to wherever, get on with her life.

He knew he was missing something. He hawked and spat. Looked at his watch.

'Fuck's sakes,' he muttered.

He saw her dead face. How she'd glared at the wall, outraged, as if she couldn't fucking well believe it, getting killed like that, like it was a total shock, completely out of the blue.

Most things are cock-ups. Things had gone pretty smoothly in the library and chapel; what had gone wrong in the lodge? Did something between her and Dubin suddenly boil over? He smoked furiously. If Dubin wasn't the perp, why had he gone AWOL?

He breathed deeply, thinking of her body dumped on the carpet, left like rubbish to be cleared up in the morning. He couldn't look her in her angry dead face till he got who'd done it.

He lit another cigarette, looking irritably at his watch again. 'Fuck's sake, Ray,' he muttered.

It was four o'clock before they set off back to Oxford. The old boy had been helpful, in the end. Dubin was an inconsiderate neighbour and Ray had listened patiently to the complaints.

The view of the street was that Dubin was psychologically damaged. He must have seen some terrible things in Iraq; there was a story he'd got caught up in Fallujah when the Yanks were running amok. He'd moved into the house maybe five years earlier and was weird from the beginning. The curtains would be drawn during the day for weeks on end, complete silence in the house, then suddenly he'd be in the street at three o'clock in the morning, twitching with drink, yelling abuse. Once he set a car on fire – his own car, it turned out. Gradually, as the months passed, then the years, he receded again into the background, surly and secretive. Now, there were women in and out of his house at all hours. Ray listened politely to all this, nodding and prompting, and at length was rewarded. On the night of the murder, Dubin had come home at about midnight. He thumped about upstairs for a while, then there was the slam of the front door and he was off again, half-running down the street with a bag over his shoulder. One o'clock, half past. Where would he be going at that time of night? No idea.

The station? The airport? Don't know. Some special place – a holiday home, a caravan?

The old man frowned, rubbed his long face with violet-tinged fingers. Deep in his throat, he made the humming noise of remembrance. 'Now I think about it, he told me once that his brother Dave had a place somewhere, that he had use of it.'

'Do you know where?'

More humming. More finger-work on the face.

'I've remembered,' he said, with a surprised smile. 'Talking to you has brought it back. Oxford. Yes, that's the place.'

TWENTY-SEVEN

'He's done something,' Ryan said. 'Or he knows something.'

They contacted Nadim as they drove back down the M40, and she fished out information from the Land Registry: a house in Marsh Cowley, under the name of David Dubin.

'He rents it out sometimes, but it seems to be empty at the moment. Off Hollow Way,' she said, 'by the business park.'

'Know it,' Ryan said at once. 'We're ten minutes away, mate.'

They were just passing Thornhill Park and Ride. They got on the ring road and accelerated south towards the car plant.

Ryan said, 'Want me to call Firearms?'

'No time. He knows we'll be after him, sooner or later. If he's there, it won't be for long. Might not get another chance.'

'What about the regs?'

Ray didn't take his eyes off the road.

'Ray? The regs.'

'Fuck the regs,' Ray said, and Ryan began to laugh.

Delayed every few yards by trucks and vans, they drove down Garsington Road, past the blank gaze of the business park's brick walls on one side and the long-winded ramble of pebble-dash semis on the other. They went through the lights into Hollow Way.

'Got to watch those vans when we get in the back streets,' Ryan said. 'Nipping in and out. Used to come here as a kid sometimes. Fucking lethal. Here it is, now.' He nodded. 'Right past the tattoo shop. Fuck me!'

'What?' Ray said, head swivelling.

'It's still there. Nearly went in once; was going to get something tribal on the back of my neck. Here we go, just here.'

Ray turned into the cul-de-sac and pulled over on to the kerb by a grey wooden fence, and they sat a moment, engine off.

'Last house on the left,' Ryan said.

'How do you know?'

'By the numbers. Evens on this side. And I used to come here, like I said. There was a guy round the corner we used to get stuff off. At the bottom, down there, there's some garages. We'd go there sometimes, hang out for a bit.'

They looked together down to the end of the road.

Ryan fidgeted. 'What do you think? Think he's here?'

'I don't know. Like I say, even if he came, he wouldn't stay long.'

'Do you think he did it?'

'I don't know. But why'd he run?'

Ryan nodded. 'Take it nice and easy then, eh?'

They got out of the car and walked down the road, looking about. It was five o'clock. Afternoon noises reached them, muffled, from the streets around – the rush-hour thrum of engines, children's laughter. It was an ordinary, quiet neighbourhood. On either side of the cul-de-sac, the houses were brick downstairs, shingled with tiles above, with frosted-glass doors: all the same, with the same air of flat indifference. They crept along, and paused.

'Window,' Ryan whispered, gesturing.

A bedroom window of the last house on the left was open.

'Do you think he's there?'

'I don't know,' Ray said.

'I think he's there. Fuck.'

'What?'

'Do you think he's armed?'

'Why do you think he'd be armed?'

'He was in Iraq. Small arms were falling into people's pockets all the time, over there. Good for contacts, too. He could give someone a yell, pick something up.'

'Can't worry about that now.'

'I should have brought the Glock.'

Ray shook his head. 'You're just going to have to kick him in the temples.'

'Joking, aren't you? I was so stiff this morning, I could hardly carry Ryan to the car.'

'Call him names, then – you're good at that. I'll cover my ears. Quiet.'

They crept forward until they came to the side of the house. There were net curtains in the downstairs windows, a broom propped outside the front door. A ginger cat appeared round the far side, stared at them and lay down, unconcerned, on the concrete to lick its groin, leg stretched in the air like a ballet dancer.

217

Ryan said, in a low voice, 'I can get to the back through the garages.'

Ray nodded, looked at his watch, held up two fingers.

After Ryan went, Ray counted down the time, then crouched past the window to the front door. No sound from inside the house. The cat stopped licking and watched him, interested, leg still disjointed. He banged on the door and the cat reassembled itself in mid-air and took off. He banged again and shouted up, his voice loud and sudden in the silence. 'Police! Open this door!'

No answer. A furtive silence. Shifting his weight out and back, he kicked the door open and ran into the empty front room, glancing round at the sofa and table, television and mirror, and then went up the stairs to the landing. From downstairs came the bursting-metal noise of the back door giving way. Ray went into the drill. He put his head into the bathroom, stepped into it, scanned round, stepped out. Moved into the nearest bedroom, backed out, went on, head high and mobile. Ryan came running up the stairs and stood next to him, and they moved at the same time – Ryan into the second bedroom, Ray into a box room – in a silence broken only by their footsteps and heavy breaths.

Back on the landing, they stood together, panting.

'Not here, then,' Ray said.

'Been here. Dirty dishes in the sink. A smell, too. He's been burning something, I think.'

'We're too late.'

The adrenaline in their bodies dissipated. They went downstairs and, in the kitchen bin, found the burnt remains of some clothing.

'Know what this is? Kitchen uniform from the college,' Ryan said. 'Jacket and cap. Told you.'

Ray found the SIM card and they peered at it together.

'Can it be repaired?'

'They can do all sorts, at the lab.' Ray put it carefully into an evidence bag and sealed it.

They sat there, at the kitchen table, Ryan thinking aloud: 'The uniform . . .'

'Yes?'

'When they went in, he had one on, she had one on. When he left, he's still wearing his. Comes back here, makes a bollocks of getting rid of it.'

'So?'

'So, what happened to hers? Not wearing it when she was found. Not anywhere.'

They sat in silence, thinking. And, as they did so, they heard a creak upstairs and looked at each other, startled.

'Fuck me, he's still here!'

Before they could move, there was the thump of feet overhead, then they ran, barging together up the stairs, falling over themselves, and, as they got to the top, the bedroom door was slammed in their faces.

'Police!' Ray shouted, and they shoved against the door, once, twice, until it broke open and they rushed inside and found a young woman halfway out of the window.

She spat in Ray's face as he grabbed her legs and pulled her into the room, the two of them falling on to the floor, where she writhed around, kicking and biting, panting and thrashing, and suddenly lay still. She began to weep, muttering in a foreign language.

'Here's a turn up, then,' Ryan said.

They sat around the kitchen table. The woman sipped water and gave them dirty looks from under thick black eyelashes. Her hair was blond and shaggy, her face strong, her make-up smudged like war paint across her prominent features.

'Do you speak English?'

'Yes, I speak English.'

'What's your name?'

'Katya.'

'What are you doing here, Katya?'

She looked at Ryan. 'Do you have a cigarette?'

He handed her one and lit it, and she blew out smoke and looked at him with scorn.

'Go on then, what are you doing here?'

'I came for my money.'

'What money?'

'Money he owes me.'

'Who owes you?'

Pushing her chair away from the table, she crossed her legs. Her face was like an exaggeration of a face, wide mouth and plump lips. She gave Ray a little shrug, settled her legs again, blew smoke. 'Dubin.'

'Where is he?'

She shrugged. 'Not here. Thank God.'

Slowly, she told her story, smoking steadily. She was a model. Dubin – she spoke of him with disgust – had never paid her for a shoot, so she'd come looking for compensation. She'd arrived an hour earlier and found the house empty.

'How'd you get in?'

Once before, she'd stayed here for a few weeks; she'd had a key made. Dubin didn't know about that. So she'd let herself in and was looking for things of value. No point in going to his house in London, she said; she'd been there once before, too, and got nothing from him but a black eye.

'Any idea where he's gone?'

She shook her head. 'He goes abroad a lot.'

'Where?'

'He likes Capri.'

'Does he?'

'He loves Capri. He was always telling me about Capri – the mountains, the sea, the colour of the water, so green, so wonderful.' She was smoking furiously and talking loudly, now. 'So beautiful, Capri. So wonderful. Capri, Capri, Capri!'

Ray was frowning.

Ryan said, 'What you up to?'

She was laughing at top of her voice, a screech. 'Ask me about Capri! Beautiful Capri!'

He caught the merest glance sideways and he turned quickly to see a shadow disappear across the yard, outside the kitchen window.

'Christ almighty, Ray! The bitch has tipped him off.'

They went out of the back door in time to see a thickset man with a holdall leap the wall into the garages beyond.

Ryan went first and gave a yelp. 'My groin!'

Ray hoisted himself up in a smooth gymnastic movement, knees to chest, and vaulted over. Dubin had reached the garages at the other side of the forecourt and was climbing a fence when Ray caught up with him. Twisting round, Dubin whipped his bag backwards and something small and heavy inside it slammed into Ray's head; he reeled back, dizzy, and fell to his knees. Dubin was swinging to hit him again when Ryan arrived and flung himself between them, catching the blow instead, high up on his shoulder. A pain ran down his side like a jolt of electricity. Squawking, he went down in a heap and, as he rolled on the ground, Dubin swung the bag again and hit him on the knee. By the time he'd struggled to his feet, Dubin was already over the fence, into a back garden, and Ray was following. Holding his shoulder, Ryan turned and ran, limping, the other way, back down the cul-de-sac.

Dubin was thirty yards ahead of Ray now, sprinting across a lawn; he ran down the side passageway of the house, pulling over bins behind him, and disappeared through a wooden gate. Ray accelerated, vaulting the bins; he struggled through the gate, ran across the forecourt in front of the house, and found himself on a street of pebble-dash semis, vans going both ways at speed. A woman with a pushchair stood on the pavement, staring at him, open mouthed, as he looked up and down.

Dubin was fifty yards away, running with frantic, heaving movements, his bag swinging round him.

There was no sign of Ryan. Ray concentrated on Dubin, ahead of him: he put on speed, running athlete-style, knees raised. He felt his eyes bulge. His blazer flapped untidily about him; for an awkward moment he tried to button it, then gave up and ran on again, arms pumping, breathing in short bursts, scanning ahead with his bulging eyes.

At the end of the road, where it joined Hollow Way, he saw that Dubin had already crossed to the other side, veering into another side street. In a second, he saw why: Ryan had appeared beyond him, coming the other way to cut him off. Ray ran off the pavement in front of a car, hand out to ward it off as it swerved, hooting, onto the opposite verge, then he followed Dubin, who ran fifty yards along the street and disappeared through a gap in a low stone wall. Ray speeded up. He followed Dubin across a deserted car park towards a fence and, beyond that, trees, gaining all the time.

Dubin went over the fence. Twenty seconds later, Ray went over. Among the trees it was suddenly dark and quiet. No sound or movement ahead – then, the familiar whip-crack of gunfire and bullet-whine in the leaves above his head, and he flung himself to the ground. Obvious, now, what Dubin had had in the bag. He wondered where Ryan was, then heard the sound of running feet and set off again, cautiously at first, gradually picking up speed, swerving between trees. The path crossed a yard at the back of a church and went on through a straight, narrow gulley between high wooden fences overhung with bushes. It was dark, but he could see the silhouette of Dubin thirty metres ahead, rocking from side to side as he hurled himself towards the light at the end of the path. His body glowed briefly when he burst into the road beyond, and there was a scream of brakes as he disappeared suddenly, sideways, in a swiping blur of movement.

Ray made it to the road moments later. Ryan was already there. A white Ford van was slewed across the far pavement and, in the middle of the road, Dubin lay unmoving, coiled on his side, bent arms on either side of his head, as if still trying to protect himself against the impact.

Shocked bystanders began to close in, hands up to their mouths. The driver of the white van was on his knees on the verge. Someone was already calling an ambulance. And Ryan and Ray stood, gasping, looking down at the body.

Ryan saw it first. 'Fuck,' he said.

Ray looked at him, and back down at Dubin. His eyes came to rest on Dubin's right hand, a sinewy incomplete bump of joints, lacking two fingers.

'Fuck,' Ray said as well.

It was clear Dubin couldn't have strangled anyone.

TWENTY-EIGHT

Eight o'clock in the evening in north Oxford: spaghetti vongole in stoneware pasta bowls, Pinot Grigio in glasses shaped like tulips, a murmur of Prokofiev from the glowing recesses of a spotlit bookcase. Ray brooded, distracted, his mind a cordoned-off scene of paramedics and medical equipment, of phone calls and interviews – all the paraphernalia and repercussions of sudden death. And, in a corner of his thoughts, Ryan – squatting in the gutter, FaceTiming his son as they waited for the ambulance, as if he was a tourist.

Diane said, 'It was on the news. Just as the Leys slips out of the headlines, there's this.'

Ray nodded.

'And now an inquiry?' She put her hand on his, small and protective.

'Standard procedure. Armed suspect resisting arrest. Not an issue.' He took the napkin from the collar of his turtleneck sweater. 'The real problem is, the whole thing was a waste of time. Turns out Dubin lost two fingers in Iraq; the guy who strangled the girl at Barnabas had two good, strong hands. So he's not our man and we're back to square one. No suspect, no ID for the victim, no idea why she was killed. I still don't understand why the Super's looks didn't turn us both to stone, when we got back to the station.'

'If he didn't do it, why did he run?'

'Panic, I suppose. Paranoia. Iraq messed him up. There'd been complaints against him before by women he worked with; perhaps this time he thought he'd go down.'

'And what about the woman you found in his house?'

'We picked her up in a Costcutter, buying cigarettes. She knows nothing about the other model. She'd been waiting for Dubin to get back from the tattoo place, where he'd said he was going to pick up some cash to pay her. Turns out he was going to pick up a Beretta 9000.'

'How's your head?'

'It's fine.'

'How's your partner? The news said he was injured, too.'

Ray shrugged. 'He took a couple of whacks, that's all. He's tougher than he looks,' he said. 'All gristle.'

Diane cleared the table and they sat with espressos on the sofa. Prokofiev was replaced by the laid-back, easy-drinking jazz of *Kind of Blue*. Ray glazed over, half his mind still in Marsh Cowley, with Thomas Dubin lying curled like a child on the tarmac.

'How are the two of you getting on?'

He stirred. 'Me and Ryan? Same as before. Won't be for much longer.' He glanced across at her. 'Misconduct inquiry.'

'Already?'

'Told you he wouldn't last long.'

She thought about that. 'Will you have to give a statement?'

He looked away. 'They call anyone they like.'

She examined him. 'Have you given a statement already, Ray?'

He jigged his leg up and down, chewed his lip. 'Yes,' he said, at last.

She let another long silence go by. 'What did you say?'

'I can't talk about it, you know that. Anyway, it doesn't matter what I said. He is what he is.' He looked at her and she held his gaze, blinked slowly. He knew that look. 'I told the truth. And the truth is, he's like a child. He can't control himself. Half the time he's sneering at people, half the time just being silly, childish.' Diane said nothing and Ray went on in the same insistent tone. 'Some of the things he does are trivial, like FaceTiming his son when he's on the job. Some of them are straightforward breaches of police conduct, textbook cases for dismissal. Doesn't matter what I said about him; he's heading for a discharge, there's no question about that.'

She was looking at him with that still, intent expression that usually accompanied a line of questioning.

Instinctively, he braced himself. 'What?'

'Do you like him?'

'No.'

He went across the room and brought back the bottle of wine, and she put her hand over her glass and fixed him with that same, still look. 'FaceTiming his son?'

'What an idiot.'

'What's his son like?'

'I don't know.'

227

'What does he look like?'

'I didn't get more than a glimpse of him. High, squeaky voice.' Ray smiled, despite himself. 'Serious little boy, though. Talking about rhinoceroses. Rhinocer-horses, actually. And he's very polite, completely different from Ryan. He told him off whenever Ryan swore.'

Her laughter crinkled the edges of her eyes. 'And what was Ryan like with him?'

'To be fair, he was . . . different. Probably he's a disaster as a father, but you can tell he's fond of his kid.'

Diane's eyes shone. 'Let's invite him round,' she said.

Ray's face went slack. 'What?'

'Both of them. Invite them round for tea.'

'No. No way. Are you kidding?'

'Come on, Ray. It'll be the best thing for both of you. And I want to see Ryan Junior, I want to hear that squeaky little voice.'

'No, no, no, no, it's wrong. You can't be serious. You haven't been listening to me. He's completely feral. Seriously. Sexist, xenophobic, you name it. Not here. Not in our house. No, Diane. Diane, please.'

She had an expression which terrified him: a thickening of skin around her eyebrows, bumps at the corners of her mouth. This expression appeared now.

'You criticise him for sneering at people?'

'I'm not sneering. I'm just—'

'For being childish?'

'Diane! Diane, wait!'

She hesitated by the door. Looking back, she nodded briefly and turned away again.

'Okay,' Ray was saying as he went after her. 'Okay, okay. Just not now, please. Later. Let's wait a bit. Diane!'

He followed her up the stairs.

At eight o'clock, the trailer park was dim under pools of weak light from lamps on wires above the caravans, like a movie set at night. Leaving his car, Ryan walked down the track between the spiked metal railings and the long mound of rubbish – mattresses, cots, toilet bowls and other garbage left by fly-tippers – until he came to the first caravan. From the ring road on the slope above came the ceaseless jolt and mumble of heavy traffic. His stomach churned. This was the place where he'd locked up his memories. Now they appeared, pale and frightened versions of himself, seven or eight years old, creeping out from the space behind the toilet block where he hid when his father was looking for him, and from the wash house, where he slept sometimes when things were really bad, and, further on, in the caravan, where he stood screaming 'Leave her alone!' as his father dragged Jade across the floor, or where he lay across the table, his head ringing from the clout his father had given him for no reason, just because he could.

He blinked to clear them and forced himself on, belching, between caravans, past the toilets, past the wash house, as far as McGregor's old place with the giant angel of mercy still high in the eaves, all flaking paint and tarnished wings. Houses lay low in the darkness, splashed here and there with dim light from the low-slung lamps. Some were small brick cubes, like public conveniences in parks; some were clip-together prefabs in cream-coloured plastic cladding, jacked up on metal stands.

On the forecourts in front of them were the Travellers' caravans. Everything was quiet and still under the muffling noise of traffic above. The place itself wasn't bad. All sorts of people lived there. But his father's obliterating shadow lay over it all.

A group of men standing under one of the lights turned towards him as he went on.

'Fuck me, it's the fucking prodigal.' A mongrel accent – part Irish, part Strangeways.

He said nothing, kept going.

'Come to bust someone, you little twat?' A conversational tone, halfway pleasant.

He left them behind, kept going, turned up the familiar path, feeling his legs start to tremble, went past the bin yard and stood at last outside the familiar door. He couldn't stop belching now, and he stood there, breathing savagely through his nose, until finally he banged on the door, and again, and again, and instinctively stepped back as it was pulled open.

He stood in the room. His mother leaned, trembling, against the sink, looking at the floor. Her face was swollen. When Ryan pulled up the sleeve of her cardigan, her arm was curdled purple from elbow to wrist. She mumbled to herself.

At the other end of the room, his father sat in his chair in his vest and pants, staring at the television. He'd sat there, staring, for the last twenty years, his hand round his plastic jug of brew, on his lap the remains of his dinner on a plate, gravy thick and dark. A big man once, he'd gradually shrunk down to bone and sinew. Only his hands were big now, thick and knuckly, outsized on his thin wrists, like separate creatures altogether, hardly human, some aspect of pit bull, perhaps. His head seemed to have shrunk too, if that were possible. He had a face like an old gardening glove, seamed and cracked. All expression had dried up. There was no life in his dull eyes.

Just looking at him, Ryan began to sweat; he felt it prickling under his shirt. He turned to his mother. 'When did this happen?'

She didn't answer, though her hand tightened round the tea towel she was holding. Her lips moved silently, prayer-like.

'When? Listen to me. When did he do this to you? Mam!'

She flinched and looked at him. Shook her head. She spoke in a tiny whisper: 'You never brought him. I want to see him, Ryan. I haven't seen him. Won't you bring him?'

'Not here. I'm never ever bringing him here. I told you. You can see him anytime, just come with me. Come with me now.'

She looked towards the far end of the caravan, shook her head.

'Leave him. Come with me. Please, Mam.'

She bent her head and started mumbling again, and he knew better than to go on.

He turned again to his father. He walked across the room. The sweat ran down his sides. He began, 'You and me,' and belched so hard he was almost sick. He swallowed. 'You and me,' he said again, louder, 'we got to have a talk.'

His father gave not the slightest sign that he'd heard him.

Ryan went over and turned off the television, breathing heavily. 'Get up,' he said.

His father continued to stare at the blank screen.

'Get up, you fucker,' Ryan said.

Without changing his expression, his father slowly lifted the jug

231

to his mouth and drank. Liquid ran over his chin and splashed on to the plate in his lap, mixing with the gravy.

Ryan clenched his lips together. His stomach liquified and he thought he might shit himself. But he forced himself forward and slowly leaned down, and, more slowly still, put his face into his father's face.

He tried to control himself. He said, in a crumbling voice he'd never heard before, 'I said I'd never come back here. Not ever. But I come back now. 'Cause you're not going to do this any more. You hear me? You're done. No more. You lay off her. You got that?'

His father's face, six inches away, was grey and waxy, pitted with tiny dents, like something left out in the rain. Red-rimmed eyes filmed over, unfocused. A smell of brew and puke.

'You listening?'

Nothing. Not even a flicker of recognition.

Suddenly, the man jerked forward, snarling, and Ryan flung his arm across his face and fell backwards on the floor.

Then he was on his feet, screaming, 'You fucker! You miserable fuck!' Then dancing in spasms. 'If you touch her again, I'll come back here in a fucking Black Mariah and I'll make sure you go down for the rest of your miserable, pathetic life, you cunt!' Then he was crying, watching his father laugh to himself, slumped in his chair, drinking again from his jug. And finally he was outside in the cold darkness, puking bile on to the concrete, while the noisy haulage trucks lumbered past, in silhouette, on the ridge above.

*

In Kenville Road, he sat at the kitchen table with a mug of sweet tea, perhaps the worst tea he'd ever drunk, trembling, and his sister held him.

'You're alright,' she said. 'It's okay.'

He finished the tea and wiped his face. 'All in all,' he said, 'I got to admit, it didn't go that well.'

They talked through their options. They could take their mother away, but they'd done that before and she always returned as soon as possible to Hinksey Point, saying she had to get their father his dinner. They could talk to social services, but they'd done that before too; their mother wouldn't talk to them, so in the end they said they'd pass the next referral straight to the police. The police had made it clear that they would involve the council, and the council had said that they would enforce immediate eviction.

'She wanted me to take Ryan round to see them,' he said. 'I told her, I'm never ever letting my son go anywhere near him. Never. He doesn't even know evil bastards like that live in the world.'

His sister nodded.

'I should probably just kill the fucker and have done with it,' Ryan said.

'Great idea, yeah – why not? Get sent down, I'll bring Ryan up on my own, you can spend the years wondering what the fuck he looks like. Honestly, Ryan, for an intelligent boy, you're incredibly stupid. Do you want more tea?'

'I really can't drink any more of this shit. Thanks, though.'

She put her hand on his head. 'Least Ryan's alright, like you say. By the way, before I forget, you got to have him early on Friday. I'm going down to London.'

'Yeah, alright.'

'You won't forget?'

'Course not.'

'You better write it on your arm. Friday.'

'Don't worry.'

She nodded. 'I'll get him for you, then.'

In Bayworth, he lay on his son's bed and Ryan lay next to him, flushed and sleepy, but determined not to lose this unexpected opportunity for a conversation.

'It's way past your bedtime, you know.'

'What *is* bedtime, Daddy?'

'Don't start that. Listen, tomorrow night, you got a babysitter coming.'

'Why?'

'Daddy's going out and Auntie Jade's busy. I'll be back later, but you'll be asleep by then, see. Anyway, I was thinking maybe we'd go to the swing park at the weekend – what do you think? And then after, maybe, we can go see Mummy.'

'Can we?'

'Do you want to do that?'

Ryan Junior nodded, as if suddenly shy. 'I want to see Mummy,' he said, very softly.

Ryan rolled over and looked at him, or not *looked* – he was too close – but felt him with his eyes, his son's pale face fuzzily close up against his, and he took him in his arms suddenly and squeezed him tight.

His son made giggly gurgling noises. 'Daddy! I can't breathe, Daddy!'

He let go and lay back again. He said, to the ceiling, 'I'll always look after you, you know that? Nothing bad's ever going to happen to you. I promise.'

His son, on his back again, looking up at the ceiling, trying to see what his father was looking at, said nothing.

'Alright then,' Ryan said. 'Tell you what, if I can stay awake, I'll read you a bit more of the *Mouse and Mole* book.'

Ryan Junior hoisted the bottle of warm milk into his mouth and waited comfortably, and Ryan opened the book and, holding it above his face, began to read.

TWENTY-NINE

Thomas Dubin's body lay in the Thames Valley Police morgue, not far from the body of the young woman with the furious expression. His brother came to identify him. No one had identified the young woman. The Superintendent called the Wilkins DIs to explain the unfortunate death of a material witness in Cowley. Something like a truce had broken out in Blackbird Leys, but, in the intensive care unit at the John Radcliffe Hospital, a man from the Leys came to consciousness with impaired functionality that might or might not be permanent; he couldn't remember what had happened to him and was generally uncooperative. The IT specialists in Forensics repaired a SIM card from a disposable phone used by Thomas Dubin. And, in the middle of the afternoon, Ryan was called into the Super's office alone.

He stood in front of her desk, watching, as she dealt with a message on her phone. Her small cropped head interested him – its neatness – as she bent forward. You can tell a lot about someone from the way they hold their head. All the Super's discipline, her unrelaxing formality, seemed concentrated in it: she wore her head the same way she wore her Detective Superintendent uniform – trimmed and tucked. He looked at the crowns visible on her shoulder epaulettes, wondering what strength of character she possessed to make it to that rank, what denials of weakness. He thought of her suppressed limp, worse in the mornings after her run, the tightness of her mouth, the fixity of her gaze.

She looked up at him and said, 'I've given a statement to the IOPC.'

It came back, then, the old feeling of being in the head-master's office, the social worker's room, and he began to shuffle and fidget.

'Which remains confidential, of course,' she said. 'Stand still.'

He put his hands in the pockets of his tracksuit bottoms, took them out again, folded his arms. 'Am I suspended, then?' he said.

'I've declined a request for your immediate suspension.'

'Why?'

She looked at him, her face unmoving. 'I'm not satisfied the testimonies gathered so far give the full picture. I've requested a second hearing. This will take place in the next few days.'

'Okay. Why?'

She looked at him again. 'You don't need to know that. You continue, for the present, as an active investigating officer, and all your focus should be on your work. Understood?'

'Yeah, alright. But—'

'No buts.' Her face was expressionless. 'You can go.'

Back in the office, he sat opposite Ray, pulling at his hangnails with his teeth, while Ray watched in disgust.

'Do you want to stop doing that? It's making me feel sick.'

'In the IOPC thing . . .' Ryan began.

'I've told you, I can't talk about it.'

'I think the Super went in to bat for me.'

Ray said nothing.

'You know her,' Ryan said. 'What's she like?'

'I've no idea.'

'Come on.'

'She's got a stellar track record. Big wins as Detective Inspector, Chief Inspector. Got the uniform job a couple of years ago.'

'Not that stuff. Her private life.'

'She lives out at Culham, near the river.'

'Married?'

'Don't know.'

'Children?'

'No idea.'

'That it? You don't know much.'

'She doesn't talk about herself.'

'You'd think, as a detective, you might've found out a bit more.'

Ray's irritability got the better of him. 'You know what I do know? Till you turned up, I'd never had a cross word from her – not once.'

'Yeah, well, maybe you just weren't trying hard enough.'

Ray bit his tongue. 'Forget it. Enough about the Super, more about *her*.'

Ryan looked at the crazy wall, bare except for a porn shot of the murder victim, a mugshot of a younger Thomas Dubin, taken in Basra, and a snapshot of Ryan Junior with a large part of a rubber shark in his mouth.

'Fuck me – we been working on this how long? And we still don't even have an ID.' He reflected. 'Still, least we got the phone stuff off that SIM.'

Data from Dubin's phone was minimal, but interesting. Several calls from a number owned by Jason Birch, on the evening of the murder, which they knew about already. One call from a number registered to Wild Mouse Entertainments, in Monaco: Mr Slick, covering his arse – the Super had been right. No doubt his call had contributed to Dubin's desperation. But there were also two text messages, sent by Dubin on the night of the murder to a third, untraceable number: the first, at 20.45, reading *did u get it ok*; the second, at 23.30, *left the gs with ron*.

'Sent to her,' Ryan said. 'Got to be.'

'I agree. The second text's obviously about her fee. He's left her money with someone called Ron.'

'Yeah. Which means?'

'He thought she was still alive. Which means?'

'He left the college separately, leaving her behind.'

'Yeah. But why? Why didn't they leave together?'

'Don't know.'

'Neither do I.'

They sat in silence.

Ryan said, 'Wait, I do know. That first text, the one at quarter to nine: *did u get it ok*. Her ring, he means. Like this: they were on their way out and she realises she's left her ring behind, says she's going back to find it, while he goes ahead on his own. Catch you up in a minute, sort of thing. Obviously, she never does. When she doesn't show, he sends her the text. Did you

239

get your ring okay? No reply. So, he leaves her money with this Ron fella. Next thing, he hears what's happened, does a bunk.'

'Okay. Good.'

They both sat in silence, depressed.

'You thinking what I'm thinking?'

Ray nodded. 'She went back to the wrong place. Her ring wasn't in the lodge. It was in the library.'

'If she hadn't made that mistake, maybe she wouldn't've got killed.'

They fell silent again.

Ray said, 'Let's say she still had the keys from Jason with her. She goes back to the lodge, lets herself in with them, goes into the study. Someone kills her. Then what? The killer leaves, locks the door with her keys and takes them with him.'

'What about the kitchen uniform?'

'He takes that as well. But why?' Ray thought about it, gazing at the crazy wall. 'I know,' he said. 'Because it's got his blood on it.'

Ryan grinned. 'Bingo. He attacks her, she fights back, he gets a slap in the face, nose bleed, whatever. When it's all over, he's smart enough not to leave it there with his DNA smeared all over it.'

'But who is he? What happened?'

'We don't know.'

'Way forward?'

'Find out who Ron is,' Ryan said.

'Could be professional – an agent, perhaps.'

'Or personal. Her boyfriend, her brother.'

'How do we find out?'

'No idea.'

They sat in silence.

'Don't you think it's odd,' Ryan said, 'that we've never had any idea *why* she was killed?'

'How can we? We don't know who she is, let alone who the perp is or what he was doing there.'

'Even so. I mean, there's no visible motive. She wasn't raped.'

'She disturbed someone, maybe,' Ray said.

'Doing what? Nothing was stolen.'

They sat in silence a bit longer, then Ray went to get coffees. Ryan said, 'Change of subject, for a minute. Back to this misconduct thing.'

'Do we have to?'

'The Super went to Canary Wharf, said her piece.'

'You told me.'

'They'll ask you, as well. Like I said. Give them a statement.'

Ray's face set oddly. 'Obviously,' he said, 'I can't speak about it.'

'Course not.'

'I'm fair,' he said.

'Course you are. Fair play's famous at all them schools you went to. It's just you don't want to talk about it.'

'*Can't* talk about it.'

'Course not. Wouldn't want to get you in trouble. Not like it matters or nothing – to you.'

'Enough.'

As Ray turned to his laptop, the office phone rang from its place in between them. Ray glanced at it and carried on typing.

Ryan glanced at Ray. 'You going to answer it, then?'

Almost a minute passed. At last, Ryan picked it up, muttering. 'Yeah?'

In the far distance, a man's voice with a heavy French accent.

'Yeah, go on. I can hear you, just about.'

The voice asked to speak with a senior investigating officer.

'Yeah, go on.'

There was a small disbelieving pause. 'You are he?'

'Let's pretend I am.'

The voice launched into an elaborate formal introduction, which Ryan had difficulty following.

'Hang on, hang on. Maybe I'm not the right fella, after all. Sounds like you want the Foreign Office or something.'

The man hesitated. As if reading from notes in a dim light, he said, 'You are not . . . Detective Inspector Wilkins?'

Ryan sighed. 'Yeah, alright, I am. One of them, anyway.'

'So. I am *bijoutier*, you understand – a dealer in jewellery. I have information about a ring.'

Ryan took a sudden close interest in the call, signalling to Ray, who watched him as he spoke.

'Oh, yeah? Go on . . . Yeah. Okay, then . . . You sure? . . . Fantastic. Hang on a sec.' He said to Ray, 'Bingo time. French jeweller sold her the ring. Remembers it clearly.'

Ray held his hand out for the phone.

Ryan ignored him, said to the jeweller, 'Yeah, go on, then, give me the name.' He scowled. 'What do you mean? . . . Yeah, but look, confidential's good, but this is a murder investigation. You understand? *Vous comprends*, yeah? We got no time.'

'I am sorry,' the jeweller said. 'These are professional requirements.'

'Face to face? Really? You're having a laugh. Where in France you based?'

The man actually began to laugh, an airy noise, very French.

'What's so funny?'

'But I am not in France.'

'Well, where are you, then?'

'Here.'

'What, in the UK?'

'In Oxford. The covered market, just up the road. It will take you five minutes to get here.'

THIRTY

Rain came down in wisps, wet-freckling the hyperbolic carving of Christ Church College's gateway and grease-staining the double-decker buses queued in front of it. Ray turned up the suede-lined collar of his herringbone sports jacket and put on a matching flat cap, positioning it carefully. Ryan put on an amiable sneer, and they walked together through lunchtime crowds up to the High Street, crossed the road to the other side and went on under some scaffolding, arguing.

'The problem with being a xenophobe,' Ray said, 'is you jump to the wrong conclusions.'

'Other way round, mate. Gives me a head start. What did I say about thousands of them being over here?'

They turned up the alley to the market and went along the southern arcade, past gift shops and cookie kiosks, to the silversmiths at the end.

'Least they've got a good English name,' Ryan said, looking up. 'Was worried I might have to get my French out again.'

'I'd leave your French where it is,' Ray said. 'I wouldn't even get it out in France, if I were you. In fact, especially not in France.'

The bell made an antique tinkling noise as they went in, and were met by a portly bald man with a baggy left eye, as if, over the years, an eyeglass had been continually screwed into it. He lifted his arms, Pope-like, in vague greeting, and his cardigan rode up over his belly.

For a while, he contemplated the posthumously taken photograph of the young woman, frowning and humming to himself. 'Yes,' he said at last. 'She is the same.'

'Sure?' Ray asked.

He shrugged. 'A little changed . . .'

'Well, she would be,' Ryan said. 'She's dead.'

The jeweller took off his spectacles and paused a moment, as if in respect. 'It is a terrible thing,' he said. He swapped their photograph for one of his own, sliding it across the glass-topped counter for their inspection. Three shots, from different angles, of a plain circular ring, silvery ochre, grooved with markings.

'Yeah, that's it,' Ryan said, straight away. 'The funny swirls and everything. Go on, then. Who is she?'

The jeweller produced a document for signature, stating that the information supplied was required in an ongoing police investigation. He pushed this towards Ray.

'I can write as well, you know,' Ryan said.

Ignoring him, the man produced a ledger from under the counter and consulted a closely printed page, running his finger down a list, humming to himself again. He looked up, hesitated, and said, with a quiet air of drama, 'Sophie Barbery: that is her name.'

There was a pause, as if in recognition of a decisive moment. 'Address?'

He shook his head.

'Telephone number? Email? Anything?'

'Alas, no.'

Ray was already messaging Nadim.

Ryan said, 'You said you remembered her.'

The man nodded, reflected. He had enjoyed his conversation with Sophie Barbery. She knew about jewellery; they'd talked about new styles and trends, revivals of older traditions. He'd explained the provenance of the ring. She'd mentioned one or two rare pieces she was looking out for and he'd made a note of them, carefully inserted (he showed them) in the ledger.

Ryan gave Ray a look. 'Collector of rare rings? Don't sound like your average porn star, somehow.'

The jeweller was indignant. Porn star! Sophie Barbery was a very elegant young woman, he said, civilised, cultured. Serious minded, he'd thought, if light-hearted. Yes, he'd sensed a capacity for fun, for good living. She'd been wearing a silk bandana and large hoop earrings, he said, pleased with himself for remembering such details, and a summer dress. Yes, yes, he had complimented her on it. They chatted; he had the vague impression she'd talked of going home to visit her family. She was – of course – a very beautiful woman. And naturally, he added, it had been a pleasure to talk to her in his native tongue.

'You can pay me later,' Ryan said to Ray. 'Absolutely knew it.'

Ray looked at the jeweller. 'She was French, was she?'

'No.'

Ray gave a sideways glance at Ryan.

'From Syria,' the jeweller said.

Ryan said, 'There you go, then. That's proper foreign, that is. Also,' he added, 'interesting.'

She'd grown up in Paris, the jeweller said, where her family had been in exile for many years. 'Political trouble.' He shrugged. Such is the way of the world.

Ray said, 'Thanks. That's all very helpful. By the way, when you met her, did she seem troubled in any way, show any signs of stress?'

The jeweller frowned and shrugged. 'I don't remember. But what difference would that make now?'

Ray belatedly realised his mistake. 'When was it you sold Sophie this ring?'

'Ten years ago.'

They both stared at him.

Ray said, 'She would only have been about nineteen.'

The jeweller concurred. 'An undergraduate.'

They stared again.

'She told you that? Which college?'

He shrugged. 'I don't think she said. One of the best, that was the impression she gave. I believed her. She was a fine young woman. All this is a terrible, terrible business.'

On the High Street, Ryan was grinning and shuffling about like a terrier with a squeaky toy.

Ray glared at him. 'Just don't say it. There's no need to say it.'

They walked on in silence.

'Told you she was foreign,' Ryan said.

Ray sighed.

247

'And an undergraduate,' Ryan went on. 'Didn't I say I thought there was some connection with the university? Posh girl, too. Got to admit it, that French guy was good value.' He threw a few dance moves on the pavement, startling passers-by.

The rain had stopped and everything shone with a dull pewtery gleam.

Ray said, 'Ten years later, she's in a porn shoot. How come?'

'Tell you what, we need to talk to Sir Grope-a-lot again about the missing picture in his study. Ten years ago – that's just the time she was an undergraduate here. What's he been hiding?'

'Remember it wasn't his office.'

'Oh, yeah. Whose office was it? Did you ask?'

'Goodman's.'

Ryan looked interested. 'Funny. From what I hear, there's another shonky bastard for you.'

They fell into their own thoughts as they turned down St Aldates.

At the station entrance, Ray said, 'By the way, before I forget . . .' He hesitated.

'What?'

'My wife wondered . . . I mean, we both wondered . . . if you'd like to come round one day.'

A panicky look went across Ryan's face. 'What do you mean?'

'You know, socially.'

'Socially?'

'Come round for tea. Bring Ryan.'

Ryan stood there, staring, and Ray was so unnerved, he instantly began to ask about dietary requirements.

Ryan interrupted him: 'When?'

'Well, whenever. What about today?'

'Can't. Sorry.'

He walked on, and Ray followed.

'You got a problem with it?'

'Course not. Got plans, that's all. Going out. Got a babysitter and everything.'

'Fine. We'll do it later, sometime.'

'Yeah.'

They walked through reception and the open-plan, got into the lift and stood there, waiting.

'A date, is it?' Ray asked, to break the awkward silence.

'Yeah.' Ryan had recovered. He grinned. 'Cocktail bar or two, one of the clubs.'

'Fancy.'

'Claire's choice.'

A few moments passed. Ray turned to him, frowned. 'Claire? Not Claire the Bursar, at Barnabas?'

'Is there a problem, Raymond?'

'Obviously – she's a material witness.'

'Not really.'

The lift doors opened and they went out, Ryan pulling ahead, Ray catching him up.

'You've got a copy of the ethical code, like everyone else. You're not to pursue an intimate relationship with a person with whom you come into contact in the course of your work.'

'If they're vulnerable.'

'What?'

'That's how it goes on, the code. I looked it up. She's not vulnerable.' He kept walking.

'I can't believe you'd do it with the misconduct inquiry going on.'

Ryan kept walking.

'You're putting yourself at risk. Compromising your impartiality. Increasing the possibility of divulging inappropriate information. Impairing your ability to carry out your professional duties. Creating a conflict of interest. I'm quoting. All these are . . . Ryan! Are you listening to me?'

'What? Sorry, I must have drifted off.'

'What about the IOPC?'

'The IOPC can fuck off. Oh, and Ray?'

'What?'

'You can fuck off, too.'

THIRTY-ONE

Eight o'clock. Ray was still at work, bent over a pool of light on his desk: a tableau painted by Hopper. One floor below, in her own anglepoise bubble, Nadim pulled data from her flickering screen.

Ray's phone rang.

'Hey, babe,' Diane said.

'Hey.'

'When will you be back?'

'Not for a while. Don't wait up. We had some good news today.'

'I saw you on the news. You know who she was.'

'Yes. Lots of things to follow up, now. The usual thing: "No time to waste, Ray." "Get on it right away, Ray."'

'Are you back in her good books? You must be.'

'Hard to tell.'

There was a pause. 'Ryan there with you?'

He took a breath. 'Ryan's not here, no.'

There was another pause. 'I assume you didn't invite him, then.'

'I did invite him. He's . . . busy this evening.'

'Did you fix up another time?'

'To be honest, he didn't seem keen; I don't know why. I'll wait a couple of days.'

'Make sure you ask him properly. Sincerely.'

'Babe. I *was* sincere. It was him being odd. He said nothing at all and then cut me off, just as I was asking him about dietary requirements.'

'*Dietary requirements?* Oh, Ray. Speak to him again. And, please, try to be natural.'

'I don't know what you mean; I'm always natural.'

He looked angrily at the phone for a moment, then got his stuff together and prepared to go to the college library, where the librarian had agreed to make the student archives available to him overnight.

As Ray was walking through college to the library, Ryan was standing at the bar in the Alchemist, getting more drinks. Rhubarb and custard sour – Grey Goose vodka, go easy on the Advocaat – and a grapefruit juice. Taking care not to spill them on his trackies, he took them through the crowded room, back to the tiny table by the window at the end, and sat down.

The whole bar pulsed with music.

He was wearing satin-look FILA-branded trackies and hoodie in orange, under an orange sleeveless puffa jacket, and he wore a Koloa Surf Company flat-brim cap, also orange. He looked like a fizzy drink. He was very pleased with himself.

'I fucking love the Westgate. Cheers.'

Claire laughed. 'This is so strange.'

'What is?'

'This.'

'Being here with me? Don't worry, I know what it is.'

'What?'

'I got curiosity value. Always had it. Comes of being so good-looking.'

She was wearing low-slung shredded denims, very tight, and a loose T-shirt with plunging neckline. She looked at him, smiling over the top of her cocktail as she sipped through the straw.

She nodded towards his grapefruit juice. 'How long since you stopped drinking?'

'Never really drunk much.'

'Any reason?'

'Yeah. My dad's a violent alcoholic.'

She looked at him for a moment, unsure whether to laugh, and glanced away. 'How's the investigation going?'

'Great. Just moving into phase two.'

She raised her eyebrows.

'Phase one: you don't know fuck all, you get the wrong end of the sandwich, turns out your partner's a knobhead, people get killed, that sort of thing.'

'And phase two?'

'Your partner's still a knobhead, but you get on a bit better.'

'Any progress in the investigation, in phase two?'

'Not really. Same in life. You just got to stick with it long enough, till it falls into place.'

She laughed then. 'I guess that's a philosophy.'

'Stamina's the only thing that counts.'

They stayed there talking for an hour or so before moving

on to the ATIK, the club in Park End Street. Ryan knew the bouncers; they went straight in, through to the Vinyl Room – all glam-rock Day-Glo leather and fender-sized chrome fittings, its booths decorated in slashing primary colours, dance floor illuminated, everything smoothed with a red glow, like the sunset lounge of a sinking ship.

'Safe, here,' Ryan said. 'They won't play any of that new shit.'

They sat at a table, with more drinks: tequila for Claire, another grapefruit juice for Ryan.

'So,' Claire said, 'is that why you became a policeman, because you had an alcoholic father?'

There was a moment when he looked at her blankly. Then he gave a scoffing little laugh. 'You know what?'

'What?'

'You look fucking fantastic. Let's go.' He jumped to his feet, grabbed her hand and led her to the dance floor.

She'd never seen anything like it. He was a cartoon. Some sort of electricity passed through him in jolts, animating him in unpredictable ways. Fixing her with an intense but unstable look, he circled her like a matador; he jostled through a series of wild hip-jerks, fell forward, nose to floor, and bounced back up again as if on elastic. Confronting her with both his hands on her shoulders, he swung his right leg vertically into the air until it touched his ear. She laughed out loud.

He loved Madonna, Britney, Kylie, Michael Jackson, the Spice Girls and all those other cheesy divas of dance-pop. He knew their moves, too. Shimmery tracksuit and puffa floating round him, the brim of his cap whipping from side to side, he did them all: cute Kylie, dominatrix Madonna, sluttish Britney. His legs came and went in a blur. He licked his lips. He mouthed the words, pouting, all the time fixing her with a look so serious it was hilarious. He was a child buzzing with carelessness. There was nothing she could do; she let herself go, into the crowded music where the laughter was.

Ten o'clock pivoted to two in the morning. Outside, in the sudden deafening silence of Park End Street, they untangled themselves in the cold breeze and she got into his terrible car and was driven out of the city, up Hinksey Hill and down Bayworth Lane, to a place she hadn't known existed.

While she went into the toilet, Ryan paid the babysitter, and when she came out, he was waiting for her in the kitchen with a grin.

'Still look fucking fantastic,' he said. 'How do you do it?'

They were on the sofa in the cold front room. She touched the little gristle of scar tissue on his cheek. 'You know what?' she said.

'What?'

'I've never done this with anyone like you before.' She kissed his mouth and put her hands under his tracksuit and felt his ribs through his shirt. His breath was hot in her ear. Her T-shirt came off and his hands were in her hair and her hands were down the front of his trackies and he loosened her belt and she arched her back as her breasts shivered out of her bra and she felt his mouth on her nipples and her jeans were round her thighs, his head in her hands as she rocked and rocked, and the room was filling up with their little moans – and suddenly she flinched and broke away.

He lifted his face to her. 'What? Did I hurt you?'

She was looking round, cocking her head on one side. 'What was that noise?'

It was silent in the house and he ran his fingers down her belly, but the noise came again and she caught hold of his hand to stop him.

'Crying,' she said, staring at him in astonishment. And then: 'There's a baby in the house.'

'Well, he's not a baby. Two and a bit. It's okay. I'll just go up and settle him back down. Won't take long.'

She shook her head, stared at him. 'You've got a child?'

'Yeah. Sorry. Should've said. Was going to, but . . . I just thought dates shouldn't be so complicated.'

She wasn't listening. 'Whose is it?'

'Mine, of course.'

She stared. 'But where's his . . . ?'

'Not here.' He paused. 'Gone.'

She was shaking her head. She tugged her jeans back up. 'Oh, God, I'm sorry.' He watched her as she put her T-shirt on. 'I've made a mistake. I'm so sorry.' She didn't look at him. 'I'll let myself out, call a cab. Look.'

'Yeah?'

'I'm sorry, I just can't do this.'

He watched her sadly. 'Yeah, okay.'

The front door banged as he went quickly up the stairs, along the landing and into Ryan's room, where his son stood, red faced and weeping, on the edge of the bed, arms outstretched, imploring, jerking out words as he panted. 'I had . . . a . . . bad . . . dream.'

Ryan held him, murmuring. 'Hey, hey, it's alright now. It's okay, Ry. Daddy's here.'

'I heard . . . a . . . voice.'

'It's okay. She's gone now.'

His son clung to him, sobbing, his damp hair against Ryan's cheek, but, in a minute or two, a great shudder went through him and he fell asleep, and Ryan put him back into bed and lay down next to him.

He should have told her he had a kid. He'd not wanted her to think him needy. But he didn't need – or want – to share his son with anyone.

The boy made tiny smacking noises with his lips and was quiet, and Ryan let out a long, quiet sigh himself and was calm again. As always, his thoughts moved quickly on to other things: they went outside, drifted like a breeze across the dark and silent fields of Oxfordshire, to a silver-coloured building, twenty miles away, where an angry dead woman had been lying on a metal gurney all this time. Now, at least, they had a name. Sophie Barbery. It suited her; it had the right sort of sound, somehow – a hint of the exotic, a flash of temper. An ID at last, a thread to pull on, something to follow.

THIRTY-TWO

Nine o'clock the next morning, Ray and Ryan stood together in the Superintendent's office. Ryan was haggard. Ray was haggard too.

'You look like shit, mate,' Ryan said. 'Your shirt's out. Never seen that before. Out on the lash?'

'College library. Came straight here. You?'

He looked away.

The Super came in, went round her desk and sat there, looking at them, and Ray began to explain what he and Nadim had discovered in the course of a long night.

Sophie Barbery, twenty-nine years old when she was killed, born in Damascus, domiciled in Paris from the age of twelve, when her family went into exile: her father, a minor minister in Bashar al-Assad's government, had been accused of financial impropriety. A cosmopolitan life of privilege. She'd attended elite schools in Paris before matriculating at Oxford.

Since her graduation, she'd moved from apartment to apartment in rich London: Islington, Richmond, Chelsea. No regular employment, but plenty of dinners and drinks, trips abroad to high-end resorts, holidays on friends' yachts.

He held up a sheaf of financial records, harvested by Nadim. 'What friends?' the Super asked.

The rich and young. They came from Milan, Mumbai, Seattle, lived in apartments in Mayfair, country houses in Hampshire and Oxfordshire, owned vintage cars, salmon rivers in Scotland, private planes. They skied in the Dolomites, cruised in the Caribbean, partied in London and occasionally got in with the wrong people.

'Meaning?'

Film-makers with well-publicised bad habits, traders blacklisted for possession of class-A drugs, club owners who went to jail for prostitution. Ray put a bunch of itemised invoices on the Superintendent's desk. 'Five years ago, she spent a couple of months in rehab.'

'What did that French guy say?' Ryan said. 'Girl with a light heart and a capacity for fun. And Daddy could fund it.'

'For a while.' Ray spread out printouts of news reports. 'Two years ago, he was killed.'

Overnight, the family money had disappeared. Straight away, there had been a marked decline in Sophie's social activity, soon becoming a sort of disquieting silence. The flat occupied in her name – in Sloane Square – had been abandoned, bills unpaid, utility supplies cut off. Where had she been living? Not known. What had she been doing?

'Porn,' Ryan said.

The Super said, 'So, we finally know who she was. But who would've wanted to kill her?'

Ryan made a helpless face.

She looked at Ray. 'Where do we start?'

'The university. Which is why I spent the night in the archives.'

She gave a brief nod of approval. 'Which college?'

'Lady Margaret Hall, where Sophie was an undergrad. But I wondered if I might find a connection with Barnabas.'

'Why? Dubin set up the Barnabas shoot, not Sophie. He was the one who approached Jason Birch.'

He told her about the feeling Ryan had had earlier, the missing picture in the Provost's study. 'And why did Dubin choose Barnabas? Why not another college? Could be she suggested it to him.'

So he'd gone, late in the evening, to Lady Margaret Hall in north Oxford, where the librarian, who seemed to live in a cubby hole next to the college library, had opened up the alumni archive for him. She was an elderly lady, with apple cheeks and a mind like a steel trap, who – unexpected bonus – remembered Sophie herself. She'd liked her, though even then Sophie had a reputation as a party girl.

'Interesting comment she made. She couldn't imagine anyone disliking Sophie – unless they were, and I quote, "some sort of puritanical fanatic."'

LMH had a lot of microfiche in their archives; he'd spent hours juggling flimsy pieces of plastic film in and out of the reader, peering at their densely typed texts, grit spots already blurring the letters on the degenerated plastic. One by one, he had located Sophie's academic schedules – the courses she'd taken, the tutorials she attended, the lectures given at the faculty.

'And?'

All her tutorials had taken place, as usual, in her own college, Lady Margaret Hall. 'Except,' he said, 'for one term in her second year, when she had tutorials at another college.'

'Barnabas?'

'Yes.'

'What tutorials?'

'International Contexts in the Early Modern World.'

'And who was her tutor?'

Ray put down a final printout on the desk, and Ryan and the Superintendent leaned forward.

'I knew it,' Ryan said. 'Ray, mate. Got to hand it to you.'

Ray turned his haggard face to him. 'You're not actually praising me, are you?'

'To be fair, I always knew you'd be good at the grunt work.'

The Super said, 'This time, I want no complaints about misconduct. You both go, but Ray takes the lead.' She turned to Ryan. 'You – you control yourself.'

THIRTY-THREE

Rain came down hard, glassy and grey, as they ran from Ray's car to the entrance and stood, dripping, under the gateway, listening to the clatter of the downpour on the flagstones outside. In the window of the porter's lodge, Leonard Gamp's face appeared and quickly withdrew. Ray shook out his umbrella, brushing splash-marks off his Burberry, and Ryan wiped his face and shoved his hands deep into the pockets of his soaked trackie bottoms.

'Know what we should do?' He pinched his nose, squeezing mucus on to the ground. 'Set up some different room.'

'What do you mean?'

'When we come here, we're always in their lodge or their office or whatever. Gives them, you know, home advantage. We got to shake things up.'

Ray nodded. 'Okay, let's do it.'

Leonard Gamp had completely disappeared; even Ryan banging on the windowpane didn't bring him out.

Ray put a hand on his arm. 'You can ask the Bursar.'

He turned to see her running in from the quad, out of a mist of rain, elfin and suited, blonde hair swishing like a fan, heels clacking. When she arrived under the gateway, she came to an awkward halt, abashed to see him, while Ray looked at them both. Their eyes slid off each other.

'Alright,' Ryan said.

'Oh. Hello.'

Her face was wet and startled, and he grinned to put her at her ease. 'Listen, you might be able to help us.' He explained about the room. 'You're the fixer, right?'

'You could set up in the SCR.'

'Don't know what that is. S for Spaniards?'

He grinned again, and she smiled back in pure gratitude. 'Senior common room, where the dons take their coffee – Spaniards and all.'

She directed them, and Ray and Ryan walked away along the cloisters, their footsteps muffled on the cold flags, while rain fell, smoking, onto the lawn of the quad, and rain-breeze swept little bits of wet through the cloister arches against their faces.

Ray gave Ryan sideways looks. 'You and the Bursar, then?'

'One thing about me: I don't bear grudges.'

As they reached the end of the cloisters, the rain came down harder still and they hesitated under the final arch, watching people caught in the quad make a dash for shelter. A man struggling with a huge umbrella decorated with the Harvard University coat of arms and the motto *Veritas* ran in and stood next to them, puffing and wiping rain around his pink face.

He greeted Ray. 'They warned me, but even so. Don't get it like this in the Midwest.'

They all looked through the cloister arches at the heavy sheets of solid air dropping in a blur, listening to the rain's garrulous voice in the gutters, smelling the strange scents coming off it, cheese and soap and doormats.

'It's only fucking rain,' Ryan said, and the man turned to him with a little twitch of alarm.

Ray said, 'Kent Dodge. DI Wilkins.'

Kent looked at him in confusion. 'But I thought you—?'

'Yeah, that's it,' Ryan said. 'We're all called Wilkins, over here. Keeps things simple. Been here long?'

'Just this year. Fulbright.'

While they waited for the rain to stop, Ryan looked him over, making him nervous.

'Got a quick question for you. Outside perspective and that. Do you mind?'

Kent looked anxious. 'If it's about Sir James, I already spoke to . . . the other DI Wilkins, and, to be honest, I didn't want to mention it, but now I'm being hounded about my battels bill. So, if you don't mind—'

'Not him,' Ryan said. 'Goodman. He's the dodgeball we're interested in, now.'

'Dodgeball?' Kent looked to Ray for help, but got none. 'Well,' he said, uncertainly, 'he's an excellent Arabist.'

'No, no, no,' Ryan said. 'What's he *like*?'

'Oh. He's strange.'

Ryan rolled his eyes.

'I guess everyone's strange, here,' Kent said. 'He's . . . difficult.'

'Difficult?'

'Stubborn. Bitter.'

Ray frowned. 'A bit more specific?'

Kent thought for a moment, his eyes darting from side to side, avoiding Ryan's look. 'Well, take the other evening.' He described the dinner for al-Medina. Despite the Provost's instructions, Goodman had immediately raised the subject of the college Koran, the repatriation of which the Saudi government had been requesting for years. It was his principled belief that the Koran did not belong in England, was in fact an example of straightforward theft. Al-Medina's response had been curt: the Saudis weren't fit custodians of the Koran. But that didn't deter Goodman. Even after Sir James tried to close the conversation down, he carried on talking. It wasn't just awkward. Goodman took it way beyond awkward. 'At one point, he even switched to Arabic so the Provost wouldn't understand. I thought Sir James was going to blow his stack.'

Ray frowned. 'You didn't tell me this before. What was Goodman saying?'

'My Arabic's pretty rudimentary. Something about getting the mosques involved. Better for them to request repatriation than the government. I think he suggested al-Medina get the Sheikh Zayed Mosque to make a demand.'

'But al-Medina had already told him the Saudis weren't fit custodians.'

'The Zayed Mosque isn't in Saudi. It's in UAE – where al-Medina comes from.'

'That,' Ryan said, 'is what we call one shonky bastard. Listen, do us a favour.' He fixed his eyes on Kent, who almost flinched. 'You know where his office is?'

'Yes.'

'Give him a message, will you? Tell him to get down here, to the SCR. Two detectives want to see him. Be good, coming from you – take him by surprise.'

Kent hesitated, caught Ray's eye, and went reluctantly towards Old Court, and, as the rain eased, Ray and Ryan stepped out of the cloisters and went across New Court in the other direction.

The senior common room seemed to have been borrowed from an old country hotel. It was fussy and faded, with pale mint-green walls above plain wood-panelling, shrivelled antique rugs on the wooden floor and sun-bleached chintz armchairs on the rugs. There was a smell of furniture polish and old ladies.

In an antique mirror, Ray brushed rain off his hair and refined the angle of his shirt collar. Ryan ambled around, peering at the paintings, scratching himself.

'What was it that woman in the library told you? About the sort of person who'd kill her?'

'They'd have to be a puritanical fanatic.'

'Well, he sounds like a fanatic to me.'

'I was thinking the same thing. But we play it straight. You heard the Super. I'll take the lead. And you behave yourself.'

Ryan picked up a dish of potpourri and sniffed it doubtfully. 'What about we go in hard instead? Maybe get a little physical?' He caught Ray's expression in the mirror. '*Joke*, for fuck's sake.'

'I'm serious.'

'You're always fucking serious. One of the things I love about you. Where we going to sit?'

They tried the chairs by the fireplace. Too far apart. The chairs by the wooden shutters of the window were the wrong height. They went around the room bickering, until there was a knock on the door and they quickly stood together behind a wooden table piled with back issues of *Gramophone Monthly* and *The Economist*.

'Come in,' Ray said, and Ameena Najib walked in with a face of fury.

In the end, they sat by the fireplace, though they were never comfortable and Ameena herself seemed hardly aware of where she was. She had overheard the Bursar say that two detectives were in college. With a trembling hand, she thrust a piece of paper at them – a photocopy of a cartoon. In it, Mohammad in heaven was waving back dead jihadis with the words, 'Stop, stop, we ran out of virgins.'

Ryan let out a laugh, which Ray immediately smothered with talk.

Ameena interrupted him. 'I wish to report a hate crime.' She had been weeping and her face seemed distorted by its wetness.

Ray attempted to pacify her, but she spoke in a rush, denouncing the cartoon, which had been left in her locker, and did not stop speaking even after Ray held up his hand. It was clear she could not. She talked on, helplessly, her English breaking down, as if giving voice to a violent outpouring of more than outrage, a cry sent up at the memory of body bags and rubble-filled streets, of the burials of parents, the rape and death of sisters, the humiliation of strangers.

'Ashley Turner has done this. I wish to report it. I know what it is – it is a crime. I wish you to do your job. There are people here who defile the Holy Book,' she said. 'Yes, here. I have seen them.' She paused to catch her breath.

Ryan handed back the cartoon and she slapped it out of his hand and it lay on the floor. He said, 'Listen, not being funny, and I know you're cut up about this, but we don't do complaints. You need to go down the station, talk to an officer there. We do other stuff. In fact, we've got stuff we're trying to do now, so if you can—'

Ameena bared her teeth at him – such a frightening gesture, he stopped talking.

Ray said, 'As soon as we're finished here, Ameena, I'll take you down to the station and help you make a statement.'

She sat, wringing her hands, the muscles in her face fluttering. In her agitation, she had pulled her headscarf half-off – a tail of it hung down over one eye, giving her a piratical look.

'Half an hour,' Ray said. 'I promise.'

For a moment, it seemed she would accept. But she stood, dismissively. 'I know your promise.'

'Don't forget your cartoon,' Ryan said.

There was a pause, like the tiny pause between stubbing your toe and feeling the pain. She said something unintelligible under her breath, then spat on to the floor and walked away.

Ray turned to Ryan. 'Christ! Can't you avoid making things worse, just for once?'

Ryan was surprised. 'What do you mean? She's bang out of order, mate. Gobbed on the floor and everything.'

'Just treat people with a little respect, will you?'

'All I said—'

'I know what you said.'

'I was just trying to—'

'No, you weren't.'

'Did you see her, though? Angry or what? Wouldn't want to be on the wrong side of her when she loses it.'

'You *are* on the wrong side of her.'

There was a knock on the door and Ray hesitated. He sat down next to Ryan and arranged himself.

'Let me do the talking.'

'Here we go.'

'He sounds just as prickly as she is, so let's keep it professional.'

'I'm not the one driving out to the Leys on my own. I'm not the one—'

Ray angrily shushed him. 'Come in,' he called, with artificial brightness.

Kent Dodge came in.

'Fuck me,' Ryan said. 'What is this? Santa's fucking grotto? Where's the shonker?'

'He won't come. I told you he was stubborn.'

'Fine,' Ryan said. 'You can take us to him.'

Kent's face did a little dance of anxiety.

'Don't worry,' Ryan said, 'we're not going to make you watch while we kick his head in.'

Ray said, 'He's joking, Kent.'

Kent gave a sickly smile.

'You can stand outside and listen to the screams,' Ryan said. 'Ever heard a man break down and beg you to finish him off?'

Ray clenched his face. 'You're not being funny.'

Ryan went past him, out of the room, and Kent and Ray had to run to catch up.

THIRTY-FOUR

Dr Andrew Goodman – fifty-three years old, fellow of Barnabas Hall, keeper of collections, senior lecturer at the Institute for Middle Eastern Studies – crouched on the floor of the collections room, surrounded by packing crates, his phone squeezed between shoulder and chin, murmuring into it, telling someone not to worry.

'I've told you before. Don't let it bother you. It doesn't bother me.'

He looked bothered. He had a long, pinched face, with a sour mouth; his eyes were exhausted and restless, naked under bony brows. His whole face looked naked and thin-skinned. In a few days, by mutual consent, he would leave both college and university, the logical but painful outcome of several years of disagreement with the Provost of Barnabas, but he was punctilious by nature, as well as awkward and disaffected, and, in a sort of savagery, he now seemed to be pushing himself to tie up all loose ends before his departure.

There was a thump on the door.

'Not now,' he called out.

The door opened and two men came in – a well-built black man in bottle-green blazer and matching corduroys, and a youth in a sloppy tracksuit.

'As I told your messenger boy,' Goodman said, continuing to pack a box, 'I'm busy now, but do please go back down the corridor to the admin office, and they'll arrange another time for us to speak.'

The youth in the tracksuit stepped forward and opened his mouth, and the black detective stepped hastily in front of him.

'Won't take long,' he said, smoothly.

They sat on stackable chairs at the back of the room.

Ryan was already fidgeting. Goodman had spent the first five minutes of an agreed fifteen-minute period explaining his busy schedule (he was packing up before leaving the college the next day and travelling abroad for an extended period). After that, he had asked them for full identification, including their lines of command. Now, he was questioning the parameters of their jurisdiction. His manner was legalistic and petty.

'Under what section of the police code is this interview taking place, please?'

Ray recited technical information which Ryan had never heard of.

Goodman said, 'Oh, well, if this is about the murder, I suggest you'd be better off talking to our Provost. It was in his study, after all, that the murder took place.'

Ryan let out a thin whine of irritation, which Ray immediately covered up. 'We're aware of your long-standing antagonism with Sir James.'

'Your point is?'

'That you may have personal reasons for directing our attention to him.'

'On the contrary, I have entirely disinterested reasons for wishing to establish the proper jurisdiction for this interview.'

Ray paused, removing a rogue piece of lint from his jacket lapel – his usual tactic for controlling his frustration.

'Respectfully . . .' he began.

Ryan, who had no such tactics of any sort, moved his chair closer to Goodman's. 'Listen to me, you shonky bastard. Stop squirrelling around, or we'll take you down to the station and question you for the rest of the fucking day about that note you sent us with Chiara Belotti's name on it.'

Goodman's face registered shock. He hesitated. 'What makes you think—?'

''Cause Forensics'll match it up with the printer in your office. It was running out of ink.'

'Are you saying—?'

'Interfering with an investigation. Which means you get to help us with our enquiries for the duration. You understand? *For the duration.* Flying tomorrow, were you?'

The skin of Goodman's face stretched tighter. His eyes went bitterly around the room, as if reviewing all the things he still had to do.

'Alright,' he said. 'Be quick. What do you want to know?'

Ray explained. From records in the archives of Lady Margaret Hall, they knew that, ten years earlier, Sophie Barbery had taken weekly tutorials with Goodman on 'Art and Culture of the Arabian Peninsula', one of the options in the 'International Contexts in the Early Modern World' course. Every week, over the eight-week term, she had come to Barnabas to spend an hour with him. They watched him as he listened.

'Tell us about her. What was she like?'

Goodman answered carefully, precisely, with a total lack of emotion. His memory was excellent. Sophie Barbery: always stylishly dressed, cheerful. Frivolous, shallow, thoughtless. A fluent Arabic speaker, obviously. French, too. But minimal interest in Arabic culture, and no interest whatsoever in academic work. Her essays were mediocre, and invariably late. 'A type all too common at Oxford, I'm afraid.'

'Type?'

'International student with money. They treat the university as a sort of finishing school.'

'A party girl?'

'I conjecture, but I don't think I'm wrong.'

'You didn't like her.'

'I'm not paid to like students. But there was something else,' he said, after a moment. 'It comes back to me. I remember thinking, at the time, she was just the sort to get herself into trouble. Not maliciously. Thoughtlessly. She had a carefree, reckless attitude to life.' His mouth curled.

'Sounds like a laugh, to me,' Ryan said.

Ray said, 'Did she come for tutorials alone?'

'No. With another girl, just the same.' He thought a moment. 'Sealy-Smith – that's it. Veronica Sealy-Smith. Isn't that delicious? Tells you all you need to know. Parents owned half of

274

Norfolk. One thing I'm not going to miss, when I leave this place,' he said, 'is the privilege, the snobbery, the unselfconscious entitlement, the—'

'Why didn't you get in touch when her picture went up?' Ryan said.

'I have a good memory for names, none for faces, particularly female ones.'

Ray said, 'Where did your tutorials take place? In your old office? The one the Provost has now?'

'No one uses that room as an office, except temporarily. I used it once for a few weeks, perhaps five years ago. Generally, it's a room for meetings. For as long as I've been here, the Provost's weekly senior management meetings have happened there. And now,' he said, looking at his watch, 'I daresay you've had your money's worth.'

Ray ignored him. 'Did she have any other connections with the college?'

'Not that I know of.'

'Any friends?'

'Ditto.'

'Anyone at Barnabas she might have kept in touch with?'

'See the above. And now we've really run out of time.'

Ryan said, 'We always leave the best questions till the end. Where were you when she was killed?'

Goodman allowed himself a smile. 'A detective sergeant took my statement, along with the others'. It will be on record, if you haven't lost it. I arrived at Burton a little before half past eight and was still there when Sheikh al-Medina left at about ten. I'm not paid to like students, nor even to be nice to them. But I am paid not to kill them.' He stood up, and they noticed for the first time how slightly built he was. Minor tremors wrinkled his taut face. 'My advice to you, if you want to know who killed her, is to find out who she'd thoughtlessly got herself mixed up with.'

And he turned his back on them.

In their office, they sat talking.

'He *was* a shonky bastard, though, wasn't he? Wasn't just me. Ray?'

Ray said nothing, bent to his work. Ryan idly flicked through some spreadsheets of information, produced by Nadim and her team, on Sophie's known contacts. A few minutes passed.

'Didn't you think he was suspicious?'

Ray kept his eyes on his screen. 'He might be a fanatic, he might even be a – what did you call him? – shonky bastard, but he's got no motive we know of. Besides, he has an alibi. Read his statement.'

'Funny, though, all that palaver at the beginning. Normal Oxford Uni bollocks, I thought at first. You know, the manner they got. Then I thought: He really don't want to answer any questions, here.'

Ray made no response. There was silence for a few more minutes.

'We keep doing this, you know.'

Ray reluctantly lifted his head. 'What?'

'Running into dead ends.'

'So, we move on.'

Sighing, Ryan settled to work at last. From time to time, he bickered with Ray – about the connection with Barnabas; about

Dubin's message, *left the gs with ron*; about the coffees and whose turn it was to fetch them. The day dwindled into afternoon, light dimmed in the windowless room and they turned on their desk lamps, throwing shadows into corners, turning the crazy wall into a puzzle of gleam and shade.

Ryan got a call.

'Yeah?'

A voice said, 'You was going to write it on your arm so you wouldn't forget. What did you do, Ryan? Leave your fucking arm at home?'

He made a cartoon face of dismay. 'Jade!'

'Coming back to you, is it?'

'Listen, it's been . . . it's been fucking mad here, all day.' He glanced at Ray, working peacefully. 'I'm coming now.'

'Too late for that, knobhead.'

'What do you mean?'

'I'm not at home.'

'Where are you?'

'Here.'

He stepped outside the office and looked down the corridor to the glass fire door at the end, where Jade stood, glaring at him, with Ryan next to her, waving solemnly.

In the office, Ryan Junior crept into a corner and stared at Ray. His padded blue hooded coat made his arms stick out stiffly from his sides. His straight blond hair, cut pudding-basin style, fell with a soft glow to the tops of his eyes.

'Daddy?'

'What?'

'You can't eat play dough.'

Ryan had a good look at him. 'Have you been eating play dough again?'

'No. Only a bit.'

Ryan caught hold of him as he squirmed, and wiped crumbs from around his mouth. All the time, his son kept his eyes fixed on Ray.

'Daddy,' he said, in a lower voice.

'What now?'

'What's that man called?'

'Him? You've seen him before. That's Ray.'

'Why?'

'What do you mean, *why*? 'Cause it's short for Raymond.'

'Why?'

''Cause it's short for the Great Raymundo. Check out the fancy jacket. He's a part-time model, I think. All the girls love him. Young women, I should say.'

Ray forced his mouth to make a smile shape.

At that moment, Nadim looked in from the corridor and, as soon as she saw Ryan Junior, she began to make a low crooning noise in the back of her throat.

'Oh my God! Aren't you adorable?' Crouching down in front of him, she began to push his hair with her fingertips, and he tolerated it with dignity.

'Daddy?'

'Nadim – that's her name. Not short for anything I know of. It's alright; she just can't help herself. She'll stop in a minute.'

'She's got brown hair.'

'Yeah. Well spotted.'

'Like my mummy's.'

Ryan said nothing to that. Picking his son up, he said, 'Right, we're off, then. Done for the week.'

Ray grunted and Nadim wriggled her fingers in Ryan Junior's face, which appeared over his father's shoulder, and he again tolerated it obligingly. Then they were gone, and Ray and Nadim heard Ryan Junior's piping voice in the corridor: 'She was a funny lady, wasn't she, Daddy?'

'Ray,' Nadim whispered, eyes shining, 'how cute is he?'

Again, Ray grunted.

'Come on, Ray. *Ray!*'

'Yes, alright. Cute.'

With a little huff of dismissal, she left him to his work, and he sat there, thinking of Diane, how she behaved around small children: the way she laughed; the creaking noises she made, like Nadim, in the back of her throat; the way she dipped her nose into their hair; the way she touched their faces with her fingertips, quivering and hesitant, as if afraid to damage them with the intensity of her emotion. Her whole body seemed to glow with it. And he thought, with a sudden slippage inside him, of the agony she would feel if the IVF didn't work.

He wiped his face and stared again at his screen.

At around seven, he called home. 'It's me. I'm sorry, I've got to get a report done for the Super. I'm going to be a couple of hours. Do you want me to pick up a takeaway on my way back?'

She didn't. She was going to go to bed early. He listened to the elusive note in her voice. Tiredness? Disappointment?

'Listen. Once I've finished this evening, I'm free all weekend.

How about we go for a walk, Sunday morning? Apparently, the weather's not going to be too bad. We can go round Boars Hill and have lunch at that pub in Sunningwell.'

She made non-committal noises and rang off, and he sat there blankly again, for a moment, before putting his hands back on the keyboard.

It was late. Outside, there was a faint whine of a siren, then no noise but the tapping of the keys.

THIRTY-FIVE

There was a cold snap on Sunday morning, white frost on Bay-worth roofs melting quickly to a wet sheen, and mist-drenched fields gleaming under a pale late-autumn sun. At the back of the house, bare trees had an old man's stiffness, frozen above a golden liquifying carpet of sodden beech leaves.

Jade called to remind Ryan he had to pick Ryan Junior up from nursery at lunchtime the next day.

'Got that?'

'Course.'

'He'll be at nursery, right. Not here. And lunchtime. You can't be late. If you're late, they won't know what to do with him.'

'Got it.'

'Write it on both arms.'

'I got it, alright? Listen, we got to go now.'

He dressed Ryan in his blue coat, yellow wellingtons and an enormous green bobble-hat which overlaid his head, soft and colourful as a cartoon animal. All the time he was being dressed, Ryan refused to let go of the twigs he had picked from the hedgerow on the other side of the road.

'They're for Mummy, aren't they, Daddy?'

'Yeah. Shall we take a jar to put them in?'

'Yes, please.'

In the car, he sat in his baby seat, waving the twigs, watching the blurring edges of trees as they went down Quarry Road, past the deer farm, into Sunningwell. The car made distressed metallic noises.

'Daddy?'

'What?'

'You shouldn't say "fuck *sake*".'

'Yeah, alright.'

They went banging into picturesque Sunningwell, with its burnt-brick farmhouses, village pond and manor house, attracting disapproving looks from an elderly couple walking their red setter, and pulled up outside St Leonard's. Ryan turned off the engine and, a few seconds later, the banging stopped. He sat there for a moment, his face tense and pale, looking at his son.

'Alright. Here we are.'

They went together through the gate, round the yew tree and past the other graves, until they got to the headstone at the end of the second row.

'There's a jar already!' Ryan squeaked.

His father said nothing, staring. *Michelle Toomey. Departed this life. Beloved.* He didn't like coming. As always, though he tried not to, he remembered the last night at the flat in London, the last moments, Shel's face going blotchy, the fish-white of her eyes, the sweating wax of her skin – not Shel's face at all, not even human – a mask, something washed up on a beach, the naked front of a head. Then the blue light swinging through the window, hands pulling him away. He tried hard to remember her real face and couldn't.

'Daddy? *Daddy?*'

'What?'

'You call Mummy Shel. And her big name's Michelle.'

'That's it. Clever boy.'

'But I call Mummy Mummy, don't I?'

He put down his hand and rested it on his son's enormous bobble-hat. The twigs stood tangled in the jar.

Ray and Diane walked hand in hand through the damp muffle of Youlbury Woods, the only sounds their soft footsteps in the mush of sodden leaves and a mournful solitary crow-bark somewhere in the mist. Ray was wearing his new Gloverall duffel coat, vintage fit, in brushed camel, Diane her old green Barbour. Everything was glassy and quiet. For a while, they talked about the IVF, going over well-known details of cost, timing and probabilities, and at last a mood like loneliness settled on them and they walked on in silence. They climbed up Matthew Arnold's Field between withered clumps of gorse, and continued along Jarn Way, through the lower woods to the Fox Inn and down Lincombe Lane to the fields above the deer farm, where they stood for a moment, looking down at the russet roofs of Sunningwell haphazardly arranged around the church below. Beyond was the Flowing Well pub, and, as they walked down the slope, they began to talk about their lunch.

The deer were gone, perhaps slaughtered for Christmas. They

crossed the road by the pond and Ray stopped suddenly outside the church gate.

'Ray? What is it?'

Diane followed his gaze to a spot in the graveyard where a youth in a tracksuit stood with a little boy. The youth turned, pinching his nose to discharge mucus on the grass, and, as he glanced over with an empty look, he froze in the middle of wiping his hand on his tracksuit bottoms, staring at them violently.

Diane said, 'Ray?'

Ray said, under his breath, 'Oh, Christ.'

They stood under the yew tree, talking, Ryan Junior peering out solemnly from behind Ryan's baggy pants. Introductions were made ('Yeah, Wilkins. Mad, innit?'), but conversation remained awkward, Ryan twitching and fidgeting, Ray making smooth, meaningless noises at the back of his throat, as if about to say goodbye and move on. Diane was transfixed by Ryan Junior; she stared at him, eyes enormous and bright, smiling, lips parted, as he dodged away and peeped out again, pulling on his father's tracksuit sleeve.

'Daddy?'

'Yeah?'

'His name is Ray, isn't it, Daddy?'

'That's it.'

'And his big name is Ray Mund.'

'Yeah, you got it.'

'And, Daddy?'

'Yeah?'

'His biggerest name is Great Ray Mundo.'

Ryan grinned. 'You're the cleverest thing for miles around, you are.'

Finding nothing to add to this, Ray looked around, smiling vacantly at the church with its wonky carved portico, the graveyard with its tilted stones and wooden benches. 'Nice spot,' he said, and wished he hadn't.

'He's not a mole,' Ryan Junior whispered to himself.

Diane crouched down suddenly and put out her hand, and they stared at each other at close range. She said, 'My name's Diane and I'm so pleased to meet you.'

He giggled, as if to excuse such embarrassing behaviour. 'Thank you,' he said politely.

'Your daddy's right,' she said. 'You're very clever.'

Encouraged, he said, in his conversational tone, 'Daddy calls my mummy Shel, and her big name's Michelle, and I call her Mummy,' he said. 'Do you want to see her?'

Ryan gave a twitch, but before he could say anything, Diane said, 'Yes, please. Will you show me?'

'Yes, I will.' He put out a mittened hand and led her away from the path, across the mild tussocks of grass to *Michelle Toomey. Departed this life. Beloved.*

They stood together, looking at the headstone: polished grey granite, its inscription brief, but still crisp and white.

'They're my twigs. But it's not my jar.'

'Beautiful,' Diane said. She could say no more.

Ryan stared up at her. 'She's dead,' he explained, in case she was confused. 'But she's still my mummy, so I can still call her that.'

Diane nodded, wiped her face. Crouching down again, she

breathed deeply, controlling herself. She put her hands on Ryan's arms and squeezed him gently. 'I don't usually tell people this, Ryan. But, a few years ago, I had a baby. And he died. Like your mummy died. But I can still call him mine, can't I?'

The little boy stared with intense interest at the tears sliding down her face. He felt an urge to touch them, but restrained himself. 'Don't be sad,' he said. 'He loves you very much. That makes you happy.'

Under the yew tree, Ryan said to Ray, 'Don't really want to talk about it.'

'I understand.'

'Overdose, if you want to know. Methamphetamine.' He sneered suddenly, feeling the dry-snot prickle of tears in his eyes, and turned away.

Ray said, 'Christ, Ryan. I'm sorry. Really.'

Diane and Ryan Junior came back to them out of the long grass, and Diane went up to Ryan and hugged him silently for what seemed like a long time, while he twitched and muttered.

'So,' she said, disentangling herself at last and speaking briskly, 'how are you getting on with the Great Raymundo?'

Ryan nodded and shrugged.

Ray made ambiguous noises.

'Playing nicely together?'

Ryan sniffed and wiped his nose. 'Thing is, I got into a bit of bother with this guy at the college. Real prick, to be honest with you. So, there's this whole misconduct thing going on. Anyway, Ray's going to speak up, so we'll see where we are after that.'

Diane glanced coldly at Ray, who grimaced at her, tight-lipped.

'And are you going to find out who killed this woman?' she asked.

'Sure. Yeah. Always the same, really. Get fuck all done the first few weeks, then it sort of falls into place.

'Daddy!'

'Sorry.'

'Well,' Diane said, 'that's a philosophy.'

'So I'm told.'

'I hope the Great Raymundo's pulling his weight.'

Ray smiled weakly and they looked together at Ryan, whose face had gone blank.

'Ryan?'

He stared back without seeing them, lost in that sensation like fainting, the soft paralysis in the last few buzzing seconds as consciousness begins to dissolve and everything disappears except for the last ideas ever to be thought.

That Ray is short for Raymond and Shel is short for Michelle.

His eyes were glazed. They could hear him breathing heavily through his nose and Diane thought he might be having some sort of seizure; she put her hand on Ray's arm just as Ryan lurched forward and grabbed Ray's coat.

'Fuck's sake, Ray!'

'Mind the toggles!'

Ryan Junior said, 'Daddy, you shouldn't—'

'*Veronica Sealy-Smith!*'

Ray avoided Ryan's manic face as he tried to prise his fingers off his toggles. 'What are you talking about?'

'Ron! Short for Veronica!'

Ray stopped struggling. 'Left the Gs with Ron! You don't think . . . ?'

'Could be, couldn't it? Friend of hers, that squirrel said. Where's she been living since getting kicked out of her own place? With a mate from college – why not? What do you think?'

Ray even forgot to check his toggles, now that Ryan had let go of them; they started to talk over the top of each other until Diane intervened.

Ray explained.

She said, 'If Ron is short for Veronica, you'll have to thank Ryan, here, for putting the idea into his daddy's head.'

They all looked at him and he put his mittens over his eyes.

His father said, 'Ry, mate, you're brilliant.'

'You're welcome,' he said. 'But, Daddy, you shouldn't say—'

'Yeah, alright, I'll stop. Promise. But, seriously, you're the dog's bollocks.'

THIRTY-SIX

Veronica Sealy-Smith, a name easy to trace, had an apartment near Sloane Square. But, next morning, just as Ryan and Ray were setting off, they were pulled into the Superintendent's office.

'News from Barnabas.'

'What's up?'

'There's been a theft from the college collection. A Koran.'

The inventory drawn up by Goodman at the end of his tenure had been checked and the Koran was found to be missing. Sir James had been informed, his disbelief rapidly turning to outrage.

'He's been on the phone to me twice already,' the Super said. 'The first time, he told me its market value's two million; the second time, three point five. Irreplaceable, he says. And a high-profile issue in UK–Saudi relations.'

'There's a security angle, too,' Ray said. 'I bet that's on his mind. Keys to the collections room are kept, like the others, in the bursary – pretty much available to anyone. Insurance will take a view about that.'

'Yes. I think that's what frightens Sir James the most.'

'And Goodman?' Ray asked. 'What does he say?'

'Goodman flew to Abu Dhabi last night. Brought his flight forward at the last minute.'

There was a pause.

'Christ,' Ryan said. 'The dodgeball's nicked it.'

'That's Sir James's view, too. Expressed almost the same way. He thinks Goodman plans to sell it – or even give it – to people over there. He's always wanted to liberate it, as he put it. We're working with the authorities in the UAE, but they haven't made contact with Goodman yet.' She looked at them. 'What do you know about this Koran?'

They told her. She said, 'Could it be connected in any way to the murder?'

They went silent.

'In any case,' she said, 'if there's no connection, it needs to be ruled out. Ray, I want you in college today, leading on the theft. Ryan, make the trip to London on your own. Keep in touch, though. I want constant coordination.'

Sloane Avenue, mid-morning. After an argument with an attendant dressed in a velvet green coat and top hat, like an historical character ('Don't you have any dignity, mate?'), Ryan left the Peugeot in a reserved spot in the Chelsea Cloisters car park and went – tracksuit flapping, trainers squeaking – into the moneyed hush of the lobby, a gleaming room of stylish angles, in black and white squares, simplistic as Ryan's Lego set. There was an atmosphere of exclusivity, effortless certainty. As usual, it made him angry. As he swaggered through, the concierge called to him from behind her desk in increasing agitation – 'Excuse me, sir! Excuse me!' – but he ignored her and went into the chrome-plated lift, sneering at himself in the mirror. He zipped his tracksuit up to his chin, rolled the collar and pulled his baseball cap round to the back. Bared his gums, checked his teeth.

Veronica Sealy-Smith lived in a million-pound one-bedroom apartment on the sixth floor. She stood in its doorway while he fished in his trackie bottoms for his badge. 'You're a *policeman?*' She had a round face and a loose lower lip, and dimples when she pouted. Her torn denim shorts, elasticated sports top and strappy wedge sandals gave her a casual, almost childish air.

She shrugged and he followed her inside.

The apartment was sleek – all white decor and furnishings, and stripped pine floors – but tiny, not much bigger than the trailer he'd grown up in, and it was a shambles, with laundry lumped against walls, and magazines in slipshod piles on spindle-legged coffee tables that looked as if they ought to be in a museum of modern design. Veronica Sealy-Smith was sleek and messy too, her slow eyes puzzled but half-amused, as if he were an unexpected aberration she could laugh about with friends later. They perched, knees almost touching, on black metal chairs in the small-paned bay window, which offered a fragmented view of the ocean-liner-sized roofs beyond.

His mistake was to assume she knew about Sophie's death. She made a noise like the gulp-choke of vomiting.

'Oh, Christ, I'm sorry. I thought you must've heard.'

Her face crumpled like a paper bag, all her shine came off and she wept, loud and wet, into her hands.

Embarrassed, Ryan went into the kitchen and got her a glass

291

of water, and she sat there, holding it as if she'd never seen one before, staring with brimming eyes while he explained what had happened.

'I knew she was going through a bad time, but . . .'

He gave her a moment to settle down.

'Listen,' he said, 'I have to ask you some questions. Can I do that?'

'Okay.'

She began to talk without his questions, in fact: she had a need to talk. She'd met Sophie at a freshers' ball when they were both new undergraduates at Lady Margaret Hall, just eighteen years old, and found they shared tastes in music, drink, boys and clothes. In their second year, they also shared a suite of rooms in college and, out of term, went on holidays together, to the Seychelles, the Maldives, Martha's Vineyard. By their third year, they were camping out together in Norfolk almost every weekend, at Veronica's family home. After that, for a year or so, they stayed close; they had the same friends, found themselves at the same places, went to the same parties.

'We were good-looking and clever – or at least well educated. And we were silly and rich.' She looked at him. 'Don't think we didn't know it. We just sort of played up to it. We were young.' She gave a broken smile. 'It seems so long ago.'

'She liked to party.'

'Yes, she liked to party. To drink, meet boys, go wild.'

'Was she reckless?'

'Yes. Yes, she was. But not frivolous. There's a difference.' She blew her nose. 'I don't know how much you know about her early life, but, when she was six years old, in Syria, she saw her grandfather killed. I mean, saw it happen in front of her. For years, her mother was ill. Ovarian cancer. The family went into exile, had to leave Syria literally in the middle of the night. You know her father was assassinated?'

'Yeah, I read that.'

'At the second attempt. The first attempt was when Sophie was seventeen – she was in the house when it happened. By the time I met her, she was desperate for fun.' She sat with the wet tissue in her hand, remembering. 'So, we had fun.'

She glanced away, through the window, a distracted, lost look.

'In a way,' she said, 'fun was something she hid behind. Actually, my favourite times were just hanging out on our own. It took me a while to really get to know her. After what she'd been through, she was very guarded. But she was really a very thoughtful person. And tough. Not kind, particularly. I think she was too serious to be kind. A survivor. I can't believe that, after all she'd been through, this could happen to her.'

'You said she was reckless, earlier. How?'

'Boys. She was so gorgeous, they just fell into the street.'

'What sort of boys?'

'Naughty ones, usually. In fact, exclusively. She said herself she had the worst taste in men of anyone she knew.'

'What about recently?'

'There were men, for sure. But I didn't keep up.' Her lip trembled. 'We didn't have that sort of relationship any more. Not that long after leaving uni, we went our own ways. For a few years, I was living abroad. When I came back, I moved in different circles.'

'She got back in touch, though.'

'Maybe a year ago. They'd finally managed to kill her father. She had money problems – serious ones. She wasn't used to that.'

'So she asked you for help?'

'Not directly. She would never do that. But she was obviously finding things hard. I loaned her some money to pay a few bills. Occasionally, she crashed here. She used it informally as an address. But we didn't get close again. I thought she'd changed, to be honest. She'd become harsher, more demanding.'

'Did she tell you what she was up to? With the modelling?'

'No. And –' she faltered – 'I didn't ask. I suppose I didn't want to find out.'

'Did she tell you anything about going into Barnabas Hall that night?'

'No.'

'But some money arrived for her.'

'An envelope, left in the lobby. It happened, from time to time. As I say, I didn't ask. I just kept it for her.'

'How often did you talk to her?'

'Once a month, maybe.'

'When was the last time?'

'Three weeks ago.'

'She talk about men?'

'Not much. I can give you the odd name she mentioned in passing, but I don't know anything about them.'

'Any stuff of hers here? Laptop, iPad, spare phone?'

'Nothing like that. A few clothes. Some stuff through the post.' She waved a hand at a small table at the end of the hall. Her mouth trembled again. 'You know what? She'd become a sad person and I didn't want to admit it.'

There wasn't much on the hallway table: a couple of unmarked envelopes containing cash; a few payment reminders from utility companies, forwarded from her old flat; flyers for beauty products, clubs, holiday homes, taxi companies.

One of the flyers caught his eye. It advertised a 'Purple Night' at a club called Wire, and someone had scribbled on it, *Why not?*

He went back to Veronica. 'This a club she used to go to?'

She looked at it, shrugged.

'Someone's written a personal message on it.'

'Could be from Hassan,' she said, after a moment. 'He was one of the guys she mentioned from time to time. I thought that was over, though.'

'Who is he?'

'He owns clubs – maybe Wire. Perhaps he was trying his luck again.'

'A naughty boy?'

'I don't know. He reminded her of home, I think.'

'Home?'

'Syria.'

Ryan raised his eyebrows. 'Interesting. Why'd they split?'

'I don't know.'

He put the flyer in his pocket and gave her his card. 'Anything else comes to you, give us a bell.'

She looked at him bleakly. 'Don't you have to do paperwork or something?'

'That's just for the bobbleheads.'

She had started to cry again.

He stood at the door, feeling awkward. 'We'll get whoever did it.' His voice was all grit and phlegm.

'Don't they all say that?'

'Yeah. But I fucking well mean it.'

Her eyes were glittery and narrow as he left.

In the elevator, he spoke to Ray.

'Got something, maybe. Don't know. Club called Wire, down near Smithfield. Guy there runs it, called Hassan, maybe had a thing with her. It's not far; might as well check him out, while I'm here. How're you doing up there?'

'I'm in the car, actually, just coming into London. Goodman's got a flat in the Barbican Centre. I'm on way to meet a friend of his there.'

'Right next to Smithfield. I'll give you a wave, if we pass each other in the street.'

The elevator doors let him out into the showroom-like lobby and he squeaked across the gleaming floor. As the receptionist called out to him again, he gave her the finger and went on towards the car park.

THIRTY-SEVEN

The club was in Long Lane, the only public sign of it a scruffy black London-weathered door, wedged between a sushi bar and an estate agent. A handwritten card next to a keypad and buzzer said *Wire*. Someone had left the door ajar. Inside was an elevator with only one destination, labelled *Wet Rock Inc.*

The lift wasn't working. As he climbed the stairs, the muffled banging of music from above grew louder, leaping into sudden definition like a wave of heat as he opened the door into a large low-ceilinged room with blacked-out windows. There was a long bar across its width and, behind, a raised stage of poles and mirrors, dimly lit, like a fish tank, where three girls in G-strings moved wearily through a sequence of gyrations to the beat of unidentifiable hip-hop. They were being watched, without interest, by the small lunchtime crowd – a few men drinking on stools at the front, and others sitting in booths round the outside.

At the bar, they said Hassan wasn't available. Ryan fished out his badge.

'Tell him to make himself available.'

One guy went off; another stayed behind, curling his lip.

'And you can get me a drink, while I'm waiting. Grapefruit juice, no ice.'

The lip curled a bit more. He took his drink to a booth and sat down to wait. Televisions high up in the corners of the room showed a news report of a bombed foreign city, smoke rising from collapsed buildings. Lower down on the walls were framed black and white signed photographs of men he took to be wannabe celebrities, acting surly for the camera, with their arms around girls. He briefly closed his eyes. The music took him back to other venues, clubs and raves he'd gone to when he was young, and, for a few moments, he saw not the booths, photographs and fish-tank stage of Wire, but places long ago, and Shel swishing her arms in the air in front of him, head swinging from side to side, that rapturous expression on her face. He remembered when, like her, he believed such moments would never end; and he remembered, later, when he didn't believe it any more, though Shel went on dancing. Then he opened his eyes again and took a sip of grapefruit juice, and the women on stage continued with their routine.

Hassan did not appear.

But Ryan found him in the photographs on the walls: a man so obviously the proprietor, surrounded by deferential looks. He had a hard, unshaven jaw, hair stiffened to a crest and a wide, white smile. He wore dark suits and white T-shirts. In the lobe of his right ear, a stud. In picture after picture, he could be seen jokily arm-wrestling hip-hop guys in booths, clasping hands with withered rockers, playing escort to sultry divas and daddy to his nervous, adoring dancing girls. In one, he was surrounded by so many, he seemed like a sultan in his harem.

Ryan stopped, leaned in to the picture. On Hassan's arm was Sophie Barbery.

It was definitely her, but different. She was sharing a joke with Hassan, half-turned towards him, laughing, her face tilted and wide open, and the people standing behind – girls and bar staff – were peering forward and laughing with her. After the photo of her dead face in the morgue, the soft-porn photos in the Provost's study, it shocked him to see her so spontaneous and carefree. Her hair had fallen back, exposing an ear, small and vulnerable as an unshelled creature.

He was about to turn away when he recognised someone else in the photo and his heart skipped a beat. She was standing at the end of the back row, also leaning forward to look at Sophie, but not laughing. On the contrary, she was staring at her with unmistakable hatred.

'Fuck me,' he said out loud.

It was Ameena Najib.

Then he was on the phone to Ray. 'No, I'm telling you, it's definitely her . . . No, I don't think they all look the same . . . Yeah, giving Sophie a look like she wanted to fucking well do her in . . . I've no idea . . . No, I'm not making a mistake . . . In the club; I'm looking at it now . . . Tell you what, I'll go get a screwdriver, take it off the wall and bring it home – how about that? Will that do you?'

Glancing round, he caught sight of two men at the bar. They were tall and stocky, their looks vaguely Middle Eastern, wearing black leather jackets and bandanas. They turned together in his direction and he saw that the taller of the two had a lazy eye.

'Hang on,' he said. 'This is interesting. Listen, got to go.'

Ray sat in a queue in Farringdon Street, staring at his phone. After a moment, he called Ryan back. No answer. The traffic shunted slowly through Clerkenwell, past converted brick warehouses and boutique shops, while he replayed the conversation in his head. *This is interesting?* He was about to try him again when, coincidentally, a call came through from Central, someone else wanting to speak to DI Ryan Wilkins – a woman from South Oxford Play Scheme. Would he take a message? He barely listened while she explained that no one had appeared to collect Ryan Junior from the nursery and that he was now being picked up by his grandparents.

Ray cut her off. 'Fine, I'll let him know.'

Calling Nadim, he explained: 'I need an address. A club called Wire, near Smithfield Market. And a spot on Ryan.'

She gave him the info and he blue-lighted the car and swung down Charterhouse Street.

'Problem?' she asked.

'Don't know yet. You know what he's like. I'm not so worried he's in trouble as causing trouble for someone else.'

Ryan reached the bar. 'Hello. Jihadi boys, innit?' He had to shout over the din of the music.

The two men stood close up to him, saying nothing, staring. They were nervous, keyed up. The smaller one did something crunchy with his jaw. The bar staff edged away.

'Remember me? Seen you outside Ameena's.'

He fished deep in his trackie pockets and pushed his badge in their faces.

'Glad we hooked up again. You can take me to Hassan. I been waiting.'

They exchanged glances and the one with the lazy eye gave a nod; they all turned together and went down the side of the bar, to a fire door at the back and out to a staircase.

The man with the lazy eye indicated upwards.

'After you,' Ryan said.

The man shrugged and went up the steps, followed by the other man, followed by Ryan, scowling and brooding. He knew he shouldn't get angry, but he could feel it in his body. He was angry with these two men who said nothing, angry with their friend Ameena Najib, angry with himself for not bringing the Glock. Behind that, other, older angers reared up, as usual.

At the top of the stairs was another door. The two men murmured to each other.

Ryan said, 'Can we speed it up a bit?'

The tall man opened the door on to a long stretch of empty roof, as the other man turned sharply and whacked Ryan across his face.

Ray left his car in the NCP car park at the Barbican and walked in the mild, damp breeze, which smelled somehow of the sea, even so deep in the city, up Aldersgate Street, into Cloth Street and along Long Lane, past hair salons and sushi bars to a plain black door, whitened by age. He rang the buzzer. No answer. The door didn't open.

Parked at an angle on the pavement outside was Ryan's Peugeot, with a yellow ticket under a wiper.

Ray called Nadim.

'He's in there somewhere,' she said.

'The point is, I can't get in. Can you get a number and attract their attention?'

He leaned on the buzzer again. No reaction. He stepped back to the edge of the pavement and looked up at the building, and, as he did, a man approached the door and began to punch in a code. Ray hustled forward.

'Members only, pal,' the man said, and Ray flashed his badge. The man changed his mind about the club and backed away down the street.

Inside the entrance was an elevator, and Ray pressed the button and waited.

Nothing happened. He looked at his watch, waited a bit longer, then pressed the button again. Nothing. Sighing, he went through a fire-escape door and began to trudge up the stairs.

Spilled across the rooftop like garbage, Ryan rolled back the opposite way – something he'd learned at kick-boxing, fifteen years earlier – and bounced on to his feet, and took another blow across the face and went down again. He tasted dirt and blood. Out of nowhere, a memory came to him of rolling on the lino of the trailer while his father stamped on him, and he felt again the shame, not of the pain, but of the way the wet slop of brew from his father's jug slathered his face. He took a boot in the ribs, it sent him slithering backwards and he put out a hand to stop himself colliding with a raised glass skylight, and hauled himself up again, panting and squinting. As the tall guy swung towards him, he ducked into him, punching low and hard to the groin, and leaned back, kicking upwards. Turning, he lost sight of the other guy, who took his legs out and he went down again, briefly, and was hauled up from behind. The tall guy hit him twice as he hung there, dazed, head sagging. His arms were behind his back. He was in pain. His vision cleared enough for him to see the London skyline jiggling faintly ahead and to watch as the tall guy retreated, picked a metal rod off the ground, and came back towards him.

Ray climbed the final flight of steps and paused a moment to get his breath back. Instinctively, he buttoned up his jacket – an American wool-blend sport coat – brushed a lapel. As he moved towards the club entrance, his phone went and he paused again to answer it.

'Babe.'

'Just checking in. How are you doing?'

'I'm fine. Down in London.'

'Much going on?'

'I'm about to find out.'

'Where are you? I can hear music.'

'Just at this place.'

'Okay. Talk to you later. Love you.'

'Love you, too.'

Standing in the stairwell, he called Ryan again, got no answer and put his phone away. Sighing, he gave a little tug to each of the sleeves of his jacket and entered the club. The music blared.

No one paid him any attention. He scanned the room, going

slowly between the tables towards the bar. There was no one there. He waited a moment, then went round the bar, looking about him. The music played, the girls danced on, the men sat, bored, in the booths.

He called Nadim again. 'I can't see him anywhere. Are you sure he's here?'

'In the building somewhere.'

He sighed. 'Why does he have to be so awkward?'

Then there was a sudden crash of glass somewhere and he jolted round and ran through a nearby fire door.

Ryan dodged as the man swung and missed a second time, smashing into the skylight again, and he butted the guy holding him with the back of his head and dragged himself free. One of his eyes had closed up; he saw the men flatly, as if at a distance, as they came across the roof towards him.

'Tell you what,' he said. 'Why don't we call it a draw?'

Then they were struggling together in confusion, their movements jerky and ill fitting, like a badly edited video. There was no space for him to kick out. He took an elbow in the nose and felt it burst, and his legs were kicked away. On his knees again, face in the concrete, he gasped for air. More dirt, more blood. Another kick flattened him out and he lay winded on the ground, curled in pain like a prawn, knowing he couldn't get up.

The two men were speaking angrily to each other. Even one-eyed and dizzy, he noticed little things – the accusation in their voices, the panic in their faces. They were frightened of what they were about to do. One of them stepped up and stood over him, still arguing as he pulled something glittery out of his belt with a snicking sound; then there was the sudden hollow bang of a door beyond, and the man pivoted away wide-eyed.

Ryan croaked as he tried to call out. He vomited a little blood and his head cleared.

When he got to his feet, he saw Ray was sparring with the two men at once, dancing on his toes, feinting and jabbing. Ryan picked up the metal rod, walked over and, taking it in both hands like a golf club, swung it into the back of the head of one of the men, who went down with a slap, like steak on a slab, and lay flat on the ground. Distracted, the other man let Ray punch him in the eyes and he fell too, arms flailing, on top of his friend. Ryan gave him a whack and then he was still.

For a long moment, there was only the noise of breathing, ragged and harsh, as Ryan and Ray crouched with their hands on their knees, staring at each other.

'They started it,' Ryan said.

Ray made a non-committal noise.

'Just in case you get asked. You know, by the IOPC.' He put his fingers up to his face and felt around. 'My nose is completely fucked.'

'Don't worry. It's not your best feature.' Ray was preoccupied with his jacket sleeve, which had suffered some damage.

One of the men on the ground started to groan and Ryan nodded at them. 'You going to cuff them, then?'

'What makes you think I've got cuffs?'

'Well, I haven't got any cuffs.'

'Use your shoelaces, then.'

'What about *your* fucking shoelaces?'

Ray lifted a foot to show Ryan his slip-on Chelseas – a Jack and Jones classic ankle boot, in tan – and Ryan began to unlace his Adidas.

'By the way,' he said.

'What?'

'Thanks. I thought maybe I was going to get my second wind. Then I thought maybe I wasn't.'

When he had finished with his knots, Ryan nodded at the trussed men. 'Let's see what we can get out of them before the bobbleheads get here. I saw these two at Ameena Najib's.'

He stood over the bigger of the two men and spoke clearly and loudly, as to a deaf person. 'Do you speak English? What's been going on? Hey, Abdul, I'm talking to you. What's the deal with Ameena Najib? Hello?'

The man stared at him with bloodshot eyes. 'Go fuck yourself.'

'Some sort of jihadi thing, is it?'

The man stared contemptuously at Ryan, who poked him suddenly in the eye, and he fell back with a scream.

'Sorry about that. Thing is, I've got issues. Anger management. Ray'll tell you. Ray?'

'It's true,' Ray said, with complete sincerity. 'He's a psychopath.'

The man's face began to buckle.

'Anyway, Ameena Najib.'

The man tried to scrabble away and Ryan put his foot on his throat.

'Ray? How long we got?'

'Ten minutes. Maybe more.'

'That's a long time to have to put up with this sort of thing.'

He stamped hard on the man's hand and heard a finger break, and the man howled again.

'Ameena Najib,' he said in the man's ear.

He put his foot on his other hand and the man spoke suddenly, a wail of grief.

'Speak English!' Ryan said.

The other man said, in a desperate blurt, 'He says we should have left her in the fucking mountains.'

Ryan sat back and looked at Ray.

There was a furious exchange in Arabic between the two men.

Ray said to Ryan, 'Wait. They're not terrorists. She's not their friend. You've made a mistake. These are the traffickers who brought her out of Syria.'

'We helped her!' the man shouted. 'And the bitch was threatening us!'

Ray said to Ryan, 'Did you read the file?'

'Not in detail. Long journey, I remember that.'

'Six months on the road. Don't know how many started, but most died on the way. I think her sister was one of them. Only a child. They dumped her body.' He looked at the two men lying on the ground. 'God knows what they did to her, after they got her here.'

'What do you mean?'

'They usually put the women to work.'

Ryan's breathing got out of whack. His eyes went funny. He saw his own sister rolling on the bit of shrivelled carpet at the back end of the caravan, Shel lying in the flat like a discarded mannequin, and he felt again the nausea of fear, a rising vomit of rage. Adrenaline rushed back and he flooded. He grabbed the iron bar and Ray jumped up and grappled with him.

'Ryan! Enough! What are you doing? Ryan?'

307

Ryan's face was blind shut as they struggled together, while the terrified men on the ground shuffled away as best they could. Then there was the hollow bang of a metal door and footsteps echoing on the rooftop as the support team ran towards them. They came apart, and Ryan tore himself out of Ray's grip and went across the roof, through the door and down the stairs.

THIRTY-EIGHT

They drove up Saffron Hill into Warner Street and across to Gray's Inn Road, heading north in erratic bursts through stationary traffic.

'Christ,' Ray said, holding on to the door. 'Do you always drive like this?'

'It's the car. You got to keep it above fifty.'

'There's a speed limit.'

'Battery goes, if you don't. Do you want us to break down or not?'

They got on to Euston Road, lurching westward through red lights and streams of oncoming black cabs, Ryan leaning on the horn and making violent gestures out of the window. On the Westway, they went faster and the engine began to bang.

'We should've gone back to my car,' Ray said.

'Too slow. Mine was right outside.'

'You shouldn't even be driving, with an eye like that.'

'I like it. Everything's a blur.'

The engine revved and banged, and Ray was thrown from side to side as they pushed and shunted ahead.

'I thought you were going to kill them, back there.'

'I was going to kill them.'

They came down the overpass at White City and speeded up again, talking about Ameena. When she had told Ryan she didn't recognise the dead woman, she had been lying. She'd known exactly who Sophie was: the girlfriend of the guy who trafficked her, who put her to work in his clubs.

Ryan said, 'You saw her expression in that photo from the club.' He jerked his head towards the back seat where it lay, still in its frame, slightly damaged from when he'd pulled it from the wall. 'She knew her. Looks to me like she hated her, too.'

'All this time, we've been assuming the perp's a man.'

''Cause of the strength involved, right? We should've thought more about the rage.'

They exchanged looks.

Ray called Barnabas and told Claire they were coming in to talk to Ameena. 'Tell her not to leave college before we get there.'

Ryan put his foot down. 'There's a gap in her file. Those ten months in the UK, for a start. I asked her about them, but she wouldn't say anything.'

Ray thought about that. 'Nadim couldn't find anything either. Any ongoing case Ameena's involved in as a refugee will be sealed.' After a moment, he said he knew someone high up in Asylum and Protection at the Home Office. 'I was at college with her.'

'No surprise there. You was at college with everyone, Ray-mundo.'

Ray made the call and left a message, and they drove out of London through the pebble-dash of Acton, the grey-slick trees of

Perivale, the windswept plain of Northolt, thinking about Ameena Najib and how much she must have hated Sophie Barbery.

Forty miles away, Ryan Junior sat in his coat and mittens on the linoleum floor of a trailer, watching the man in the chair. The man was staring at him. He had eyes like an animal, watchful and unkind. Occasionally, he drank from a plastic jug, but the animal's eyes never stopped watching, not even when the jug was lifted to his face. Over by the sink, an old woman was crying. At his nursery, Ryan had been told that she was his grandmother, but he didn't know why she was crying now. She made a grizzling noise like a frying pan.

He didn't know who the man was.

He didn't know where his daddy was, or Auntie Jade.

He didn't know where he was either, and he didn't like it. There was a smell like a toilet smell coming from the man's jug. It made Ryan's mouth quiver like it did when he was going to cry, though he struggled against it.

The woman was murmuring and hiccupping, saying something to the man about just wanting to see somebody, and, although he didn't understand her words, he felt he ought to know what the noise of them meant. The man didn't say anything at all. The animal's eyes stared at him and Ryan's lips quivered and the woman carried on making her noise, and finally he understood what her noise meant. It meant she was frightened of the man. His mouth finally buckled.

Through the Chiltern Gap, they swept down the long slow bob-sleigh curve of the M40 on to the plain beyond and went past fields streaked with shadows under the low sun. Ray got a call from the UAE to tell him that Goodman's journey had been traced as far as al-Ain, on the border with Oman, to which he had driven in a car hired in Abu Dhabi. A reservation for the following three nights had been made in his name at a hotel in Abu Dhabi, site of the Zayed Mosque.

Ray said, 'Al-Medina has a home in al-Ain.'

'Dodgy as fuck. Knew it.'

Then the call came in from Ray's friend at the Home Office, and they listened to her on speakerphone as they drove through the gathering dark towards the faint amber blush of Oxford.

It was a story of almost unrelieved distress. Ameena's father had paid a little over thirteen million Syrian pounds, to men he had never met before, to take his daughters – Ameena, aged twenty-two, and Anushka, thirteen – out of Syria, to the UK. His three sons were no longer alive. The two girls left Aleppo in a minibus, crossed the border into Turkey at Kilis, and travelled non-stop along the coast to Antalya to pick up the faster route, through Denizli, to the western port of Izmir. There, they waited for a month. Anushka fell ill and they ran out of money, borrowing some from the men who travelled with them, which came with certain conditions. At last, they attempted the sea crossing to mainland Greece. Twenty people set out in an inflatable dingy; five came ashore at a rocky beach a mile south of a village called Kymi. There, they waited another month, sleeping in caves. Ameena and Anushka ran out of money again, and more was borrowed, with more conditions. Anushka was ill a second time and, a few days after they began to travel again, she died; her body was left behind in the mountains above Berat, in Albania.

Three of the original party remained, but they were joined by others along the way, travelling in a succession of trucks through Montenegro, Bosnia, Austria, Germany and on to Calais, in France. At last, they arrived in the UK, where Ameena was told how much she owed the men who had brought her and was put to work in various clubs in London, an illegal immigrant in a city patrolled by vans bearing the slogan *Go Home or Face Arrest*, and told never ever to make an attempt to contact the authorities. Most girls, the authorities estimated, never did. But Ameena, it seemed, was different. Ten months after arriving in London, she turned up one morning at the offices of Refugee Action in Belgrave Road, wearing a man's overcoat over a nightdress, and was taken to a safe house while her case was evaluated by the Home Office.

Ray asked about the owner of the clubs.

Hassan Awad was thirty-four years old, a Syrian national with a British passport, domiciled in London for the past seven years. He owned three clubs and two 'entertainments businesses' at the sleazy end of the market. Twice, he had been investigated for serious fraud, once for drug trafficking, and Interpol has also been involved in investigating his activities. For the last six months, he had been the subject of an investigation into human trafficking, led by the National Crime Agency, but it had run into technical difficulties and it seemed unlikely charges would be brought.

'Ameena testified?'

'Yes, she did. Very bravely. We're certain she was subject to intimidation.'

'But nothing's going to happen?'

There was a pause. 'I'm afraid not.'

Ryan said, 'I read she was put on a watch list.'

There was another pause. 'Yes, that's correct. We fear she may have become radicalised.'

'Well, what the fuck did you expect?' Ryan said, and Ray finished the call before he could say any more.

They drove on, past Sandhills and the park and ride.

'What do you think happened, Ray?'

'If she came across Sophie in college that night?'

'The trafficker head-honcho's girlfriend. Suddenly there.'

'A million-to-one chance of it happening.'

'Bit of a shock.'

'As if God put her there.'

'We've seen what she's like when she loses it.'

'You think she saw her, followed her to the lodge, confronted her?'

'Motive, means, opportunity, Ray. We know she went to the lodge. Suppose she thinks to herself she'll just tell Sophie how God's going to judge her and her slaver boyfriend. There's an argument, it gets out of hand. All that rage.'

'Didn't you say she was at the lodge at eight? Too early for the murder.'

'Eight-ish. Only person corroborating that, though, is Jason. And he's a muppet. Suppose he was twenty minutes out? And Forensics said themselves that ETD's not definite.'

They drove through St Clement's. Ryan opened the glove compartment and fumbled out a pair of zip cuffs.

'I've used up my laces already, so you better have these.'

'We're not going to need cuffs.'

'You've seen her when she gets angry.'

'When we get there,' Ray said, 'just let me do the talking.'

Three miles away, Ryan Junior began to sob. He didn't want to, he tried to stop it, but sobs filled him like giant hiccups and made it hard to breathe. The old woman lay on the floor, where she'd fallen after the man had hit her. Her face was wet and red. She'd raised one arm, and held it there, now, as if she couldn't remember what she'd been going to do with it. The man stood, swaying, above her. Ryan stopped looking at the man's eyes and looked at his hands instead, twisted and raw, like clumps of roots.

He could smell the jug, but he couldn't see it any more; it had fallen out of sight.

His words came out with the sobs: 'I . . . want my . . . daddy.'

The man's hands swung big and low as he turned. 'I'll give you your fucking daddy.'

The sobs jerked him hard. 'You . . . shouldn't say . . . *fucking*.'

The man came towards him.

They drove up the High Street.

'What do you mean, *why*?' Ray said. 'Because we need to be calm.'

'I can be calm.'

'You weren't calm back there. You were going to kill those men with a metal bar – you said so yourself.'

'Nah, I was just fucking with you.'

'You've got to control yourself.'

'Funny, that's what the Bishop said when I was going to throw him off the top of Salisbury Cathedral.'

315

Ray looked at him.

'I'm fucking with you again.' He drove on. 'Couldn't even get him up the stairs,' he said. 'Too heavy.'

They waited at the pelican crossing by St Mary's and Ray said, 'By the way, nearly forgot, there was a message for you earlier, from a playgroup, about Ryan. You were meant to pick him up.'

Ryan stared at him. 'Why didn't you tell me before?'

'Well, for one thing, I was busy saving your life and—'

'Fuck!'

'Calm down, it's okay. They said his grandparents were picking him up.'

Ryan slammed on the brakes and Ray's head hit the windscreen.

'What did you say?' Ryan's voice was different – loud and curt.

Ray stared at him. 'That his grandparents were—'

He was flung sideways as Ryan swung the car on to the opposite side of the road and floored the accelerator.

'Ryan!'

They screamed between cars, horn blaring, and shot through a red light at the top of St Aldates, scattering pedestrians.

'*Ryan!*'

They went past the end of Blue Boar Street and, a few seconds later, the police station, picking up speed all the time, other cars pulling up on to the pavements to get out of the way, and Ray held on to the door, yelling at him.

'What's going on?'

'His grandad's a psychopath. He's more likely to kill him than look after him.'

Ray opened his mouth, and closed it again when he saw Ryan's face. They roared, banging, down the Abingdon Road, mainly on the wrong side. Ray finally fumbled the blue light on to the roof and called for backup. As they swung, screeching, round the bend at the bottom of the road, his phone rang.

'Babe, I'll call you back.'

'I'm out shopping, I thought I'd ... I can hear the siren. Where are you?'

Ryan shouted, 'We're here!'

Ray said quickly, 'Hinksey Point. There's a bad situation. It's Ryan, his son. Later.'

Then they were going over Redbridge and swinging into the trailer park entrance, slithering to a stop.

THIRTY-NINE

Ryan ran, and Ray ran after him, along the tarmac between trailers. Kids sitting on motorbikes watched them pass; one of them shouted something about the FBI. On the ring road above, headlight beams raked the dark sky.

Ryan ran in a panic, fighting his tracksuit, which swung sluggishly around him. His unlaced trainers flew off. He thrashed on, moaning to himself, till he reached the trailer and flung himself on the locked door, beating on it, shouting. Inside, there was a high-pitched wail, immediately smothered, and he banged again, tugging at the door, clubbing it with his hands and arms.

Ray reached him. 'Police!' he called. 'Open the door!'

For a moment, there was silence inside, then a single piercing cry: 'Daddy!'

'*Ry! Ryan!*' Ryan beat wildly on the door, which would not open.

A small crowd of people gathered round, watching silently.

Together, Ray and Ryan heaved themselves against the door and it sagged open with a squeal of metal.

Ray dragged Ryan back. 'Wait!'

Ryan struggled fiercely to free himself and Ray held him tight, their faces pressed together.

'You're not going in there like this. *Ryan!* Listen to me. You wait for me here. Understand?'

Ryan continued to struggle, but Ray held him.

'Wait for me!' Ray said again. 'I'll bring him out. No one's going to harm him. I promise.'

Ryan stopped struggling. He wept openly, biting his lower lip, and Ray let go of him and went up the steps into the trailer.

It was a single-room space, kitchen at the near end, seating beyond. In the middle, there was a woman on the floor; she turned her bleeding face away, as if in shame, as Ray stepped forward to where a man stood, clutching Ryan by the collar of his coat, like a badly wrapped package. In his other hand, he held an empty bottle. His face was dead, the remains of a face, grey and exhausted, and he looked at Ray with dead eyes.

Ryan made a mewling noise, and Ray gave the boy a smile and put his finger to his lips.

'Put the child down,' he said quietly to the man.

The man made no move, but his grip tightened; Ray could see the skin stretching across his knobbly yellow knuckles.

He held out his badge. 'Put the child down now.'

There was no sign that the man had even heard him. Ray talked on softly, telling him that he was going to put the child down, that Ryan was going to be safe, that the woman on the floor was going to get the treatment she needed, that things were going to work out.

'But first I need you to put the child down,' Ray said, and stepped forward.

The man lifted the hand holding the bottle, and Ray stopped, his eyes fixed on the man's eyes, in them nothing but dull malevolence, like the last blank second of silence before the smash of glass. After a moment, Ray took another step forward.

'I need you to put him down now,' he murmured.

He took another slow step forward and the man sneered – his face suddenly looking like an older version of Ryan's – and let Ryan Junior drop on to the floor. Ray snatched him up and went rapidly back through the trailer and gave him to Ryan, who was waiting outside with Diane, who had appeared out of nowhere.

'Daddy!'

He clung, big-eyed, to Ryan, who walked away with him, patting him all over, his face startled and panicky. Diane put her hand over her heart and Ray nodded and went back inside the trailer to the man, and read him his rights.

All the time, the man's eyes never left his. At last, he spoke, a sticky voice full of bits: 'What kind of policeman you call yourself?'

'Detective Inspector.'

'Still a fucking nigger.'

Ray cuffed him with the ties from Ryan's car and steered him outside. Ryan and his son were nowhere to be seen. In the distance, he heard sirens. Then, the woman in the trailer let out a sudden cry and, leaving the man by the door, he hurried back inside. She lay, fighting for breath, on the floor. Her face was full of old bruises and a deep new gash under her hairline,

320

and as he leaned over her, she touched his face with her hand, muttering words he couldn't catch.

'It's okay,' he said. 'It's over.'

Then, from outside, he heard his wife scream.

A little way off, Ryan was clubbing his father with a half-brick, beating his face and head with meaty thumps as the man staggered and snarled. Sprinting over, Ray caught hold of him and they struggled violently together, Ryan still lashing out wildly with the brick, before Ray managed to pull him away.

'Enough! Ryan!'

He didn't seem to hear. He fought him.

'*Ryan!*'

'I'm alright,' Ryan said, fighting on.

'Stop!'

Diane appeared briefly from behind the next trailer, holding Ryan Junior, and swiftly turned away again. Beyond her, two constables came running up the tarmac.

'Ryan, backup's here,' Ray said. 'You have to stop now.'

Ryan nodded, panting, as Ray held him tight. 'I'm alright.' Gradually, he stopped struggling. 'I'm alright now.' He suddenly went limp and swayed in Ray's arms, gasping for breath, while Ray shouted instructions to the constables.

A crowd of kids from the trailer park stood, staring, or talked on their phones. An ambulance was arriving.

'Over, now,' Ryan said in a calm voice.

Keeping an eye on him, Ray let him go.

'Ry's okay,' Ryan told him.

'I know.'

'Your wife's got him.'

'Yes.'

'She's going to take him to my sister's. She'll be back by now.'

Ray nodded. 'You go with her.'

'No, I'm okay now. Normal.'

Ray looked at him sceptically. He did not look or sound normal.

'Thing about me is I calm down really quick. Let's get to Barnabas.'

'That's a bad idea. You're not thinking. What about your mother?'

'I'll see her at the hospital.'

Before Ray could reply, he got a call and stepped aside to take it. 'What?' he said. 'When? . . . No, we're not at the college yet. A detour,' he said. 'How long? . . . Can't it be held up? Christ.'

He turned back and said to Ryan, 'We've made contact with al-Medina. He wants to talk about Goodman. Nadim's got a video call set up for me.'

'I'll drop you off on my way to Barnabas.'

Ray looked at him for a long moment. 'I still think you should go home, Ryan.'

'What about Ameena? Come on, Ray. After what we found out, she's in the frame for Sophie. What happens if we don't make contact now, and tomorrow she's gone missing or whatever?'

'We have to talk,' Ray said. 'About what just happened.'

'Talk later. No problem. Let's get going.'

Diane came over and Ryan hugged his son tight. 'Be a good boy with this lady, alright? She's going to take you to Auntie Jade's. Not for long. I'll be back soon.'

His son nodded. He put up his mouth to be kissed, and Ryan kissed him and turned to Ray. 'Come on, then.' He set off for his car.

Ray and Diane whispered together for a moment.

'How come you're even here?'

'I was up the road, at Sainsbury's. When you said it was something to do with the little boy, I didn't think, I just came straight over. Are you alright?'

He glanced towards Ryan, in his car, trying to get it started. 'Yes. But he's not. He just hasn't realised yet. Look how many witnesses there were.'

'Surely—'

'He's on a misconduct already. It looked like he was trying to kill him.'

Ryan had got his car going. He called over and Ray gave Diane a last look and walked away, and she stood, holding Ryan Junior's hand, watching him go.

FORTY

At Barnabas, Claire took Ryan over to the SCR, where Ameena was meant to be laying out things for the fellows' afternoon tea. But she wasn't there.

'Did you give her our message?'

'Yes.'

'What did she say?'

'I don't think she said anything. But she knew you were coming.' She looked at him awkwardly. 'Are you alright? What happened to your eye?'

'Caught it on the end of this other guy's boot.'

She made a face, half-sympathetic, half-horrified.

'You should see his boot, though. Wouldn't be surprised if the boot's in hospital.'

She didn't smile. 'Are you sure you're alright? You seem a bit . . .'

'Funny old day, that's all.' He put his hands behind his back so she couldn't see them trembling. He felt dizzy, there was a noise in his ears. From time to time, a memory of

Ryan's scream from inside the trailer came to him. He couldn't remember much else.

They went together to the bursary to consult Ameena's work schedule. At two o'clock: in the music room to arrange things for a reception in the evening. At three: in the SCR. At three thirty: in the Burton Suite, laying tables for dinner. At four: in the hall with the rest of the staff to hear the announcement about the theft. At four thirty: preparing for evensong in the chapel. But she was in none of these places.

'I don't understand,' Claire said. 'What can have happened? Where can she be?'

Ryan stood for a moment in silence, trying to think. Something had gone wrong. 'Where's her locker?' he said at last.

Staff lockers were in the stores, the mouldering rubble-walled room near the Stable Yard door. As Jason had told them earlier, it was full of equipment, kit, fuel, bags of old clothes and a hundred other miscellaneous items with specific technical uses. Under the high arched window at the far side were the lockers; the door of one of them was ajar.

Ameena Najib's.

'That's strange,' Claire said.

Inside was a rucksack, some gloves and a headscarf, a small bag of toiletries, a devotional paperback in Arabic, two packets of paracetamol – and several photocopies of obscene cartoons of Muhammad, which Ryan removed and showed to Claire.

She looked at them, bemused.

'Same thing happened a couple of days ago,' he said. 'She went wild before; she must be fucking well off the scale now.'

'Someone's put them here to upset her?'

'She thinks Ashley.' He rummaged around in the locker and took out the rucksack. 'Hello, what's this?' He took out a bunch of keys.

Claire said at once, 'It's the missing bunch from the bursary.'

Ryan was already out of the room; he went fast down the passage towards the hall and ran down the steps to the kitchen, Claire running behind awkwardly on high heels. When she got there, he was already talking to her staff.

No, they'd never seen the cartoons before. No, they didn't know where Ameena was now. Someone thought she'd gone.

'Gone where?'

The girl shrugged. 'She came in and took off her uniform.' She pointed to where it lay on a counter.

'When was this?'

'About half an hour ago.'

'Anyone actually see her leave?'

Someone had seen her go over to the utensils dump, which was on the way out – a range of narrow drawers in the corner, near the door. When he went over, Ryan saw at once that one of the drawers had been left open. The drawer containing knives.

He looked round at them all. After a moment, he said, 'Can't see Ashley. Where's Ashley today?'

Claire said, 'Called in sick. She's at home.'

And now his fucking car wouldn't start. It died and died again, and he beat the steering wheel, swearing, while Leonard Gamp watched complacently from under the gate. He was still dizzy and his eye was hurting again and the noise in his ears was worse, but he didn't think about any of that. He thought about Ameena

Najib, with a knife taken from the utensils dump, walking home to where Ashley Turner lay in bed.

He was beating the steering wheel again as Leonard Gamp peered in, saying, 'You've flooded the carburettor now, that's what you've done,' and he was just about to get out and slap him when another car pulled up alongside, driven by Kent Dodge, who wound down the window and said pleasantly, 'Engine trouble?'

He was taken by surprise when Ryan ran over, yanked open the door and forced him over to the passenger side. He made a series of unintelligible bleating noises.

'Shut up,' Ryan said.

Ignoring Kent's frightened owlish face next to him, he pulled away and swung violently through Oriel Square on to the High Street.

Kent said, in an almost reasonable voice, 'I think I should tell you that this is a hire car and—'

He was flung sideways into the door as they swerved down St Aldates, speeding up, and his face crumpled as cars loomed suddenly towards them when Ryan pulled out to overtake, before whipping back in again. At the junction with Thames Street, they slithered, tyre rubber screeching, round a turning double-decker bus, and went on, faster, towards Folly Bridge, cyclists leaping off their bikes on to the narrow pavements.

Kent began to mutter to himself, some sort of good-luck chant or prayer, interrupted when Ryan's phone went off and he tossed it over.

'Can't talk when I'm driving, can I?' he said. 'Against the law.'

Kent spoke tentatively into the phone. 'Hello? . . . No. My

name is Kent Dodge. I'm an American, I'm—' He listened. 'Yes, he's here. But he's driving.'

He paused to scream as they went, without braking, round the ninety-degree corner into Western Road and crunched to a stop.

'Yes,' he said, when he could, panting a little and on the verge of tears. 'Goodbye.' He handed Ryan the phone. 'Someone called Detective Superintendent Waddington.'

Leaving him in the car, Ryan ran, talking into the phone as he went, towards the courtyard at the back of the college house.

The Super understood the situation instantly. 'Ambulance and backup are coming now,' she said. 'Talk me through it. I want to know what's happening.'

He ran on, talking quietly, up the steps. 'Door's open. Going inside now. Hallway clear. Going into the living room. Fuck.'

'What is it?'

'Things all over the place. Chairs overturned. Table smashed.' He tiptoed on quickly, peering around. 'In the kitchen, now. Stuff smashed here, too. Fuck! There's been some sort of fight.'

'Any sign of Ashley?'

'No.' He went back through the living room to the staircase. 'Going upstairs.' He went carefully up, listening and peering about. Halfway up, he stopped. 'Door's open, up there. Can't hear nothing. Going up now. Looks like her room. Okay, I'm going in.'

There was a long pause.

The Super's voice said, 'What is it? Ryan? *Ryan?*'

Ryan's voice came back, at last: 'I'm too late. Sorry.'

'She's dead?'

'No good way to say it.'

There was a pause.

'Any sign of Ameena?' the Super asked.

There was another pause.

'Sorry, didn't make myself clear. It's Ameena who's been killed.'

'*Ameena?*'

'Strangled, looks like. Same as Sophie Barbery.'

He glanced over towards the doorway, where Kent Dodge had appeared, white faced. The American looked down at Ameena, his eyes rolled up and he slumped sideways.

FORTY-ONE

Ryan and Ray stood talking at the station entrance, while squad cars and vans went in and out, blue lights swirling, past the group of journalists with their microphones and cameras, waiting like trainspotters on the street. News had got out; more journalists waited on the other side of Folly Bridge, where the distant lights on the paramedics' wagons blipped steadily in the dark.

The first thing Ryan asked Ray was about Ryan Junior, and Ray told him he was with Jade already. He nodded, looking distracted, as if he wasn't really listening, and then carried on, twitchy and lit, describing the scene at Western Road.

'Should've seen her face, Ray.'

'We can talk about this tomorrow.'

Ryan ignored him. 'Colour of it. Tongue out. Eyes like they'd sort of boiled over.'

Ray engaged. 'The same as Sophie, then.'

'Yeah.'

'Same perp?'

'My first thought.'

'Why would he kill Ameena?'

'Shut her up, maybe.'

'She knew something about Sophie's murder?'

'Could be she saw something.' He glanced up and caught Ray staring at him. 'What?'

'Are you alright, Ryan?'

'Yeah. No. Just . . .' He fell silent; his hands wouldn't stop trembling and he put them under his arms and squeezed. He had a feeling of vague dread, which he pushed away. There were things he had to face, he knew, but they were too large, too painful. He couldn't begin to think of his son without flooding, so he babbled on about Ameena Najib.

'Suppose she saw him that night, the perp.'

'Why didn't she speak up straight away?'

'Maybe didn't realise what she'd seen, till now. Or maybe . . .' He drifted off. 'Remember what she said to us in the SCR? That weird shit about, what was it, *defilers?*'

Ray remembered: '*There are people here who defile the Holy Book – I've seen them.*'

'That's it. What's all that about, eh?'

He could no longer stop his hands trembling; he could feel them vibrating through his tracksuit sleeves, no matter how hard he squeezed them.

Ray was looking at him again.

'What?'

Ray looked away, embarrassed.

Ryan talked on, as if talking was the only way to keep everything else at bay. 'Her phone was there, Ray, on the floor, next to her, like she'd been calling someone. What do you think? Maybe she'd called them to tell them what she remembered. And her laptop, Ray. Did I tell you? Her laptop was open. She'd been looking at some sort of Arabic thing – religious, I don't know.' He hugged himself, shivered. 'Ray? Ray, mate? Are you listening or what? This is shit, but we're getting close now, I can feel it.'

He caught Ray's glance – that embarrassed sideways look again.

'What's going on?'

Only then did he see the constables. Three of them stood in front of him together and one of them said, 'Ryan Wilkins, I am arresting you on suspicion of causing grievous bodily harm to Ryan Wilkins Senior at Hinksey Point. You do not have to say anything, but it may harm your defence if you—'

Ryan grabbed his jacket collar and the other two constables stepped in.

'What the fuck! The cunt kidnapped my son!'

Ray tried to intervene and was pulled away.

Arms pinned behind his back, Ryan continued to yell. He twisted his head round and glared backwards at Ray as they cuffed him and led him away. Flashbulbs went off in the street; some of the journalists had spotted the commotion. When Ray turned to go inside, the Super was waiting for him in the doorway, and he went towards her, breathing heavily.

FORTY-TWO

That evening, they had a late supper: Moroccan tagine with harissa and mangetout, and sourdough bread. Ray brought out a nice Sauvignon Blanc and they had half a glass each and didn't feel like any more. They sat, looking at each other.

'I'm proud of you,' she said. 'You went in and got him out.'

Ray sighed, nodded.

'But could he really go to prison?'

'Certainly he could.'

'Surely extenuating circumstances . . .'

'The situation was under control; his father was already cuffed. There were a dozen witnesses – half of them will say it looked like he wanted to kill him. It did.' He pushed away his glass. 'Anyway, it's the end of his police career. If I were him, I'd be worrying now about my son.'

'What do you mean?'

'I hope he gets a sympathetic lawyer. There are custody issues around violent fathers.'

'But he was trying to protect him.'

Ray shrugged, looked the other way.

'You think he brought it on himself, don't you?'

'Not all of it.'

'Ray?'

'You can't deny he has problems controlling himself.'

'He controls himself with his son. I've never seen such a happy little boy.' Her eyes swam. 'Did you see him? He was so brave. As soon as he saw his daddy, he felt safe.'

Ray sighed. 'They'll look at his record of service – the thing with the Bishop in Salisbury, the behaviour that triggered the misconduct charge here. It's not as if no one's given him a chance. He got off, in Wiltshire. And the Super's gone in to bat for him here. Twice. To be honest, she's spent pretty much all her political capital on him and she's not going to be thanked for it. In fact, it wouldn't surprise me if it's used against her. Anyway,' he said, 'she can't do anything for him now. And I can't think about him either; I've got to think about the case. It's all got confused again.'

There was a silence after this.

Diane said, anxiously, 'But what will Ryan *do*?'

Ray shook his head, sighed. He got up and began to clear the table.

'Daddy?'

'Yeah?'

'You're squeezing again.'

'Sorry. That better?'

'That's a bit better. Thank you.'

They lay together under the tractor-motif duvet, looking up at the ceiling.

'We're having a conversation, aren't we, Daddy?'

Ryan began to squeeze again and stopped himself. He patted his son all over instead: his tummy and arms and toes, all zipped up in his towelling sleepsuit; his soft, fine hair; his tiny nose with its pristine little nostrils. Giggling, the boy began to wriggle, spluttering a little on his bottle.

He still hadn't said anything about what had happened to him at Hinksey Point; he didn't answer Ryan's questions about it. Where had the experience gone? Ryan wondered. How deeply was the memory of it embedded in his mind? He lay there, as his father watched him, placidly drinking milk from his bottle.

What had happened was all Ryan could think about – a not-thinking of churning feelings, anger, fear and, most of all, guilt. His suspension from active duty, imposed a few hours earlier by the Super, didn't enter his mind at all, wasn't important.

'Listen, Ry,' he said. 'I know I'm a dipstick, right?'

Ryan Junior hesitated, not sure if 'dipstick' was a forbidden word.

'But what happened today will never, ever happen again. I promise you. I mean it.'

His son said nothing, calmly scrutinising the ceiling.

'Don't matter if you don't want to talk about it.'

Still his son said nothing.

'It's just, when I saw you, when Ray brought you out, I knew I was going to look after you better now, always and always. You understand? Like, forever. Never let you go.'

He looked to see what effect this speech had had on his son, who carried on sucking milk, his pouty mouth around the teat, his eyes half-closed.

They lay in silence for a while.

Ryan Junior took the bottle out of his mouth and said, in a conversational voice, 'I didn't like the smell.'

'What?'

'I didn't like it, what was in the jug. But I like Ray,' he said. 'He's nice. He's not a mole,' he added, and popped his mouth back on the bottle. A moment later, the bottle slipped out of his hands as he fell asleep.

Christ, Ryan thought, I am so fucking lucky.

And then, regretting the profanity, he said, 'Sorry,' out loud.

FORTY-THREE

Next morning, Ryan went to his sister's, as usual. Now that he was suspended, he didn't have to, but it felt like the right thing to do. He sat in the kitchen, drinking tea with Jade, while Ryan Junior watched television in the front room.

'You absolute knobhead.'

He fiddled with his mug.

'Fucked up again, didn't you?'

'Yeah, alright. No need to rub it in.'

'So, what happens now, genius?'

'With a bit of luck, he goes down. Abduction. Domestic. Whatever.'

'And what about you? Are you going down?'

'Come on, Jade. I did what any dad would've done.'

'Ryan! You tried to kill him with a half-brick.'

'That's a point. And, you know what?'

'What?'

'I think, just one more go at him, I could've done it.'

337

'You're a total fucking complete knobhead. Do you want more tea?'

'I don't know how you drink this shit. We're going to the swings in a minute, anyway.'

'How is he, this morning?'

'Good. Amazing. He keeps on about Ray and Diane, Ray's missus. He hasn't talked about what happened in the trailer at all.'

'You're lucky to have him.'

'You don't have to tell me.'

'What happens with the misconduct thing, now?'

'Yeah. Haven't really thought. Might be a bit . . . I don't know. I'll have to have a word with the Super. I think Ray might speak up for me.'

'Really?'

'He's alright. Just a bit up himself. I mean, fuck, he went in and got Ray out. Did you hear what Ry told me?'

'What?'

'They had a kid that died. Fucking awful. Feel sorry for him, now.'

'What about the investigation you was working on?'

'Don't know. Maybe there's a way I can . . . Don't know, to be honest. It's strange, 'cause it'd got much worse, in a way, but there was something, I don't know, like it was all about to fall into place. Maybe I'll give the Super a bell, see if I can stay on to finish things off. Nothing to lose.'

He called his son, who came dawdling in from the front room with his coat and hat still on and his usual solemn expression.

'That's a nice lady, yesterday, with the hair, wasn't it, Daddy?'

'Yeah. Shall we go to the swing park now?'

'Yes, please. She gave me a sweet.'

'Why'd she give you a sweet?'

He thought about that for a long time. 'I expect I was good,' he said, at last.

'You're always good, you are. You're a good boy. Except when I can't get you to shut up at bedtime.'

'Shall we have a conversation now, Daddy?'

'We can have a conversation at the swing park, if you like.'

'Yes, please.'

It was windy at the swing park, and the equipment was wet. It was still early; they were the only people there. He sat on a bench, thinking about Ameena Najib – the dark, congested, thick-eyed stare of shock, so like Sophie's – and wondered again if she'd seen someone on the night of Sophie's murder, a defiler.

Ryan called out to him, bird twitterings of excitement, and he watched his son run from swings to climbing frame to see-saw, blue coat buckling round him in the breeze. He watched him climb the steps of the slide with the exaggerated and serious care of a mime artist. Watery clouds coalesced above the grey rooftops of the Kennington houses and the sun broke suddenly from some unexpected source in the dark sky, dividing the strip of grass beyond into brilliant yellow phosphorescence and inky black shadow, and he sat, fiddling with his phone, wondering if he should call the Super.

In the end, he thought better of it and went to chase Ryan round the sandpit, and when he stopped to get his breath, he saw the Superintendent standing at the gate, watching him. At first, he thought she was a figment of his imagination. Then, he put Ryan on the roundabout and went over to her.

'How'd you know I was here?'

'I'm police. I can find people.'

They sat together on the bench, the Superintendent alert and upright in her uniform, a muscle jumping in her cheek, Ryan giving her sideways looks.

'Always meant to ask. What is it? Arthritis?'

'Sciatica.'

'It's a bastard. Jade gets it, sometimes – she's only thirty.'

The Super did not say how old she was.

'Nice little boy,' she said, after a while.

'Yeah. Fucking genius, too – you should hear him. You got kids?'

'Five. All boys.'

'Christ. That's a whole five-a-side team.'

'Grown up, now. They don't play football.'

There was a long silence, broken only by Ryan's chirruping from the climbing frame, where he stood on the second-highest rung.

'I was thinking about Ameena and—'

'You'll be discharged – that's what I came to tell you.'

'Oh, right.'

'I'm sorry. But there's nothing I can do.'

'Yeah. Well. Brought it on myself, didn't I?' He wiped his nose and sniffed. 'My own worst enemy, I know that.' He paused. 'But I was wondering if maybe there'd be an appeal.'

'There won't be an appeal. And I think it's very unlikely you'll ever work for the police again.'

'Will charges be brought?'

'It's possible, yes.'

Ryan Junior waved excitedly from the highest rung of the climbing frame, and he made himself wave back.

'I've written references for you,' the Superintendent said.

'Okay. Cheers. And thanks for . . .'

'Thanks for what?'

'Going in to bat for me at the IOPC.'

'You know I can't comment on that.' She stood up, wincing imperceptibly, and straightened her uniform. 'I'm sorry it's over. But I'm obliged to warn you: don't attempt to contact Ray, don't try to continue with the investigation. You won't be doing yourself any favours.'

He said, 'It's not about me and my favours, though, is it?'

They looked at each other for a moment.

'It's about a couple of murdered women,' he said. 'And the twat who killed them.'

She gave the slightest of nods and, without saying any more, turned and went away, limping slightly, through the gate and across the grass, a spare, upright figure in irreproachable uniform; and Ryan went across the concrete towards his son, who looked at him and waved.

FORTY-FOUR

The name of Ray's new partner wasn't Wilkins. It was Watkins. Ray and the Super waited for him in her office, talking about Sheikh al-Medina, to whom Ray had spoken by video link the previous evening.

'He denies meeting Goodman, has no interest in meeting him. He said he didn't even know Goodman was in the UAE.'

'Do you believe him?'

'Yes.' Throughout their conversation, Ray had picked up the Sheikh's personal antipathy to the English Arabist. 'And I believe him when he says he has no interest in the college Koran either. It's a holy relic for the Shia; for years, it was owned by the Imam Ali Mosque in Iraq, a Shia shrine. Al-Medina's Sunni.'

'So, is Goodman meeting another buyer?'

'We don't know. He's somewhere in Abu Dhabi, though not at the hotel he'd originally booked.'

'Are you getting support from the Emirates?'

'They're being very helpful. But they haven't caught up with him yet.'

The Super went behind her desk and sat. There were footsteps in the corridor. She said, 'By the way, I have to advise you not to have any further contact with Ryan while he's under investigation.'

'He hasn't—'

'I don't need to know what he's done or hasn't done. I only need to advise you.'

'We're going to miss his ideas,' Ray said.

The Super looked at him coldly.

He held up his hands. 'Understood,' he said.

There was a knock on the door and DI Robin Watkins came in. He was a pale-faced man with stiff gingery hair, a ginger beard and prominent eyes. Quiet by nature and hard-working, he was on loan from Berkshire. Like Ray, he was an Oxford alumnus. Unlike Ray, he wore clothes without distinction – standard chinos and a plain shirt. Introductions were perfunctory; they settled quickly to a review of the situation and forward progress, Ray talking, the Super interjecting and Robin listening in silence, eyes bulging slightly.

Forensics had provided a preliminary report on Ameena's death. It was very likely she'd been murdered by the person who murdered Sophie.

'First question, then. Why?'

Robin leaned forward. 'The timeline puts Ameena there, or thereabouts, on the night Sophie Barbery was killed. Perhaps she witnessed something. The killer had to shut her up.'

Ray agreed. 'It's got to be our first line of enquiry. She was in college, she even went over to the lodge to fetch that bag of clothes. It's possible she saw something suspicious, maybe even saw the perp.'

'But didn't realise it at the time?'

'Until yesterday.'

'Why? What happened yesterday?'

Ray outlined two areas of immediate enquiry. Firstly, to map out more precisely Ameena's movements on the night when Sophie was killed – where she had been, who she had talked to, what she had seen, etc. Secondly, to reconstruct the last moments of her own life, reviewing her phone use, search history and anything else of relevance.

'Ryan thought she might have been trying to tell someone something. So, a working hypothesis. Something happened to Ameena yesterday afternoon in college – perhaps the cartoons, perhaps not – to trigger a memory about the night of Sophie's murder. She got agitated. She rushed home and tried to make contact with someone.'

'Who?'

'Someone in the Arabian Peninsula – we don't know who yet.'

'How do the traffickers fit into this?'

'We don't know that, either. There's a warrant out for Hassan Awad.'

'And Ashley Turner has nothing to do with any of this?'

'I don't know about the cartoons, but Ashley wasn't even in the house when Ameena went back; she'd gone to her sister's, in Carterton. Anyway, there's no sign Ameena was looking for her. No knives were missing from the Barnabas kitchen. When Ameena got home, what she immediately started to do was look things up on her laptop and make calls. The question we have to answer is: what did Ameena witness on the night of Sophie's murder?'

The Super asked Robin if he had any further thoughts. He hadn't. The meeting broke up.

At the same time, Ryan was crossing Cabot Square towards 10 South Colonnade, on the way to his IOPC interview. He was met inside the building by two constables, who relieved him of his phone, asked him to sign various documents and, at length, led him to the twelfth floor, where he was escorted to a glass-sided room in the middle of a large expanse of well-populated open-plan desks, like an empty fish tank, on stage, in a crowded auditorium. He felt – and looked – like a football hooligan being ushered into custody. He met his legal representative, Tracy Turner, brisk and businesslike in a navy trouser suit, and the three IOPC officials running his case, investigator Alec Todd, senior solicitor Meg Ayers and director of people Tisi Phou. Once they were all settled inside the room, two constables took up bouncer positions at the door.

The recorder was switched on, they announced themselves in turn, and Todd began by summarising the purpose of the IOPC's inquiry, to determine the validity of a complaint received from Sir James Osborne, Provost of Barnabas Hall in Oxford, that DI Wilkins of Thames Valley Police had, on multiple occasions, broken the police code of conduct. It was not, he stressed, an inquiry into a more recent incident of alleged violent conduct, which would be investigated in due course. Long portions of the code concerning issues of diversity and human rights were read out. Todd had a thickened, catarrhal voice, but he spoke slowly and firmly, while his colleagues kept their eyes on their own screens, as perhaps they were trained to do, and Ryan sat there, looking bored.

'Any comments, before we proceed?'

'Yeah.'

'What?'

'It's *Ryan*.'

As Todd hesitated, Ryan said, 'There's another DI Wilkins. You don't want to get me mixed up with Ray. He's done nothing wrong.'

Todd proceeded, without further comment, to specific instances of DI *Ryan* Wilkins's misconduct, beginning with the occasion on which Ryan had addressed Sir James as, quote, 'a sordid little fuckrat', unquote.

Tracy Turner interjected: 'My client is advised that he need not, here, confirm or deny personal recollections uncorroborated by witnesses.'

'We have witnesses.'

'He's a fuckrat, anyway,' Ryan said.

Tracy Turner withdrew her advice and Todd proceeded. As always, Ryan soon stopped listening. The outcome of his hearing was a foregone conclusion, and, given what had happened the day before, it made little difference to him. Gazing into the middle distance, he spoke only to give automatic answers to the cut-and-dried questions, hearing in the man's tone other voices, in other rooms, long ago, the same falsely impersonal note of accusation. He couldn't stop himself thinking of Michelle, who was so often with him or waiting outside for her turn. Michelle Toomey, raw pikey from the West Country, half-grown-up and still skinny, with bare legs and rough skin and a dirty smile. From the age of thirteen to nineteen, a lifetime of innocence on the edge, they'd stuck together through chaos, clinging on to each other, laughing,

346

lurching in and out of control, like novice skaters at the ice rink, as if they'd never grow up but would live forever as children, with nothing worse than skinned knees.

Somewhere in the background of his mind, Ryan noted that Todd had concluded his remarks and the solicitor, Ayers, had taken over.

It wasn't even like they were in love, more like being a part of each other. For six years, they were inseparable, in and out of Hinksey Point, dosshouses, squats in tower blocks, campsites in former warehouses, bars and clubs and raves in fields.

In due course, Ayers handed on to the director of people, Phou – another trivial disturbance in Ryan's mental distance.

But it turned out they wouldn't live forever, weren't inseparable, would get more than skinned knees. At first, the only difference between them was that he didn't have a taste for weed; later, when she started on pills, they used to argue; he could feel the change begin in her like a change in his own body. Then she got pregnant; he thought it might bring them closer, but it did the opposite. As soon as Ryan was born, she started taking pills again – Molly first, then Spice and flake, ice at last. He watched her turn into a stranger, a matter of a few short months. In the clubs, at the raves, even as they clung together, her face was the same but her expression was someone else's. As if she disappeared into the crowd. Or was it him that disappeared? She didn't talk to him, didn't look at him, didn't even recognise him as she lay staring up at him from the floor, the red lights of the club turning into the blue lights of the ambulance, her face twisting into the last shock of all.

There was a faint buzz in his ears as Phou concluded her remarks.

Like Sophie Barbery's dead face, like Ameena Najib's dead face, Michelle Toomey's face stuck in that final contortion, that last horrible mistake. He hadn't protected her, hadn't been able to save her. He'd done nothing. Guilt flooded him, and that too was a familiar emotion.

He leaned forward, surprising his interviewers. He said, 'Listen, there are dead women here, right? Let me finish the investigation. I don't care what you do to me after. Just give me a bit of time.'

There was a frisson of embarrassment, as if he'd just farted.

Todd said, 'I'm sure you understand, that's not how it works.'

'The twat who did it's still out there,' Ryan said. 'Don't that bother you?'

They carried on putting laptops into briefcases, avoiding eye contact.

'They're dead,' he said, helplessly. He was on his feet, now. 'He killed them 'cause he could, like they was trash. Please,' he said, 'let me finish. I was getting close, I could feel it.'

Even his lawyer avoided eye contact, and he stood there, ignored like a child while the adults cleared their things away. He couldn't stand it. Turning away, he made for the door.

Phou said, 'Not yet. The escort will take you.'

Ryan gestured impatiently at the constables waiting outside the door, and she said, 'It needs to be the ones who brought you in. Protocol.'

'Who the fuck cares? Bobbleheads all look the same.'

Phou made a disapproving noise, and Ryan sat down again, wiping his nose with a finger.

And drifted off.

Then they were telling him to get up. Was it a minute or an hour later? He couldn't tell. He didn't hear them at first; he wasn't there any more; he was in the zone of suspended certainty, with the three dead faces, all the same, telling him something, something obvious.

Same beauty gone ugly.

Same pain.

Same fury.

He could hardly tell them apart. He came out of his trance, already on his feet. 'Hey! Yeah, you. Give us your phone, will you?'

Phou looked at him in surprise. 'Pardon?'

'They took mine. I got to call someone. Just had an idea. It's urgent.'

He was trembling, eager faced, slightly mad. Ignoring him, she turned her back and left.

'Fuck's sake!' he shouted. 'I got to call Ray!'

The bobbleheads moved in.

'What the fuck is wrong with you people?' he shouted, as they strong-armed him and took him away, the men and women working at the surrounding desks all pausing to watch him go. And he understood that this was how it always was, always would be, and he gave up struggling and let himself be pushed out of sight.

Ray was still in the office when his phone rang. It was seven o'clock, hushed. Robin was with him, diligently working through the forensics report on the crime scene of Ameena's murder. Ray looked at his phone; it was the fifth time Ryan had tried him, and, after a moment's hesitation, he picked it up and went outside.

'What are you doing?' he whispered as he walked down the corridor. 'No contact. You know I can't speak to you.'

'No worries, mate, it's a purely social call. How's tricks? What's the new guy like? Forensics report come through yet?'

Ray went through the door at the end of the corridor and down the stairs. He was alone, but he still looked up and down the stairwell before he answered. 'Yes, it's come through. Robin's going through it now. Listen, you need to calm down.'

'Robin? He the new guy? What's he like?'

'He's fine.'

'So, who were the Islamicists she was trying to contact?'

'Seriously, Ryan. Can't you let it go?'

'No. Who were they?'

Ray sighed. 'Turns out they're a bunch of students; they stage protests. We got some more transcripts from Ameena's phone. It seems she linked up with them that night, when al-Medina got mooned at. Anyway, when she was killed, Ameena was trying to contact them again. She didn't get through. She left a voicemail saying she'd got terrible news for them, and a text saying the same thing.'

'That it? *Terrible news*?'

'Yes. No explanation.'

'What about her laptop?'

Ray explained that Ameena had accessed various Islamic sites – religious, mainly, but also tourist sites – all in Arabic. Briefly, she'd browsed websites full of images of mosques, religious arte- facts, books, paintings, scrolls and pilgrimage sites, but it wasn't clear exactly what she was looking for, or if she'd found it. 'And we don't see how any of this connects to Sophie.'

'Maybe it don't.'

Ray paused. 'What do you mean?'

'Listen, I've had a thought. Just came to me. You know how we could never think of a reason why Sophie was killed? Well, maybe there wasn't one.'

'Explain.'

'Maybe Ameena was the real target.'

There was a silence.

'Why was Sophie killed, then?'

'Thing is, these foreign chicks, they all look the same.'

'Oh, for Christ's sake, Ryan.'

'It's what I always say, Ray. Most things are cock-ups. Imagine it, for a minute. Ameena's going round college that night, she sees the perp up to something. Don't realise it at the time – but the perp sees her, *he* knows what she's seen, *he* can't risk her realising, so he goes after her. But it's dark, misty, rain coming down, maybe he don't know the college too well. He thinks he's lost her. Then, he gets lucky – sees her going across the quad in her jeans and kitchen uniform. Looks just like her, anyway – she's even wearing that funny little cap that looks like Ameena's turban – so he follows her to the lodge, slips in after and – bingo! – he's got her. And then – fucking unbingo! – it's the wrong girl.'

There was a long pause while Ray considered all this. He said, 'Really? I'm not sure. Anyway, it doesn't help us answer the question. *Who* did she see that night? *What* was he up to? We still have absolutely no idea.'

'Yeah. But I been thinking—'

'Maybe you've been doing too much thinking. You've had a crap time of it. You need to take time out.'

'No, but Ray—'

'I'm serious. Drop it.'

As he spoke, there was a sound in the stairwell, slight and somehow deliberate, and, when Ray turned to look, the Superintendent was standing there, looking down at him.

'Your wife again, Ray?'

He put his phone in his pocket and climbed the stairs, following her to her office and waiting by the door as she sat behind her desk.

'I said no contact. He's under investigation.'

He stood there in silence.

'Any contact you have with him now is expressly against regulations.'

He nodded.

There was a long pause. The Super's expression didn't change. Ray knew how seriously she took the regulations and the thought came to him that she wouldn't hesitate to enforce them.

Then she spoke: 'So, what did he have to say?'

FORTY-FIVE

In the stores, Jason Birch took an almost empty can of Lynx deodorant spray out of his locker and put it in his holdall. For a moment, he paused, glancing wistfully round the room – rubble walls always damp, metal lockers with their squeaky hinges – listening to the familiar clatter and murmur from the kitchen next door, then he reached again into his locker, took out a half-eaten packet of salt and vinegar and put it carefully in his bag, next to the Lynx. He was clearing out his stuff before leaving.

As he slowly filled his bag, he couldn't stop himself thinking of Ameena. He had a superstitious sense of her presence nearby, as if she'd stepped across from the kitchen to stand behind him, silent and no less scornful than when she'd been alive. He felt she waited only to accuse him. Resisting the urge to turn round, setting his pulpy face to neutral and draining his mind of difficult thoughts, he focused on his locker, fishing for the Arsenal fanzines at the back – and nearly screamed when someone coughed behind him.

★

They sat on stools among the equipment and supplies, Jason gazing round unhappily while the fed explained that he wanted him to remember exactly what Ameena had told him on the night of the first murder – specifically anything that had disturbed her in any way. It was the fed with the medical plaster across the bridge of his nose and the sharp eyes and unexpected questions.

'I already talked to a detective this morning. Big, ginger fella.'

'Now you're going to talk to me.'

Jason felt himself start to sweat. 'Yeah,' he said. 'Thing is, and I told him, I don't really remember now.'

The fed thought otherwise. 'Start with old Money-Nuts. He'd upset her, you said.'

'The Sheikh, yeah.'

'How?'

'Dunno.'

''Cause of something she'd seen him do? Something she heard him say?'

Jason began a series of helpless gestures and the fed gave him one of his looks. He made an effort to concentrate. 'Hang on, let me think. She said something about . . . something about him being on the phone when she went in with the drinks. So, yeah, maybe she'd heard him say something. And I said to her, "Don't matter how many wives he's got, 'cause he's just a—"'

'Don't worry about what you said, Jason.'

Sweat ran into Jason's navel. Again, he had the unpleasant image of Ameena looking at him with exasperation. It was an expression he'd been on the thick end of many times.

It seemed to be his turn to speak again. He said, without much conviction, 'She didn't like him, that was the thing. She was proper frightened of him.'

The fed was getting impatient. 'I want to know *what she heard him say.*'

Jason drew a blank. 'He's a defiler, though,' he said, suddenly remembering.

The fed gave him an interested look. 'Sit still while I think. Don't move.'

Jason perched on his stool, trying to breathe quietly. The fed seemed to have drifted off. With surreptitious movements, he wiped his forehead and unstuck his Arsenal shirt from his belly.

Ryan had drifted into the zone of imagination, where things lack meaning and make themselves more obvious. Images and sounds, a small, neat room, a man on the phone, a girl with the tray of drinks. Arabic being spoken, the girl understanding. What did she hear him say? Something that frightened her. A name? People, cities, towns, places she recognises, Damascus . . . her home town.

Ryan said sharply, 'Did she mention Kafr Jamal?'

'Who?'

'A town.'

'No.'

Ridiculous. She wasn't frightened of al-Medina. *He* was frightened of *her* – he sent his bodyguard after her. In any case, both Sheikh and bodyguard were in Arabia when Ameena was killed.

He fixed his gaze on Jason again, who had spent the last few moments perfecting an expression of injured innocence, inadvertently making himself look suspicious.

'I told you what I remember,' Jason said, hopefully.

Ryan nodded. 'Let's forget about the Sheikh. Go back a bit. Where did you run into her?'

His face twitchy and his breathing shallow, Jason made an effort. 'Over by the Great Hall, there.'

'More detail.'

'She was sort of hiding in a corner.'

'Why?'

'I don't know. She was upset, like I say. She had her phone out, looked like she was trying to make a call, and I said something about not getting a signal. You know, being helpful.'

'Then what?'

'Just chat, really.'

'I'm warning you, Jason.'

'Okay, alright. I told you what she said about the old Sheikh.'

'Forget the old Sheikh. She mention anyone else she'd seen?'

'I really don't remember.'

'I swear, Jason, if you say that again—'

'Oh, yeah, the Provost. She mentioned him, alright? Way he looked at her.'

'Forget him, too. She'd seen her family murdered, her sister die in the back of a truck, I don't think she'd get upset if someone looked at her wrong.'

Jason's pulpy face bunched and unbunched. 'Well, there's no one else.'

'Where else did she go that night? Where was she before the lodge?'

His face perked up. 'She'd got lost, that was it! All them little new corridors.'

'What are you talking about?'

'Conference suite. But nothing happened there.'

'Where in the conference suite?'

'I don't know. Collections room.'

He paused. 'Collections room?'

Jason was on the back foot again; he wiped his eyebrows with his sleeve. 'She just opened the door by mistake, that's all she said.'

The fed got off his stool and took a step towards him, and Jason heard his own voice rise a register: 'She just opened the door and Goodman was there, she said. He didn't say anything to her and off she went. She was late by then, see.'

He stopped, alarmed. The fed's eyes had gone funny; they glazed over briefly, like he'd seen a fish's eyes do once, then cleared fiercely.

'Jason, I want your attention now. Think very carefully. That word Ameena used: "Defiler".'

Nervous about any sort of test, Jason winced. 'Yeah? Summit to do with the toilet, innit?'

'Did she say, "Defiler of the Holy Book"?'

He perked up. 'Oh, yeah, that's right, I'd forgotten. Yeah, "Defiler of the Holy Book", that was it. I don't even know what it properly means, but . . .'

He trailed away, listening to the fed's running footsteps in the passageway outside.

Ray was sitting at the conference table with the Superintendent, Deputy Chief Constable, principal lawyer, chief press officer and various other members of senior management when his phone rang. He glanced at it and killed the call and went on listening to the chief press officer talk about reputational fallout from the recent disturbances in Blackbird Leys.

His phone rang again and he turned it off without looking at it. The Super glanced at him, and he put on a non-committal expression and they both turned back to the chief press officer.

After a moment, the Super's phone rang. She listened for a moment, then turned and spoke quietly: 'Nadim needs you, Ray. Yes, now.'

He knew Nadim was out of the office that morning. Nodding, he excused himself and went out of the room, calling Ryan from the end of the corridor.

'For God's sake. Not at work! What is it?'

'Ray! The defiler!'

'What are you talking about?'

'Defiler of the Holy Book!'

'I don't know what—'

'Goodman, that shonky dodgeball!'

Ray went through some doors, into the stairwell. 'Stop shouting. Everyone in the building can hear you.'

'Listen, then. Someone upset Ameena that night. She told Jason.'

'We know. Robin spoke to him, first thing. We're going to talk to al-Medina again.'

'Non-starter, mate. Listen, before she met al-Medina, she got lost in the conference suite. Went into collections by mistake. And who do you think was there?'

'Well, it would have been Goodman.'

'Doing what?'

Ray paused.

'Defiler of the Holy Book,' Ryan added.

Ray said slowly, 'You think Ameena saw him stealing the Koran?'

'Timing works. When was the last time it was seen? That afternoon, right?'

'Yes, that's true.'

'When did she rush home? Just after staff'd been told it'd been stolen. Announcement at three o'clock. I remember it from her work schedule. *That's* when she realised what she'd seen that night. Tell me what she started to look up on her laptop when she got home.'

'Images. Religious sites, artefacts.'

'Any of the college Koran?'

Ray blew out his cheeks. 'One of them was, actually.'

'Come on, Ray. Think about it. If she saw him packing it up, she wouldn't've guessed straight away that he was stealing it, but it would've spooked her. Defiler of the Holy Book. Actually handling the Holy Book, shoving it in a crate. Goodman, that hinky bastard, he knew – course he did – that, as soon as she realised what he'd been doing, she'd raise the alarm. He would've been straight after her, fanatic like that – no one's going to stop him doing the right thing. Only, he got the wrong end of the sandwich with Sophie!' He was out of breath by now. 'Ray!' he panted. 'It works out.'

Ray collected himself. 'You're forgetting something obvious.'

'What?'

'Goodman was already in the UAE when Ameena was murdered. He couldn't have killed her.'

Ryan's panting went on, diminishing slowly.

'Sorry,' Ray said. 'Listen, Ryan, don't you think it's time to let it go?'

'And let you and Ginger Nut sort it out?'

'Seriously. You shouldn't even be in Barnabas,' he said.

'What makes you think I'm in Barnabas?'

Ray heard the Barnabas clock striking the hour in the background. 'Seriously, Ryan,' he said again. 'I thought you were going to your second tribunal this afternoon.'

'Just about to. Do me a favour, though, will you? Just one thing? Check up on Goodman.'

'He flew to UAE. We know that.'

'Yeah, but—'

'He's still there. Nadim's been plotting his movements.'

'Just check for me, that's all I'm asking. Don't give up on it.'

Ray said, 'I've got to put a stop to this. Sorry, Ryan.'

'Ray, mate!'

'Enough, now. Go to your tribunal. Don't call again.'

Ryan went into New Court and walked round the quadrangle twice, distracted and agitated. The masonry walls of the library, charmingly pale, the plum-coloured chapel windows glowing in the winter light, did nothing to soothe him. He stared unfocused for a moment at the grass of the quadrangle, then jogged over to the porter's lodge.

He banged on the window. Leonard Gamp looked up and immediately settled his features into an aggrieved expression.

'Kent Dodge,' Ryan said. 'Where's he hang out?'

Gamp left a long pause before answering, as if considering whether to answer at all. 'We don't usually supply that information,' he said.

Ryan said, 'I don't usually slap provocative old fuckers round the head. But I sometimes do.'

Gamp sneered a long sneer. 'New Court, staircase three,' he said at last. 'Is where he had his rooms,' he said, after another moment. 'But,' he added, with aggravating slowness, 'he leaves college today, so unfortunately you may have missed him altogether. In which case, I simply can't help you further.' And, with that, he got to his feet and retreated with painstaking slowness round the back of the screen at the far end of his room.

Ryan went back out into New Court and the first person he saw was Kent Dodge, coming round the quad, carrying a large bag. Kent seemed to see him at the same time, because he hesitated and showed signs of wanting to retreat, but Ryan shouted to him and, with a nervous expression, he came on.

'I'm a little busy,' he said, before Ryan could say anything else. 'So, if you don't mind—'

'Simple question. Won't take long.'

Kent's face sagged. 'I don't mean to be rude, but every time I help you out, I get into trouble. I'm already in a dispute with the college about my battels bills; now, my hire-car company is demanding payment to cover the damage and—'

'Did Goodman talk to al-Medina about selling him the Koran?'

Kent Dodge stopped talking.

'At the dinner,' Ryan said, 'when he was speaking to him in Arabic, did he say anything that might have been about selling it?'

Kent Dodge put down his box, giving the question thought. 'Not really,' he said.

'What's that mean?'

'I mean, it definitely did not occur to me at that time.'

'But it occurs to you now.'

'Only because you've raised it. No. As I remember, what he was wanting to explore were methods by which the Sheikh, or an institution, such as a mosque, as I mentioned, might come to an arrangement with Barnabas to acquire it.'

'Meaning it was available.'

'Only in principle. But, as I say, the Sheikh wasn't interested.'

'Not my point.'

Kent shook his head. 'Look, Goodman wasn't my favourite guy, he was pretty unfriendly, and uptight and all, and I know he was a nut about repatriating the Koran, but, honestly, I don't think he'd do anything illegal.'

As Ryan considered this, a call came across the quad. Jason Birch, also carrying a large bag. He made his way over.

'Glad I caught you,' he said, ''cause I just remembered something else. Don't know if it's important.'

'Go on, then.'

'Don't know if I understand it, really.'

'Don't be shy about your stupidity, Jason.'

'Well, when she said she'd seen Goodman, she made this funny gesture.' He put his fingers together in circles and held them over his eyes. 'It's been puzzling me.'

Ryan looked at him. 'That's the universally recognised hand gesture for glasses, Jason. Spectacles.'

'Yeah, but . . .'

'But what?'

'Goodman don't wear glasses. Funny, innit? And I got a feeling she said something else too – I can't get a hold of it somehow, though.'

Ryan took a close interest. 'Try,' he said.

'I been trying. Honest, I have.'

'Try harder, Jason.'

'I been trying so hard, I feel sick.' There was a silence in which he heaved a number of expressions, one after another, into his shapeless face.

Kent cleared his throat. 'You know,' he said to Ryan, 'if you've got all these questions for Goodman, why don't you just, like, ask him?'

''Cause he's fled the country, that's why. Disappeared. That's your fucking dodgeball for you. He's done a bunk.'

Kent frowned. 'I don't think so.'

Ryan looked at him sharply. 'What do you mean?'

'Well, I saw him in Cornmarket Street yesterday.'

Ryan looked as if he was going to say something, then he looked as if he wasn't. He turned and ran for the lodge.

His face still furrowed, Jason said, 'If only I could remember what she said. It's on the tip of my whatsit.'

Kent said, 'You know, there are plenty of things about my time here that I'm going to be glad to forget.'

It was the middle of the afternoon before Ray picked up Ryan's message. He and Robin had spent a couple of hours discussing the images Ameena called up in the moments before she was killed. Three of them were of Korans, one of them the Koran in the Barnabas collection: an open spread of pages, yellowing parchment decorated with neat black lines of loops and squiggles, shadowed by smaller loops in red. English commentary noted the date, provenance and significance in Shia history. There was a sentence about its market value. But Ameena's reason for calling it up was unclear; her Internet search had been restless and rapid, as if she hadn't found what she was looking for. Their conversation had ended inconclusively and Robin had gone off to Western Road.

Alone, Ray listened to Ryan's new message. Trying to calm himself afterwards, he sat for a moment, uselessly tapping the desk with the edge of his phone, but at last he left his office and went along to COMINT to find Nadim.

'Ray! How are things? How's the new guy?'

'Fine.'

She squinted at him. 'You're not missing the old guy, are you?'

He ignored her. 'Question for you. Just checking. Goodman's still in the UAE, right?'

She hesitated. 'Working assumption, yes.'

He hesitated too. 'What do you mean, "working assumption"?'

'We think he's in or around Abu Dhabi, but, to be honest, we haven't had eyes on him since al-Ain. The Emirates guys are still trying to catch up.'

'Don't we have GPS?'

'Lost after al-Ain.' She looked at him curiously. 'What's up?'

He stood for a moment, frowning, as the niggle of a worry worked its way into him. 'Any chance he could be back in the UK?'

Nadim raised her eyebrows. 'Very low probability.'

'But possible?'

'Well, we haven't been checking inward travel data, so, if the Emirates guys missed an outward journey, it's just about possible.'

He swore under his breath. 'How quick to catch up?'

'Without knowing his travel arrangements, not quick at all. He could have been incoming from anywhere. What's going on, Ray? What makes you think he's back here?'

'Ryan's left me a message saying someone at Barnabas said they saw him in Cornmarket Street yesterday.'

'I thought Ryan was off the case.'

Ray was already calling him. No answer.

Nadim said, 'Isn't he in his tribunal this afternoon?'

Ray looked at his watch. He paced about. 'This is ridiculous,' he said, at last. 'Have you got Goodman's Oxford address?'

Sandford-on-Thames lies five miles downriver from Oxford, a few strips of houses alongside the main road to Dorchester. The narrow street of Riverview, perched above a sloping green, is a line of toylike red-brick cottages, originally built for workers at the nearby paper factory, but apartments now, overlooking the picturesque lock.

Ray left his car on the grass, walked to the end house and knocked on the door.

No answer.

Through the letterbox, he had a narrow view of pine floorboards, lime-green wallpaper and framed photographs of historical scenes. Envelopes and flyers were piled up on the doormat.

There was a side gate, which he tried.

It was locked.

The next-door neighbour confirmed Goodman's absence. 'Went a few days ago. Going to be gone a good long time, he said to us. Not back till after Christmas.'

Ray sat in his car again, thinking. His niggle didn't go away. At last, he backed out of Riverview and headed for Barnabas Hall.

He hadn't been to the bursary before. He went along the cloistered walk adjoining New Court, the stone tunnel cold and colourless, now, in the fading afternoon light, through Old Court and under an archway into a small garden laid out in the shadow of the chapel wall. Opposite was a terrace of cottages, and he ducked through the middle door and found Claire sitting at a desk in a low-ceilinged room at the back.

'Hello again.' She flushed slightly to see Ryan's partner.

Ray explained himself.

'I was told he'd gone abroad.'

'I just need to verify it.'

She let Ray have all the college's contacts for Goodman, which turned out to be identical to the ones Ray already had.

'Okay, fine,' Ray said. 'I need to talk to Kent Dodge, then.'

'You're not being very lucky, I'm afraid. He's left college, too. Went this afternoon.'

'Do you have a number for him?'

He stood in the little garden to make the call, and when it was clear it wasn't going to be answered, he gave up and went back inside. For a moment, he felt he'd done as much as he could. But the niggle remained, and persistence was his own special quality.

'Do you have any other contacts for him?'

'I'm afraid not.'

He gritted his teeth. 'Forwarding address?'

'No.'

'Do you know where he was going?'

'I don't. How urgently do you need to speak to him?'

'I don't know yet.'

He stood in thought, while Claire searched online.

'Here's his page in the Art History Department at Harvard,' she said. 'That's where he came to us from. You could try them. They might have a different private number for him.'

'Okay. Thanks.'

Ray went out into the garden again. The light had failed almost completely now; shadows thickened the chapel wall and smothered the flower beds. An invisible bird sang, monotonous and insistent. Ray had a conversation with two different administrators unfamiliar with personnel in Humanities before reaching the departmental secretary. By now, he was irritable.

'British police. I know Dr Dodge is in the UK, but I need to contact him.'

But there was a continuing, exasperating problem.

'No,' he said. 'Please. You don't understand. If you can't give out the number, I need you to get in touch with him yourself, straight away, and tell him to contact me.'

But the problem was Ray's.

'Mister,' the lady said, 'you're not listening. I don't have a number. And I don't have a number because I don't have *him*.'

He paused. 'What do you mean? He's a member of your department.'

'So *you* keep saying. *I* ain't never heard of him.' And she put down the phone.

Ray went back inside to Claire.

'Any luck?'

He looked at her thoughtfully. 'He came to you on a Fulbright, I think.'

'That's right.'

'There must be paperwork connected with that.'

'Sure.'

'Can I see it?'

He looked through the various documents – an application form, a CV with Kent's picture, and several letters, including a testimonial from a Professor Solomon Weissman at the University of Michigan.

He stayed in the room to call, this time. It was a brief conversation. The Department of Art and Architecture at Michigan had no Professor Weissman. Had never had a Professor Weissman.

There was long silence in the room after he hung up. The niggle was now in a rage. With Claire, he stared at the picture of Kent Dodge on his CV. His eyes focused and narrowed.

'What is it?' Claire said.

He was breathing heavily. 'Something Ryan said.'

'About Kent?'

'No. About Goodman.'

'What?'

'Jason told him something: Goodman doesn't wear glasses.'

Claire thought about it. 'No,' she said. 'He doesn't.'

Ray turned back to the document on the screen, to the picture of Kent Dodge, who was staring back at them with eyes magnified by large, round, black-framed glasses.

FORTY-SIX

Michael Chiffolo left his bicycle in the crowded racks of the leisure centre car park, where it would be anonymous, put his bag over his shoulder and walked down Field Avenue, through the shadows. The street was dark; lamps broken in the riots had still not been repaired. Vans and pickups parked on the verges were dim approximations in front of the larger approximations of maisonettes, shallow in shadow, as if temporary, like portside containers stacked for imminent departure. Pausing for a moment to clean his glasses, he told himself not to worry, and went on again more cheerfully, feeling – almost relishing – the finality of the moment of the last risk of Kent Dodge.

Kent was not his first self-invention. There had been others, beginning in childhood. In St Louis, Missouri, where he'd had an unfortunate start in life, it had been natural to deny the apartment above the dirty bookstore and the mother drinking short dogs in her chair, and the gap where his father should have been. Friends came to him as easily as his lies; they were part of the same world, after all, and, in his fictions, he was polite, clever and honest. People trusted him. He looked the part, his manners were good and people had a fanatical desire to believe in the convenience of the world. He wasn't interested in money, in the beginning; he just wanted to live differently. At thirteen, he obtained a scholarship for orphans to a private school, a deception lasting almost a year, in which time he developed a bitter love of the educated upper-middle classes, where he did not belong. Academia in particular attracted him. His own academic record was poor, but, at the age of eighteen, on the strength of several carefully constructed educational certificates, he was admitted (on a full bursary for the children of veterans) to Truman State University, lasting two semesters, followed by nearly a year at the University of Missouri, then a brief but wonderful month at Duke, where he began to believe that, if he did not belong among these intelligent, trusting people, they could be made to think he did.

His interest in money came later, as, bolstered with plausible qualifications, he applied for travel awards and research grants, and he saw – with initial incredulity – how easy it was to move without effort or responsibility from short-term position to short-term position, at first within North America, and later abroad, where testimonials from fictitious Ivy League professors were good currency, and congenial Midwesterners were warmly welcomed. Of course, he hated them too, the thoughtlessly fortunate – he always had. He laughed at them as he sat at their high tables, eating their elaborate dinners, running up bills he would never pay, buying aeroplane tickets on their dollar, charging his hotel accounts to their educational foundations. In Paris, a chance conversation with an antiquarian dealer first made him aware

371

of the value of his visiting-scholar access to the libraries of rare books, such as the Institut Henri Poincaré or the Bibliothèque de la Sorbonne. From the archives of the Sharjah Museum of Islamic Civilisation in the Emirates, he acquired several Islamic coins and Koran manuscripts of interest to private collectors in Berlin and Cincinnati. And, here in Oxford, he'd been presented with the biggest opportunity of all.

To be crude about it, his primary motive was money: it would make possible a new life for him. No more applications for stipends and grants, just a leisured mingling with the people he so loved and hated. But, in a curious way, he also felt he owed it to the college – to its chuntering Provost and his superior wife – to steal the thing, if only to relieve them, a little, of their self-satisfaction. College security was so pathetic, all it required was a minimal amount of daring and his usual outfacing of the facts. What he hadn't anticipated at all was the excitement, the nerve rush of danger, the hilarity of risk.

Because, of course, it had gone wrong almost immediately, lurching into a comedy of coincidences and pratfalls. First, the blundering migrant from the kitchens who opened the door – which, after all his caution, he had forgotten to lock – at just the moment he was taking the Koran out of its display case, and who, even more hilariously, was one of the very few people who could instantly recognise the book for what it was. Then, the other girl in the kitchen uniform, who looked just like the first one, hur- rying towards the lodge, it seemed, to tell the Provost what she'd seen. Even in the rush of his adrenaline he'd noted her outraged bewilderment – soon superseded by his own bewilderment, as he realised his mistake. After that, there had been the long wait and close watch to find out if the original kitchen girl would realise what she'd seen, a little goading with the cartoons – an insurance policy – to make her seem unstable and untrustworthy, and the keys in her locker, of course, but it all ended abruptly with the announcement of the theft, which arrived, with great comic timing, just a couple of days too early for him to be safely abroad. Then, in speeded-up slapstick: the scramble to catch up with her as she fled back to her house; the reward, finally, of silencing her (less bewildered, in the end, than the other girl, but just as outraged); and then, as if the whole thing were scripted for laughs, the second pursuit, immediately retracing his steps, with the insane English policeman – so bizarre, he'd found it difficult not to break out laughing.

And still it continued, even now, with the unexpected comic turn of the fat janitor. It was time to bring the joking to an end, however. The janitor needed to be silenced before he remembered whatever else the kitchen girl had told him.

He glanced at his watch as he walked down Field Avenue: he had just enough time before heading to the airport to catch a flight to Kuala Lumpur, where his buyer was waiting for him. It was dark and still in the street, but downstairs lights were on in the end maisonette. He went up the cracked concrete driveway and, pausing for a moment to settle himself one last time into the manner of earnest, affable, uninteresting Kent Dodge, he knocked on the glass pane of the door.

Ryan opened it.

FORTY-SEVEN

'He's not here, mate. Popped out to get some cigs. Come in.'

He found himself shutting the door behind him and following the detective down a narrow hall by the staircase, into a small front room in which the only furniture was a black leather easy chair and a large wall cabinet containing a giant-screen TV. The thought came to him that this was what rooms in prisons were like, and he frowned. He was puzzled by the appearance of the detective, but not frightened. It didn't do to be frightened. It would break the spell, and the spell was everything.

He said, 'I just came by to drop this off.' He held out the copy of the Arsenal fanzine which he had taken from Jason Birch's locker as a precaution. 'No need to wait for him, though. I'm on my way to the airport, actually. Tell him I said bye.'

For a moment, they just looked at each other. As usual, the detective looked much more like a criminal than a policeman, pure poor white trash, skinny and crude in sweatpants, baggy jacket and a baseball cap slung on backwards, in a manner not seen in the US for several years.

'Yeah, alright,' the detective said, 'no problem.'

He'd already turned away when the man spoke again.

'What you going to do with the Koran, by the way? Just asking.'

Slowly, he turned back. Wrinkled his brow, smiled.

It was important to smile.

'Excuse me?'

The detective was scratching his groin through his pants; it really wouldn't have been a surprise if he'd produced a baggie of weed and tried to sell it to him. He winced; he'd become more fastidious, over the years.

'Got a buyer already? Or you going to hawk it round? They're animals, over there, you know – you'll probably get your throat cut.'

He was partly waiting, partly still deciding. He felt a familiar rush inside and up his arms, but forced himself to stand still and shake his head. 'I don't know what you—'

'It wasn't Goodman nicking the Koran, it was you. Turns out *you're* the dodgeball.'

'You've totally lost me.' Even as he spoke, he had the disconcerting feeling that he'd forgotten to stop smiling. He bent and carefully put the fanzine on the arm of the chair. A nice touch. 'Listen, I'll just leave this here.'

But the detective wouldn't shut up. 'You had access to the collections room, you told me yourself. And you were that bit late getting to the drinks, weren't you? Quarter to nine-ish. The Provost was leaving to make his call as you arrived. So, no alibi for the time of the murder. We should've pushed you on it, to be fair, but the way you got us looking the other way was nice, very nice – all that about the Provost going off towards his lodge, Goodman chatting in Arabic to Money-Nuts at the dinner. It was only when Jason give us a nudge, just now, I started thinking. Goodman don't wear glasses. But you do.'

The grinning detective was a bit much to take, so he took his glasses off and began to clean them. He was a punctilious cleaner – he loved all the stupid little touches that made him normal, until it was too late. He put his glasses back on and unzipped his bag, glancing inside it quickly.

'I know what you're thinking,' the detective said.

He smiled again. 'Do you?'

'Oh, yeah. You're thinking I can't prove any of this, I'm basically just pissing in the wind. But, you see, I remembered something else I should've been thinking about. What Ameena was doing at the lodge, that night.'

He affected to take a polite interest. 'And what was she doing?'

'Picking up that bag of clothes for charity.'

A little thrill went through him to hear it. He knew, now, what would happen. He began to flex his fingers.

Still the detective went on – he simply wouldn't shut up. 'Forensics always said they couldn't be exact about the time of Sophie's death. More like quarter past than half past, I reckon. In other words, you'd already killed her by the time Ameena arrived.'

The excitement was unbearable, but he shook his head soberly. 'I was lost before. Hope you don't mind me saying, I'm even more lost now.'

'Killed her and had time to think about getting rid of the unform.' He grinned again. 'What could be better than stuffing it in a bag of grubby old clothes? And, a few minutes later, Ameena turns up and carts it away – like she was actually helping you get rid of the evidence. Off it goes to the kitchens, to the charity shops, never to be seen again. Nice little improvisation. Fucking bingo.'

'Bingo?'

'All very unprovable, I know. Except no one got round to taking the bag to the charity shop. It just sat in the stores all this time. And look what I found in it.'

He bent down and fished in a rucksack and pulled out an evidence bag containing a crumpled kitchen uniform.

'And you know what? This is the best bit, to be honest. There's blood on it. See? Ten to one, it's yours. So, anyway. I reckon job done, proof-wise. Know what I mean?'

It was a setback, no denying it. But manageable. That, exactly, was the beauty of improvisation. One last thing to be tidied away? No problem. All the time the detective had been grandstanding, Chiffolo hadn't stopped smiling. Now, his smile was broader than ever, he could feel it stretched across his face like Scotch tape. 'Okay, asshole,' he said. 'I totally get how pleased you are to think you know stuff.'

The poor white trash detective looked sneery and pleased with himself.

'But, here we are, just the two of us, and what have you brought to the party, unarmed English-type police guy?'

He almost laughed to see the dumb-ass detective instinctively put his hand into his sweatpants pocket and take it out again, empty.

Reaching inside his bag, he took out the carving knife he'd brought from the college kitchen.

It was odd how the guy didn't do anything. Just stood there, hands in pockets, scratching his groin. Trailer-park trash.

'I'm getting on that plane, you understand, and no shit-for-brains . . .' His smile faltered just a moment. Something wasn't quite right. Some tiny part of what was happening had come loose, like a misplaced note in a piece of music, like the almost imperceptible shadow of a feeling that tells you it's a dream and you're about to wake up.

He lurched round blindly, too late, as Ray, standing behind him, hit him hard and knocked him out.

'Fuck me, Ray,' Ryan said, as they stood there, looking down at the figure on the floor. 'What took you so long? I thought you was never going to get here.'

'Don't start.'

'I left the back door open and everything. All you had to do—'

'For Christ's sake, give it a rest. Are you going to cuff him?'

'How can I cuff him? I'm not even a fucking policeman any more. You cuff him.'

'You think I had time to stop and get cuffs?'

'We'll have to ask Jason, then.'

Ray shouted up and there were footsteps on the stairs. Jason appeared, looking shaky. Obediently, he went off to find something suitable.

'Got him in the end, though, eh, Ray? Eh, Raymond?'

'Yes.'

'Told you it was a cock-up.'

'Yes.'

'And turns out he's foreign, too, so chalk me up another one.'

Ray shook his head and sighed.

'Don't worry,' Ryan said. 'Last time you'll ever have to work with me. Silver linings, eh?'

Ray said nothing to that.

Jason came downstairs and they tied Kent Dodge's hands together with a phone-charger cable, then stood around in silence for a while. At last, there was the sound of distant sirens getting closer.

'By the way,' Ray said.

'What?'

'I always meant to ask you. What did you actually do to the Bishop of Salisbury?'

Ryan squinted and sniffed, ran his hands round the waistband of his trackies. 'Straight up?'

Ray nodded.

'He slipped on a kerb.'

'What?'

'I was giving him a lot of verbals, to be fair, but I didn't touch him. He just went over backwards. Three witnesses give testimony they'd seen me clobber him.' He shrugged. 'Thing is, Ray, people see what they want to see. Like with Kent Dodge, there. I'm a knobhead, I know that. But I'm not the knobhead people think I am.'

Then, the front door banged open and the firearms team crashed into the house, shouting for calm and drowning out any further conversation.

THREE MONTHS LATER

In the interview room, prisoner in custody Michael Chiffolo was sitting on the other side of a security screen from his criminal defence solicitor, discussing his forthcoming trial, the date of which was still not yet fixed.

Since a violent attack on his former solicitor a month earlier, Chiffolo was not allowed close physical proximity to visitors. He had let his hair and beard grow long, which gave him an unkempt, unstable air. His usual chinos and Thomas Pink shirts had given way to sweatpants and T-shirts. He rocked to and fro in his chair and, when he spoke, his voice was over-loud at first, flaking away into silence. After so long playing others, he had been reduced to being himself, and it was unbearable. His solicitor had not brought good news: it did not appear likely that the court would find police contamination of evidence in the matter of the kitchen uniform.

'You think that asshole knew what he was doing?' Chiffolo said.

'In this instance, it appears he did.'

'Then find some other fucking instance.' Chiffolo's leg pumped up and down.

Despite repeated requests, the US consulate had declined to provide him with an American attorney. No legal advice, no financial assistance. All they had offered were regular visits from a member of the clergy of his choice. In the meantime, the British police were liaising with their counterparts in Paris and Abu Dhabi.

'Do your job, asshole,' he said.

They sat there facing each other through the screen in silence.

The Provost of Barnabas was sitting in the college chapel with his guest, Batyr Khodjayev, owner of Uzbekistan's largest producer of cement, listening to English madrigals. The singing was superb, but he remained nervous; the Uzbek was so expressionless, so taciturn, it was hard to make him out. The man had a habit of picking things up – the silverware at high table, for instance – and summarily inspecting it. More seriously, only the day before, the Provost had heard rumours of financial irregularity in Khodjayev's cement business: an American-led international task force was investigating 'high-level corruption'. Already, he'd received a dozen perturbed emails from colleagues in the university.

The singing built to a bright finale, dissolved to a contemplative peacefulness. He escorted Mr Khodjayev out of the chapel and through the drizzle, round the Fellows' Garden towards his lodge, where a traditional English cream tea would be served. Regrettably, his wife would not be there; she had extended her visit to her sister in Kent. Was it his imagination or did she sound distant when they talked on the telephone? She had proved irrationally angry when she discovered that he was responsible for the temporary removal of that ten-year-old picture of the gaudy, in which he appeared, grinning and avid, next to the attractive young undergraduate Sophie Barbery, though he had assured her that there had been nothing between them beyond a little harmless chemistry. Its removal had merely been a precaution while the intrusive investigation was still running.

Mr Khodjayev had halted to examine (with his usual disdain) one of the old-fashioned lamp posts, and the Provost had to stop himself telling him that it hadn't worked for months. After a moment, without speaking, they went on again.

In her office at the St Aldates police station in Oxford, Detective Superintendent Waddington put down the phone and sat a moment, reflecting. She had just been told by the Police and Crime Commissioner that her services were no longer required. She had rejected the offer of a consultancy role and all that remained to sort out now was the announcement of her departure.

Janine came in with a cup of tea. The Super thanked her and asked after her little boy. Alone again, she straightened her jacket and sat upright in her chair; the low-grade pain, which never left her, niggled and nibbled, and, as always, she put it out of her mind. She picked up the phone and called the director of public relations.

The five surviving members of Ameena Najib's family sat in the makeshift room built among the ruins of their house: Amira, her youngest sister; the twins, Fatima and Latifa; her mother,

Iman; and her father, Jamal. They sat on cushions where the floor was covered with rugs retrieved from their old house. The floor was concrete, the walls breeze blocks, all grey. There were no windows, only a hole in the wall, screened with a sheet of transparent plastic, leading to the place where they slept. There was a wire rack for crockery in one corner of the room, a television on a chair in another and the sort of bags used to line bins hanging along the walls. They sat, passing round a photograph of Ameena, while each person in turn recited the al-Fatiha, the first chapter in the Koran, for the soul of the deceased. There was no body to wash and bury, however, no funeral and no singers to sing at it, no slaughtered ram or meal with bulgar for the poor. They had only just been told of Ameena's death, in fact, and she was already buried, far away, in a country where they had hoped she would be safe.

From the back of his limousine, Emir Sheikh Fahim bin Sultan al-Medina gazed with heavy-lidded eyes at the picturesque frontages of the narrow Cambridge streets as he travelled to Pembroke College, where he was due to meet the Master to discuss endowing a university Chair of Human Flourishing. What he saw met with his approval. After his experience in Oxford, he preferred Cambridge – smaller, less surprising and safer. His advance enquiries about security had been answered to the satisfaction of his new bodyguard, who occupied the front passenger seat of the limousine, also scanning the streets, his radio kept close to his mouth. His old bodyguard, who had left his employment shortly before being exposed as a traitor, had not yet been traced, though it was only a matter of time.

The car pulled off Pembroke Street into the small car park cleared by arrangement of all other vehicles, and the Master himself stepped forward to welcome them.

DI Ray Wilkins drove away from the Children and Family Centre in Rose Hill, where he had spent an hour with a representative of the Family Solutions Service, giving a voluntary statement in support of Ryan Wilkins's continued care of his son Ryan. The FSS had been working with the Wilkinses, exploring the best options for the little boy, including care and fostering. It had dragged on, but Ray had now been assured that, with all their enquiries finally completed, the service would be making the recommendation that the child remain with the father. Who knows, it might even have a bearing on the retrospective review of Ryan's discharge, which had recently got underway.

In the car, he put on Bach, then, with a change of heart, Smokey Robinson. As he went past the car plant on the ring road, he began to sing along.

Some weeks had passed since he was officially reprimanded by the IOPC for his 'failure to provide and maintain adequate standards of behaviour in his subordinate officers'. After a brief, unremarkable partnership, Robin Watkins had returned to Berkshire. His replacement was a young woman called Livvy, whose up-to-the-minute views and pointed way of speaking made Ray uncomfortable. Now that the Super was leaving, he felt, somehow, a little left behind.

At home, he went into the kitchen to kiss Diane, who was making butter chicken. He picked at the courgette and asparagus salad, talking about the FSS and the Super, until he realised she wasn't listening.

He looked at her. 'What's the matter?'

'I'm pregnant,' she said.

In Paris, Sophie Barbery's younger brother, twenty-three-year-old Michel, opened the package that had arrived from the family attorney in Damascus. Since Sophie's death, he was the only surviving member of the family, except for his grandmother, who had never, in any case, involved herself in business matters.

Before he began to read through the documents, he thought for a moment of his sister, whom he had hardly known. She was so much older than him and he had been away at school so much. From others, he had received the impression that she was a bad example, frivolous, even dangerous. Yet, in his own vivid, if few, memories, she was a young woman of casual sophistication, funny rudeness and sudden, bright laughter. He remembered her appearing for a day in the middle of a family holiday in St Tropez, taking him out in the evening to a club, buying him a beer. They had walked, very late, along by the harbour, while she talked flippantly about London and the people who lived there. '*Vis la vie sans regrets*,' she said. 'You never know what will happen.' And she had laughed to see him take her so seriously, though even then he could tell she really laughed to hide her own seriousness.

At the swing park, Ryan Junior went on the slide again.

'Watch, Daddy! Are you watching?'

Sitting upright in his red corduroy dungarees, he slid very

slowly halfway down and stopped. 'This slide doesn't work,' he said matter-of-factly.

Ryan, distracted by his phone, waved at him as he began to speak. 'Yeah, Wilkins. Yeah, it's about the security job.' He walked around the playground, head down, talking. 'That's right,' he said. 'CID, yeah. Detective Inspector . . . No. Discharge . . .'

Ryan Junior was calling him again from the swings, his piping voice clear as birdsong, and he waved and turned back to his phone and hissed into it, 'Yeah, I know they *call* it dishonourable . . . Yeah, but if you read what they said . . . Yeah, well, if you read it again . . .' He glared at the phone. 'You can read, right? You know what, forget it . . . Yeah, well, *I'm* sorry you wasted *my* fucking time.'

He sat down on a bench with his eyes closed and, when he opened them again, Ryan Junior was sitting next to him, his legs sticking out in front of him. He held out his hand and his son took it.

'Daddy . . .'

'Yeah, alright. Surprised you could hear what I said from all the way over there. You must have ears like an elephant.'

'No, I don't.'

'I didn't mean really.'

'Daddy?'

'What?'

'A conversation is always pleasant.'

'It's always pleasant with you.' He put his phone in his trackie pocket. 'There's some tossers I don't ever want to talk to again.'

'What's "tossers", Daddy?'

'People what don't know how to have conversations.'

387

They sat there in companionable silence. It was a cool evening, the sky a washed-out blue veiled with white wisps of clouds, the air empty. Two youths slouched by, one of them boasting to the other about his trainers. 'Know how much they cost? More than you.' He threw a stone and a bird in a bush made snapping, throaty cries.

'You know what?' Ryan said.

'What?'

'Sometimes I don't even need a conversation.'

He still had twenty hours of community service to do, but he didn't think of that. He didn't think of his father, serving time at Her Majesty's pleasure, or his mother, fretting incoherently at Jade's, or the low-paid security jobs he couldn't get, or the unlikely chances of a review into his discharge going his way.

He didn't think of anything. He squeezed his son's hand.

'You and me, mate,' he said. 'What could be better?'

ACKNOWLEDGMENTS

All books are collaborative and it gives me great pleasure to acknowledge the help I have received in writing this one. Thanks are due to the following. My agent, Anthony Goff, who has given me invaluable support now for over thirty years. My world-class publisher at riverrun, Jon Riley, who had the idea of writing this book before I did. His editor Jasmine Palmer, whose efficiency made everything so much easier. Penelope Price, whose exceptional copy-edit has, on so many pages, saved me from myself.

Thanks also to my daughter, Eleri, who was thorough (and, by and large, tactful) in pointing out basic errors. To my son Gwilym for supportive noises off. And finally, and above all, to Eluned, my wife, who has put up with me for half her life.

Read on for a sneak peek at the second book
in the DI Ryan Wilkins Mysteries

THE BROKEN AFTERNOON

Coming in 2023

ONE

Poppy Clarke, four years old, standing in the sun-dazzled gateway of Magpies. Giggling.

Deep in the heart of rich Oxford, Garford Road glowed in the heat, a moneyed hush of rustling copper beech, murmuring voices of girls from the private schools, muted conversations of construction workers at the Edwardian villas under renovation – and Poppy's laughter ringing out bright as summer birdsong as she danced on the spangles of sunshine in the gravel driveway of her nursery school, waiting for her mother at four thirty on a July afternoon.

It was a game, their usual game. She knew where he was, she could see his shadow on the bright pavement. Pausing, she watched carefully as she knew she was supposed to. Her eyes shone. She clapped her hands. She jumped round in a circle, all dimples and ribbons in her red and black pirate costume, the season's craze. Still smiling, she shook her head sternly and wagged her finger. Covered her eyes with her hands, snatched them away, and burst out laughing again.

Briefly, she turned and looked at the nursery building behind her, where her mother was talking to a friend, but there was nothing to see there except a boring empty doorway, so she turned back to the street. She looked shyly, but only pretend-shyly, really she was watching between her fingers in that clever, sly way she had, and soon she was giggling and jumping up and down, until, when beckoned, she skipped forward. And when her mother came out a few moments later she had gone.

Panic set in.

TWO

Ten hours later, five miles away, in a poky shed-like office smelling of motor oil and instant coffee, night-watch security guard Ryan Wilkins broke the long hours of his shift by catching the news on repeat. Two o'clock in the morning, night rain creeping with tiny claws across the plastic roof. He turned up the volume and leaned in.

On the screen his former partner, Detective Inspector Raymond Wilkins, flanked on one side by the new Superintendent and on the other by the Thames Valley Police crest in gilded carpentry, fronting a presser. A little girl gone missing. Her picture appeared, an irresistible advert for the human race with her blonde curls and dimples, her bunched cheeks and shining eyes, appropriately pleased with herself in pirate costume, eye-patch and cutlass, ribbons and sash. Vanished from outside her Oxford nursery while her mother talked for no more than two minutes to her teacher in the lobby. A picture of the nursery appeared too, a snippet of sculpted beech hedge and immaculate lawn – another advert, for parental serenity, priceless at fifteen grand a year.

From which, in broad daylight, a little girl had been snatched. Upper middle-class England was freaking out. In the echoey conference room journalists shouted questions over each other.

DI Wilkins said they were following a lead but declined to give details, and Ryan turned him off and sat there in the sudden quiet staring out of the window at the rain-crackly darkness of the van compound beyond. He could imagine the situation. A news shout so quick wasn't ideal, things were still too messy, but the timetable of sensational cases was driven by the media. A lead? If real, probably the father; Ray pointedly hadn't mentioned him and the disappearance of very young children was mostly the result of parental disputes. Ray would be good at dealing with that, smooth and tactful. He'd looked good on television too, no denying it. Cameras loved him, tall and black in his uniform; they loved his serious features, educated tone, the way he paused between sentences, the firm shapes he made with his strong hands, the resolute look in his handsome eyes. The thinking woman's law enforcement.

Ryan considered his own reflection in the window. Skinny white kid in nylon uniform, a discount purchase from mywork-wear.com. He looked at his overlarge nose and attention-seeking Adam's apple, quick eyes under scratchy brows, shiny smear of scar tissue down his left cheek, a grimace about to happen, a fidget coming on somewhere – Ryan Earl Wilkins, twenty seven years old, trailer park rat boy, one of the youngest ever Detective Inspectors in the Thames Valley force, dishonourably discharged three months ago, now working nights at Van Central, off the Botley Road. Boom. Hero to zero in three minutes. Or two and a half.

Still, Ryan was never down for long, he always revived, without warning or indeed reason, his optimism an inexplicable part of him, unasked for, like his nose, his fidgets or his beloved son, Ryan Junior, three years old, by far the calmest and most discerning of all the Wilkinses, asleep now at home with his Auntie Jade. Grinning at the thought of him, Ryan was turning on his broken-backed swivel chair to put the kettle on when his eye was caught by a tiny blip in the corner of the security screen. Gone almost before it had happened, but not too quick for Ryan. Things stuck to his eyes. Another quirk.

He stared at the screen for two minutes more. Nothing. Only the unvarying van compound, an area of grizzling darkness, of rental vans stored between railings, a big box of toys put away at bedtime, a dead zone of silence, complete stillness. Except, just momentarily, a brief tremor in the texture of the shadow of a Ford Transit. A little jolt of interest went through him. He initiated the required security procedure, activating the police response and logging the time, checking the codes for the doors to the offices and workshop. All fine. Everything was nice and smooth – until he tried to switch on the compound floodlights. Not a glimmer. After a moment he began to rummage in a drawer of his broken-down desk for a flash-light.

Outside, silvery rain was drifting down on a fine breeze scented with diesel, and Ryan followed the beam of his torch across the concrete forecourt to the metal gates, still securely padlocked. As he went, he mentally reviewed the last few hours for signs of anything out of the ordinary he might have missed. There was nothing he could think of. When he'd arrived at ten there had been a van left on the forecourt – usually there was at least one – and he'd driven it inside the compound and parked it and locked it, as per, and given the pen a last look round. Everything had been secure; he'd double-checked the gates. He looked about him now. The compound was surrounded by a two-and-a-half metre high palisade fence in galvanised steel, pretty much burglar-proof. Perhaps an animal had got in, one of those muntjac deer from the water-meadows at Hog-Acre. He'd seen them on the pavements among the surrounding warehouses, strange creatures, dog-like, with foreshortened front legs and raised hind-quarters, creeping along as if in shame. He scanned the ground ahead as he unlocked the gates and went inside, listening. The vans around him seemed to bulge forward in the torch beam as he waved it slowly to and fro, walking down the narrow channels between them. He came to a halt at the end of a line and waited a few beats, listening again. Nothing but the whisper of rain on van roofs. And then, five metres away, very softly, a scrunch of gravel.

He switched off the light and went quietly back along the row towards the entrance, and a shadow movement on the other side of the line of vans seemed to keep pace with him. At the end he waited a moment, then stepped smartly to the other side.

The figure looming in front of him was big, six six at least, and bulky, head hooded. When Ryan appeared, he flung his arms out and canted forward with a grunt, but Ryan was quicker, shining a light at him with one hand, taking a picture with the other before he could flinch away.

There was a panting pause as they confronted each other, a moment of unexploded-bomb uncertainty when things could still go either way.

Ryan said, 'Go ahead, kill me with a spanner why don't you? Murder first degree, ten to fifteen in Grendon, no parole, come out in time to waste the rest of your fucking life on street meds.'

More panting.

He tensed himself.

Then the figure spoke, a deep sticky voice. 'Done Grendon already.'

Ryan hesitated; a flutter of recognition went through him. 'Mick Dick?'

The man lowered his hood and showed him his face, trembling. Those familiar puffy cheeks, those bloodshot eyes, lopsided mouth. All distorted now in fear. Terror.

'Mick Dick! What you doing here?'

All the man could do was moan. Passing a big hand across his face, he brought it away shaking. Shook his head, dumbly suffering. He didn't seem able to speak. Something was wrong with him. Ryan stood there shocked, puzzled, trying to remember when he'd seen Mick Dick last: maybe not since school, when they were both sixteen, when Mick was still promising, boxing heavyweight in the Nationals, trying out for Wantage Town, and Ryan was running wild at the raves and in the clubs.

'What the fuck's the matter with you?'

Still no reply. Moans.

'Jesus Christ, Mick Dick. Didn't even know you were out.'

He'd read about it at the time. Aggravated burglary, minimum five at Grendon, category B facility out in Bucks. Nice lad, Michael Dick, but easily led, always doing favours for the wrong people. Some weakness let the violence in. They said the man he'd attacked during the burglary was in a coma for

399

a fortnight.

Looking at Ryan with his blood-shot eyes, he finally spoke. 'Two months. Trying to get work. Every day, man, knocking on doors.' He moved his tongue around his lips. 'Get something soon. But this. This is fucked up. I can't be here.'

'Yeah well, don't want to let you down too badly, but you are actually here, and you need to tell me what the fuck you're doing.'

'I'm telling you, Ryan, it's a mistake.'

'Listen. You got about five minutes before the bobbleheads get here. You can explain to them if you like.'

There was a faint noise wafted on the breeze, sirens.

Mick Dick was shaking his head wildly; he said in a rush, 'Ryan, Ryan, man, can't go back. They put me away for long this time. Got a little girl, four, five, she grow up without me. Ryan!'

'Calm down. I need to know what you're doing here. Say something I can understand.'

'I got nothing, I done nothing, I swear.' He spread his arms. 'Check me out, man. It's just . . .'

'Just what?'

He looked ashamed. 'I got nowhere to stay. She kick me out till I get my shit together.' He gestured hopelessly at the sky. 'It's raining, man.' In his voice nothing but defeat. An ex-con on the street.

'You been sleeping in vans?'

He said in a sullen whisper, 'I done it, other places. There's always one left unlocked. But not here, man, you locked up tight.' He gave Ryan a closer look. 'What you doing here anyway? Thought you went for a police.'

'Never mind that. Show me again.'

He put his light on him and Mick Dick turned out his jacket pockets, his trouser pockets, stood there humble and defenceless as if convicted already. Nothing but his phone, wallet, bunch of keys, papery scraps of rubbish scattering on the ground.

'That's it, that's everything.'

The sirens were closer now.

'Ryan, man. Got to help me out.' His mouth was loose with fear. Terror, again. 'My little girl, Ashleigh,' he said. Plucking at his lips with his teeth.

Ryan looked at him.

'*You* know,' Mick Dick said softly. 'I can see it.'

'Know what?'

'Know what it's like. Be out of luck.'

Ryan thought of Mick Dick aged sixteen, taking his boxing seriously, doing what he was told, forgetting to think for himself; he thought of handsome Ray on the screen, of himself in the fuggy shed where he spent his nights. There was no sound of the siren now, only the long, rising engine-whine of acceleration coming along the stretch of Ferry Hinksey Road two hundred metres away.

He had thirty seconds to decide. Do the right thing, do the wrong thing.

'Go on then. Fuck off. Don't come back till your luck's changed.'

Mick had already gone. Moved easily for a big lad. Of course he was practised: slipping in and out of places is what he'd gone down for.

The squad car was on the forecourt and Ryan ambled out to meet them. Two bobbleheads known to him only by sight.

401

'Good news, boys,' he said. 'No need for heroics. Turns out, just one of those little deer things got in. Thanks for your time and that. Always nice to have a spin, eh?'

And watched them drive away.